THE HALF SISTERS

GERALDINE ENDSOR JEWSBURY was born in Derbyshire in 1812, one of six children of a cotton manufacturer (later insurance agent), and his cultivated wife. The family moved to Manchester when Geraldine was about 6, and her mother died soon after. Geraldine spent most of her life in Manchester till 1854, and became very familiar with the social transformations caused by industrialism. She also became preoccupied with questions of religious belief, questions which took on a particular urgency for her as a single middle-class woman with no social role beyond that of keeping house for her father and brother. Such concerns led initially to a close friendship with the social critic Thomas Carlyle and his brilliant wife Jane, and eventually to a career as a novelist. Her first novel, *Zoe: A History of Two Lives* (1845) caused a stir with its radical treatment of religious doubt, while her next, *The Half Sisters* (1848), was equally outspoken about the constraints of all kinds governing women's lives. Among her other novels, *Marian Withers* (1851) deals with industrialism, and *The Sorrows of Gentility* (1856) examines inter-class marriage. Geraldine Jewsbury also co-edited and co-wrote the memoirs of Lady Morgan, an important woman writer of an earlier generation.

Geraldine Jewsbury became a prominent literary figure, counting among her friends the Huxleys, the Kingsleys, the Rossettis, and John Ruskin. She was the first woman to enjoy a position of influence as a publisher's reader, and also reviewed over two thousand books for the notable weekly journal the *Athenaeum*. She died of cancer in 1880, aged 68.

JOANNE WILKES is a lecturer in the Department of English, University of Auckland, Auckland, New Zealand.

OXFORD WORLD'S CLASSICS

*For almost 100 years Oxford World's Classics have brought
readers closer to the world's great literature. Now with over 700
titles—from the 4,000-year-old myths of Mesopotamia to the
twentieth century's greatest novels—the series makes available
lesser-known as well as celebrated writing.*

*The pocket-sized hardbacks of the early years contained
introductions by Virginia Woolf, T. S. Eliot, Graham Greene,
and other literary figures which enriched the experience of reading.
Today the series is recognized for its fine scholarship and
reliability in texts that span world literature, drama and poetry,
religion, philosophy and politics. Each edition includes perceptive
commentary and essential background information to meet the
changing needs of readers.*

OXFORD WORLD'S CLASSICS

GERALDINE JEWSBURY

The Half Sisters

Edited with an Introduction and Notes by
JOANNE WILKES

Oxford   New York
OXFORD UNIVERSITY PRESS

Oxford University Press, Great Clarendon Street, Oxford OX2 6DP

Oxford New York

Athens Auckland Bangkok Bogotá Buenos Aires Calcutta
Cape Town Chennai Dar es Salaam Delhi Florence Hong Kong Istanbul
Karachi Kuala Lumpur Madrid Melbourne Mexico City Mumbai
Nairobi Paris São Paulo Singapore Taipei Tokyo Toronto Warsaw

and associated companies in Berlin Ibadan

Oxford is a registered trade mark of Oxford University Press

First published as a World's Classics paperback 1994
Reissued as an Oxford World's Classics paperback 1998

British Library Cataloguing in Publication Data

Data available

Library of Congress Cataloging in Publication Data
Jewsbury, Geraldine Endsor, 1812–1880.
The half sisters / Geraldine Jewsbury : edited with an
introduction by Joanne Wilkes.
p.   cm.—(Oxford world's classics)
Includes bibliographical references.
1. Actresses—England—Fiction.   2. Sisters—England—Fiction.
3. Wives—England—Fiction.   4. Women—England—Fiction.
I. Wilkes, Joanne.   II. Title.   III. Series.
PR4825.J7H35   1994   823'.8—dc20   93–29306

ISBN 0–19–283757–5

1 3 5 7 9 10 8 6 4 2

Printed in Great Britain by
Cox & Wyman, Reading, Berkshire

CONTENTS

INTRODUCTION

WE might approach the concerns of *The Half Sisters* by recalling a more famous novel which appeared a year earlier, in 1847. In Charlotte Brontë's *Jane Eyre*, the heroine, restless after several years at Lowood school, takes up a position as governess at Thornfield Hall. But after she has spent some time confined to the society of her pupil Adele and the housekeeper Mrs Fairfax, the quiet domestic routine there palls, so Jane yearns for 'the busy world, towns, regions full of life' she has never seen. And her predicament is one she sees as characteristic of women:

Women are supposed to be very calm generally: but women feel just as men feel; they need exercise for their faculties, and a field for their efforts as much as their brothers do; they suffer from too rigid a restraint, too absolute a stagnation, precisely as men would suffer; and it is narrow-minded in their more privileged fellow-creatures to say that they ought to confine themselves to making puddings and knitting stockings, to playing on the piano and embroidering bags. It is thoughtless to condemn them, or laugh at them, if they seek to do more or learn more than custom has pronounced necessary for their sex.[1]

Jane Eyre is attacking here a widespread assumption of the mid-nineteenth century—that women and men were intrinsically very different, and should therefore have very different roles in society. Or, as it was often put, they should occupy distinct 'spheres'—men being meant for the public sphere, and women for the private. Women were thought to be fragile beings, easily swayed by emotion, and possessing limited intellectual capacities, indeed little in the way of 'faculties' to 'exercise'. They lacked the toughness and resilience needed for success in business, the professions, or public affairs—and so these were rightly the preserve of the sex 'naturally' endowed with strength of mind and body. But women's innate gentleness, docility, anxiety to please, affectionateness, and talent for dealing with minutiae, made them ideally suited to performing or supervising domestic work and to making the home comfortable for the men of the family. In the

[1] Charlotte Brontë, *Jane Eyre* (1847; repr. 1980), 110–11.

middle and upper classes, women were expected to remain at home, supported by husband, father, or brother, rather than venture beyond the private sphere to get a living. If obliged to work out of economic necessity, they were more or less confined to teaching, governessing, or working as paid companions. The professions, civil service, and 'white-collar' jobs in industry and commerce were closed to them, while joining the thousands of women factory workers, servants, or agricultural labourers would entail losing caste. Not surprisingly, the restricted employment opportunities for single women and the social value attached to women's domestic role meant that marriage was seen as women's primary goal, and those who remained single were often despised as 'old maids'.

The circumstances and ideas described here were certainly not peculiar to the 1840s: they already had a long history, and less extreme theories about innate differences between the sexes are still with us. Yet the concept of 'separate spheres' seemed all the more relevant, even necessary, to a society in the throes of unprecedented industrial expansion. The rapid growth of manufacturing and of manufacturing towns and cities in the first half of the nineteenth century created not only the notorious expanses of jerry-built slums for the working classes, but also a middle-class way of life where the sexes might have little to do with each other. Manufacturers and businessmen could be preoccupied for long hours each day with their factories and firms; the women of their households would take no part in these, would see little of their menfolk, and would be expected to devote themselves to household concerns. But conventional interpretations of women's function took on an added inflection from the period's ambivalent attitudes to that famous Victorian value, 'work'. In general, work was considered both morally improving to the individual and beneficial to society, yet it was recognized that constant engagement in the world of buying, selling, and striving to get ahead might have a hardening, even corrupting effect on men. Hence the home and the wife at its centre came to be celebrated as a refuge from the stress and the temptations of the commercial and industrial world. A further development of this idea was that women, being sheltered from the damaging influences of the public sphere, might remain untainted and thus be able to exert a moral influence on their menfolk. Conduct books for women, in which the period was prolific, could wax lyrical about the softening, purifying, elevating powers of womanhood.

But just as many tomes celebrated conservative attitudes to women, a number of writers forcefully attacked such preconceptions: notable texts were Marion Reid's *A Plea for Women* (1843), Anne Lamb's *Can Woman Regenerate Society?* (1844), and the American Margaret Fuller's *Woman in the Nineteenth Century* (1845). The 1840s was a period of questioning and upheaval on many fronts—religious, intellectual, social, political—and what had come to be termed the 'Woman Question' was up for debate. Opponents of the status quo argued that women should be treated as rational beings, with the same intellectual potential as men, and be educated accordingly; also, that they should have greater employment opportunities open to them, so as not to have to subject themselves to the degradingly desperate pursuit of husbands. These writers pointed out too that the concept of contrasting 'spheres' for the sexes was so pervasive, not because it reflected their innate characteristics, but because it was convenient for men. Among novels of the period, *Jane Eyre* is, as we have seen, concerned in part with the 'Woman Question', and the heroine does eventually move beyond Thornfield and exercises her faculties to achieve both moral and financial autonomy. But *The Half Sisters*, probably more extensively than any nineteenth-century novel before George Eliot's *The Mill on the Floss* in 1860, explores and exposes the damaging effects of the period's conventional beliefs about women. It was also a subject about which Geraldine Jewsbury was well qualified to write.

Her parents were Thomas Jewsbury, a cotton manufacturer from Measham, Derbyshire, who became a Manchester insurance agent, and his wife Maria, née Smith, a woman of some cultivation. Born in 1812, Geraldine was the fourth of the six surviving children, and the younger of the two daughters. At the time she wrote *The Half Sisters*, she had lived in Manchester for most of her life, though she was familiar with other parts of England: the family had still been in Measham during her early childhood, while she had spent several years at a boarding school near Tamworth, and had visited London. In 1832, when Geraldine was 20, her elder sister Maria Jane, who had run the household since their mother's death in 1819, married and went to India, and Geraldine was left in charge. She kept house for her father till he died in 1840, and from then on for her single brother Frank. (When Frank married in 1854, Geraldine moved to London.) It is likely that the town of 'M——' in which Alice Helmsby in *The Half Sisters* grows up is based on Manchester, and that the novel's descriptions of its way of life reflect the author's response to aspects of the town's middle-class milieu, albeit not necessarily to her own family. Weary after long days spent at their businesses, which engross all their energies, the men want nothing more at home than to make themselves comfortable. Hence wives and daughters are expected merely 'to manage the house well, and to see that the dinner was punctual and well appointed; to be very quiet, and not talk nonsense, or rather to talk very little of anything'. Ill-educated and with little but trivia to focus on, the women in general are petty-minded, and the younger ones 'pretty, trifling, useless beings, waiting their turn to be married' (Vol. 1, Chapter VIII). Women are meant to adhere to social codes based on notions of propriety and respectability, but there seems to be no moral or rational basis for such codes, and the real, underlying aim of a woman's life amounts to marrying the most prosperous man within reach and living in a home filled with material evidence of his prosperity. A few years later, another Manchester-based woman writer with whom Geraldine Jewsbury was acquainted, Elizabeth Gaskell, was also to register in her novel *North and South* (1854–5) the dreary materialism of 'woman's sphere' in the new industrial cities. At a dinner-party the heroine, Margaret Hale, is inspired by the men's strong sense of purpose, but finds the women dull, and notices how they gear their conversation to showing off the concrete evidence of their husbands' prosperity.[2]

As her portrayal of Alice's world suggests, Geraldine Jewsbury was a woman who sought to delve beneath appearances and to question commonly accepted standards and beliefs. Her first biographer—writing in the early 1930s when there were still people alive who could recall her—comments on her 'restless and consuming curiosity to get at the workings of things and to see

[2] Elizabeth Gaskell, *North and South* (1854–5; repr. 1982), 167.

behind the scenes'.[3] By the time she reached her late twenties, she had come to a spiritual crisis: the religious beliefs of her community seemed dry and unsatisfying, followed mindlessly and enjoining 'Duty' on her as a matter of social convenience, but offering her no sense of any world beyond the material. Her questioning of these codes meant that she eventually lost her faith in God, while nursing her father in his last months brought on anguish over both the meaning of death and the purpose of her own life. But this mental and emotional turmoil also ended up making her a writer.

Geraldine Jewsbury's crisis of faith was by no means unusual for the period, and she, like many others, found solace in the works of Thomas Carlyle. But Geraldine Jewsbury, in her characteristically enterprising fashion, went a step further, and wrote to the author about her predicament. Carlyle was impressed by the letters, and so began what was to become a lifelong friendship between Jewsbury and both Thomas Carlyle and his wife Jane.

Carlyle's works of the 1830s enjoined on readers the need to subsume their emotional and spiritual anguish into work—and his influence had much to do with the way Victorians often invested work with a religious significance. He told Geraldine Jewsbury that 'doubt is always a disease; we are not here to doubt and ask, but to see and do'.[4] She never in fact ceased to 'doubt and ask', but succeeded in expressing her doubts through her work—initially, the work of writing the first of her six novels.

Zoe: A History of Two Lives, published in 1845, explores the religious experience of Everhard Burrows, a man who achieves eminence in the Catholic Church only to lose his faith in the Church's teachings (albeit not in God). As a result, he finds it difficult to give his life direction and meaning, although (like the author) he finds an outlet for his ideas and feelings in writing. The novel implies that no Christian doctrines of any denomination can be validated by external evidence, and this understandably upset some readers. Another source of scandal was that Everhard, a priest, falls in love with the heroine Zoe, a married

---

[3] Susanne Howe, *Geraldine Jewsbury, Her Life and Errors* (1935), 5.
[4] Thomas Carlyle to Geraldine Jewsbury, 26 Apr. 1840, in Susanne Howe Nobbe, 'Four Unpublished Letters of Thomas Carlyle', *PMLA* 70 (1955), 878.

woman, and she reciprocates, albeit their love is never consummated. *Zoe* was considered so likely to injure the morals of young men that it was placed in a dark cupboard in Manchester Library, and even the more cosmopolitan Jane Carlyle was surprised that her friend had so little concern for conventional standards of decency. During the composition of the novel she advised the author to temper its explicitness, but Geraldine had to confess that she found it hard to make the book 'proper-behaved', and very truly remarked that she had 'no vocation for propriety, as such'. Jane admired the work none the less, praising Geraldine to a correspondent as a 'profound and daring speculator' who was 'far too clever to do nothing in her day and generation'.[5]

To some extent, *Zoe* foreshadows *The Half Sisters* in giving some attention to the limitations of women's lives: for example, it shows the heroine being induced to enter into a loveless marriage partly because she has no outlets for her intellect or her energy. But it is a rather incoherent novel, much of its energy dispersed into long digressive subplots. One gets the impression too that Jewsbury has displaced onto her male protagonist Everhard the difficulties that women in particular might have with finding a sense of purpose in life.[6] And although Zoe and Everhard are separated for much of the novel, the book implies that it is love which is the source of meaning in a woman's life. What she was to do in *The Half Sisters*, her next novel, was to confront directly the discontent which many women felt about the narrowness and emptiness of their existence. She was also to examine the role of love in their lives, asking whether women could attain happiness without love—whether pursuing worthwhile work might develop sufficient sense of achievement and independence to make them less reliant on relationships with men. One of her half-sisters, Alice, is given a conventional, middle-class upbringing and marriage, while the other, Bianca, pursues an acting career as a single woman. The novel's treatment

    [5] Geraldine Jewsbury to Jane Carlyle, 1844, in *Selections from the Letters of Geraldine Endsor Jewsbury to Jane Welsh Carlyle*, ed. Mrs Alexander Ireland (1892), 145; Jane Carlyle to Jeannie Welsh, 25 Dec. 1842, in *Jane Welsh Carlyle: Letters to Her Family, 1839–1863*, ed. Leonard Huxley (1924), 66.
    [6] See Norma Clarke, *Ambitious Heights: Writing, Friendship, Love—The Jewsbury Sisters, Felicia Hemans, and Jane Welsh Carlyle* (1990), 164.

of the issues it raises is ambiguous, for reasons which will be discussed later, but the author's dissatisfaction with her society's assumptions about her sex is very clear.

The standards to which Alice has been brought up to conform offer her neither moral guidance nor any sense of purpose. Her mother devotes herself to trivial household tasks, and expects Alice to do likewise, while any other talent a woman might have—such as an ability to draw or play the piano—is valued only as an accomplishment to be displayed at social gatherings. All Mrs Helmsby's advice to her daughter is geared to making her successful according to social codes which she and her friends never question, and these decree that a girl can never be admired for her personal qualities, only for ensnaring as early as possible a wealthy husband. The community's religious beliefs are equally desiccated, so that Alice never gains 'a single strong abiding principle of right or wrong to govern her as by a moral necessity' (Vol. i, Chapter XXXI). In these circumstances, it is not surprising that she is attracted to John Bryant as a man who can free her from her single state while (apparently) despising the ignorant and narrow-minded people of M——. But her marriage merely protracts her misery. She sees little of her husband, and he mistakenly seeks to protect her from his business worries, thereby making her feel both neglected and useless. Her life offers her no activity more meaningful than giving orders to her housekeeper, arranging her ornaments, sewing, reading popular novels, and visiting uncongenial people. Never presented with a motive that could give energy and direction to her life, Alice is so cowed by her conditioning that she is afraid to question, let alone rebel against, the beliefs which confine her. That hers is not an isolated case is illustrated by the narrator's forthright comment, that women

are crushed down under so many generations of arbitrary rules for the regulation of their manners and conversation; they are from their cradle embedded in such a composite of fictitiously-tinted virtues, and artificial qualities, that even the best and strongest amongst them are not conscious that the physiology of their minds is as warped by the traditions of feminine decorum, as that of their persons is by the stiff corsets which, until very recently, were *de rigueur* for preventing them 'growing out of shape'. (Vol. i, Chapter XXVII)

Jewsbury is obviously showing the dreary reality that could lie behind the sentimental contemporary rhetoric about woman's domestic 'sphere'. She also extends this criticism by arguing, through both Alice's strong, independent half-sister Bianca and the latter's admirer Lord Melton, that women's upbringing is determined, not by their innate qualities, but by masculine self-interest. A bit over half-way through the novel (Vol. 2, Chapter II), Lord Melton and his friend Conrad Percy argue about what women should aspire to be. Conrad had earlier been attracted to Bianca, but has reverted to a much more conventional ideal of womanhood—an ideal which will later inspire his disastrous liaison with Alice. For Conrad, a woman should be 'quietly at anchor by her own fire-side, gentle, low-voiced, loving, confiding'. She is a delicate, graceful being who would both help her husband and defer to his guidance; her timidity and sense of propriety would preserve her from 'eccentric originality'; she would eschew evil, not because she understood what is was, but 'instinctively', out of 'exquisite taste'. Lord Melton launches into an attack on this mindset, arguing that it assumes that women do not exist for their own sake, but for men's. They are constantly warned against saying and doing certain things simply because they are not graceful or becoming or agreeable—in other words, because men disapprove. Rather than being considered as individuals with inner spiritual, intellectual, and emotional lives, plus capacities to develop, women have their qualities and talents 'modified, like the feet of Chinese women, to meet an arbitrary taste'. It is as if they are meant to be 'flavoured with virtues and tinctured with accomplishments, just up to the point to meet the taste of the day, but never with the intent to strengthen their own hearts and souls'. That is, 'they never were intended to lead a purely *relative* life'—and in putting this phrase into Lord Melton's mouth, Jewsbury is no doubt targeting directly the most prominent writer of conservative conduct-books for women, Mrs Sarah Ellis. In her best-selling *The Women of England* (1838), she had declared that women were 'from their own constitution, and from the station they occupy in the world, strictly speaking, relative creatures'.[7] According to Melton, the outcome of so-

---

[7] Mrs [Sarah] Ellis, *The Women of England: Their Social Duties, and Domestic Habits* [1838], 149.

ciety's pernicious treatment of women is that their idle, trivial, rudderless lives make them diseased and restless, and Bianca later develops this point. Of unmarried middle-class women, she says that they 'spend their days in the same kind of trifling that slaves in the East amuse themselves with, till some-one comes to put them into a harem' (Vol. 2, Chapter VI). Without some kind of worthwhile employment, their unsatisfied powers will consume them.

A further dimension to Jewsbury's demystifying of traditional assumptions about women in this novel is her revelation of how women who do successfully follow the social codes really perceive men. For all her parroting of contemporary truisms about the desirability of marriage, Alice's mother Mrs Helmsby has no genuine reverence for the supposedly superior sex. She warns her daughter against showing too much affection for her fiancé, since men are egotistical, untrustworthy, and inclined to be complacent; rather, she should stimulate his love by appearing cold and reserved. Marriage is in reality a sort of power game between the sexes where men enjoy nearly all the advantages—the only leverage a woman has comes from playing hard-to-get, and rather than deferring to her husband, she should exploit such little power as she possesses. The way the inequalities between the sexes in marriage encouraged deviousness rather than devotion in wives is brought out even more clearly in the advice Alice is given by her sister-in-law Margaret Lauriston. Mrs Lauriston tells her about men's habitual egotism and desire to dominate women, and urges her to contend with this, not by openly defying her husband, but by ensuring that she always conceals from him any knowledge of which he could take advantage. She may give the appearance of trusting him, but should never do so in reality. Indeed women have little choice but to behave in this way:

'Men made their own laws; it is not our fault that they are suspicious, ungenerous, and selfish; if they choose to be such, we are obliged to take them as we find them, and make the best of them. (Vol. 1, Chapter XIV)

All this suggests that women do not by nature look up to men or see themselves as innately 'relative creatures', yet often recognize the value of appearing to do so in order to live as comfortably as possible. It is women like Alice, genuinely seeking guidance from their husbands and too honourable to 'manage' them, who end up lonely and unhappy. Moreover, assumptions about women's nature and the system of separate spheres which they underpin may ultimately work to the detriment of men as well. John Bryant is an intelligent, upright, well-meaning, and loving husband—more than can be said for Lauriston—but his experience gives him no way of understanding Alice's feelings, and he cannot recognize that she would welcome an outlet for her ennui in sharing the business worries that so preoccupy him.

As a follower of Carlyle, Geraldine Jewsbury does present Bryant's diligence and ardent sense of duty towards his work in a positive light: he is certainly a more attractive figure than the idle, fickle, dilettantish Conrad. But unlike Carlyle, she believed that women too should have the opportunity to contribute both to their own self-development and to society: in fact she gives to Conrad Carlyle's idea that women should make themselves into a 'beautiful reflex' of a man's best qualities, only to have her hero Melton undermine this notion. By setting Bianca's life against that of Alice, she highlights the beneficial effects of an independent career on a woman's life.

Arriving in England at the age of 16 with an ill, insane mother and no living friends or relatives to turn to, illegitimate into the bargain, Bianca has much to contend with, and adopts her career initially to preserve herself and her mother from destitution. But the need to work for her living gives her strength, and she benefits as well from never being exhorted to worship the empty commonplaces that bedevil Alice's life. Indeed she becomes so self-reliant and purposeful that she does not need to make a habit of consciously invoking the standards that guide her. Rather than being confined to a way of life which society considers natural, she can develop her potential in a genuinely natural way. Rather than being protected from the practical world of work, she is constantly in the thick of it. Moreover, she develops a passion for acting itself, declining Alice's offer of a position as a nursery-governess, because acting gives her an outlet for her tremendous energies, as well as a sense of power over an audience. She is conscious too that the theatrical profession has never been sufficiently valued either by British society in general or by its own members, and so aspires to improve it by her example, dedicating herself to embodying as effectively as possible the conceptions of the great playwrights.

Jewsbury's choice of acting as a vocation for her career-woman heroine has several implications. On the personal level, it reflects her own interest in the theatre. In particular, while writing *The Half Sisters*, she was friendly with the noted American actress Charlotte Cushman, who played in England in the mid-1840s. Jewsbury's conception of Bianca certainly owes something to Cushman, a hard-working and dedicated actress who devoted herself earnestly to her career and had a great respect for her material, especially Shakespeare's plays. One of her notable roles was actually as a character called Bianca, in Henry Hart Milman's *Fazio*. Cushman had also impressed Jewsbury with her capacity to conquer her love for an unworthy man, an aspect of her life which influenced the portrayal of Bianca's relationship with Conrad.[8] (Cushman in fact chose never to marry.) As well as all this, acting was probably the only career open to women in the 1840s where they could achieve the same prestige and level of pay as men, at least in the higher echelons—a fact that enhances the contrast between Alice's dependent obscurity and Bianca's independence and fame. The theatre world was (and is) such that women's wages were not depressed by direct competition with men's, but were much dependent on the box-office appeal of individuals.

Acting was also the profession which took women furthest outside the private sphere, since by its nature it depended on the open display of their talents for money. It is interesting that William Charles Macready, the leading actor of the 1840s and another friend of Jewsbury's, believed that a conventionally educated woman could never become a great tragic actress, since she was brought up to conceal her strongest feelings.[9] But this element of public display, given the period's assumptions about women's fragility and the importance of female chastity, meant that actresses were often associated in the public mind with prostitutes: Conrad, whose attitudes epitomize those Jewsbury

---

[8] See Joseph Leach, *Bright Particular Star: The Life & Times of Charlotte Cushman* (1970), 65, 165–7, 203, 209–10.

[9] Diary entry for 8 Sep. 1845, in *Macready's Reminiscences, and Selections from his Diaries and Letters*, ed. Sir Frederick Pollock (2 vols.; 1875), ii. 266.

seeks to undermine, declares to Melton that 'a woman who makes her mind public, or exhibits herself in any way' is 'little better than a woman of a nameless class' (Vol. 2, Chapter II). Jewsbury wishes to show, however, that the purpose and occupation which a career can give a woman, plus the strength and self-reliance it can develop, will offer her something to preoccupy her besides love, and thus act as a safeguard against sexual temptation. So she puts Bianca into the profession with the most pervasive reputation for promiscuity, only to demonstrate how her resilience and sense of vocation help to keep her chaste. And if this can be true of an actress, the novel implies, then it could also apply to another category of women whose intrusion into the public sphere made their reputations dubious—female authors.

Yet the novel goes further: it suggests that being deprived of both worthwhile work and a chance to develop her faculties actually fosters Alice's adulterous feelings for Conrad. Alice has been shown from the outset to have latent intellectual abilities and artistic tastes which have been stifled by her upbringing and her environment. Conrad's appeal for her is not purely sexual, but derives partly from his association with a world outside her experience. Indeed he first makes a strong impact on her by introducing her to that most unerotic of poets, William Wordsworth—but in the absence of any other outlet for her feelings and aspirations, these inevitably become sexual. One of the main points the novel makes is that restricting women to lives of domestic trivia guided by unexamined truisms is an ideal prescription for leading them to flout the most powerful Victorian social taboo of all.

The radicalism of the book's attitudes to the 'Woman Question' emerges all the more clearly if we consider a couple of earlier texts dealing with the same issues which would have influenced it. One of these, Madame de Staël's *Corinne, or Italy*, published in French in 1807 but rapidly translated into English, would have been very familiar to readers of the 1840s, particularly women. The other, a novella of 1830 called 'The History of an Enthusiast', was by Geraldine Jewsbury's only sister, Maria Jane.

Corinne focuses on a pair of half-sisters—Corinne, who is half-Italian, and the entirely English Lucile; even by calling her novel *The Half Sisters*, Geraldine Jewsbury would have recalled *Corinne* to many readers' minds. Corinne is a woman of extraordinary artistic talents of all kinds who, after being hemmed in by rigid English rules of propriety for several years, returns to Italy and becomes the country's foremost living artistic genius. One reason for the novel's popularity was that it allowed conventionally educated English girls to imagine themselves as Corinnes, and in *The Half Sisters*, Alice misses dinner through being absorbed in *Corinne*, the narrator commenting that the first reading of the novel is 'an epoch a woman never forgets' (Vol. 1, Chapter XI). Yet if Alice is inspired here by the example of Corinne, it is not for long enough to quell her constant feelings of guilt at transgressing social codes.

The aftermath of Alice's reading of *Corinne* actually serves to lock her into the role of the novel's other half sister, Lucile, who is given a conventional English upbringing and aspires to be simply a quiet, docile homebody. For, while hurrying back to her mother in a guilt-ridden state, Alice encounters Bryant, and her anxiety to appease her mother adds to the eagerness with which she accepts his proposal. Thus Jewsbury emphasizes how hard it is for a woman of Alice's conditioning to challenge her lot, even with the inspiration of *Corinne*. Yet both *The Half Sisters* and *Corinne* deploy half-sisters as protagonists in order to make the same point, a point about women as such. For, since half-sisters have a parent in common, but only one, they can be expected both to resemble each other and to differ, and this relationship stands for that between one woman and another. That is, women in general are not all the same, albeit one of the many deficiencies in their socialization is that they are treated as if they were. On the other hand, even women whose conduct is considered most unwomanly do share underlying qualities with the most feminine of their sex, as some apparent differences between women can result more from nurture than from nature. Neither Lucile nor Alice has the great artistic talents of Corinne or Bianca, but each does possess capacities which have been repressed by her upbringing and way of life.

The basic story-line of *The Half Sisters* has much in common with *Corinne*, but the later novel modifies the plot to present a more optimistic view of women's potential than de Staël's. Like

Conrad Percy, *Corinne*'s male protagonist Oswald Nelvil is initially attracted to the artistically gifted half-sister. Yet he eventually finds that she challenges too radically his basic assumptions about women's role, so he transfers his affections to the more domesticated one. In de Staël's text, however, Corinne's loss of her lover is fatal. She had always seen her artistic talents as almost worthless unless they brought her love, and when Oswald abandons her for Lucile, they atrophy, and she herself soon pines away to the grave. *The Half Sisters*, by contrast, implies that a woman with a vocation to occupy her mind can gain some satisfaction from this, and is thus less dependent on a man to give her life meaning. While in love with Conrad, Bianca certainly aspires to please him, but this is never her sole motive, and when things go wrong, her misery can even enhance her performances. Although her later love for Melton does make her feel that her career alone cannot fulfil her needs, devotion to acting has helped her to overcome her passion for Conrad and to turn to a man who at least sympathizes with her aspirations. Also a challenge to *Corinne* is the way the domesticated half-sister who has won the other's lover ends up suffering much more from the effects of love than her rival. Furthermore, whereas in *Corinne* the narrow-minded Oswald is presented as the typical British male, *The Half Sisters* offers us not only his literary heir Conrad, but also the enlightened Lord Melton, not to mention the well-meaning Bryant, who (unlike Oswald) is finally capable of recognizing his own limitations.

If *The Half Sisters* questions some of the implications of *Corinne*, it reverses even more clearly the apparent moral of Maria Jane Jewsbury's 'History of an Enthusiast'. By the time Geraldine Jewsbury embarked on her own literary career, her sister was long dead. Accompanying her husband William Fletcher to India, she had died of cholera at Poona in 1833. She had been a prolific writer, but a proposal to bring out a posthumous collection of her articles had to be shelved because they had been published anonymously, she had taken the originals with her, and Fletcher would not answer any of the Jewsbury family's letters. It would be surprising if all this did not make Geraldine doubtful about marriage! In any case, she retained a great deal of respect for Maria Jane, both as a sister and a writer, and regretted that she had not lived to guide her own literary endeavours. Yet the messages which Geraldine must have derived from her sister's writings about independent careers for women were very ambiguous, and *The Half Sisters* is in part an attempt by Geraldine to come to terms with Maria Jane's legacy.

Twelve years older than Geraldine, very devout, and left to bring up her younger siblings in her teens, Maria Jane often wrote to her younger sister at boarding school. The overall burden of these letters (preserved in the John Rylands Library of the University of Manchester), is that Geraldine should control her emotions, eschewing ambition and thoughts of fame, since these encouraged vanity and selfishness, and might ultimately endanger her prospects of eternal salvation. They bear witness to contemporary writers' constant practice of recommending to women certain Christian virtues, such as humility, selflessness, and dutifulness, as if they were particularly suited to females, while strenuously attacking behaviour in a woman motivated by any sense of her individuality, or desire for self-actualization. Maria Jane adapted these and other letters into a collection where piety and meekness were even more stridently enjoined on readers, published in 1828 as *Letters to the Young*. Yet the published letters gave their author literary renown, while the originals are interspersed with news of Maria Jane's publications, even quotations from favourable reviews.

'The History of an Enthusiast' is part of a collection of novellas called *The Three Histories* which came out in 1830; Maria Jane was 30, and had already published (as well as *Letters to the Young*), a collection of poems and prose sketches called *Phantasmagoria* (1825), and a book of poetry, *Lays of Leisure Hours* (1829). The story's heroine, Julia Osborne, is given a very narrow, domestically orientated education by her grandmother, but has her reading extended by the good offices of the local clergyman, Mr Percy. Eventually she becomes a writer, and attains great success in London. Yet the man she loves, Mr Percy's son Cecil—note the surname he shares with Geraldine's Conrad—never returns her love, wedding the gentle and home-loving Mary. Julia feels her talents dry up (like Corinne's), and comes to envy unambitious, happily married women. Although the story presents Julia's struggles for a literary education very sympathetically, it also suggests that by becoming a public figure, she has sacrificed not only her beloved but her essential femininity. Yet it is also open-ended, with some hint of recovery for Julia in the last pages.

The Three Histories was Maria Jane Jewsbury's best-selling work, so that ostensibly she achieved her own literary ambitions by writing books attacking literary ambition. But as Norma Clarke has shown in her study of the Jewsbury sisters, it was difficult for women writers in the early nineteenth century to avoid accommodating themselves in some way to prevailing assumptions about female ambition. Besides, women writers also internalized such assumptions themselves, so that their inconsistencies were not the result of hypocrisy, but evidence of very real inner doubts about the validity of what they were doing. The difference between Maria Jane's Julia and Geraldine's Bianca shows the younger writer challenging the idea that a career for a woman unsexes her or dooms her to painfully unrequited love. Nevertheless, no more than her sister could Geraldine Jewsbury escape misgivings about how far she could subvert traditional assumptions.

To begin with, *The Half Sisters* really stops short of making specific demands about career paths that should be opened to women. In his argument with Conrad, Melton says that he is not interested in women's 'rights' to become soldiers, lawyers, or MPs, so much as their right to 'grow up freely, and to have their natural characters developed as God made them'. Later, in his three-way discussion with Bianca and his sister Lady Vernon, Melton claims that what women really need to do is to review what they have been taught, and to 'consider what is a real matter of conscience, and what only a matter of convention'. Bianca speaks fervently about what her own career has meant to her, and argues that women should have a purpose in life. But apparently this is not so as to make them independent and self-reliant, but to produce 'a race of wives and daughters far different' from those of the present, women who could 'aid men in any noble object by noble thoughts, by self-denial, by real sympathy and fellowship of heart'. Such a sentiment would have been by no means too radical for Mrs Ellis. On the other hand, the novel does seem to acknowledge its own tentativeness: Lady Vernon complains

that Bianca and Melton are restricting themselves to safe gener-
alizations, and says that if women did stop short at analysing their
own condition, half of them would simply want to hang themselves on confronting the pointlessness of their lives (Vol. 2,
Chapter VI).

Jewsbury also seems over-anxious to show that Bianca's ambitions are not primarily motivated by any desire to gratify her ego.
She portrays the beneficial influence of Bianca's career on the
development of her personality, but the self thus created is not
fostered for its own sake, but in the service of what is presented
as a higher cause. To begin with, Bianca acts so as to support
herself and her mother and to show her love and gratitude to
Conrad. Later, even though she does come to enjoy her power
over an audience, there is much more emphasis on her ultimate
aim of serving and elevating her art. That is, she exists 'relative'
to a spiritualized conception of her profession, if not always
'relative' to other people. And the odd interlude involving Melton and the singer La Fornasari, scarcely connected with the rest
of the novel, seems there to highlight the difference between the
woman artist who submits herself to her art and the one who
exploits it for the sake of wealth and admiration. Moreover, since
La Fornasari has apparently adopted out her child to pursue her
career, the novel seems at least partly to endorse contemporary
fears that, if permitted careers outside the home, women could
selfishly neglect what were considered their primary and indeed
'natural' duties. Yet by using La Fornasari to define what Bianca
was not, Jewsbury may well have rendered more acceptable to
her contemporary readers the claims she was making for women
via her actress heroine. It is also possible that some of the novel's
most radical arguments about women were more palatable to her
readers because they came from the mouth of a man, and a lord
at that!

The ending of the novel is puzzling, since it appears that
Bianca quite calmly abandons her career on marrying Lord Melton. Henry Chorley, reviewing the novel for the *Athenaeum* in
1848, thought this showed that Conrad had been right about
women's nature all along.[10] This is unlikely to be what Jewsbury

---

[10] The *Athenaeum*, 18 Mar. 1848, 289.

had in mind: perhaps she is again accommodating herself to her readers, concerned about how much she can get away with. Or is she possibly demonstrating, in the face of popular prejudices about actresses, that the qualities Bianca's career has developed in her can be adapted to life in the aristocracy? Or is she finally uncertain about a career as a lifelong focus for a woman's life?

Geraldine Jewsbury herself never married. She was rather given to passionate entanglements, and Jane Carlyle certainly believed her eager to find a husband. Indeed, during the writing of *The Half Sisters*, she proposed unsuccessfully to Charles Lambert, a French socialist leader—but given her intense interest in the public sphere, she conceivably saw such a union mainly as an entrée into politics. She produced four more novels, dealing with such urgent contemporary issues as industrialism and the self-made man (*Marian Withers*, 1851), inter-class marriage (*The Sorrows of Gentility*, 1856), and even hereditary insanity (*Constance Herbert*, 1855). She also reviewed about 2,000 books for the *Athenaeum*, and was the first woman with an established career as a publisher's reader. Long before she died in 1880, she had a secure position as a woman of letters, and was justifiably proud of what she had achieved. Her friends had come to include the Huxleys, the Kingsleys, the Rossettis, and Ruskin, while she had also met the Brownings, Tennyson, and Charlotte Brontë.

For all the inconsistencies in her novels, Geraldine Jewsbury was unusually aware of how, like Alice, she and her contemporaries had been shaped by their conditioning and would never break completely free of its influence. None the less, their apparently formless and sometimes futile struggles represented an encouraging sign of things to come. About a year after *The Half Sisters* was published, she was optimistic and prescient about the future for women, writing to Jane Carlyle in words which deserve quoting at length:

I believe we are touching on better days, when women will have a genuine, normal life of their own to lead. There, perhaps, will not be so many marriages, and women will be taught not to feel their destiny manqué if they remain single. They will be able to be friends and companions in a way they cannot be now. All the strength of their feelings and thoughts will not run into love; they will be able to associate with men, and make friends of them, without being reduced by their position to see them as lovers or husbands. Instead of having appearances to attend to, they will be allowed to have their virtues, in any measure which it may please God to send, without being diluted down to the tepid 'rectified spirit' of 'feminine grace' and 'womanly timidity'—in short, they will make themselves women, as men are allowed to make themselves men . . . I do not feel that either you or I are to be called failures. We are indications of a development of womanhood which as yet is not recognised. It has, so far, no ready-made channels to run in, but still we have looked, and tried, and found that the present rules for women will not hold us—that something better and stronger is needed . . . There are women to come after us, who will approach nearer the fulness of the measure of the stature of a woman's nature. I regard myself as a mere faint indication, a rudiment of the idea, of certain higher qualities and possibilities that lie in women, and all the eccentricities and mistakes and miseries and absurdities I have made are only the consequences of an imperfect formation, an immature growth . . . A 'Mrs. Ellis' woman is developed to the extreme of her little possibility; but I can see there is a precious mine of a species of womanhood yet undreamed of by the professors and essayists on female education, and I believe also that we belong to it.[11]

---

[11] Geraldine Jewsbury to Jane Carlyle, 1849?, in *Selections from the Letters of Geraldine Endsor Jewsbury to Jane Welsh Carlyle*, 347–9.

NOTE ON THE TEXT

The Half Sisters was first published in two-volume form by Chapman and Hall in 1848. There were two further editions in Jewsbury's lifetime, both in one volume: one published by Chapman and Hall in 1854, and another published as Vol. 230 of The Parlour Library in about 1861. As there is no evidence that Jewsbury made any alterations to these latter editions, I have used the first edition as copy-text. The spelling of the original has been retained, except in a few cases where ambiguity might result for modern readers. Punctuation has also been modernized, and a few misprints silently corrected.

SELECT BIBLIOGRAPHY

Place of publication is London unless stated otherwise.

Editions

Of Geraldine Jewsbury's novels, the only one reprinted this century has been the first, *Zoe: A History of Two Lives* (3 vols.; Chapman and Hall, 1845). It appeared in 1975 in Garland's series, Victorian Fiction: Novels of Faith and Doubt, and in 1989 as a Virago Modern Classic. Publication details for Jewsbury's other novels and children's stories are as follows:

Angelo; or The Pine Forest in the Alps (Grant and Griffith, 1855, dated 1856).

Constance Herbert (3 vols.; Hurst and Blackett, 1855; new edn., [1882]).

The Half Sisters: A Tale (2 vols.; Chapman and Hall, 1848; other edns., 1854, [1861?]).

The History of an Adopted Child (1852, dated 1853).

Marian Withers (serialized in *Manchester Examiner and Times*, 1850; published in 3 vols., 1851).

Right or Wrong (2 vols.; Hurst and Blackett, 1859).

The Sorrows of Gentility (2 vols.; Hurst and Blackett, 1856).

Letters and Other Primary Sources

Many of Geraldine Jewsbury's letters to Jane Carlyle were published in *Selections from the Letters of Geraldine Endsor Jewsbury to Jane Welsh Carlyle*, ed. Mrs Alexander Ireland (Longmans, Green, & Co., 1892), while four of Thomas Carlyle's early letters to Geraldine Jewsbury have appeared in Susanne Howe Nobbe's 'Four Unpublished Letters of Thomas Carlyle', *PMLA* 70 (1955), 876–84. Both sides of this correspondence are held in the Alexander Turnbull Library, Wellington, New Zealand (Geraldine Jewsbury, MS Papers 544; MS Carlyle Acc. bk. 15, 1258). This library also holds Jewsbury's numerous letters to Walter Mantell (1857–80, WBD Mantell papers, MSS 83); extracts have been published in Joanne Wilkes, 'Geraldine Jewsbury, Walter Mantell, and Race Relations in New Zealand', *New Zealand Journal of History*, 22 (1988), 105–17. Jewsbury's letters to *Athenaeum* editor W. Hepworth Dixon are in the library of the University of California (Los Angeles). Maria Jane Jewsbury's letters to Geraldine from 1827 to 1832 are held in the John Rylands University Library of Manchester.

Geraldine Jewsbury's 609 reports to Richard Bentley as a publisher's reader (1858–80) are in the British Library (Add. MSS 46, 653–5). Some of them are quoted in Jeanne Rosenmayer Fahnestock, 'Geraldine Jewsbury: The Power of the Publisher's Reader', *Nineteenth-Century Fiction*, 28 (1973), 253–72. Her reviews for the *Athenaeum* (1849–80) are listed in Monica Correa Fryckstedt, *Geraldine Jewsbury's Athenaeum Reviews: A Mirror of Mid-Victorian Attitudes to Fiction* (Acta Univ Uppsala; Uppsala, 1986).

Biography, Criticism, and Background Reading

Baker, Michael, *The Rise of the Victorian Actor* (Croom Helm, 1978).

Branca, Patricia, *Silent Sisterhood: Middle Class Women in Victorian Homes* (Croom Helm, 1975).

Carlyle, Jane Welsh, *Jane Welsh Carlyle: Letters to Her Family, 1839–1863*, ed. Leonard Huxley (John Murray, 1924).

—— *Letters and Memorials of Jane Welsh Carlyle*, prepared for publication by Thomas Carlyle, ed. James Anthony Froude (3 vols.; Longmans, Green, & Co., 1883).

[Chorley, Henry Fothergill], Review of *The Half Sisters*, *Athenaeum*, 18 Mar. 1848, pp. 288–90.

Clarke, Norma, *Ambitious Heights: Writing, Friendship, Love—The Jewsbury Sisters, Felicia Hemans, and Jane Welsh Carlyle* (Routledge, 1990).

Davis, Tracy C., *Actresses as Working Women: Their Social Identity in Victorian Culture* (Routledge, 1991).

Ellis, Mrs [Sarah], *The Women of England: Their Social Duties, and Domestic Habits* (Fisher, Son, & Co., 1838).

Foster, Shirley, *Victorian Women's Fiction: Marriage, Freedom and the Individual* (Croom Helm; Beckenham, 1985).

Fryckstedt, Monica Correa, 'Geraldine Jewsbury and *Douglas Jerrold's Shilling Magazine*', *English Studies*, 66 (1985), 326–37.

—— 'New Sources on Geraldine Jewsbury and the Woman Question', *Research Studies*, 51 (1983), 51–63.

Gorham, Deborah, *The Victorian Girl and the Feminine Ideal* (Croom Helm, 1982).

Hartley, J. M., 'Geraldine Jewsbury and the Problems of the Woman Novelist', *Women's Studies International Quarterly*, 2 (1979), 137–53.

Howe, Susanne, *Geraldine Jewsbury: Her Life and Errors* (George Allen & Unwin, 1935).

Jewsbury, Maria Jane, *Occasional Papers*, ed. with a memoir by Eric Gillett (OUP; Oxford, 1932).

Leach, Joseph, *Bright Particular Star: The Life & Times of Charlotte Cushman* (Yale University Press; New Haven, Conn., 1970).

Rosen, Judith, 'At Home Upon a Stage: Domesticity and Genius in Geraldine Jewsbury's *The Half Sisters* (1848)', in *The New Nineteenth Century: Feminist Readings of Underread Victorian Fiction*, ed. Barbara Leah Harman and Susan Meyer (Garland; New York, 1996), 17–32.

Rowell, George, *The Victorian Theatre, 1792–1914*, 2nd edn. (CUP; Cambridge, 1978).

Surridge, Lisa, 'Madame de Stael Meets Mrs Ellis: Geraldine Jewsbury's *The Half Sisters*', *Carlyle Studies Annual*, 15 (1995), 81–95.

Trudgill, Eric, *Madonnas and Magdalens* (Heinemann, 1976).

Wolff, Robert Lee, *Gains and Losses: Novels of Faith and Doubt in Victorian England* (John Murray, 1977).

[Woolf, Virginia], 'Geraldine and Jane', *Times Literary Supplement*, 28 Feb. 1929. Repr. in her *The Common Reader: Second Series* (1932) and in her *Collected Essays*, vol. iv (Hogarth Press, 1967), 27–39.

A CHRONOLOGY OF GERALDINE ENDSOR JEWSBURY

1799 Marriage of Geraldine Endsor Jewsbury's parents, Thomas Jewsbury, a cotton manufacturer of Measham (Derbyshire), and Maria Smith.

1800 Birth of Maria Jane Jewsbury, Geraldine's sister and mentor.

1812 Geraldine Endsor Jewsbury born, 22 August.

1818 Thomas Jewsbury fails as a cotton manufacturer, and the family moves to Manchester, where he becomes an insurance agent.

1819 Mrs Jewsbury dies soon after giving birth to son Frank. Maria Jane takes over running the household and bringing up her five surviving siblings.

1820s GEJ attends the Misses Darbys' boarding school at Alder Mills in Tamworth.

1825 Publication of Maria Jane's first book, *Phantasmagoria, or Sketches of Life and Character*.

1828 Maria Jane publishes *Letters to the Young*, partly based on her letters to GEJ at school.

1830 Maria Jane publishes her last and most successful book, the series of novellas, *The Three Histories*. One of these, 'The History of an Enthusiast', will be a major influence on *The Half Sisters*. GEJ spends a year in London with her sister, studying French, Italian, and drawing, with a view to earning her living as a governess. But she also meets Maria Jane's literary circle, including the novelist Maria Edgeworth.

1832 Maria Jane marries the Revd William Kew Fletcher on 1 August, and soon afterwards leaves for India, where he is a chaplain to the East India Company. GEJ is left to manage the household for her father and brother Frank.

1833 Maria Jane dies of cholera in Poona, India, on 4 October.

1830s During the latter part of this decade, GEJ, feeling intellectually and spiritually isolated, struggles with religious doubt, trying to combat a Materialist view of life. She gains some consolation from reading the works of Thomas Carlyle.

1840   GEJ writes to Thomas Carlyle in April, initiating a correspondence. Her father dies; she continues to keep house for Frank.

1841–   Visits the Carlyles in March, and begins a long-standing friendship with Jane Carlyle. Embarks on *Zoe*, initially in collaboration with Elizabeth Newton Paulet; Jane Carlyle finds the novel too outspoken, but is instrumental in having it accepted by Chapman and Hall.

1844   GEJ has published in the *British and Foreign Review* her translations of articles on Dante and Thomas Carlyle by Italian writer/patriot Giuseppe Mazzini.

1845   *Zoe: The History of Two Lives* causes a minor sensation because of the way it deals with religious doubt and with love between a priest and a married woman.

1846   GEJ befriends American actress Charlotte Cushman, one model for Bianca in *The Half Sisters*.

1846–7 Four articles and a story by GEJ published in *Douglas Jerrold's Shilling Magazine*: they cover class differences, the treatment of servants, and the pressures on women to marry for mercenary reasons.

1847   GEJ proposes by letter to French socialist leader Charles Lambert—without success.

1848   *The Half Sisters* published. In May, GEJ visits Paris because of the revolution which has broken out there.

1849   GEJ embarks on her long career as reviewer, primarily of fiction and children's books, for the *Athenaeum*.

1850   GEJ's article, 'Religious Faith and Modern Scepticism' published in the *Westminster Review* for January. She begins contributing to Dickens's *Household Words*, in which she will publish 17 tales by 1859.

1851   Novel *Marian Withers* published.

1852   Publication of GEJ's first children's story, *The History of an Adopted Child*.

1854   Frank Jewsbury having married, GEJ moves to Chelsea to be near the Carlyles.

1855   Publication of GEJ's novel *Constance Herbert*, and of her children's story *Angelo; or The Pine Forest in the Alps*.

1856   Novel *The Sorrows of Gentility* published. GEJ falls in love with Walter Mantell, a New Zealand colonist. He fails to reciprocate, and returns to New Zealand in 1859, but he and GEJ correspond until her death.

1858   GEJ begins her long career as publisher's reader for Richard Bentley.

1859   Publication of *Right or Wrong*, GEJ's last novel. Writer Lady Morgan, who has been preparing her autobiography for publication with GEJ's help, dies and leaves her a legacy.

1862   Publication of *Lady Morgan's Memoirs: Autobiography, Diaries and Correspondence*, which GEJ has partly written, and also co-edited (with W. Hepworth Dixon).

1866   Jane Carlyle dies on 21 April. GEJ moves to Sevenoaks (Kent) for the rest of her life.

1867   GEJ begins friendship with John Ruskin.

1871   Government refuses GEJ a Civil List pension, despite the support from many scientists and men of letters, plus numerous Manchester identities.

1874   GEJ granted a Civil List pension of £40 a year, for services to literature.

1880   GEJ dies of cancer in a London private hospital on 23 September, aged 68.

THE HALF SISTERS

A Tale

TO

JANE WELSH CARLYLE

AND

ELIZABETH NEWTON PAULET

*This book is inscribed,
by their affectionate friend,*

GERALDINE ENDSOR JEWSBURY.★

Green Heys, Manchester,
February 14, 1848.

VOLUME ONE

CHAPTER I

On a bed, scantily hung with faded print, lay a woman apparently in extreme suffering. A girl about sixteen stood over the fire, carefully watching the contents of a small pan; at length it seemed sufficiently prepared, and she poured it into a tea-cup, and approaching the bed where the sick woman lay moaning and restless, she addressed her in Italian, and endeavoured to raise her up; but the woman shook off her arms and hid her face in the pillow, like a fretful child endeavouring to escape from its nurse.

'Come, Mamma mia,' said the girl, 'I have made you something delicious, something you like very much, won't you eat it, now I have got it ready with my own hands?'

'No, no,' said the sick woman, in a querulous tone, and burying herself still more among the clothes, 'I won't be teased; let me lie still, and then we will go and see him.'

'See whom?' asked the girl.

'Him whom we came to see—came from Italy to see, who will take care of us, and never let us leave him. He will be glad to see us; it is so long, so long since we parted, and he has never seen thee. I have nursed thee and kept away from him till thou wert grown a beauty. I have kept away all these years to surprise him at last, when thou wert grown tall and beautiful. I should have died when he left me but for the hope of this; and now that I am so near him I feel frightened; I dare not get up and go to him, I should die with too much joy. All yesterday I kept thinking, perhaps he will come here; but I see he had no presentiment to bring him; I must go to him. See,' she continued, drawing a pocket-book from under her pillow, 'read there, read there, I will have no secrets from my child now.'

'Is there any money in it?' asked the girl.

'Yes, all I have,' replied the mother, 'but no matter, he has plenty, he always used to give me plenty, we shall want nothing now, and we shall have no more sorrow.'

The girl looked anxiously at the contents of the pocket-book, with which she had never before been intrusted; she found some old letters, a lock of light hair, an address written upon a card, and about five shillings in money.

'Is this all?' asked she, anxiously.

'Yes, yes, but he has plenty; if this pain in my head would only cease, I would get up; but I cannot.'

'Will you not take some of this nice arrow-root?' said the girl, coaxingly.

'No, no, I tell you, but I will see *him* presently.' She then fell off into a doze, moaning the whole time, and clutching the bed-clothes with her long, thin fingers.

The little inn where they were staying was very noisy—bells were ringing incessantly. There were callings for different individuals from the top to the bottom of the house, the tramping of heavy feet along the passage, and up and down stairs. The window of their room looked on to the stable-yard, and they could hear the noise of the horses' feet, and the whistling of the ostlers; the smell of the stables ascended; and an all-pervading odour of tobacco and spirits made altogether an association of sound and scent most irritating and oppressive. The sick woman had sunk into a stupor, but still seemed obscurely sensible of the annoyances around.

The girl first put the little room to rights, and then sat down at the foot of the bed with a cup of milk and a slice of bread. She had not sat long, before the doctor, who had been sent for early in the morning, entered. He was a grave hard-looking man, with cold indifferent manners; and the appearance of poverty about the room did not tend to give him any additional blandness. He stepped at once to the bed-side, and rousing the patient, proceeded to question her without much gentleness.

'How long is it since she was herself?' he asked abruptly of the girl. She did not understand him.

'I mean,' said he, 'is she usually in her right senses?'

The poor child, shocked and stunned by this horrible suspicion, which entered her mind for the first time, could not reply.

'Come, come, I cannot wait here all day,' said the doctor, 'I have other places to go to. Have you perceived your mother growing childish? because, though there is some fever, I don't see that she is exactly delirious.'

'She is not so sensible as she was at home; she has seemed changed since we came here—she will not get up nor be dressed. I don't know what to make of her.'

'Ah well, young lady, it is as well you should be prepared for the worst; your mother will never be herself again, in my opinion; she seems quite weak in her intellects, and if you have any friends,* you had better communicate with them, for you are too young to be left with such a charge. Just now she is overcome with fatigue and excitement, but she is in no sort of danger. I will see her again to-night, and send her a little medicine, which you must give her regularly. Let her sleep as much as she will, and keep her quiet. Good morning to you.'

As the door closed after him, the child sank on her knees beside the bed, sick with fear. A horrible future had just disclosed itself to her—her girlhood was strangled by this sudden fearful anxiety, and the life curdled in her heart. All that had struck her as strange in her mother's conduct, and which she had forborne to question, attributing it to sorrow, was now revealed in its full significance. All the complaints she had uttered about being watched by enemies, and which had excited her daughter's sympathy, now seemed a horrible confirmation of her fears; and when she recollected all her mother had that morning told her of the vague motives which had brought them from home, and thought of the slender means that remained to them, her heart trembled and died within her.

She sat thus overwhelmed for several hours, during which she became laden with as many years. At length, the heavy necessity which had at first stunned her, acted as a stimulus; besides, in the deepest sorrow there is always a reaction towards hope. People who are called to suffer much have always great elasticity of heart, for without that it must give way and break.

'After all,' thought she, 'the person named in the address may live near here, and may help us. Any way, he will put us into the way of getting home, and once there I can work.'

Her nature began to recover from the despondency in which she had well nigh been overwhelmed. She began to rise to the surface of her sorrow, instead of being plunged, like lead, beneath it.

CHAPTER II

IT was assize time,* and the town of L——was filled with an inroad of visitors, witnesses, and barristers; every inn was occupied, and more than occupied; and very fastidious people at other times were now glad to find accommodation in very second-rate places.

The landlord of the 'Blue Bell' was lounging at the door of his small tavern, when he was accosted by a dashing-looking youth, followed by a porter carrying a leathern portmanteau. The landlord felt instinctively that he had been round the whole town before coming to him, and therefore thought without dismay on the one small back three-cornered chamber, which alone remained untenanted. He knew it was the only one to be had in the place.

'Happy to see you, sir—town very full—beds worth a guinea a piece. Yes, sir, yes, by the most singular good fortune the parties for whom I had orders to reserve it are unable to attend—only heard an hour ago, or would have been snapped up fifty times. Walk this way, sir; a charming room, you see!—a little small or so, but a beautiful aspect.'

The new comer shrugged his shoulders. 'Well, well,' said he, 'I suppose there will be a time when one ought to be thankful to have a place in Purgatory. Will that window open?'

'Yes, sir, that top pane swings back on a hinge, and will let in a charming current of fresh air.'

'For Heaven's sake admit it, then, for I am half stifled. Have you a sitting-room at liberty?'

'Why no, sir, I am sorry to say they are all engaged; still, if you would not object, I think I could accommodate you. There is a gentleman in the "Sanded Parlour", who, I am sure, will be very glad to admit you to a share of it. He is a most respectable man—comes here very often—I have known him for years. He is the manager of a circus, and has a travelling company; he has just been to make some new engagements. He opens next in Birmingham. Sometimes I've had half the troop, horses and all. We would be glad of your company in the bar; but the "Sanded Parlour" is more comfortable.'

The stranger yielded to his destiny, and allowed himself to be conducted to the 'Sanded Parlour'. A man, apparently about forty, a stout, coarse-looking, and rather pompous individual, in a dark green cut-away coat, with a bright full stock, and showy pin, stood with his back to the fire-place.

'Mr Simpson,' said the landlord, entering, 'I have taken the liberty to assure this gentleman that you will allow him to join your company, as there is no other room at liberty.'

'Certainly, sir, certainly; pray make yourself at home. Assize time is like misery for making one acquainted with strange bed-fellows—*room*-fellows, I should say—but it's all a matter of no consequence.'

The stranger bowed rather haughtily, and taking up a news-paper which lay on the table, desired the landlord to let him have a grilled fowl and tea directly.

The manager of the circus put his hands in his pocket, and began to whistle to himself as he looked out of the window; and the young man sat turning over the old softened provincial newspaper, whilst the sand crackled and grated under his feet every time he moved, in a way to try the nerves even of people not particularly fastidious. He kept up a true Englishman's si-lence,* and endeavoured to turn his share of the room into his castle, by surrounding himself with an impassable moat of stiff-ness and reserve.

The tea and grilled fowl made their appearance at last. The landlord placed them on the table, but did not offer to withdraw, in spite of the surprised and impatient looks of the young man.

'Mr Simpson,' said he, addressing the first occupant of the room, 'perhaps you will give me your opinion as to what I had best do in a little matter that has just occurred. When I went out of the room just now, a young girl, who arrived here with her mother three days ago, came to me in the bar,—not crying, but quite pale and desperate like. She is from foreign parts, and it was as much as I could do to make out what she said, though she does speak English after a fashion. It seems her mother came over to England in search of some relation, I suppose, but I cannot just make out who or what. She had been in a queer melancholy way, and since she came to England she has got worse, and has now got a nervous fever or something; and this young thing, her daughter, came to me to tell me what I suspected, namely, that their money has run short. She put these gimcracks into my hands to sell, and asked me to help her to some work. I could not help feeling sorry for the poor thing. Her mother will never be any sort of protection to her, for the doctor who was sent for to her, says she is quite childish. I feel very sorry, for I had a daughter just that age myself once, but I cannot keep them here when their money is all done; a man must live by the fruit of his labour, and I cannot afford to give mine away. I thought, perhaps, you, sir, or this gentleman, might understand her tongue, and make out whether she has any friends.'

'What does she look like?' said Mr Simpson.

'She is rather dark complexioned. I thought at first she might have been a play-actor, for she made me understand by her looks and actions I don't know how. If you happened to have a place open in your company now, her fortune would be made.'

The younger stranger had paused from eating, and had put down his paper to listen to this conversation. It was an adventure he had not calculated upon, and he began to get stoical to the gritty floor and the grinding of the table and chairs when they were moved.

'Can we see her, landlord?' said he, 'perhaps we may make out something.'

The landlord retired, and in a few minutes returned, leading in a young girl of about sixteen, in a black silk dress, high to the throat, and the folds confined with a band round the waist. She had the unformed undeveloped figure of a girl, but her face was full of beauty—large liquid grey eyes, that looked with an intent and earnest meaning beyond her years; a profusion of hair, of that blueish black, so rarely seen, was twisted round her head and fell in tresses over her neck; her face was deeply flushed as she entered the room, but there was a composed reserve in her manner.

'Tell these gentlemen,' said the landlord, 'all you have been saying to me, and may be they will help you.'

The young girl seemed to nerve herself by an inward effort. The younger stranger addressed a few words of Italian to her—her eyes flashed with pleasure—poor child, it was as if she had already found a friend! She spoke quietly and slowly, and told him that her mother, who had for several years been in a feeble state, both of body and mind, was haunted with a desire to come to England, and had hoarded up every farthing she could get; but that her uncle, with whom they lived in a small sea-port, had always watched her carefully to prevent her leaving the house; that he died a few weeks back, and then her mother seemed suddenly to rally her faculties and bodily strength,—disposed of the property her uncle had left; took a passage for herself and daughter in a sailing vessel to England—to see a friend, she told her daughter, who would provide for them both; but that, since leaving the vessel, she had become more imbecile every day, and now, from fatigue and excitement, was too ill to leave her bed. The child's voice slightly quivered as she said this; but she recovered herself, and said she was very anxious to get some work, as there would be much to pay before she could get back home.

'What is the name of this friend of your mother's, my poor girl?'

The child handed him a soiled and crumpled card, on which was written,

> Phillip Helmsby,
> Messrs Helmsby and Co.
> Iron Masters, Newcastle.

He handed it to the landlord, who shook his head.

'Phillip Helmsby,' said he, 'has been dead these two years, his wife and daughter have left these parts, and the Works have passed into other hands.'

'What does he say?' asked the girl, anxiously.

The stranger repeated it in Italian. The child clasped her hands in an agony of despair—she did not know herself how much she had hoped.

'Very good, indeed!' said the manager, 'that attitude is very effective. Do you know any one else?'

She shook her head, and seemed quite stupified with what she had just heard.

'Tell me what I must do?' said she, appealingly to the stranger.

' 'Faith, that's more than I know,' said he, in English, to his companions. 'What are we to do with the poor thing? there seems nothing wrong.'

The landlord, who had been considering for some time, said at length,

'Well, it's a queer business, but my mind misgives me terribly. When Phillip Helmsby came home from foreign parts, on the death of the old gentleman, there was talk of some beautiful lady he had left behind, and it *was* said by some he would marry her, but he took the partner's daughter and a mine of money instead; that girl has a trick of Phillip Helmsby's face,—I could not think who she reminded me of. I have seen him many's the time as he passed through the town. It would not surprise me if the poor thing upstairs had given them the slip at home and come to seek him. Ah, Phillip was a wild one before he married, and there's no saying what he had to answer for.'

Whilst the landlord was piecing out his romance, Mr Simpson was coming to a resolution. Clearing his voice, he turned to the stranger:

'Tell her,' said he, 'that I am manager of the Birmingham Circus—a man well known, and, I may say, respected. I want a female who can act in dumb show; and if she will agree to come with me, I will give her ten shillings a-week* and teach her her business beside. She shall be a regular member of my company, and draw her salary weekly; it's more than she's worth now, but she will improve and be useful, and she may work it out then. I don't want to be hard on her, as she will have her mother to keep. She may do on ten shillings, as I shall find her in stage clothes, and those Italians can live on nothing.'

When the offer was repeated to the girl she could scarce find words to express her gratitude, but the eloquence of her looks and gestures quite satisfied the manager that he had made a good bargain.

The stranger took out his purse, and counting out five sovereigns, he put them into her hand, telling her their value in English money.

'By what name may I pray for you?' said she.

'Conrad Percy,' said he; 'and you, how are you called?'*

'Bianca Pazzi,' replied she; 'there is no danger of my forgetting you,' and raising his hand to her lips, and curtsying to the others, she left the room.

'Give the poor thing her trinkets back, Mr Landlord,' said Percy, 'and tell me what her bill is likely to be.'

The landlord in the warmth of his heart had the moment previously been on the point of declaring he would charge her nothing, but this offer from one who seemed able to afford it was too great a temptation. Still he tried to keep up the appearance of a virtue.

'As good deeds seem the order of the day, I will let you off very easy, though, as I said before, beds, just now, are worth gold, and there has been no end of running about after these people—still right is right, and I can do a kind thing as well as my neighbours, so we will say fifteen shillings for both board and lodging.'

Conrad threw down a sovereign, and bidding the landlord give her the difference, ordered his own bill, saying he should start early the next morning.

When left alone with the manager he said,

'I feel confident, sir, that every care will be taken of that poor girl, to see she comes to no harm; and if ever she needs a friend there is my card. I assure you I feel deeply interested in her.'

Conrad was very young, and there was something pleasant to his sense of manliness as well as his good nature in standing forward as the friend of a pretty little girl.

'My good sir,' replied the manager, pompously, 'you are very young, indeed; almost a boy; and at your age, men ought to be all faith in the good side of human nature; but I know the world, and have left off expecting any good from it. Still the girl seems a good girl enough, modest and all that, but there's no saying what she may turn out,—women are such jades! Bless you, I could tell you such stories,—but that's neither here nor there; the feelings you have shown do credit to your heart, and I will keep my eye upon her, so that if she goes wrong it shall not be for want of the best of good counsel. If ever you come to Birmingham I hope you will inquire for me. I am pretty well known; my company is most talented, and my stud of horses wonderful. I always seek for genius wherever I can find it, and do justice to it; and no doubt our young *protégée* will become illustrious in time; but it takes a deal of time to polish up a reputation, and there is much to learn, for ours is a profession, sir, to which people must be born, as one may say, and yet they have never done learning it.'

Mr Simpson would willingly have treated his hearer to a dissertation on 'High Art', but luckily for Conrad the landlord entered with his bill; he was glad to escape, and, taking up a bed-candle, desired he might be called in time for the early coach. Mr Simpson stretched out his hand with an elaborate friendliness, and said, 'Farewell, my dear sir, rely on me that our interesting *protégée* shall have every justice done her. We shall see each other again, and talk of this remarkable evening; good night, and farewell, my very dear sir.'

He looked at the card as soon as he was gone, and read—'Conrad Percy, St John's College, Cambridge'.

CHAPTER III

IN an extremely neat sitting-room, without one particle of taste visible in the arrangement of the grave substantial furniture, sat the wife and daughter of the late Phillip Helmsby of Newcastle, engaged on a large piece of household needle-work. A book-case, filled with books of uniform size and binding, stood in a recess by the fire-place; but none were lying about. An engraving of the Princess Charlotte, and another of her husband,* hung against one of the walls; some ornaments of old-fashioned Dres-den china, little Cupids with blue scarfs, and pots of roses, stood on the chimney-piece, marshalled at equal distances on each side of a plain time-piece. All the chairs stood in their lawful places against the wall; none of those idle, lounging, pretty inventions for being comfortable, encumbered this singularly prosaic-looking room. A brisk fire in a shining black grate was the only thing that did not seem subdued down to the level of the presiding spirit of decorum. A blotting-book, and an inkstand upon it, stood on a table in the centre of the room; and at a small work-table by the window sat the two ladies, with a large wicker pannier full of 'mending' between them.

The elder lady was a plump, composed, grave matron, with a pair of large round black eyes, which looked on every thing and saw every thing, but had the peculiar faculty of giving no indica-tion of what was passing within. She was dressed with scrupulous exactness, in a black silk gown, and a net cap with lilac ribbons; her complexion was rather fair, and her features delicate, yet it would be difficult to say whether she was good-looking or not. The younger figure was a slight drooping girl about fourteen; her hair was braided under her small and beautiful ears; she was not exactly pretty, but she had soft lustrous eyes, and all her features expressed delicacy and sweetness. She appeared a docile, gentle creature; and an expression of earnest, though immature intellect, shone on her countenance. On seeing the two together, the first impression was of wonder, how characters so different could be mother and daughter. After being for some time diligently occu-pied with her work, the young lady exclaimed, with vivacity:

'There, thank Heaven! this tedious work is finished at last. I have taken the last stitch, and now one can go out; it is quite a sin to be in the house such a beautiful day.'

'Alice!' said her mother, in a dry, precise tone, 'how often am I to tell you that those strong expressions are highly unbecoming in a young woman; it is extremely wrong in you to have such a distaste for useful occupation. What have you to expect all your life? If you marry, and become the mistress of a family, you will find yourself woefully deficient; but, indeed, what prudent man would ever think twice of such a flighty young woman? I have long felt uneasy at your way of going on: every day more and more neglect of your duties, more and more dislike to the sober-minded condition of life in which you are born. Your life will be domestic; you are neither to be a fashionable woman nor an authoress; therefore your excessive devotion to books and accomplishments will bring no useful results, but only unfit you for your duties, and fill your mind with fancies. I quite looked forward to your coming home from school to be a comfort and companion to me; but I am sorry to say I find you neither one nor the other.'

'Dear mamma!' said Alice, with the tears springing to her eyes.

'Yes, my dear, you may look, and you may say "dear mamma," but what I tell you is true. You do all I tell you, no doubt; but then you appear to take no interest in any thing; you seem to care nothing for the house, nor for my troubles with the servants; you don't see after them; and though you do just what plain work is wanted, you do nothing as if you liked it. And as to being a companion to me, I might as well talk to a stone—except, indeed, that you make a contemptuous face, and look as if I, your mother, bored you to death! And then, to see how you behave to the people who come to the house. There is good Mrs Jones, for instance, you almost insulted her only last night.'

'Because', said Alice, 'she is both vulgar and impertinent: perhaps I could have stood that, but it put me out of all patience to hear the malicious construction she put on Miss Gally's marriage.'

'Well,' said her mother, tartly, 'and what gives you the right, I should like to know, of setting yourself up in judgment against your elders, picking and choosing what you like, and what does not meet your fancy? By the way, I paid eightpence for a letter for you this morning*—who was it from?'

'My old governess, Mrs Hunt,' replied Alice.

'It is very good of her to take so much trouble about you,' said her mother, in a slightly discontented tone. 'Where is it? Let me see it.'

Alice handed the letter to her mother, feeling, she hardly knew why, that she would rather not have shown it.

'Well, it is a very nice sensible letter; and it is all quite right for Mrs Hunt, who keeps a school, and whose bread it is, so to speak, to talk to you about improving yourself, and keeping up your studies; but I wish now that you are from under her care, she would say something about your duty of attending to your domestic concerns, and your useful employments. You have done with your school-books now, and though I do not object to your practising an hour a day—nor to keeping up your drawing, if you would only make it practical, and paint me some screens for my drawing-room, or a cabinet for the library, or a chess-table, or something that would be really useful—yet you spend all your time in sketching from nature, and never making them into finished drawings by mounting them on card-board—so that one might have a portfolio to show one's friends; the other night I was quite ashamed to have nothing but your school drawings to show the vicar's lady, and you refused to let her see what you have been working at all by yourself. And then you sang, as I never heard you sing before, as if we were all fools together, and not good enough for you to keep company with.'

Alice remained quite silent, for she felt there was some justice in her mother's complaint; in a few minutes, however, she said,

'You told me to remind you about calling on Mrs Haslitt; would not to-day be a good day, as it is so fine?'

'That is not so badly thought of,' said her mother; 'but mind you make yourself look very nice, for you are growing quite a sloven, and Mrs Haslitt is a most particular person. I shall ask her where she gets her groceries; I shall deal no longer with Bradkin, his tea is very bad.'

Alice left the room, and soon returned duly arrayed to her mother's satisfaction, who speedily joined her in all the dowager dignity of a Chantilly veil and a velvet cloak, trimmed with sable.

CHAPTER IV

PHILLIP HELMSBY, the father of both Alice and Bianca, was the son of an extensive iron master in the neighbourhood of Newcastle. When quite a young man, his father sent him to Genoa on business connected with the house, and whilst there, he became passionately enamoured of a beautiful Italian girl, the daughter of the friends in whose family he lived. He endeavoured to obtain her hand in marriage, but both families raised a storm of objections—*his* father would not hear of a Papist for a daughter-in-law,* nor would *her* father consent to her marrying a heretic. Whilst the heads of each family were thus contending on points of orthodoxy, the young lovers took matters into their own hands. The girl, a passionate Italian, had loved the young Englishman before she saw any sign of its being returned, and she had wearied the Madonna with prayers that the heart of him she loved might become hers.

Prayer is the great consolation of men in religion; but it is a mercy that the hearing and granting of it is placed in the hands of the Highest, and quite beyond man's control,—for who can look back on his past life without trembling, when he thinks on the mad and fatal petitions he has offered up, and reflects on what must have been his destiny had they been granted!

The prayer of the young Italian was apparently heard,—for the one she loved declared his love for her, and in the wild, almost fearful, joy she felt, she made offerings at all the shrines of the Virgin in Genoa.

When the opposition to which we have alluded was raised, she hesitated not, but gave herself to her lover without the sanction of either her parents or the church. She loved him with a passionate entireness which prevented her feeling any sense of shame or degradation—she fled from her home and joined her lover at Leghorn, whither his father's mandate had removed him. They lived together for about a year and a half, nobody taking much heed of them. She was a wild-hearted gifted creature, with all good qualities except *common sense*—the only virtue that in this world brings any sort of practical reward along with it. She lost sight of herself altogether, idolising him, and all that belonged to him—seeing nothing as it really happened to be, but every thing as it ought to have been.

When a woman loves with an engrossing passion, and is by nature entirely ungifted with coquetry, it is ten chances to one but that in a very short time she becomes a great bore to the man on whom she bestows it. The *abandon* becomes in time an insupportable burden, for she throws herself on her lover with all the confiding weight of helplessness.

The Italian was too much engrossed with her own affection to consider the appearance and becomingness of things;—the relations between men and women in this world will not stand too much reality being heaped upon them. A morbid love of power in the shape of cruelty lies at the bottom of every human heart; and when either a man or woman is invested with absolute dominion over the happiness of another, that very instant, 'like tares sown by the Evil One', comes the inclination to tyrannise.

This young Italian had beauty, genius, generosity, and a whole mine of precious things in her character, not scientifically balanced, but poured out in lavish profusion on her English lover, whose slower nature seemed to provoke her to still more abounding love, in order to quicken him to her own intensity. She was utterly unconscious of the magnitude of all the sacrifices she had made, and lived on, enwrapped in a fiery element of love and devotedness.

At the end of about eighteen months his father died, and he was re-called to England to settle the affairs of the partnership.

The parting was vehement and passionate on both sides; he left her, promising to return in a few months and carry her to England and make her his wife—and he was quite in earnest at the time he promised; but, though he would not own it, yet in his secret heart he had begun somewhat to weary of this passionate love. He was an Englishman after all, and loved quietness.

Arrived at home, all the complicated affairs of the partnership had to be gone into. The three months were of necessity lengthened into six—into twelve. The real work that now devolved upon him made his Italian life seem dreamy and childish;—and after all, getting money does seem to the natural man of more importance than love, however desperate. Several long journeys

had to be taken, and his acquaintance with the Continental
languages devolved them upon him.

Love can only thrive in idleness, and he was overwhelmed
with business from morning till night; whilst the skill necessary
for carrying out extensive operations, the calculation, the foresight needed, and a large number of workmen to control, all
contributed to blot out his Italian dream.

Then, too, he felt the incongruity there was between the
smoky dingy town in the neighbourhood of which he was
obliged to reside—the stolid, hard, all-engrossed men amongst
whom he was thrown; men with no idea of literature beyond a
newspaper, or the monthly part of a novel, which they bought
just as much because it seemed a good amount for their shilling
as for the tale—and the beautiful country, elegant environs, and
the lovely creature he had left behind. Whilst he shrank from
inflicting such a lot upon her, he regretted that a mad passion and
the facility of Italian life had seduced him into entailing such an
embarrassing tie upon himself—then, too, she was a Catholic, a
word of abomination as great as that of Socialist.*

The memory of his mistress became gradually divested of its
most winning attributes; he began to fancy her a passionate,
fantastic, wayward child, who would bring ridicule upon him; in
short, he had already had as much love as one man can stand in a
lifetime, and had begun to feel the charm of getting money.

She, on her part, used to write him passionate love-burning
letters—all her days were passed in dreams of his return, and there
was one *secret* which she kept to tell him until he wrote to fix the
joyful day for rejoining her. She had never brought him a living
child; when he left her, she was not herself aware that there was
a prospect of her becoming a mother; when she did become
conscious of it, she did not tell him, lest the disappointment
which had once before been theirs should happen again; and
afterwards, she determined to keep her secret till he announced
his return.

That announcement never came;—before twelve months had
elapsed, he had grown weary and impatient of his position, and
determined to make an end one way or the other. He opened his
case to his elder partner, a kind-hearted man, much esteemed for
his sound judgment and solidity of character.

No satisfactory result ever comes of either giving or taking advice. What in one man would be a wise and natural mode of conduct, in another, even in similar circumstances, is forced, hard, and altogether unsuitable. So every man would do well to follow his own sincere instinct; that which in his inmost soul he feels it right to do. When a man asks advice on a point of right or wrong, there is a *warp*, a *bias*, towards which he desires to be impelled, and he asks counsel for the sake of lessening his own responsibility. So it was with Phillip Helmsby.

His partner was too much a man of the world to be scandalised, but he thought it his duty to persuade him to give up a dangerous connexion, likely in all ways to compromise his respectability; and Phillip Helmsby ended by fancying himself a victim to necessity, and endeavouring to think that there was as much kindness to her, as consideration for himself, in what he was about to do.

He wrote, to tell her that he could not bring her to England:— it was a letter just to drive the person mad to whom it was addressed, whilst a third party seeing it, would have declared it an excellent, kind, reasonable letter. There it is! If there be one thing more utterly insupportable than another in this world, it is to receive reasonableness and kindness at the hands of one from whom we expect *love*, given as a *substitute* for love. Poor Theresa, not being a reasonable woman, never attempted to reply to this letter. A handsome sum of money was paid to an Italian banker for her use, and her brother, who resided in a small Italian seaport, took her to live with him. Her child was about two months old; when the letter came, it had been named Bianca; and now her whole idea seemed to be to bring it up carefully and to carry it to England to claim its father, when it should be old enough. This idea kept her from destroying herself in the first frenzy of her grief—but her faculties gradually declined; the memory of her desertion died away; and the idea of taking the little Bianca to its father filled her heart alone.

Phillip Helmsby knew nothing of all this; perhaps, had he done so, he might have acted differently—but there is no telling.

As it was, in about six months after he had broken with the Italian, he lawfully married his partner's daughter, with a large fortune; a very well-conducted young lady, and one not at all likely to weary him with any passionate demonstrations; but she was a clever housekeeper, and kept his establishment in excellent style.

He became a patron of the arts, and filled his house with pictures, statues, and objects of *vertu*.* Although his wife was proud of having her house a show-place, yet that hardly counter-balanced the plague of keeping so much 'ornamental furniture', as she called it, in order. She was not an unkind woman, but she had an intensely prosaical heart; however, as we said, Phillip Helmsby had had enough of passionate love, and he thought his wife a very sensible woman.

They had only one child, Alice, and in her the father's heart was centered. She stood beside him like the best part of his life; she seemed to him the ideal of all he had ever dreamed, himself 'in finer clay'; the child, a sweet endearing little thing, was passionately attached to him; and this *legitimate* tie kept his mind from ever wandering towards poor Theresa. He did not live long, however, for he died rather suddenly, when Alice was about twelve years old.

By his will, his wife and her father were constituted his daughter's guardians. All his collection of books, pictures, &c., were sold and dispersed, except a few of inferior value, and some books which she thought might be useful as her daughter grew up.

The Works, too, were disposed of, and Mrs Helmsby and her daughter went to reside in a large manufacturing town, where she had some relations.

CHAPTER V

IN spite of all that has been said about the happiness of childhood, of its being a recollection of the better world from which we came forth, it is to many a most purgatorial entrance into life; and to them, a return to a state of childhood would be more dreaded than any Hindoo or Egyptian transmigration.

The childhood of Alice had not been a happy one. There had been no positive unkindness; but children do not understand the value of what we call solid comforts; kind words, smiling looks, sympathy with their little pains and pleasures, are all they understand; a harsh word or chiding tone conveys more pain than a grown person can understand.

Alice had always been a singular child, and her father's death had thrown her altogether in the hands of persons quite unable to understand or train a child of her disposition. She was not clever; never said or did any of those precocious wonderful things mothers are so proud of repeating; she was always a quiet, thoughtful, dreaming child; she never desired companions of her own age, but delighted in playing by herself; she would sit for hours under the shadow of a tree, watching the green light stream through its branches; she would leave any play she was engaged in to creep to the window-seat in the nursery, there to watch the sun set, firmly believing it was the gate of heaven; she would sit gazing at the changing light, and the large stars suddenly starting into sight on the confines of the dim orange-coloured mist, and the dark, clear, crystalline blue of the coming night, and the moon growing gradually more clear as the daylight died out, till her large blue eyes dilated with awe, and she grew frightened at being alone, and yet did not dare to venture out of her recess, but sat with a sort of pleased terror until her nurse broke the spell by carrying her off to bed; nor would she sleep unless the blinds were all drawn up, in order that when it was moonlight she might see the quiet mysterious light pour a flood of radiance through the room, and the shadows of the tall trees tossing about on the walls.

As she grew older, she was haunted by a sense of hidden meaning in all she saw, and was baffled and perplexed in her weak endeavours to understand more than was seen. The common tasks she was set to learn, seemed to have a spirit she could not seize, and this bewildered her and kept her from attaining the common cleverness of most children; but there was a constant striving after something not set down, which the lessons did not express, but seemed to contain.

When she was at play, her doll-bonnets of leaves, her chains of rushes, dust gardens, and pebble houses, were really clumsy compared with those of her companions; but there was a feeling, a striving after some meaning she could not express, which made a difference between her work and theirs.

One fine moonlight night, her nurse coming softly into the nursery, overheard her praying to the *moon* 'to take her up there, it looked so beautiful'; and when the orthodox nurse, much scandalised, told her she was worse than a heathen, she said she 'had always been told to pray for what she wanted, and then God would give it her, and she wanted to live in the moonlight or the sunset for ever!'

When she grew a little older her mother sent her to a boarding-school, in the hope she would grow more like other children. The regular employment and constant bustle of being with twenty other young people, seemed for awhile to deaden her vague dreamy fancies—the spirit of emulation was roused, and she became very ambitious to excel her companions; but when, after a few years, she had worked her way to be considered the first in the school, the commonness and insignificance of what she had done suddenly struck her; she felt ashamed of having been so much excited in pursuit of a prize for attaining a knowledge only a little less imperfect than that of her companions; she felt disgusted and dissatisfied; a sense of baffled effort depressed and distressed her; and none of those around her could understand the vague, undefined, restless aspirations that filled her heart. No one could speak a word to direct her towards an object worthy of her.

Her mother withdrew her from school before she was quite fourteen, in order that she might learn to be useful, and not get her head stuffed too full of book-learning, which never did a woman any good yet.

From the specimen we have given our readers, they may judge of the extremely unpromising aspect of her condition at home.

Indeed, whether she or her poor unknown half-sister Bianca were in the worse position for all that regards real help and training for the lifetime opening before each, it would be hard to say. God is good and life is strong.

CHAPTER VI

IT was not till five days after her meeting with the manager of the circus, that Bianca and her mother arrived in B——, on the top of the heavy stage. Her mother was quite unable to travel; and they had been detained at the inn, till what between the doctor and the expenses of their prolonged stay, Bianca's reserve fund of five sovereigns was reduced, when she had paid the coach fare, to one. The landlord, however, gave her some refreshment for the journey, and a bottle of home-made wine for her mother; and also recommended her to the care of the guard, who promised to give an eye to her when they got to B——.

In this world men cannot resist the temptation of making money when they have an opportunity, or turning aside from a bargain; but there is a great deal of good-nature for all that. The landlord's conscience smote him for taking any thing from the poor friendless child, but it was in the way of his trade, and he could not help it; still he tried to justify himself, by giving her some scraps of food for the journey, and a recommendation to the ostler, a friend of his, at the inn where the coach stopped, begging him to see her into honest lodgings: so, on the whole, perhaps Bianca fared quite as well as if the landlord of the 'Blue Bell' had strained his generosity by going contrary to his habits, and had let her off without further charge than the bill already discharged by Conrad;—for we all know that when we feel constrained to do a good deed rather beyond our strength, our soul is, as it were, half choked in the attempt to swallow it, and, instead of feeling nourished and refreshed, and experiencing that sense of satisfaction which is said to be the accompaniment of good deeds, a fit of splenetic humour is generally the actual result, a sort of sulky protest against our conscience, for being so *exigeante*,* and there is not a scrap or a remnant of good-nature left for the accidental need of the occasion. So, as we said, it was quite as well for Bianca, considering she was a child and a stranger, and going unprotected to a large town, that the landlord's generosity expanded in what was to cost no money—he took some trouble, and great credit for it, as it was ever after to figure as one of the benevolent incidents of his life.

They arrived without accident at B——, and where the coach was to put up for the night. The guard put Bianca and her mother inside the coach, and told them to sit there till he could attend to them.

Bianca, who had entertained a vague idea that as soon as she arrived at B——all her difficulties would be at an end, felt her heart sink at the sight of all the strange faces and the crowded streets, which she contemplated from the coach windows as the weary minutes passed away. Her mother had been persuaded to come to B——, by the assurance that he she sought was gone there; and now she was eagerly looking at every passer by, in the hope of seeing him. At length a vague terror seized the hither-to brave-hearted girl; she seemed suddenly to realise the forlorn, desolate state she was in; she fancied her only acquaintance, the guard, had gone away and forgotten her; and what between fright, fatigue, and the reaction of the excitement of the last few days, she gave way, and burst into tears. Her mother did not perceive it; she was watching them light the lamps in the street.

At length the guard came to the door of the coach, saying:—'Well, did you think I had forgotten you? I have been rather long; but, come, come, we must have no crying, that will never do; it never helped a body—you must keep up a good heart. See, this is the ostler you brought the letter to—not that he can read it, but I have explained all about you, and he thinks, if so be you won't mind mounting a few steps, he has a room in his own house you could have. Come, wipe up your eyes, and let us be walking. I'll see you safe myself before I leave you.'

The guard had been refreshing himself with hot brandy-and-water, and he was in a very comfortable, good-natured frame of mind. There are so many more accidental things in this world than premeditated ones! He flung away the end of his cigar as he spoke, and lifted Bianca out of the coach.

'So this be the young woman,' said the ostler, holding his lantern to her face, 'and that there her mother, I take it. Well, I reckon, if they can make themselves content, we can take them in. Where are their traps?'

Swinging the small trunk upon his shoulders, he began to stride along; Bianca, the guard, and her mother following. After walking some distance, they came into an old-fashioned narrow street, out of which they turned into a court, and at the top of the court they stopped before a tolerably decent house; the door stood half open, a clean, tidy-looking woman, in a blue bed-gown and a check apron, was laying a cloth on a round table, and a frying-pan was on the fire, steaming and spluttering forth savoury odours. She seemed disconcerted at the sight of so many.

'Well, missis,' said the ostler, entering, 'do you think as how we can do with these here two ladies to lodge up stairs? Mr Smith, the "Blue Bell", sent them to me.'

The woman looked very cross, but said: 'I reckon they may, if they're not too grand; but a decent single man would pay better, and be only half the trouble. But lor! Mr Simms, who thought of seeing you here? I am sure, if they are friends of yours, we will be happy to take them.'

The good-looking guard was the ostler's grandest acquaintance, and his appearance softened matters wonderfully.

'I am sure they can be nowhere better than with you, ma'am,' replied the guard.

Placing her frying-pan on the hearth, she took up the candle and showed the way up-stairs. The room to be let was at the top of the house; it contained a single bed with blue check curtains, a couple of chairs, and a small table; there was a fire-place, and on the mantle-shelf stood, by way of ornament, two rude plaster images, painted as gorgeously as Indian idols; there was a pot of flowers in the window-place, and the walls had not lost all trace of whitewash; on the whole, there was an air of comfort and decency about it, not common in that class of houses.

'Now, young woman,' said the ostler, 'I don't want you to be imposed upon by no means; if you conclude to take this here room, you will pay eighteen pence a-week; and, if you think it too much, you are free to seek another, but any way, you had best stay here to-night.'

'You might go further and fare worse,' said the guard. 'You had best make a bargain, eighteen pence is not out of the way.'

'I want to take no advantage, it's what we get for it.'

Bianca, who had great difficulty in comprehending the strong Warwickshire dialect, signified she would be glad to stay there, and, at the direction of the guard, paid the first week's rent in advance; on which the woman began to have a better opinion of the speculation, asked her to sit by her fire down stairs, and inquired what she would like to eat. A small packet of tea and sugar being amongst Bianca's stores, she made her a comfortable cup of tea; and in less than an hour Bianca and her mother had taken possession of their new abode, and were both sleeping as soundly as fatigue could make them.

Bianca was up betimes the next morning, and after dressing her mother, and getting breakfast, she asked the woman to direct her to Mr Simpson, the manager of the circus. This did not seem to augur too well to the woman, who looked very suspiciously as she gave the necessary information.

Fortunately, she had not far to go, and without much difficulty she found the house where he and his wife lodged. With a beating heart she knocked at the door, and was admitted to where they were at breakfast.

'Well, my girl, so you are come at last, are you? How comes it you are so long after time? It has been very inconvenient this delay. I have had to keep back the new piece, and if you had been one day later I must have filled up your place, and then what would you have done?'

Bianca explained that her mother's state of health had made it impossible for her to travel sooner.

This, the manager knew was very likely; but he had got so much into the habit of not believing the excuses of any member of his troop, that, from mere force of habit, he said—

'Well, well, no doubt you have plenty of excuses; I have only to do with the fact; you are after your time, and you understand that, if I chose, I should have the right to cancel your engagement; however, you must mind better another time; recollect, always, I am punctual to a second. Nothing to be done without it in our line.'

He spoke in a sharp, bullying tone, not from any unkindness or ill temper, but because he had got into the habit of shouting both to his people and his horses; and he was obliged to be peremptory in his business. Poor Bianca was not accustomed to

hearing harsh tones, and not understanding all he said, began to
fear she had committed some terrible crime. Her deprecating
look pleased Mr Simpson, and restored him to the perception of
the excellent bargain he had made.

'This is the young woman I spoke of, my dear, so highly
recommended to my care by my distinguished friend Mr Conrad
Percy, when he was my guest at Newcastle.—Have you another
cup of tea in the pot? I dare say it is some time since she had her
breakfast.'

'Oh!' said Mrs Simpson, taking no notice of her husband's
hint, 'she is, is she? Well, you know best whether you are going
to have a dumb girl in all your pieces, or else you must teach her
to talk, for nobody can understand what she says—for my part I
think you have made a foolish bargain. That Dupréz would have
done very well, if you had only managed her; and you will find
out your loss; but it is no business of mine.'

Mrs Simpson, who was one of the corps of female equestrians,
was a tall well-formed woman, with a hard bold face and a
defying pair of black eyes: she had a slight toss with her head, and
she looked as if she could get up a storm at a moment's notice.
Ever on the watch for the smallest slight, at the least provocation
she would burst out in words as pelting as hailstones. She was
fully impressed with the dignity of her position as manager's wife,
and did not incline with any favour towards the striking-looking
foreign damsel, whom her husband had picked up in a way she
could not, or would not, understand.

'Now, my girl,' said Mr Simpson, as he emptied his last cup of
tea, 'it is quite time for us to be going. You will recollect,'
turning to his wife, 'that there is no rehearsal of the "Thessalian
Virgins" to-day, this "Dumb Girl of California" will take all the
time; but you will be in time to ride with the troop. They never
form as they should do except you are with them, my dear.'

'You are mightly flattering all at once,' said his wife, tossing
her head.

As they went along, the manager tried to impress upon Bianca
the great favour he was conferring in giving her such an arduous
part for her *début*. To which Bianca listened in profound silence.

Bianca did not know what a circus was; and the sudden change
from bright sunlight into a close dim place, the light struggling

through the canvass roof and the spaces between the boards, was quite bewildering; and the smell of the horses, the lamps, the saw-dust, and the peculiar odour that pervades all theatres, nearly stifled her. The greater part of the troop had already assembled.

'Come, now ladies and gentleman,' said Mr Simpson, 'are you all prepared to begin? This is the young lady I have been expecting, and, as she is a foreigner, who cannot speak our tongue, I beg to recommend her to your good offices—she takes the part of the Dumb Girl.'

The business of rehearsal now began in earnest. Bianca remained standing where she was, till she should know what she had to do. At first she felt afraid of the horses, but as nobody else seemed to have that idea, or to think such a thing possible, she became gradually reconciled to their vicinity, and she kept quiet, much wondering what she would have to do in all the bustle that was going on. At last the manager came to her.

'Now, my good girl, attend to me. That man there,' pointing to a dissipated-looking youth, in a ragged shirt and a plaid stock, with a very scanty front, but who had an indescribable air of jaunty self-complacency, 'that young man there is your lover; you must watch beside him when he sleeps, and defend him against an assassin; you must try to awake him, but, as you cannot speak, nor scream, it is only natural you should not succeed, but you will only be the more distressed. Now just think how you would feel if it were a real sweetheart in such a position, and you have only to do accordingly.'

Bianca, little as she knew it, had been intended by nature for an actress. She got directly into the spirit of what she had to do. Her ineffectual attempts to arouse her lover, who slept with a most supernatural soundness, her agony and her struggle with the assassin were so earnest and natural, and her attitudes so effective, that Mr Simpson was lavish of his praise. Then there was a skirmish, and Bianca had again to rescue her lover, and finally get killed herself, falling under the horses' feet. It was a long confused business altogether, such a tumult of shouting and swearing, falling into confusion and beginning again, going over the same thing a dozen times, until Bianca, who had eaten nothing since early in the morning, was nearly fainting with fatigue and exhaustion. However, the rehearsal came to an end at last, and the manager, who was really good-natured, and in a very good humour with her besides, sent out for some porter and a crust of bread. Then, as the day was fine, a grand procession of the horses and the troop round the town, preceded by the band, was the next business. The troop, all dressed as much like natural men and women as their wardrobes permitted, riding two and two, made a touching tableau, emblematic of the fraternal love and amity which pervaded the body. Mr Simpson brought up the rear in a lofty phaeton, drawn by four beautiful spotted horses, and Bianca, smartened up to meet his notions of Italian costume, was seated beside him.

Bianca was stunned, bewildered, and ashamed of her conspicuous position, and of the wonder and notice they obtained from the crowd; but she had no sort of alternative, all those around her seemed to take it as a matter of course, and before the ride was over, the people she was amongst seemed the realities, and the people in the streets through which they passed appeared the show.

At length all came to an end, and Bianca, stupified and weary, was at liberty to go home, with strict charge to be very punctual at rehearsal the next morning.

Bianca was not sixteen when she became one of the circus troop. She had never received any direct instruction or education in her life, except a little English from her mother, and a little reading and writing from an old priest in the village. She was a Catholic, as all Italians are; but no sort of extraneous good had been instilled into her, nor artificial notions of any kind; she had been left to grow up exactly as it pleased Nature. None of her faculties or feelings had developed themselves when she left Italy; she seemed as closely shut up and unawakened, as a flower that is still imprisoned in its calyx, and has not yet shown a trace of its rich leaves to the sun; she had come to no sort of self-consciousness; and the constant attendance she was in upon her mother, the spectacle of her dejection and suffering, had damped all her youthful spirit, and prevented her ever knowing the glee and joyousness which is the normal state of childhood. She was grave and still; it was almost painful to behold the unnatural thoughtfulness and prudence with which she attended on her mother, and kept their little household in order; it was the spectacle of rosy youth becoming colourless before its time by contact with the cares of life. She loved her mother intensely; and seeing her always sad, she had felt that all gaiety was out of sympathy—and children are capable of sympathy with those they love, to a degree never found either in lovers or friends in after life. With the natural egotism of sorrow, her mother had kept Bianca constantly with her; it was the only solace she had, and she was not aware how she was blanching the most brilliant and sunny portion of her daughter's days. Her own fine intellect, which had been a rich untilled field, became weaker and weaker, till, as we have seen, it ended in almost childishness. The shock that came on Bianca that fearful day beside her mother's bed, when the knowledge of her helplessness came in its full extent upon her, quenched the last spark of youth from her heart; henceforth, the burden and anxiety of providing for the passing day came upon her; she was face to face with destitution, and with nothing but her own hands to stave it off herself and her mother. A strong and indomitable resolution—an energy that would shrink from nothing, was then first roused; it was the strong bass note of her nature, the finer harmonies were not yet unloosed. She had no idea of vanity, or of getting admiration, or of displaying herself in any way; her sole idea of the circus was, that it was the means of earning a certain number of shillings, on which she might support her mother; it never occurred to her whether it was a mode of life she would like or dislike. She had only the fixed idea that she must do her best in all she had to do, in order that this mode of subsistence might not be closed against her.

Bianca had never been at any sort of theatrical representation in her life, and a few nights before her own appearance she took her mother to see the performance. The preparation behind the scenes was so coarse and unpleasant that Bianca had felt very little curiosity to see the result produced.

But she was startled by the change she found in all things; the dark, dirty circus, lighted up with brilliant gas lights, seemed to glow with bright and radiant colours: the coarseness of the decorations was not perceived; in the gorgeously and picturesquely attired heroes and heroines of the scene, she could not recognise the dingy, sallow, slovenly individuals whom she met at rehearsal; the horses had always been noble creatures, but now they seemed only in keeping with their riders; the effect was brilliant, and the tawdriness and paltriness of the dresses and trappings did not appear when seen from the proper point of view. Bianca felt a glow in her heart; and as the horses and riders disappeared one after the other, dashing behind the mysterious pink satin curtain which hid the exit under the stage, she could hardly believe it led to nothing better than she had seen in the morning.

The *idealism* of her profession had struck her, and henceforth it was not the unmixed drudgery it had been.

The night of her own *début* came at last; she had not felt much anxiety about it, for the *necessity* that was upon her allowed her very little alternation of hope or fear. When, however, she stood for the first time before the blinding lights and the oppressive presence of so many hundred human eyes, her whole being seemed turned to stone; she would have run away if she could only have moved. The people applauded her, but that only frightened her more. Two energetic words from Mr Simpson broke the spell that was on her, and restored her faculties; she felt she *must* do her work. In a few minutes she became engrossed in what she had to do, and gradually forgot all about the audience. The piece went off very well, and Bianca did her part admirably, with the exception of a few mistakes in the business of the scene, very excusable in a novice. She had got over her fear of the horses, and her '*death*' was very effective, and brought great applause; which gave her great satisfaction, because she felt her livelihood was now secured. She had proved herself worth her wages.

CHAPTER VII

AFTER Bianca had learned to ride, and could speak English a little better, she was promoted to more important business. She began to feel a fascination, even in that low grade of her profession, which carried her through hardships, annoyances, and drudgery. There was a constant excitement and sense of adventure; even the dead heavy reality of her life at home was surrounded by a fictitious atmosphere; it was only one scene in a drama, of which she did not yet know the *dénouement*. A sense of her own powers gradually made itself felt, and there was a pleasure in the exercise of it. At first when she went to the circus she had no idea beyond doing her best; but a spirit was soon roused within her, what she had to do in each piece became a reality for the time, and she flung herself into it with all her force. Many were the jeers she received from the rest, for giving herself so much more trouble than was needed.

Accident had thrown Bianca into this line of life; but we are obliged to confess she continued in it from choice.

Within a few days of her arrival in B——she sought out a Catholic priest (her mother had become exceedingly devout since her desertion), and Bianca instinctively looked for her priest as for a friend to whom she might go for counsel in any perplexity. There was a Catholic church not far from their lodging, and the priest, a benevolent looking old man, soon felt a strong interest in both the mother and daughter. He was much shocked at Bianca's mode of life, and exerted himself to get her some more creditable employment; after a few weeks he succeeded in obtaining the offer of a place in a shop, and a lady of the congregation promised to supply her with as much needle-work as she could do. But in the first place Bianca could not sew; and in the next, unfortunately, the charm of her profession had begun to work. She could not make up her mind to leave it. She felt a blind instinct that obliged her to continue in her present course, even at the risk of offending the good old priest, who had taken so much trouble for her. The benevolent lady with her plain work, turned her back at once on Bianca, and would have

nothing more to do with her, considering her lost to every
chance of respectability; but the old priest, though sadly grieved,
thought she would all the more need his warnings and watchful-
ness, so, although he looked very grave, he still continued his
visits to her mother, and after a while, finding Bianca regular at
her duty, and in all respects conducting herself extremely well, if
he did not become reconciled, he at least ceased to try to persuade her to leave her way of life, and contented himself with
watching that she got into no mischief. Mr Simpson, to do him
justice, kept a vigorous hand over his troop, so that nothing
flagrant was carried on. It certainly was not a particularly exalted
school of refined morality; they all belonged to the lower orders,
and their general conduct was the average of that of people of
their class. The respectable public who went to see them, considered them *en masse* as dissipated disorderly vagabonds, whom
it would not have been creditable to know, or altogether safe to
admit to the neighbourhood of their silver spoons. Separated
from them by a glittering row of gas-lights, seeing them only
dressed up in whimsical and tawdry costumes, the frequenters of
the circus hardly considered the actors as human beings; content
with being amused when they went, they did not even look for
any morality more exalted than that they should abstain from
burglary or disturbing the peace of the neighbourhood; the
actors, in their turn, lived in a world of their own; and if they were
dimly conscious of the degraded estimation in which they were held
by the respectable daylight inhabitants, they repaid it by supercilious indifference; nobody feels degraded in his own eyes by his
profession, be it what it may; they were a community amongst
themselves, and all of much the same opinion as to the importance of their business; and on the whole felt themselves rather
superior to those who came to see them.

Bianca kept chiefly to herself—not from any sense of superiority, but because no one in the troop attracted her. People can
only take in from surrounding influences what they have an
affinity to receive. At first her reserve was attributed to pride, and
was bitterly resented. Though not one in the troop, except the
riding-master and Mr Simpson, cared one straw whether they
exchanged a word with her or not, yet they did not choose any
one to set up to be better than the rest, and they set themselves

to punish her for it in the thousand ways which a community has of making an individual miserable, against whom it has a dislike. Without knowing how she had incurred it, Bianca found herself the object of every sort of covert malice and persecution. No one would speak to her; she saw nothing but mocking looks, sneers, and, as far as they dared venture, of practical ill-treatment. One night, in the ring, she was thrown from her horse, in consequence of a malicious trick, and was carried, bleeding and senseless, from the circle. Mr Simpson made rigid inquiry, but the offence could not be brought home to any one. This was rather a fortunate incident, in the end; for Bianca showed so much real good-nature, such an absence of all wish to get any one into trouble on her account, that the tide was turned in her favour. Her progress from a martyr to a heroine was as summary and reasonable as those transformations usually are. It was owned that she had never taken advantage of her favour with the manager to do any one else an ill turn. The women found she never interfered with their lovers, or laid herself out to attract admiration; but, on the contrary, was ready to help them in manufacturing of their finery; she had a natural genius for costume, and could make up picturesque dresses out of the most shabby materials, which was a most convenient talent. And then it was discovered that she supported her insane mother, and that it was to hasten home to her she had always hurried away from the circus; and, finally, as to her promotion to the best business in the pieces, it was agreed on all hands that she took so much more pains and trouble than any one else was willing to do, that no one could wonder if she succeeded better; besides, there was the mollifying circumstance, that her salary was not raised in proportion, for Mr Simpson was not a generous man, and he insisted on her working out the 'over-payment', as he called it, which she had received before she became useful. Now, all these good qualities, and all these reasons for not ill-treating, had existed from the beginning, but her companions were now in a humour to do her justice; their ill-nature had had its fling, and was appeased, and they were now disposed to go as far in the opposite extreme. As soon as she was able to reappear in the circus, Bianca found herself received with enthusiasm by her companions. The man who was the actual perpetrator of the trick which had so nearly proved fatal, had been denounced by the rest, glad of a scapegoat, and dismissed the company. Henceforth, Bianca's path was smooth; a sort of consideration and pre-eminence was tacitly awarded her, and her only difficulty was to solve the daily problem of supporting herself and her mother on twelve shillings a-week; that, and her business at the circus, was more than enough to employ her, and keep her clear of the innumerable cabals, intrigues, and *tracas- series** going on around her.

As to Bianca herself, she had a hidden source of life and comfort she would have revealed to no one, and which was the secret of her singular discretion, and indifference to all the admiration that offered itself: it was, the memory of the graceful, handsome Conrad, who had appeared like an angel to her in her deepest need. He had made, as was only natural, an indelible impression on her heart. The hope of seeing him again, kept her up under all her vexations, and the idea of pleasing him was at the bottom of all her exertions. He was the ideal hero to whom she acted, he was the type to which she referred all the qualities attributed to the heroes in the pieces they acted; and as her consciousness of power in her profession increased, her only idea was, that it would be something to display to him. It was with reference to him she valued it. This secret sentiment grew and increased in strength every day. She did not know where he was to be found, nor in what condition on life he was; but she never, for a second, wavered in her firm conviction that he would find her again; about the probable when and where, she did not perplex herself.

The company was not always stationed in the same town; they had a regular circuit; and though the coming or going of an equestrian troop seems even less than unimportant to the town, it was an essential affair to them, and their business to make it so considered by as many in the town as possible. After various removals, they at length came to M——, about twelve months after Bianca had joined the company.

CHAPTER VIII

To return to Alice and her mother, whom we left long since on their way to call on Mrs Haslitt. On their arrival at that worthy lady's they were ushered into the drawing-room, which was rather small in its dimensions, but the furniture and appointments were of the most sumptuous description. The walls were covered with highly-coloured and richly-gilt paper; the window-curtains were of light blue and silver brocaded satin, but carefully preserved by chintz covers; the carpet was velvet pile of the most highly decorative pattern; marble slabs, richly gilt bronze sconces, and two large mirrors were dispersed about the room; a cut glass chandelier, rather too large for the size of the room, hung from the ceiling; a few splendidly bound books furnished the heavily carved rosewood table; an exquisitely designed French time-piece was on the chimney-piece; the steel grate was quite dazzling in its brilliancy, and a comfortable fire was blazing in it; nothing could look handsomer or more comfortable. No one was in the room when they entered, and they had full time to look round.

'Well,' said Alice's mother, 'Mrs Haslitt keeps her house more elegantly than any one else I know; it is quite a show to see it! I am sure I wonder how she manages to make her housemaid keep all her things so nice. Ah, Alice, I wish, instead of tossing up your head at Mrs Haslitt, you would take pattern by her, it would be better for you. How proud I should feel to see you mistress of such a house as this! If any worthy young man would but come and offer you such a home, I hope you would not go and frighten him away with your nonsense, just because he did not happen to have so many fine fancies as yourself. It is all my prayer to see you happily settled before I die; but sometimes I fear you will disappoint all my hopes. If young Mr Haslitt now should happen to come in, do, pray, be civil to him, and don't look as if you did not know what you were saying. If you only knew how ignorant it makes you look, you would not do it. And, besides, what right have you to set yourself up, I should like to know?'

Her harangue was here cut short by the entrance of Mrs Haslitt herself, dressed in a rich green satin dress and Brussels lace collar, fastened with a gorgeous brooch,—had it not been for these, she might have been mistaken for the housemaid. She was a tall, homely-featured, cross-looking woman, and addressed her guests in a strong provincial accent.

Alice's mother began, by hoping they had not called at an unseasonable time.

'Oh dear, no, ma'am,' said Mrs Haslitt; 'but I have been so flurried this morning, that I fear I have made you wait. Would you believe it, ma'am, my housemaid, whom I thought such a treasure—I have found out in an intrigue with one of the men at the Works! She has been in the habit of letting him into the kitchen when we are all in bed of a night!'

'There is no being up to the depravity of servants and such people,' said Alice's mother, in a sympathising tone. 'How did you find her out?'

'Quite by the merest accident, ma'am; I happened to have the toothache last night, after I was in bed, and I got up again, as I did not like to disturb the servants, and came down stairs myself for a clove of ginger. I fancied I heard voices, and walked very softly right into the kitchen, and there found my lady, sitting as comfortable as you please, on one side of the fire, and Andrews on the other, and a jug of hot ale on the table between them! I declare you might have knocked me down with a feather! However, I soon ordered him out, and walked my hussey up to her own room, and locked her in. And what do you think she had the impudence to tell me this morning, when I pointed out to her the shamefulness of her conduct? She said servants were as much flesh and blood as their mistresses; and that, if I had allowed her to receive him at proper times, she would not have let him in on the sly. She pretends he is going to marry her, but I don't believe a word of it. However, I turned her out this morning, and she may go courting where she pleases, I'll have none of it in my house. As I told her, I hire my servants to do my work, and not to entertain followers. This makes the third housemaid I have had in four months. I am sure I slave myself to death in looking after them, and yet cannot get my work done, which is rather hard, considering there are three women servants, and only Mr H., my son, and myself. But they are all a set of lazy, ungrateful, deceitful sluts. I declare if I leave my tea-caddy unlocked for an hour, I find it half emptied; and as for bread, butter, and beer, there is no end to their wastefulness; look after them as one will, there's no having one's eyes in every place at once. I declare it's scold, scold, scold, from morning till night, till I am quite worn out, and no good comes of it.'

The two discreet matrons now launched forth in a declamatory duet on the iniquities of the race of servants in general, and their own specimens of them in particular, till any stranger hearing them talk would have felt as one might be supposed to do if our natural eyes were suddenly gifted to discern the numerous animals and unknown monsters infesting a drop of water, as seen in the oxy-hydrogen microscope.* In the midst of their discourse the son of Mrs Haslitt came in—the same young man to whom Alice had been desired to be civil. He was tall, light-complexioned, heavy-looking, rather handsome. He was very hungry, and wanted his dinner directly, that he might get back to the mill without delay; so he did not look remarkably pleased at the sight of visitors in the drawing-room—nevertheless, he bowed and took a chair beside Alice; which her mother perceiving, redoubled her eloquence to Mrs Haslitt, in order that the young people might make up as much agreeable conversation as they chose, which did not however promise to be much, for Alice continued to read one of the ornamental books she had taken from the table. At length, catching the echo of a more than usually bitter tirade, he ventured to say:

'Well now, there's my mother on her everlasting subject! I declare she makes more noise and bother about managing her three women, than I and my father do over four hundred men. I declare I feel sorry sometimes for our servants, they seem scarcely considered like human beings; I cannot make out how it is they can be so bad as she says, unless they are worried into it. I tell her sometimes she is like the old woman in the fable, who used to make her maids get up at cock-crowing to spin, and all they thought of was circumventing her every way they could think of;—but women do not seem to have any feeling for each other.'

Alice looked at him with some complacency, and asked him how he managed his men; and he was about entering into all the particulars of what he did for their comfort, for it was one of his hobbies, when Alice's mother rose to take leave, pressing both mother and son to fix a day for coming to see her.

Arrived at home, poor Alice hoped she might have a little time to herself, and after dinner sat down to 'Sismondi's Literature du Midi',* but had scarcely found her place when her mother entered the room.

'Oh, Alice, what are you there at your reading again? Well, you may keep your book for just half an hour, and then do set to work to something useful. You might make Fido a collar; I have mentioned it two or three times. There now, make good use of your time, it is just half-past four now, and you may read away till five o'clock.'

Alice was only called away twice from her book, once to look for a lost key, and once to fetch some old linen from the bottom of a chest at the top of the house. It cannot be denied that all this was very worrying. At first Alice had endeavoured, by sitting up at night after she had retired to her room, to find time for her favourite employments; but her mother was a housekeeper of the old school, and would not for the world have gone to bed without first perambulating the house, and seeing with her own eyes that every fire and candle was safely extinguished: so Alice had no chance of spoiling her eyes by midnight study. The only available time she could call her own, was before her mother came down to breakfast in the morning; and as if it had been decreed that all the mother's good qualities should be special points of annoyance to the daughter, Mrs Helmsby was a perversely early riser. And yet she was not wilfully unkind; had no intention of tormenting her daughter in all this; she was to the full as much perplexed and troubled by Alice and her taste for reading and unprofitable employments, as Alice was by her mother's matter-of-fact, worrying industry, about things which a servant might have done equally well. Mrs Helmsby thought it her duty to discourage her daughter's fine fancies, as she called them; and Alice, to do her justice, had very little skill or tact to recommend them to her mercy.

Alice was a type of a very numerous class of English women, whose fine qualities, for lack of wise guidance, evaporate amid the common material details of household life, leaving them ineffectual and incomplete—grown children without the grace of childhood. She had a soft flexible nature, which shrank from blame rather than aspired to win praise; she had a kind of morbid conscientiousness, which made her fancy herself in the wrong whenever she met with a want of sympathy; and she was really miserable at feeling herself so different to those around her. She shrank from all outward manifestation of taste or feeling, except when sanctioned by some one to whom she looked up. Gentle, timid, unenterprising, yet with indomitable tastes, and a refinement of nature almost amounting to fastidiousness, she resembled a choice and graceful plant, which, for want of support, trails along the ground, putting forth its delicate tendrils in all directions to find something higher and stronger than itself round which to cling. She every day became more restless, dreamy, and melancholy, deepening at times into positive depression; the good that was in her lay rather in capacity, than in any definite well-developed qualities. Under wise guidance, she might have been trained into a valuable character, but wise guidance is precisely the blessing that seldomest falls to a woman's lot. Certainly her clever, worldly, bustling mother was not the one likely to afford it.

There was one object amid all that surrounded her which alone seemed in sympathy with the vague yearnings and dim aspirations of her nature, and that was an old picture, which had been saved at the general dispersion of her father's collection. It had been recently deposed from its place in the dining-room, to make room for a portrait of Mrs Helmsby, taken in the most stylish turban and best fitting gown that Miss Higgins, chief milliner and dress-maker to the town of——, could invent for the occasion. Alice begged to have the unhoused picture placed in her own room; she had loved it from a child; it seemed to have a mysterious sympathy with the vague emotions which lay dumb and oppressive at her heart; it was an opening through which she escaped from the contact of the dull, harsh, common details by which she was hemmed in on all sides. It represented a Spanish convent amongst mountains, surrounded by dark tall trees, growing out of the crags that lay piled on all sides covered with long green moss; a clear dark twilight was spread over the whole, which gave a strange and weird-like stillness to the scene. Alice knew nothing about pictures, but her whole soul was athirst after the ideal, and there was that in the picture which it soothed her to look upon. She had the sensibility of genius without its creative power; she had not force enough to break through the rough husk of her actual life and assert her inner soul; she had not the gift of utterance in any way, and the life was almost choked out of her by the rank, over-fed, material prosperity which surrounded her.

Society in a prosperous commercial town, is a raw material not worked up into any social or conventional elegances. Some of the very highest qualities are latent there, but lying quietly like gold in its native vein, not recognisable even when disinterred by those who are conversant only with it as it appears worked up by jewellers. Labour has never yet been made to look lovely, and those engaged in labour have nothing picturesque or engaging in their manners. Alice had nothing of a philosopher about her, and therefore saw nothing but that which was obvious, and which jarred on her somewhat morbid fastidiousness. The men engaged all day in business operations on a large scale, frequently with several hundred workpeople to manage, were not likely to feel any interest in small refinements and elegancies for which there was no tangible use. Consequently female society went for very little. To manage the house well, and to see that the dinner was punctual and well appointed; to be very quiet, and not talk nonsense, or rather to talk very little of any thing; were the principal qualities desired in wives and daughters. Any attempt to show off, or attract attention by a display of graceful prettinesses, would have called forth comments rather broad than deep. They were tired and harassed when they came home from business, and were in no mood for any thing more exalted than to make themselves comfortable; their energies were all engrossed in *one* direction, namely, towards their business, which was the object 'first, last, midst, and without end'* of their life; and they were not up to taking any trouble for the sake of society. The women being thus thrown chiefly amongst each other for companionship, had not a high tone of thought; for women never elevate each other, but fall into a fraternity of petty interests and trivial rivalries. They each extolled their own husband, and adopted all his opinions, only with less good sense and more exaggeration. The young ladies were pretty, trifling, useless beings, waiting their turn to be married, and in the meanwhile, doing their worsted work, and their practising, and their visitings; and were on the whole nicely dressed, quiet, well-conducted young women, with as little enthusiasm as could well be desired.

CHAPTER IX

ALICE was now about twenty. She was not at all popular amongst her own set; the young ladies declared she was 'insipid', and the young men pronounced her 'conceited'; so that her mother had the mortification to see all the 'good matches' in the neighbourhood 'snapped up' by girls very inferior, as she in her heart owned, to her Alice—who, if we are to confess the truth, had never received a single offer. The good lady, though the quintessence of decorum, had entertained great hopes that, by a little prudent encouragement and management, young Mr Haslitt might be induced to propose. He had indeed been heard to declare that Miss Alice could make herself very agreeable if she chose, and was not in the least proud when you came to talk to her; he had stood up for her on all occasions, and had paid her a good deal of what is called attention, and Alice disliked him less than any body else; but, in spite of all these promising symptoms, a young Scotch girl, who had come on a visit to his mother, carried off the prize before Alice's mother was more than aware of her arrival. Young Mr Haslitt had proposed and been accepted; and on her calling to invite Mrs Haslitt and her visitor to a pic-nic, she learned the tidings, which dashed her castle in the air to the ground, and almost deprived her of presence of mind enough to offer her congratulations. She returned home in no very good humour, and throwing herself into a large chair, began to fan herself with some violence.

'How tired you seem, mamma!' said Alice, approaching to remove her bonnet.

'And no wonder,' said her mother; 'here you let me go toiling and slaving myself for your good, and you neither move hand nor foot yourself. Well, well!'

'Will Mrs Haslitt come, mamma? I have been making the jelly, and it is quite brilliant. You must taste the milk-punch. I think it is capital, and a glass will do you good after your walk. I have finished all you left me to do, and I think you will say I have succeeded pretty well.'

Alice left the room, and soon returned with a *pâté* and a glass of the milk-punch, which she had prepared for the pic-nic.

'Well,' said her mother, somewhat refreshed, 'I must say you have worked well; but only to think that young Haslitt is engaged to be married to that young Scotch lassie! I fancy it was all made up before she came here. He met her last year when he went to the Moors shooting; and I must candidly say he is throwing himself away. A more dawdling, ordinary-looking young person I never saw; I wonder what it is he sees in her, for my part.'

'Dear mamma, now just put your feet up on the sofa till dinner-time, and tell me all you have heard. You may as well rest while you are talking, you know.'

'Well, I don't mind if I do; there, I am quite comfortable; now sit down yourself and I will tell you. I had always in my own mind laid out that young Haslitt for you, Alice. Well, that is all passed, but I am sure he admired you. I had scarcely sat down, and was just giving my invitation, when the young lady came in. "Give me leave," said Mrs Haslitt, "to introduce to you Miss Mackintosh, my daughter-in-law that will be." You may think how surprised I was! I declare I could hardly speak for a minute, and then of course I said all that was proper, but indeed she looks a very unfit person for him, and then I invited them both, and they will come, and young Haslitt of course won't fail; but I declare I don't care whether he does or not. When people are courting, they are no company for others; we must look up some young men, or it will go off very stupidly.'

'What is the Scotch lady, like?' asked Alice.

'Oh, nothing at all out of the way—she does not seem to have a word to say for herself.'

'Well, I hope they will be happy,' said Alice; 'but upon my word I always feel as if it were such a risk to run. How terrible it must be, if, after you are married, you should see any one you like better than your husband!'

'My dear Alice,' said her mother, turning round so suddenly that her bonnet fell off the sofa and pitched on the bird of Paradise plume, 'my dear Alice, never let me hear such a shocking speech again. What would any gentleman think who had heard you? When you are married it will be your duty to love your husband more than any one else in the world; and no young woman with a well-regulated mind ever thinks of doing otherwise.

Such an idea is quite shocking. A well-conducted modest woman would no more think of any man except her husband, than she would think of getting tired of her own father or mother, and wishing for somebody else; she must be very depraved, indeed, if such an idea comes into her head.'

'Well, but,' said Alice, gently, 'a husband is not like a father or mother given to one by Providence; you take him on your own judgment. If I, for instance, had married that young Haslitt, as you seem to have wished, I am sure I should have got very tired of him, for I could not have loved him, and should only have taken him because he was a good match; and if he should have lost all his money in business, what would have become of me?'

'I don't like to hear your head running on love so much,' replied her mother; 'it is a thing none but silly girls talk about; and, whatever you do, never let a gentleman hear you; men don't like it; it looks forward and impudent; and besides, my dear, I can tell you, though you may not, perhaps, believe me, that however hot love may be at first, all that goes off fast enough, and it makes no difference at the end of six months whether you married for love or not, provided always you have chosen prudently, and have a respectable, steady, sensible man for your husband; whatever men may be before marriage, they all fall out of love pretty soon afterwards; it is to your children you must look, and not to your husband; for if you expect him to be in love with you, and make much of you, the sooner you get rid of that idea the better; it is a silly romantic notion only found in novels.'

'Then must I neither love my husband, nor any one else?' replied Alice, disconsolately.

'Of course you must; don't I tell you it is your duty to love him, but in a sober, rational way; life was given for something more important than loving, and such nonsense. I wish I could see you more sober-minded.'

'I often wonder what life *was* given us for,' said Alice.

'La! how you talk,' replied her mother; 'any one to hear you would think you a fool. That is the way you lose yourself. This life was given you to do your duty in, of course, there is no difficulty in seeing that; to fill up your time with useful employments. You have very wrong and wild notions of life; it is very different to what you expect; you have an idea of liking this and not liking that, but what have you to look forward to, I should like to know, but marrying some honest, respectable man, who will support you decently in the sphere in which you were born. You say you could not like young Haslitt—what is it you expect? a nobleman to come in a coach and six to make you an offer? I wish I could see you cured of these flighty notions and more sober-minded.'

'But why must I marry at all?' said Alice.

'For what else do women come into the world,' replied her mother, 'but to be good wives? Poor profitless, forlorn creatures they are, when they live single and get to be old; unless indeed they are rich enough to keep up an establishment, with a parcel of dogs and cats and parrots. Depend upon it, Alice, if a young woman is lucky enough to be married to a steady, respectable young man, it is the best thing that can happen to her; and then she is something in the world.'

Here dinner cut short the worthy matron's harangue. Afterwards, when they returned to the drawing-room, her mother (who had talked herself into a good temper, for we all feel good-humoured when we have succeeded in giving utterance to what strikes us as being very sensible) said,

'You have not prepared your dress for Mrs Dickson's dinner-party on Thursday; when I was in town this morning I got the satin; go and fetch it whilst there is daylight, and whilst you are busy we can have a little rational conversation.'

Alice fetched the dress, and began to take out the sleeves, the shape of which required altering.

'I did not buy you a new dress,' said her mother, 'for I expect there will be a *soirée* when the Association comes, and Miss Higgins, the milliner, told me there was likely to be a great change in the material of evening dresses, so I thought it would be better to wait. But as I was passing the shop door, Mr Bruce stopped me to say he had received an assortment of the sweetest French goods; and though it was monstrously dear, I could not resist this scarf; I thought you would admire it so much. Is it not beautiful?' continued she, unfolding it. 'I declare that business of young Haslitt quite put it out of my head before dinner.'

The scarf, which was really beautiful, was duly admired and thankfully received by Alice, for no woman is insensible to the acquisition of a piece of finery, although comparatively few have the taste and patience to pay the minute attention necessary to dress well: but any body is competent to put on a scarf or a turban; the minute finishing touches in dress as in art show the master, and masters in no pursuit are plentiful.

'I wonder who will be here for the *soirée*,' said Alice; 'it is such a pleasure to see distinguished men, even though one may not be able to understand all they talk about.'

'I don't know, but they say there is a *chance* that the Queen will come, and I don't see why she should not come here as much to see learned men, as go to the races;—it would be a comfort to see the *real* bonnet and shawl she wears!'

'It is raining,' said Alice, shortly after, 'and it is lecture night besides; do you think you are prudent to go, mamma?'

'It is a very unpleasant evening,' replied her mother, 'but I don't like to miss, on account of the example. If we are not punctual at church, how can we expect the poor people to be? But I really think the poor people about here require more good example setting them than in any other parish; and yet they are no better that I can see. I sometimes wish there were no poor people, and then one would not have so much responsibility for being better off; it would be happier for *them*, poor things, for they have little enjoyment as it is, God help them, in spite of all we can do!'

'But staying away this one wet night will do no harm,' said Alice, gently; 'and as I shall go, the pew will not be empty.'

'No, no, my dear, it is a bad thing to break through a habit; we are all so apt to be self-indulgent; staying at home to-night would only make it harder to go another time; one excuse always admits another. We will have our tea when we come back—it will be something comfortable to look forward to. Wrap yourself well up, and mind you put on your strongest shoes.'

Mrs Helmsby caught a bad cold at the lecture; and the pic-nic, from this cause, and a variety of other circumstances added, did not come off; which she the less regretted, as she told Alice, because it put her out of all patience to see that young Haslitt look so soft and foolish with that Miss Mackintosh.

That failure in her matrimonial speculations was a heavy blow and a great discouragement to the worthy lady—especially as she was obliged candidly to own that the balance of perfection was decidedly in favour of Alice.

CHAPTER X

THE day of Mrs Dickson's dinner-party arrived, and Mrs Helmsby was sufficiently recovered from her cold to attend it; and at the appointed hour, she and her black velvet dress, and her diamond ear-rings, appeared in Mrs Dickson's drawing-room; Alice dressed in pale pink satin, and without any ornaments at all, was with her, looking as pretty and lady-like as possible.

Mrs Dickson was in the habit of giving a great many dinner parties; one differing from another as Lamb or Venison happened to be the presiding dish, or as it was the turn of Mr and Mrs Haslitt or Mr and Mrs and Miss Mason, to be invited; but all had a strong family likeness in being all equally sumptuous, the plate equally massive, and the guests equally heavy to match. Alice had grown to fancy it a matter of course that all dinner parties should be dull; it seemed to her as essentially an unalterable etiquette, as that there should be soup and fish.

About ten of the guests had assembled when Alice and her mother arrived—all people who were in the habit of meeting; but, in a few moments a stranger entered, a tall solidly built middle aged man, with an extremely quiet air; he addressed the mistress of the house in a remarkably gentle voice, and with a manner quite different to that of any one Alice had ever seen before. He had been announced as Mr Bryant; several gentlemen gathered round him, and began to talk of the markets, the state of the country, and whether the harvest was likely to be well got in, as if no such beings as women were in the room. Whilst Alice was sitting watching the new comer, the mistress of the house came to her and said, 'Well, Miss Alice, I have got a new beau to-day, you see! He is rather old for you, to be sure: but he is a very nice man, for all that; and I want you to talk to him because he is very clever, and has travelled a great deal, and you know so much history and geography that I quite depend on you for keeping him amused during dinner.'

'Where has he been travelling?' asked Alice.

'It is where has he *not* been! My Mr Dickson tells me that he has been establishing iron works somewhere, where hardly any body has ever travelled even; but you must ask him at dinner.'

Here the entrance of the remaining guests in rapid succession put an end to her conversation, and dinner being shortly afterwards announced, little Mr Dickson offered his arm to Mrs Helmsby, and Alice was escorted down by a bluff, square-headed, elderly gentleman, given to telling venerable jokes and stories, that with a different disguise of names and places had, no doubt, figured from the days of Odin; but he chuckled over them with as much glee as if they were fresh from the mint of human whimsicality.

'This way, Mr Glenton,' cried Mrs Dickson, 'let Miss Alice divide you and Mr Bryant; I cannot do without my young favourite in my neighbourhood—I call her my princess. Mr Bryant, let me introduce you to her. We are only plain people here. You must not compare us with the fine ladies abroad.'

Here the bustle of getting seated at table having subsided, the business of dinner commenced, and put a stop to good Mrs Dickson's flow of talk.

Mr Bryant did not appear at all disposed to test Alice's stores of history or geography, for all his attention seemed given to assisting Mrs Dickson to dispense her dishes; besides, her other neighbour seemed inclined to talk for the whole table. When the ladies returned to the drawing-room, Alice was placed at the piano by Mrs Dickson, and entreated to play something; whilst the elder ladies either dozed, or settled family receipts,* or talked of their servants;—what young ladies there were gathered together and discussed Mrs Ellis's novel,* and thought the heroine a very natural character, but that it was doing a great deal, certainly, to give up her fortune;—and then another asked if any one intended to go to the Chemical Lectures to be delivered next week,—and many things of the same sort: till coffee came, and then some of the gentlemen made their appearance, and Mr Bryant amongst them; he came and sat down by Alice at the piano, and asked her whether she gave up much time to music;—then he began to tell her about some Bohemian students, with whose singing he had been much struck when in Germany. He was very quiet, but Alice felt him at once to be very different from all the people who surrounded her, and was much more interested than she had ever been before; but still he was so quiet, she felt rather afraid of him. Silent, quiet people, have a charm and mystery about them which gives them a great advantage over more demonstrative mortals;—nobody knows exactly what they think, nor the impression made on them by any thing; all within them has the prestige of an oracle; the extent of what they indicate is unknown, and what little is uttered goes so far! Every body has felt the charm of a kind, or even of a reasonably civil expression; from one of these reserved, silent persons; 'it is not much', is the common expression, but from so-and-so it means 'a great deal';—it is like signing a blank cheque on our self-complacency.

Alice soon felt this charm, and by little and little began to feel a most unusual degree of interest in both what she heard and in what she herself was saying, for she was asking questions to which she felt very desirous to have an answer. He told her about his recent journey into Hungary, to a part which has never yet figured in any hand-book for travellers, and about a most singular race of people flourishing there, who belong to no known nation, and might pass either for the one of the lost tribes of Israel, or as the original gypsy stock, from which all the others have wandered forth on the face of the earth. A race of idealised gipsys, however, if such they be; living an allowed and recognised life, under no fear of the magistrates, and quite free from the sins of poaching and robbing hen-roosts. He had arrived at one of these villages during fair time, and he gave Alice a graphic account of a picturesque procession in which the handsomest girl in the tribe was carried through the village crowned with flowers on the last day of the fair, and of the strange dances and *polkas* which closed the festival. Alice's imagination was completely captivated by the vision of that wild and lonely country in its utter isolation from the rest of the world—surrounded by those mysterious giant mountains, and that strange unknown tribe of people, with no filiation amongst the other families of the earth. She could have sat and listened for ever, but a general move amongst the guests had commenced, and her mother amongst the rest had risen to depart. Alice returned home in a dreamy reverie. The stranger, with his cold passionless manner, and kind, quiet voice, and the new things she had heard that night, were mingled in her dreams, till she awoke with the fright of finding herself carried through the air over impassable mountains, and placed where no human being could approach her! She went down stairs the next morning, a new creature; the dull monotony of her life had received a quickening impulse; she had found an object on which all the pent-up passionate affection of her unoccupied dreaming heart might be poured forth;—it required but a touch for the lava torrent of her soul to burst out, and bear down all the small frozen barriers with which she had been surrounded. William Bryant became the hero of her desert! Her cheek was flushed, and her eye sparkled the next morning when she descended to breakfast. People must have been *ennuyé** within an inch of final suffocation, before they can know the blessing of something to interest their faculties. Her mother hardly knew what to make of it; but as she went about her usual avocations with an energy not usual, she could not find fault; and, in fact, her maternal vanity was gratified to perceive the attention her daughter had received from a person of much more importance than all the young Mr Haslitts or Mr Smiths, or Mr Oldfields in the town, put together. It was in high good-humour she sat down to her daily stitching after breakfast.

'Well!' she said, 'Alice, I must say we had a charming dinner-party yesterday. I never saw any thing go off better. Did you remark that pretty new side dish in the second course? I must ask Mrs Dickson for the receipt, and it is as nice as it looks; those sweetbreads were dressed in quite a new fashion—recollect, my dear, we have some our next dinner-party;—and, by the way, we owe one now to a good many people. I should like to have it whilst that Mr Bryant is in town. Mrs Dickson said he was staying over the Association, and that he will read a paper about something; he seems a very nice man, quite the gentleman. Do you know, Alice, he reminded me a little of your poor dear father.'

'Ah!' said Alice, 'then that accounts for his being so very agreeable.'

'What were you and he talking about so fast?' asked her mother.

'He was telling me all about his travels, mamma,' replied Alice, blushing; 'he has been abroad a great deal.'

'Yes, so I heard,' said her mother; 'I managed to pick up a good deal about him from Mrs Dickson. She says he is very rich, and has just established large iron-works in some outlandish place; so far off they can hardly get to it. He is very well connected, and lives somewhere in Lancashire.'

Alice listened with great interest to all this gossip, and even volunteered to call on Mrs Dickson for the receipt, in order that the cook might have time to practise it before the party. Mrs Helmsby nodded sagaciously to herself; it was the first time she and her daughter had ever felt any real sympathy together. Notes were written and sent out. Mr Bryant graciously accepted— which was all Alice cared for. Nevertheless, she did not see him again until the *soirée* of the Association, for she had gone out to inquire after somebody's cold or rheumatism the day Mr Bryant called on Mrs Helmsby! The disappointment may be imagined; but still the *soirée* was in sight, which was to pay for all, and with the prospect of the dinner-party, Alice could not be very miserable.

At length the *soirée* arrived. Alice felt very much dissatisfied with her own appearance; but her mother declared she looked very nice, and for once, we are inclined to be of her mother's opinion. She was dressed in white tarlatan, over white satin; a small wreath of myrtle in her hair was all the ornament she wore; and with her face a little flushed, she had all the animation of look she generally wanted.

The large room in the town-hall was brilliantly lighted, and thronged with elegantly-dressed women and all the respectability and gentility of the town and neighbourhood. Many strangers were there from all parts; and every eye was turned on the *savans*,* who had attended the Association, and who were walking quietly about, very little impressed with the effort that was made to do them honour, looking, indeed, rather bored than otherwise, as they blandly attempted to give intelligible replies to questions (put by those lucky enough to get an introduction) which required the knowledge of a life-time to be compressed into a portable answer, that might be carried away like a receipt for venison sauce.

Alice remained amongst the crowd of nicely-dressed young ladies, with bouquets in their hands, and wreaths in their hair, each with a separate personal freight of hope, vanity, and importance, but all massed together in an undistinguished throng, like the points in a mosaic brooch. She had one hope, that Mr Bryant would come and speak to them; and that was all the stake she had in the evening. But time wore on; and Alice, who had hitherto pertinaciously kept beside her mother, afraid to move, for fear of losing the one important moment, was at last obliged to leave her place. An elderly gentleman, a great friend of her mother's, approached and offered her his arm, to walk through the rooms, promising to point out all the grand people. Her mother, pulling her lace shawl over her shoulders, rose at once, and Alice, with a sigh, had to follow her example. Every young lady there had far rather have had a dance, and thought it a great pity such a charming band should be wasted; walking about, and looking at curiosities, or even at learned men, was in their opinion a very dry substitute for their usual allowance of dancing and flirtation. And many of the young men were of the same opinion; they could only hope that the mayor would let them have one little dance at the end of the evening. Alice and her mother, and their escort, threaded their way through the crowded rooms; and, at last, in a doorway, talking to a knot of professors of various sciences, her eye discovered Mr Bryant; but though he recognised them with a pleased bow, he did not attempt to break off his conversation, and the movement of the crowd carried them away in a different direction. But in about half-an-hour, whilst they were in the refreshment-room, Mr Bryant again approached; at first he did not see them, and began to eat an ice at another stand. Alice pointed him out to her mother, who boldly accosted him. Mr Bryant seemed quite pleased to have been recognised—said he had not perceived them, and putting down his plate, offered his arm to Alice.

'How do you manage to get on with all these people?' said he, after a few moments' silence.

Alice started—it was the first time she had ever heard them called anything but highly sensible, respectable persons, a great deal better than herself. She was too much abashed to reply immediately.

'I suppose,' continued he, 'you would parody the words of Bacon, and say, "Some are born stupid, some achieve stupidity, and some have stupidity thrust upon them!"*—which latter is your own case. It is when you see a great gathering like this that you perceive the uncultivated state of social habits amongst the English; there are, no doubt, exceptions, but social talent is not indigenous amongst them; they are all incumbered with themselves, and consequently, don't move well; there is all the dead material for enjoyment, but no life to set it going. However, I must say, I can stand any thing but your superior and respectable people. I have been a long time out of England, you know, and that must be my excuse. I can stand dulness *au naturel*;* I consider it as I would any other human affliction—blindness, or lameness, or what not; but, when it will arrogate to itself a superiority, and claim a sort of apostolical succession from the wisdom of Solomon, and set up little fancy anathemas on everything, and everybody, who are not, like themselves, "measured from the standard of Cornhill", I confess I get out of all patience and all charity! I know you to be a good listener, Miss Helmsby; and some pitying Providence, or rather some instinct, has led me to you, for I am just now quite savage at all the nonsense I have heard to-night. So much innate vulgarity and stupidity I never heard before. As men of business and enterprise, Englishmen are wonderful. Do not suppose, for a moment, I underrate the sterling granite qualities, the real *stuff* that lies in them—but that does not come out in a *soirée*; they make no show; they lie like gold, quietly in the mine, ready to be dug out; but your provincial *superior people*, who have attained a small reputation—oh, those are terrible! I have just been listening to one of them, who was speaking to C——the geologist, and propounding his "Asses' Bridge" as if it were a new revelation. I left him in despair; but, if C——do not pick his way through the Mosaic theory of creation, and keep his chin cleverly above the waters of Noah's deluge, he will be held up as a heathen man, and be attacked for his insidious principles.'*

'Do you think the man he was talking to able then to hold him up?' said Alice, extremely comforted by this tirade, which gave utterance to her own feelings.

'Well, true, you're right, that is his chance; it is a sort of compensation for many blunders, that when a man has gained a name for any thing he may hide under the shadow of it, it gives him a *prestige*, and enables him to put down impertinent questions with words. C——is a great friend of mine—have you ever seen him? Do you know many of the distinguished visitors by sight?'

'No,' said Alice, 'I would give a great deal to have them pointed out to me. I like to speculate on their faces.'

'Well, then, if Mrs Helmsby will trust you with me, we will make a *voyage autour de la chambre*.'*

Mrs Helmsby had reached a vacant place on a bench, and readily consented to remain where she was until they returned.

Mr Bryant pointed out to Alice every one of any note, and gave her a succinct account of what they were distinguished for. Alice found herself talking quite at her ease, and speaking the things that had so long been hid in her heart; and it was a new, inexpressible pleasure to be listened to, and replied to, as if there were nothing either strange or reprehensible in her ideas. Her companion made clear her meaning to herself, and brought so much kind good sense to bear on her vague, unformed, floating notions, that it is no wonder if Alice, charmed with his gentle voice and manner, felt all her vague aspirations more than realised, and destined from this evening to wear the shape and aspect of Mr Bryant! True, he was a good deal older than herself, but she fancied that half the charm.

'I fear,' said Mrs Helmsby, the next morning, as they sat over their work as usual, 'that Mr Bryant is not too sound in his religious views; I fear, from something I heard, that he is by no means a regular churchgoer; indeed, Mrs Dickson told me he had been heard to say that he required a *rest* on Sunday, and could not stand going to church twice a day! You did not happen to ask him whether he was a member of the Church of England, did you, Alice?'

'No,' replied Alice, quietly, 'I never thought about it. I should not suppose he would ever be likely to do any thing that was not right.'

'I don't know that,' replied her mother; 'he has been abroad a long time, and there young men are either apt to be led astray, by popish delusions and soul-destroying heresies, as Mr Wright calls them, or else to fall into the fatal snare of infidelity and human reason; but I shall not rest till I have asked him.'

'My dear,' resumed Mrs Helmsby, after a pause, during which she had been carefully adjusting a petticoat body—'my dear, have you got that receipt from Mrs Dickson? I should like to have it for our party—we must begin to arrange what we will have;

there are only four days till the twenty-third.' Then she wandered off into the regions of the land of Goshen,* settling her roast and boiled, her fishes and fowls; having determined in her own mind to give the very most elegant dinner that had ever been seen in M——. To her surprise she had a most zealous adjutant in Alice, who seemed as anxious as herself that the dinner should be perfect. She could not make it out. 'Ah! Alice,' said she, half reproachfully, 'there would be some pleasure in giving dinners, if you would always support me in this way.'

The dinner-time arrived, the guests came, and every·thing went off as well as possible; but Alice little suspected that Mr Bryant left their house fully convinced that Alice was exactly the woman he wanted for a wife! He was not in love with her, but he thought her a charming lady-like young creature, with plenty of sense, if she were taught to use it; in short, his judgment was quite convinced he might look a long time before he found any one else so suitable; that was the grand point with a man like him, and there was no doubt but that he would fall in love afterwards quite as much as was necessary.

In the meantime, Alice and her mother were to go to Matlock the following week, and he had to break his purpose to his only sister, and to arrange his affairs so as to be able to take a holiday.

But an offer of marriage is far too important a thing to introduce at the end of a chapter.

CHAPTER XI

THOSE who have read that delicious old book, Amory's 'Life of John Buncle',★ will know that the north of England once was full of unexplored wildernesses, impassable mountains, mysterious caverns, leading to the bowels of the earth; and, difficult as it may be to believe, yielding adventures second to nothing in the 'Arabian Nights'. It is not very much more than a century since he lived, and all his wonderful journeys and romantic discoveries have been explored in their length and breadth, by turnpike commissioners, if not by railway surveyors,★ and the mysteries have been subdued by statistics, till one knows where every road leads, and we are allowed to entertain no doubt about the turnings of the longest lane; every foot of ground is known, and there is no hope left of being able to *lose oneself*;—and that, as every body must have felt, is a dreadful drawback on the pleasure and excitement of finding oneself in a wild romantic *looking* country. It is wild and unknown to *us* alone, and our ignorance is going to be speedily enlightened by guide-books, teaching us all the walks, and drives, 'and points of view'. The convenience and the cultivation, the civilisation and all that, is, of course, a wonderful improvement, and shows the progress of the species in a way that ought to rejoice one's philanthropy; for, 'as man is no longer an individual, but a species,' as Fanny Wright tells us,★ we all have an infinitesimal investment in the rise of human perfection. Still all the *hope* is taken out of travelling now. We know, beforehand, all we are going to see; and we, for our parts, cannot help wishing it were possible to set out like the heroes of old to seek our fortune, and walk to the end of the world, without knowing the history and geography of what we were going to find.

Derbyshire, in spite of its wonders being written down in the chronicles of guide-books, has still a look of mystery, with its peak and its caverns, and its Druidical remains; it seems as if it really had been, at no distant time, the abode of gnomes and spirits, who are even yet scarcely dispossessed of their ancient holdings. Men and women seem intruders living in the ruined abodes of a different order of beings. Good Mrs Helmsby had no speculations of this kind, as she and Alice journeyed *en route* to Matlock, one fine afternoon, about ten days after the dinner party.

'I hope, Alice, we shall find Saxton's a comfortable house, and that the beds will be well aired; that is the great drawback in travelling; one can never feel quite safe.—Well, I must say, that really is very pretty, indeed. Look, Alice, at those white houses, upon those rocks, nearly hidden with the trees.'

But Alice was silent. She was drinking in the sight—feeling, for the first time in the presence of the power of nature, crushed down before the mute aspect of superhuman beauty and majesty, which made all human utterance irreverent; taking her, for the moment, out of herself, away from her own hopes, and fears, and personalities,* to feel overwhelmed before the grand inorganic majesty around her. The first sight of any scene that strikes us as really grand, touches our ideal; stuns all the small personalities within us: and bows us before the grandeur of a power which stands revealed before us impassive, incommunicable, pressing on our senses, but utterly unmindful of us, separated from us by a gulf of everlasting silence—for there is neither sound nor language which we may interpret, or by which we may draw nigh to it. All we have ever hoped, or feared, or desired for ourselves, seems then so pitiful and worthless, that our impulse is to fling ourselves down before the vast dumb aspect of nature, leaving time and chance to happen as they may. Alice felt choked with emotions she could not have expressed; but she leaned out of the chaise window to conceal from her mother the tears that coursed each other down her cheeks.

They arrived, at length, at Saxton's hotel, at Matlock, as all the village lay bathed in the golden lightning of the descending sun. The dinner-hour was passed, but an early tea, and a chicken, in their own room, was a not unpleasant substitute. When they joined the company at supper, Mrs Helmsby recognised, in a comfortable, portly, well-dressed woman, an old school-fellow, with whom she had once sworn everlasting friendship, which, however, had not survived the wear and tear of the first twelve months after leaving school. Circumstances separated them, and absence had almost made them forget each other, until this unexpected meeting at a *table d'hôte**★** stimulated their dormant sensibilities. It was a very pleasant meeting on both sides; they had not met for more than twenty years, and in that time they had married, and were now both of them widows; both had got wonderfully well over their loss, and both were very comfortably jointured.

Alice had the most reason to rejoice in this encounter, for it not only put her mother in an excellent flow of spirits, but she had so much to tell, and to hear, and to talk about, that Alice was left to follow her own devices, and ramble and explore as much as she pleased; added to which, Mrs Fernly (her mother's new-found friend) was an active, comfortable woman, with a great notion of enjoying herself, and seeing every thing that was to be seen; and, as she had learned the best rides and drives, she was proud to take her friends about; and a little pony chaise belonging to the house was put into daily requisition. She won Alice's heart altogether, by allowing her to read out her subscription to the circulating library, whilst she was talking over old times with her mother.

One day Alice had taken her book—it was a volume of 'Corinne',★ which she was reading for the first time—and had clambered up to the spot called the 'Romantic Rocks' in guidebook parlance; they resemble an immense mountain shivered into a fantastic skeleton, and covered with a tanglement of shrubs, and creeping plants. Seated in a cleft of rock so narrow, that she could scarce see the sky above her for the ivy that hung across, she was quite unconscious how the time flew by. The first reading of 'Corinne' is an epoch a woman never forgets, and Alice never lifted her head till she had come to the last line in the last page of the volume, and then it struck her she had been away a long time; on looking at her watch she found, with dismay, it was long past the dinner hour. She is not the first whom that book has beguiled into a breach of punctuality; but that would have been no comfort, even had the thought occurred. She started up and began to hasten to the inn, with a fear lest the scolding in store for her might be coupled with a prohibition of any more books from the library. It is very provoking to be brought back to such disagreeable realities; but one is never so sure to meet with a jar, as when one has been absorbed in a very highly wrought novel. She was crossing the fields with a rapid step, and lifting her head to see how she should best clamber over a somewhat awkward stile, when her eyes encountered, certainly the last person she expected to see—Mr Bryant! He sprang over the stile with great eagerness. 'You little know,' said he, smiling, 'the excitement your absence has caused; your mother and her friend have ordered the pony carriage to scour the country in search of you. Dinner has been over these two hours.'

Alice was too much embarrassed to give a very definite answer, but murmured something about her book, and not knowing it was so late. 'Is mamma very angry?' asked she.

'Well, I hardly know,' replied he, smiling, 'she had become uneasy, and perhaps when she finds you safe and sound, and that you have been in no sort of danger, she may be indignant at your having excited so much needless sensibility. If you were to sprain your ancle, now, she would quite forgive you.'

But poor Alice looked confused, and distressed, and so evidently thought she had been guilty of a grievous breach of decorum, that Mr Bryant ceased to rally her, but walked silently beside her for some time. Her embarrassment seemed to communicate itself to him. He had come to Matlock with every intention of proposing to her, and this was as fair an opportunity as he was ever likely to have. He had certainly intended to prepare the way a little, but then the thought of saving her from the scolding she evidently dreaded, was the small incident that determined him to risk his declaration at once. He had not any great fear of a refusal, but still 'making an offer' is always a nervous thing, it is throwing every thing on the 'hazard of the die'. He made one or two efforts to speak, but no sound passed his lips. They at length reached a place where the pathway branched off, one path leading to the inn, and the other through a small grove of trees, to the river side. Three more steps, and she would have turned to the right, and three minutes more would have ended their walk at the inn-door. He made a desperate effort, and said, in a husky voice, 'Alice—Miss Helmsby, I mean—will you play the truant a few minutes longer—there is something I *must* say to you, will you hear me now?' He took her hand, and gently drew it through his arm, which she was too much agitated to resist, and led her down the other footpath. Alice felt the arm she was leaning on tremble.

'I fear,' said he, after another pause, 'that I am premature; if I am, forgive me. I came to this place only to see you; I have no other business here, and unless you bid me stay, I shall depart again to-morrow morning. I am come to put my fate in your hands, Alice. Do you think you can ever like me well enough to *marry* me?' He took the little hand that hung upon his arm; it trembled, but was not withdrawn. 'Will you not speak to me *one* word, Alice? Will you tell me that you will try to like me? you have not seen much of me yet; but from the first moment I saw you, you have been to me, what no woman ever was before. Tell me—may I remain in Matlock, or must I go away tomorrow? I do not ask you to say you will have me now; I will have as much patience as you can wish; but will you think of what I have said?'

Alice's tears were falling abundantly, and she could not have spoken, had her life depended upon it; but Mr Bryant seemed to be able to interpret her emotion; he pressed the hand he held to his lips, and said, in a whisper, 'God bless you, Alice, you have made me very happy.'

He did not now attempt to prolong their walk. On reaching the inn, Alice disengaged her arm, and passed rapidly to her own room, altogether stunned and bewildered. She was sensible of no feeling but the desire to be alone. Luckily her mother had not returned, and she was not interrupted till tea-time.

CHAPTER XII

'ALICE!' said Mrs Helmsby, entering her daughter's room, 'I very much dislike your passion for locking yourself up in your bed-room during the daytime; it looks affected, to say the least of it; and now, pray, may I hear why you were absent from the dinner-table, where had you gone, and what were you doing?'

'I am very sorry, mamma,' replied Alice, 'I had taken out a book when I went to walk, as the day was so fine, and I sat down to read amongst the rocks, without observing how the time passed.'

'Very romantic, indeed!' said her mother; 'but if there be one thing I dislike to see in a young woman more than another, it is love of singularity; indeed, it is the only impropriety a well-brought-up young woman has it in her power to commit, but it paves the way for every thing that is wrong. If a young woman allows herself to be different to other people, she throws herself out of the path marked by propriety, and has no guide but her own giddy head; so no wonder if she, sooner or later, goes wrong; it does not even surprise people. "We expected no better," is the cry. It is no mark of superiority, Alice, whatever you may think; it only exposes your ignorance in the eyes of sensible people, and let me tell you, that, of all things, gentlemen dislike all approaches to eccentricity or singularity in a young woman's conduct; they may be very polite to your face, for they find their amusement in it, but no gentleman would *marry* a girl who set up to be remarkable.'

Alice made a very pretty but rather scornful mouth at this climax.

'Ay, you may look as saucy as you please, Alice, but what I tell you is quite true; with all your airs you have not received a single offer of marriage, and that is the criterion of whether the men admire you. It is true you are very young, and have plenty of time before you, but the day may come when you will wish you had listened to me. Suppose any gentleman had seen you sitting reading by yourself amongst those rocks, he would have thought you just wished to be remarked.'

All the delicious reveries in which Alice had been steeping her heart, were rudely destroyed by the coarse prosaic reality of her mother's discourse, like the rosy and golden clouds of sunset which thicken into leaden vaporous masses of darkness, without the majesty of night.

'I have something to tell you, mamma,' said she at length, feeling the desperate necessity there was that her mother should be made acquainted with the occurrence of the morning, although it seemed almost sacrilege to mention it after such an exordium.

'Well, what is it?' said her mother, after waiting in silence about a quarter of a minute,—'Make haste, or the tea bell will ring, and you are not dressed yet! Will it not keep until bed time?'

If the reader can recall the time when he, a small child at school, was called upon for a barely-learned lesson—how he went slowly up to the master with eyes lingering to the last moment on the task which hovered on the brink of his comprehension—when the sudden jerk with which his book was taken, scared away all that was so nearly entering in, leaving him blank and stammering!—he can then sympathise with Alice when so compendiously desired 'to make haste'.

'Mr Bryant joined me as I was coming home,' said she, in a faltering voice.

'Mr Bryant!' interrupted her mother, 'what *can* have brought him here! Did he tell you?'

'Yes,' said Alice, with some difficulty forcing herself to speak; 'he told me—he asked me—in short, he made me an offer.'

'My dear Alice!' cried her astonished mother, as soon as she could take breath after such an announcement, 'my dear Alice, why did you not tell me this at once, instead of letting me find fault with you for half an hour, when you had such a piece of news as this! Let me hear all about it,—what did you say to him, and how did it all come about? I declare I had no suspicion of such a thing, though in general I have a tolerable insight into such matters. But first I will order tea to be brought up to us here, and you shall lie down whilst you tell me.'

Mrs Helmsby rang the bell, drew the sofa and a large arm-chair to a comfortable proximity, and settled herself down for a regular gossip.

'Now, my dearest Alice,' said she, at last, when the tea-tray had been brought and the waiter had retired, 'tell me all about it, and do not miss any thing. I declare it makes me feel quite young again. Ah, Alice! when you have a grown up daughter you will know how proud it is to feel she is admired as she should be! None but a mother ever really cares for her girl's success;—but now begin—tell me first is your tea sweet enough?'

'Quite so, thank you, mamma,' replied Alice—rather worried, if the truth must be told. Her mother's gossipping tone jarred on her feelings; however, thus adjured, she spoke, and gave a circumstantial narration of the events of the morning; but her own heart, her own thoughts, she could not lay bare; they were tender blossoms which contracted and almost withered beneath her mother's coarse version of maternal affection.

'Well, my dear Alice, I must say you have behaved very properly indeed, and shown great discretion, and I am very much pleased with you;—of course, Mr Bryant is a very good match for you, perfectly unexceptionable in every respect, but I shall not let him think he is to have you for the asking; it will not do to seem too keen about him; men are all quite set up enough in their own esteem; and of all things a young woman must never let her real sentiments appear;—the best of men are not to be trusted—they are our natural enemies, and always ready to take advantage of any thing they see in their favour;—so, my dearest love, just let me give you a hint never to allow him to feel to sure of your partiality. You are going to marry him, and that, as Dr Gregory* says, is quite a sufficient mark of preference. A little reserve and coldness makes a man's love burn all the more briskly; they never care for that of which they are certain.'

'I am sure,' said Alice, warmly, 'that Mr Bryant is a very different sort of man; I am confident that no one ever repented of trusting him.'

'Well, well,' replied her mother, kissing her and patting her check, 'it is all quite right that you should think so.'

At this moment the waiter appeared, bringing in a note for Mrs Helmsby. She read it, and handed it to Alice. It was from Bryant, begging the favour of an interview with Mrs Helmsby, at any time she would name in the course of the evening.

'Shall I say in half an hour, Alice?'

'Yes, mamma, whenever you think best.'

Mrs Helmsby and Mr Bryant had finally an interview that evening, which concluded to their mutual satisfaction. Mrs Helmsby had the supremest self-complacency in the manner in which she had acquitted herself. When she came to consider the matter, she was convinced that she had conducted it with the most sagacious diplomacy: she had concluded by telling Bryant that 'she would never force her daughter's inclination, but that if he could succeed in winning the affections of Alice, she had never seen the man to whom she would so willingly commit her happiness, though it would cost a great pang to part with such a dear companion,' &c., &c. All which Bryant perfectly understood, and made the requisite assurances about 'honour and happiness'. He, of course, obtained permission to plead his cause with Alice, and the result was that when a few days afterwards they quitted Matlock, she was the affianced wife of Bryant.

CHAPTER XIII

ALICE found her position at home materially changed for the better; she had become a person of importance, her desires and opinions were humoured in every way. Bryant, by sanctioning them, gave them quite a different aspect in her mother's eyes, who became suddenly enlightened on her daughter's merits, and began to fancy that they had never been duly appreciated by the circle of her acquaintance. She even began to suspect that she was superior to all the young ladies whom she had so perseveringly held up to her as models—to be sure, she was going to make a much better match than they had any of them achieved for themselves. It was not her mother alone, the whole neighbourhood began to regard her with deference, as the future mistress of a handsome establishment, and the dispenser of dinner-parties and dances.

It is unfortunate, but it generally happens, that people become sensible of our merits at the precise time when it is most a matter of indifference whether they do or not: possibly, to teach us that what we really *are* is the only essential point whilst, whether we are admired is of very little consequence at all. It is difficult to become indifferent to the sympathy of those around us, it seems like the response of an oracle to sanction what we do; but, after all, sympathy is a luxury, and not a necessity; the natural craving we have for it had need to be carefully watched, lest it should degenerate into a sentimental vanity. We must all of us learn to lead our own life, according to the best of our ideas, and the best manner in which we can realise it, whether we have to encounter good report, or evil report. 'The favour of man bringeth a snare,' as wise King Solomon declared, long ago. The intense yearning after sympathy, and the habit of fancying all to be wrong which did not come with the sanction of other people's opinion, was the weak part of Alice's character, although the source of much in her that was delicate and graceful; it gave that confiding, clinging, beautiful helplessness, which was the fascination of her manner: but still it is *strength*, and not graceful weakness, that is to be desired: defects of character have often a beautiful aspect, and virtues present, in some points of view, the defects of their qualities.

Alice, however, had, for the present, found all that her soul had thirsted for so long. Bryant was several years older than herself, and whatever opinion he expressed came to her with the weight of authority. Every body who spoke of him seemed to regard him as a man of superior sagacity in all matters of business; she heard men quote his opinion to give weight to their own; his character stood high on all sides, so that she had no misgivings about his worth. The quiet impassiveness of his manner, mingled as it was towards her with a tenderness and gentleness that had a touch of the paternal in it, possessed a peculiar charm for her more demonstrative and passionate nature. There was a certain mystery about it—so much more was implied by his calm speech than the words expressed, and every word of affection seemed an inlet through which she discerned an infinite world of love lying beyond.

Under this new order of things she bloomed into fresh life and vigour; her faculties for the first time dared to assert themselves, and expand to their natural growth. She had an affinity with all that was beautiful and refined: without knowing what was meant by an *ideal*, she had unconsciously lived in aspirations after it. It seemed to her that the new life now opening to her would realise all her vague dreams.

Bryant was really become most sincerely attached to her; he listened with ready and admiring interest, as with a confiding shyness she poured out to him all the hoarded aspirations of her soul; he thought her very charmingly romantic, and he told her histories of his travels and of the incidents of his past life, to which she listened with Desdemona-like avidity,* whilst he thought that when she grew older, and had seen more of the world, she would gain common sense, and 'become more like other people'. Most fortunate was it for the safety of poor Alice's dreams that he never gave this hope words!

Alice was terribly annoyed by being told on all sides that 'she was going to make an excellent match'. Had Bryant been the most insignificant of his own clerks, on a salary of a hundred a year, she would have rejoiced in the opportunity of proving to him that she married him for his own sake, and she was much afraid lest some of these speeches should come to his ears, and that he should take a disgust to so much worldliness. Her mother especially showed a disposition to drive in all things as good a bargain as possible. But Bryant perfectly understood the disposition of both mother and daughter; and whilst he behaved with the most profound civility to Mrs Helmsby, and acceded to all her propositions, he registered a mental vow that there should be as little intercourse as possible with his dear mother-in-law when he was once fairly married!

He used all his influence to bring matters to a conclusion as speedily as possible; and, at length, that grand marriage preliminary, 'making the wedding clothes', was put in hand.

Mrs Helmsby had determined in her heart that her daughter should have the most splendid outfit that any bride on record had carried out of the town, and as many sempstresses and mantuamakers were set to work as would have sufficed to fit out all the heroes of the 'Niebelungen Lied'.* She who had objected to letting Alice take drawing lessons on the score of extravagance, cheerfully spent thirty guineas on a Brussels lace veil, and felt no economical pang when she ordered a sumptuous skyblue velvet dress, saying, 'It would be so serviceable.'

We are not going to give a list of Alice's 'wedding clothes'; there is no precedent for it except in the case of Harriet Byron, who married Sir Charles Grandison;* but we beg our readers to believe that it was a superb trousseau. All being prepared, the last flounce finished, and the last seal affixed to the settlements, the wedding itself was allowed to take place. Alice looked very lovely in her veil and wreath of orange-flowers; the wedding breakfast comprised 'all the delicacies of the season'; and Alice and Bryant set off for a short tour through France and Switzerland.

Mrs Helmsby was very much affected at parting with her daughter; but the necessity there was to clear away in safety all the additional glass and china, and to count up the silver spoons, proved a salutary distraction to her mind; whilst the proud anticipation of seeing Alice 'sit for her company', prevented the present moment feeling gloomy.

In London a slight disappointment awaited Alice to temper the almost excessive flow of her happiness. Bryant found there letters awaiting him, the contents of which rendered his presence at home necessary, and put a stop to their projected tour; but he promised Alice that if he could snatch time in the spring she should still see Mont Blanc.

Alice, in the meanwhile, was very well contented, after a few days in London, to accompany her husband to the mining districts of Wales, whither his business called him, and to have a brief sojourn amid the minor grandeurs of Snowdon.

Bryant had an only sister, who, for some years, had kept house for him, until she married a wealthy man, with the finest house, the most extensive grounds, and the largest hot-houses and conservatories in the county. This sister had not been able to grace the marriage breakfast, as she was out of England at the time, but she had now returned, and a letter, which, after travelling for some days after Bryant, at length reached him, expressed her earnest desire that he and Alice should pay her a visit, as soon as they could arrange it. Bryant earnestly desired that his sister and Alice should like each other; and, as there was yet a fortnight before their 'at home' fell due, he thought they might as well spend it at his sister's house, which being only seven miles on the other side of his Works, would allow him to come to and fro without difficulty. Alice was rather dismayed at the prospect of encountering this sister, of whose elegance and importance she had heard so much; but Bryant wished it, and it never occurred to her to object. Accordingly, Bryant wrote, accepting the invitation, and fixing the day for their arrival at Matching Park.

Mrs Lauriston, Bryant's sister, was a woman of about six-and-thirty. Her figure had precisely that carriage and *embonpoint** which people think essential to the reputation of being 'a fine woman'. She dressed always remarkably well, and might be called handsome, although her features were not regular; her manners had a glossy suavity, which, at a little distance, looked very like kind-heartedness, whilst her voice had a tone of good-humoured cajolery, which was rather pleasant than otherwise. She was, moreover, very well bred, and could have edited a manual on the abstruse points of etiquette.

She met her brother and Alice on their arrival at the head of the staircase. A glance at the graceful drooping figure of the latter, as she clung to her husband's arm, satisfied her, and she embraced her with a sufficient effusion of sensibility.

'My dear new sister, welcome to this house!—My dear John,'* continued she, giving a hand to her brother, though without abandoning Alice, 'how happy you have made me! How I rejoice to see you both under this roof!'

'God bless you; my dear Margaret,' said he, in a faltering voice. 'May you and Alice ever be sisters!'

'That is my dearest wish,' replied she, as she glided into her superb drawing-room.

Alice was bewildered with her emotions; she could not look round her; still she thought her sister-in-law very beautiful, and felt sure she should love her extremely.

Mrs Lauriston narrowly scrutinised every movement of Alice, though she affected not to notice her shyness.

'Well, my dear, and what do you feel the most disposed to do?' said she, in a tone of friendly vivacity, 'will you rest a little here, and take a little refreshment, or will you at once proceed to your dressing-room? We dine at seven; there will only be ourselves; I thought we should be happier alone; we have all our friendship to make; though I do not expect to find much *ice* to break,' concluded she, taking the hand of Alice with a smile, which displayed a row of the smallest and whitest teeth in the world.

Alice preferred going at once to her room.

'Well, then, my dear Bryant, you must excuse us awhile,' said his sister, drawing the hand of Alice through her arm as she led her away.

Alice was conducted to the bed-room she was to occupy; it was sumptuously furnished with everything that could be needed or dreamed of for use or luxury. It opened into a small boudoir dressing-room, fitted up *en suite*, and abounding in fanciful chairs, tables, and *chefs-d'œuvre** of the art of upholstery: it commanded a lovely view of the park, and there was an opening, through which some hills were seen in the distance, which relieved the level richness of the ground near the house; a stand of choice plants, and a book-case full of elegant-looking volumes, completed Alice's delight.

'What charming rooms!' she exclaimed. 'I never saw any so pretty, it is like reading a novel to come into them!'

'I am delighted, if you are pleased, my dear Alice; I hope you will find everything you need; I wish you to consider yourself at home.'

This was a very kind speech and pronounced in a very sweet voice; but Mrs Lauriston had an absent look in her clear grey eyes, which were wandering over the flower-stand, and Alice felt the warm impulse to express her thanks suddenly checked—she hardly knew how.

'I will ring for your maid, my dear,' continued she; 'but do not make a state toilet, we shall be alone—and besides you are so pretty, that dress will be wasted. You will find me in the drawing-room; I will go now and keep poor Bryant company until you return to us.'

Before her maid arrived, Alice amused herself with inspecting her apartments more nearly; she seemed to breathe more freely in the atmosphere of refinement that surrounded her; her love of beauty eagerly caught at all that was in affinity with it. The exquisite taste which presided in the arrangement of the rooms, had subdued the richness of the decorations; the sense of their expensiveness was lost, and no thought of the upholsterer's bill was suggested by them.

Alice's mother had always been in the habit of spending a handsome income,—the chintzes, damasks, and furniture, were all the richest that could be got for money; still they conveyed no more meaning than when they were in their native warehouse— a dull, uninteresting *mediocre* look pervaded the whole house; the result was very inadequate to the money expended upon it. Here, on the contrary, a gay *fête*-like aspect glowed everywhere, combined with an air of elegant comfort, which made Alice fancy she had fallen upon the sort of home she had yearned after.

In the midst of all this, her maid appeared, and the business of dressing commenced.

'Well, Simmonds,' said Alice, 'and what do you think of this place? Have they made you comfortable down stairs?'

'Oh, yes, ma'am, thank you. I am very happy indeed; this is just the pleasantest and beautifullest place I was ever at in all my life, everything is so cheerful and pleasant—it is quite a comfort to be amongst it; my room is fit for a duchess, and the servants seem all very agreeable; and I am sure Mrs Lauriston is every inch a lady, and so pleasant spoken! I met her as she was going to the drawing-room, she smiled, and hoped I would do all I could to make you feel comfortable and at home. I am sure I hope our house will be half as nice.'

Alice listened to this tattle, and fell into a reverie wondering what her own home would be like. A sense of her own importance dawned on her for the first time, as she thought that she, too, was going to be the mistress of a handsome establishment, and would have as much money as she chose, to do whatever she pleased with it.

When Alice re-entered the drawing-room, it wanted but a quarter of an hour to dinner-time. Mrs Lauriston was dressed, and looked, as Alice thought, like a duchess, in her rich black satin and Brussels lace.

'Come and sit here, my sweet Alice,' cried she; 'how lovely you have made yourself! really I think Bryant may feel very proud of his wife, at least *I* do of such a sister! We must be great friends, Alice. I shall not feel satisfied unless you love me very much.'

Again the sweetness of this honey speech was marred by the expression of the speaker's eyes, which were critically inspecting the make of Alice's dress. Alice timidly pressed her white dimpled hand, and thanked her for her kindness. The French clock struck seven, and Mr Lauriston entered as it ceased. He was a grave, reserved-looking man, with a bald head, and a lean stooping figure; he wore a gold double eye-glass round his neck, and was dressed in a full suit of black; a white and beautifully plaited cambric frill peeped under his waistcoat, and joined his equally white cravat.

'My dear Mr Lauriston, let me make you acquainted with our new sister-in-law,' said his wife, presenting Alice as she spoke. 'You know how often I have sighed for a sister, and now you see Heaven has heard my prayer.—Alice, my love, this is Mr Lauriston, my husband, and your brother.'

Mr Lauriston made a low bow, shook hands with Alice—said he was very glad to see her, and proud of such an acquisition to their family—congratulated Bryant, who entered at that moment, on his wonderful good fortune in securing such a wife— and then, with the air of a man who has acquitted himself towards his creditors, he inquired from his wife whether the dinner were not behind-hand. The sound of the gong luckily obviated a reply, and, presenting his arm to Alice, he led her to the dining-room.

The dinner-table and the dinner were in equally good taste with all that Alice had yet seen. She was interested in watching the arrangements, and taking a lesson from all she saw, against the time when she would have to preside over her own table. This occupied her attention, and prevented her feeling the element of heavy silence which Mr Lauriston had introduced. He paid her all the requisite courtesies of the dinner-table; but he had the air of being always on his guard, and there was a weight of reserve and caution in every line of his face, which made his taciturnity quite portentous. It was impossible to utter a sentence under this influence, of which you could not feel certain whether it were dulness or wisdom; and it caused a mysterious sense of oppression in those subjected to it—an uneasy speculation as to what his thoughts were like—a point on which he was never known to enlighten any one. Even the bland *empressement** of his lady fell dulled and stagnant, like a stone into the Dead Sea, without causing a ripple.

It was the custom at Matching Park to retire to rest early. They had a short sojourn in the drawing-room after coffee; and then the wine and water and bed-candles made their appearance. Mrs Lauriston accompanied Alice to her room, told her she was sure she was a prodigious favourite with her husband, and that she must not mind his being so silent, as it was constitutional; and after hoping that the next day would be fine, and that Alice would find her room comfortable, she embraced her once more and glided out of the room.

CHAPTER XIV

THE next day Alice was duly taken over all that was to be seen in the house and grounds. There is always a freemasonry amongst women about the mysteries of housekeeping and servants, and in recounting their several experiences. Alice naturally enough had none to impart, but she was a reverent listener to the household wisdom that fell from Mrs Lauriston's lips; and her naïvely expressed admiration for all she saw gratified that lady extremely, who was well pleased to find that her pretty sister-in-law was not stiffened into notions of her own dignity, and evidently never dreamed of setting up any rivalry with Matching Park. With all her suavity Mrs Lauriston had a pitiless insight into the short-comings of others; her bright grey eyes could penetrate, like those of a cat, into the darkest corners; and she was not without the velvet paws, armed with sharp claws, to drag all she saw into the light, whilst she tossed and patted and tormented her victims with an air of such irresistible graciousness, that even they were in doubt whether she really meant to be disagreeable. But some-how it always happened that whenever any one, seduced by the tempting softness of her manner, reposed any of their distresses in her gentle bosom, they invariably repented of having done so before the day was done—not that she made any particularly mischievous use of confidences, but there was an unfathomable reserve underneath her friendliness, and her eyes looked absently into space with a sweet smile at the very crisis of the communica-tion. With all her *empressement* of manner, she had not a grain of enthusiasm; she was covered all over with a sort of moral glass-case, which kept her precious emotions fresh to the eye, whilst it protected them from all contact with trying realities.

'I really feel quite nervous as to how I shall get on with my house-keeping,' said Alice, when they were seated at their work-table, 'and the idea of sitting for company has something terrible in it. I do not like to see people I do not care about.'

'If they are good acquaintances you need think of nothing further, very little liking will answer every purpose,' replied Mrs Lauriston; 'but you are such a dear, sweet, enthusiastic creature, that you will quite wear yourself out if you insist on liking all the people you know.'

'Ah! but I know the annoyance of living always amongst people who do not care for any of the things I do. I feel so happy now that I have some one to look up to and trust in, and to whom I may come for counsel whenever I am in doubt. Bryant will guide me in all I ought to do. Do you know that feeling of always wishing to do right, and yet somehow feeling that you are always doing wrong?'

'How enthusiastic you are!' replied Mrs Lauriston, with a vague smile.

'It is so delightful to belong to one who is wiser than oneself,' said Alice, 'one has such a sense of safety.'

'My sweet Alice! you are talking like a girl in love! You will never manage your husband if you let him think he is wiser than you are! You will make yourself a slave directly; and if once you put such a notion of your submissiveness into his head, you will never be able to eradicate it. Husbands are always quite ready enough to believe themselves wise.'

'But,' replied Alice, 'surely one's husband is always one's best friend?'

'My dear Alice!' cried Mrs Lauriston, with vivacity, 'a man can *never* in *any* relation be *really* the friend of a woman, and there is no good in trying to make a friend out of any of them; the best of them will take advantage of whatever you say or do. A woman must *never* trust a man: she may *seem* to do so as much as she likes, but woe to her! the instant she really lets him see or know any thing about her, except just as it *suits* her that it should be seen and known. Luckily, men always believe just what a woman tells them; they have no sense to see any thing for themselves, and they understand nothing but what is made visible to them.'

'But,' said Alice, 'surely to one's husband one may think aloud; of course a married woman would never dream of making a friend of any other man.'

'Well, my dear, try it, and see the sort of life you will lead for your pains. My dear Alice, you have married my brother, and what I am saying is quite as much with a view to his happiness as to your own. I have been married a long time, and I give you this piece of experience, never tell your husband, in an impulse of confidence any thing which there is a chance he may not admire; if at the moment he happens to be in a good temper, he may seem to stand it pretty well, but depend upon it he will recollect it against you on the first *accès*★ of ill-humour. Of course, I do not mean that you are to deceive your husband; I only mean to tell you, that as men only see things in the light they are put to them, you must be very careful always to present your facts on the *right* side. How should I live with Mr Lauriston, who is reserved, suspicious, and *miserly*, to the last degree, unless I used great judgment with him? My brother is a different sort of man altogether; but if you pour out to him any of your romantic notions about love and friendship, it will make him think you childish, and he will never feel any respect for your judgment.'

'But all this sounds very painfully,' cried Alice; 'am I to have no friend?'

'A woman ought never to make intimate friendships out of her own family,' replied Mrs Lauriston; 'there are always family secrets which ooze out to one's "dear friend"; they are confided in affection, and recollected in revenge, because, sooner or later, the best friends always quarrel; it is very silly to make confidences, for our "intimate friends" always have it in their power to say the bitterest things against us. If you are afflicted with an *épanchement du cœur*,★ it is not safe to indulge it, except to a mother, or a sister. I am talking frankly to you, because I can read your character; you will not make a bad use of it; and besides, I am endeavouring to save you, as I would endeavour to catch hold of a person whom I saw about to walk into a pond—if I could do it without risk to myself.'

'I almost wish you had allowed me to fall into the "pond" in peace,' said Alice, 'you have made me feel as if I had eaten of the "tree of knowledge" and committed sin.'

'Bah! my dear, you are a child. Men made their own laws; it is not our fault that they are suspicious, ungenerous, and selfish; if they choose to be such, we are obliged to take them as we find them, and make the best of them. But come, let us have a drive in the park, and do not allow your sweet face to look so perplexed; when you have lived in the world a little longer, you will find realities, "things as they are" to be, of more importance than dreams of love and friendship. By the way, talking of love, what dress do you intend to wear, when you receive your company? If you have it here, I should like to see it. *Mais allons.*'★

The painful impression produced by the foregoing conversation long depressed the spirits of Alice, and produced a sense of *guiltiness*, as if she had become partaker in some vague undefined evil. The purity of her soul had been desecrated. She detested all she had heard; but she could not regain the happy, trusting unconsciousness, with which she had arisen in the morning. During their drive she was silent, and the admiration she expressed for the really lovely country was cold and flat. She was ill at ease with herself, and Mrs Lauriston half repented the candour which had rendered her so uninteresting.

When Bryant returned, the first impulse of Alice was to tell him all that had passed between Mrs Lauriston and herself, but she checked it instantly; she had no right to exhibit his sister in a disadvantageous light. She rejoiced in her reticence, when Bryant, breaking the silence her deliberation had caused, said:

'My dear Alice, I am delighted to see that you and my sister get on so well together. She is a most superior woman, and has an excellent judgment; there is no one to whose opinion I would sooner listen upon all matters within her reach. She has had a good deal of experience in society, and I think that, until you become accustomed to your new position, you had better go to her in any perplexity which may arise; in all matters of housekeeping, and household arrangements, I never saw her equal; in the midst of apparent profusion she is not without an elegant thrift.'

His speech caused Alice a strange annoyance, which she could not have explained to herself, much less to her husband. After a pause, she replied—

'I hope I shall always do what pleases you in all things; but do you not think Mrs Lauriston is rather worldly in some of her notions?'

'What do you mean by worldly, my Alice? My sister Lauriston knows the value of outward things, and the goods of fortune; she puts a just appreciation upon appearances; she is not romantic, certainly, which is fortunate for her own happiness, but she has an excellent heart; and you must agree with me, that a woman like Alice Bryant would have been wasted on a man like Mr Lauriston?'

Alice smiled, and was comforted by this compliment.

Bryant continued. 'Her husband is not the man I would have chosen for her; it was a disappointment to me when she married him; but she was always ambitious, and marrying for love would not have satisfied her. I do not think she sees his defects so clearly as others do; any way, she fills her station with great propriety, and seems perfectly contented with it.'

At this juncture the dressing bell rang, and there was no time for further conversation.

Alice was left to reconcile this new knowledge to her soul as well as she could. They remained a little more than a fortnight at the Park, in which time Alice had not succeeded in being able to love her sister-in-law. The elegance and refinement which at first had struck her so forcibly, came in the end to seem as circumscribed in their significance as her old environments at her mother's house.

An atmosphere of *self* pervaded all the details of Mrs Lauriston's life, making all things vulgar. Alice even began to sigh for her old familiar homeliness amid the cold elegance of Matching Park. She was uneasy at finding nothing in sympathy with the hidden world of her own heart, to meet no sort of recognition of those sentiments and aspirations which haunted her like gleams of a former existence. She felt chilled to the soul, in the midst of all that wealth and unbounded indulgence could procure of external enjoyment. She rejoiced in the prospect of going to her own home, where, at least, she hoped to be able to break through this circle of ice, and live with Bryant according to the dream of her own heart. At length the day of their departure came. It had been arranged that Mrs Lauriston should return with them, to give Alice the support of her presence, through the trying ordeal of 'sitting for company'; and also, to afford her judgment and advice on the arrangement of her visiting list, she being well acquainted with the various claims to consideration possessed by all the families in the neighbourhood.

Alice was, on the whole, rather glad of this. Nervously afraid of doing wrong, with confidence in every one's judgment rather than her own, she felt thankful to Mrs Lauriston for undertaking the responsibilities of her social *début*.

The bridal party made their first appearance at church, to the great satisfaction of the whole congregation, who had been

anxiously expecting their advent. The elegance and beauty of the
bride, her superb Brussels veil, and the stylish dignity of Mrs
Lauriston, earned unqualified approbation. Some who were disposed to raise objections observed, that Mr Bryant was older than
they deemed advisable for the husband of so young a creature;
but that was not a point which could be rectified, so they
considerately added the saving clause, that there was no accounting for tastes, and that elderly men generally made indulgent
husbands. On the whole, the gossip that went on concerning
them that day was marked by strong approbation.

Then followed that mysterious purgatory which is *de rigueur* in
all civilised English marriages, 'sitting for company'. All went off
extremely well; crowds of well-dressed people came in their
carriages to the bridal levée, to look at Alice, to look at the house,
to drink chocolate, to depart and criticise.

'Well!' said Alice, at the close of the second day, 'white kid
gloves and bride cake will seem to me like a bad dream realised,
from henceforth. Oh, my dear Bryant, why can they not let
people marry in peace, and be happy, without chaining it to such
a leaden weight of obligation! What shall we do this evening to
celebrate the conclusion of our toils?'

'The most advisable step would be, to eat our dinner in the first
place,' said Bryant, 'and then I fear I must leave you for an hour.
I have some business that is indispensable.'

'Well, at least, I will never look bride-cake in the face again,'
said Alice; 'and recollect, this business is only to take you away
for an hour—not one moment longer!'

'Is she not a sweet natural creature, Margaret?' said Bryant,
looking after his wife as she left the room.

'Indeed she is,' replied his sister; 'I quite adore her for her
freshness; but she is not yet alive to all the advantages of her
position in the world as your wife.'

CHAPTER XV

CONRAD PERCY, and a college friend of his, were lounging down the principal street of M——, on a dusty, sultry afternoon in June.

'My dear Conrad!' cried his friend, 'must we actually remain in this cursed place till to-morrow? We don't know a soul, and are poisoned with the smoke. I vow I have not seen one decent man or woman since we arrived; every body is walking as if on life and death—there is nothing to look at, and we have nothing to do. I cannot make out what you are stopping for;—why cannot we go on to the Lakes to-night?'

'My good fellow,' replied Conrad, 'don't be so disconsolate—it makes me quite melancholy to hear you. I have told you at least a dozen times, that we must stay till to-morrow, because we got in after the bank was closed (it is one of their confounded holidays), and neither you nor I have money enough in our purse to pay our coach fare;—does that satisfy you?'

'Somebody could surely be found who would cash your cheque.'

'My dear fellow, these people of business would only see two plausible swindlers in dashing fellows like you and me. I don't know a soul in the town, and can give no reference—so just be peaceable, and don't grumble: it is of no *use* to rebel against destiny.'

'Well,' said the other, after a pause, 'as people *do* live here, there must be something to live upon—I do not mean bread and cheese, but some sort of amusement—something to keep the soul from stagnating, or drying to brick-dust. Bah! do let us get out of this smoke; see! if we cross over the road it will pass over our heads—it is dreadful!'

'We certainly do not breathe

'An ampler ether, a diviner air,'★

said Conrad; 'but this smoke does something, streaming from that tall chimney. What do you say to seeing a factory?—it will help to pass the time.'

'Well,' replied the other, 'be it so; but if the outside be so villanous, what will the interior be?'

They proceeded a few steps with this intention, when they were overtaken by a procession of equestrians from the circus, exercising their horses, and showing themselves. The band, in gaudy liveries, and sitting in a sort of open omnibus, were playing to the great delectation of a crowd of women and children, who came running out of every street. The two friends turned to gaze also, glad of any event to break their *ennui*. The *cortège* was brought up by a radiant-looking phaeton, and Conrad was startled by receiving an elaborate bow from the very magnificently-attired individual sitting in it, and who, at the same moment, ordered the whole procession, in a voice of thunder, to 'halt!'

'By Heaven, Conrad!' said his friend, 'you have found an acquaintance at last. Who is it?'

'The devil knows,' replied Conrad, in an annoyed tone; 'let us move on.'

'Oh, no!' said the other, 'politeness for ever! We must not turn our backs on this Magnus Apollo,* who has stopped his course and descended from his chariot to seek us.'

Mr Simpson, for it was none other, had by this time reached the two friends.

'My very dear sir,' said he, offering to Conrad his dirty but dazzling hand, all covered with Birmingham rings, 'permit me to rejoice in this unexpected meeting. I knew you instantly. I never forget a face I have once seen, and yours is not one to be forgotten, even without the interesting occasion of our first meeting. Your *protégée* has done you credit—she has real genius. She is not with the troop to-day; but you will honour us in front to-night. All the officers patronise us with their presence to-night; you are come at a fortunate time. Your *protégée* will be enchanted. She has often asked whether we should go to where you live. She is a wonderful girl.'

In the course of this voluble discourse Conrad had recollected without difficulty the hero of the 'sanded parlour'.

'Ah!' said he, with as good a grace as he could assume, though sorely annoyed at the publicity of the thing, 'I hope the little Italian is well. Is she still a dumb girl, or have you taught her to speak English? Is her mother alive still?'

'My dear sir, she is a genius. Most astonishing talent, and has kept herself perfectly respectable. I told you I would keep my eye upon her, and I have done so. But you will come and see us to-night. If you will tell me your hotel, I will have the honour of sending you half a dozen tickets, and will keep places in the reserve box.'

A crowd had gathered by this time, to see what was going on, and to hear how circus people talked.

'Yes, yes,' said Conrad, impatiently, and moving away, 'I will not fail to come. But you need not take the trouble to send.'

Conrad's friend, who wanted to plague him, said, quite loud enough to be heard, 'Thank you, Mr Simpson, send them to the Royal Hotel.'

'You may rely upon me, my dear sir,' cried Mr Simpson, as he sprang upon his lofty seat, and gave the word to proceed, just as a policeman was crossing the road, and bid them 'move on.'

'Well, Conrad, and who is this Italian miracle? Faith, this delay has been more lucky than one could have hoped. I am dying to see what she is like.'

'She was a young Italian girl,' said Conrad, annoyed at his companion's tone, 'whom I met with at an inn in the North, twelve months ago. She was in great trouble. Her mother, who was mad, had fallen ill; and somebody they had come to England to seek, turned out to be dead; so you may fancy she was badly off. I helped the poor thing with a trifle of money, and made a bargain for her with this man, who also happened to be there. It was one way of gaining a living. She was little more than a child then—not fifteen; I wonder what she is like now. She was very interesting and modest-looking then; but she will have lost all that, I suppose.'

'We will go and see,' replied his companion. 'Now let us go back to dinner, I am hungry; and now we have an object to look forward to, I don't feel half so bored as I did. How very little one wants in this world, and we do not get it!'

When Bianca learned the *rencontre** of the morning, she was, as we all are when we unexpectedly come upon our dearest wish, not half so glad as she expected; it threw her into a tumult of feelings she could neither express, nor understand, amounting almost to physical pain. At last, the true woman's instinct made itself felt; a woman's first impulse is always to dress for her lover, and out of the chaos of new sensations that bewildered her, one made itself speedily articulate, a determination to get a new dress out of the manager. There was not much time to manufacture it, but she was clever at inventing costumes, and very quick in a rough effective manner of realising them.

Mr Simpson was in a capital humour, and very desirous that his *protégée* should appear to advantage, so she found him in an unusually liberal mood, and obtained without difficulty an un-limited supply of white spotted muslins, silver tinsel, with some sky-blue ribbon, and a new pair of Greek sandals of a similar colour. Out of these materials, she achieved a costume that surprised even herself; she did not know what it was that had inspired her with a refinement and delicacy she had not dreamed of before; all that had hitherto contented her, now seemed mean and coarse, when brought into actual contact with one moving in such a different sphere. She felt for the first time to measure the distance between them, and her dress was contrived to meet what she fancied would be his taste; she looked forward with a sort of pleased dread, to showing him what she could do, and determined to excel herself.

Dressed in her fresh pure-looking costume, her magnificent black hair arranged so as to exhibit all its beauty, her cheeks too flushed with anxiety to stand in need of rouge, she made her entrance on the scene. Her eyes soon found out Conard and his friend, when all her powers seemed suddenly to forsake her; she felt dreadfully frightened, and her impulse was to rush off the stage; though that was not possible, and, in a few moments, the effect of habit resumed its sway, yet she did not recover so far as to act so well as usual; she was constrained and embarrassed, and had not the *abandon* and earnestness which was her great charm; all she was saying and doing suddenly seemed to become so foolish and stupid, now that she fancied *him* listening to it. Mr Simpson was provoked, but as saying so would have made her worse, he prudently held his tongue.

The occasion which Bianca had so long looked forward to was now come; but instead of the delight and happiness she expected, she felt more wretched and depressed than she had ever done in her life, and would gladly have sat down and cried.

After the first piece on the stage, came the scenes in the circle, in which she had a good deal of pantomime to do. Relieved from the insipid mawkish stuff she had been obliged to utter, her spirits began to rise, and she did herself more justice. Conrad and his friend were both startled by the power she showed. It was the sight of Conrad's face that restored her energy; she heard *his* applause as she passed round, and was up to the mark instantly.

'Upon my honour that girl has real talent,' said Conrad; 'she will do something one of these days if she goes on.'

He flung a moss-rose to her, as she passed beneath where he sat; she made an effort, and recovered it, before it fell to the ground. The audience fancied it a *tour de force*, and applauded mightily, and other flowers were dropped by aspiring youths; but Bianca had already disappeared behind the pink satin curtain.

'A glorious girl, in faith,' said Conrad's companion; 'let us go behind and speak to her.'

It was a scene even more motley by night than by day. But Bianca was not there, she had left the circus immediately on quitting the ring. Mr Simpson, however, in a dress something between that of a footman and a field-marshal, came up to them, expressing regrets, and hopes, and fears, enough to have furnished a whole generation of the human race in times of ordinary vicissitudes; winding up with—

'Well, my dear sir, and what is your opinion of our *protégée*? She was not in force to-night in the earlier part—she seemed frightened—the first time I ever knew her so. I think the idea of appearing before you embarrassed her. But she pulled up towards the last, I thought.'

Conrad and his friend paid all the expected compliments, not only to Bianca, but to the whole establishment.

'Yes, sir,' replied Mr Simpson, with complacent gravity, 'every man has some model he proposes to himself—Buonaparte is mine. I never accept excuses. I never allow my people to fail: and by expecting nothing less than perfection, I secure excellence, at least. He was a wonderful man, sir, Buonaparte! I am generally supposed to resemble him in person, as it is my ambition to do in mind.'

'It is equally striking in both,' said Conrad, with perfect gravity; 'but I should like to see Ma'mselle Bianca. Do you know where she lives? and at what time I should be most likely to find her to-morrow?'

The manager felt an undefined fear, that an interview between Conrad and his *protégée* would end either in his losing her services altogether, or in being obliged to pay a higher rate for them; so he tried to evade the question. But Conrad persisted, and at last got the requisite information, with which he took his leave.

The next morning Conrad repaired early to the address he had received,—he went alone, as he did not choose his travelling companion to go with him.

As Bianca's salary had not been raised beyond the original twelve shillings a week, the lodging she and her mother now occupied was in no respect superior to the one we formerly described; in fact, poverty had made inroads even on the few comforts they then possessed. It is no easy matter to keep two persons in food, clothes, and lodging, on twelve shillings a week; her few trinkets had gradually been disposed of, to supply accidental deficiencies as they arose,—and her salary had been anticipated for several weeks. Poor Bianca was suffering under that most wearing of all human ills—anxiety about money; that worst fruit of the tree of knowledge—the utmost value of a shilling! It was about nine o'clock when Conrad went to visit her, and she was preparing breakfast. A cup of chocolate for her mother; a little milk and water, with a slice of bread, for herself. Their small apartment was already swept and straightened for the day. Her mother, wrapt in a large shawl, sat in a rocking-chair beside the fire, still retaining traces of the beauty she had formerly possessed. Bianca was much grown since Conrad had last seen her; but he was shocked to perceive, by daylight, that she looked gaunt and thin, as if she had not sufficient food. She was dressed in a pink gingham gown, high in the throat; and a black apron, pinned to a point in front, showed her round slender waist.

She started so violently when Conrad, having knocked, entered, that she upset the whole of her breakfast; the blood rushed to her heart, which felt as if it would never beat again; and this girl, inured to appearing nightly before hundreds of spectators, stood with trembling limbs and downcast eyes before Conrad, unable to speak, unable to move a step.

'I could not leave the town, without informing myself of your welfare, mademoiselle,' said Conrad, with a respect which surprised himself, 'and I hope I have not come at an unseasonable hour. I am obliged to continue my journey in an hour, which must be my excuse.'

All which Bianca had thought, felt, pictured to herself that she would say, when the opportunity of seeing Conrad should come, faded from her memory now; she could only stammer an invitation to be seated; the one glance, as she lifted her eyes to his face, and suddenly withdrew them, perhaps supplied Conrad with the true meaning of her abrupt and broken words, for he sat down quietly, and gave her time to recover herself. He addressed her mother (who looked uneasily at him) in Italian, and told her he had the honour to be an old acquaintance of her daughter's. She at first brightened a little at the sound of her native tongue, but her attention soon wandered, and she began again to rock herself. Bianca now found her voice, and expressed all the gratitude she felt for the services he had rendered her.

'I have long desired,' said she, quietly, 'for the opportunity of telling you this, and now that it has occurred; you see how awkward I am at expressing it; but there is not a day in which I have forgotten you.'

Conrad could not reply by any common compliment; he felt too strongly interested in his *protégée*.

'Tell me how I can serve you further,' said he; 'by this time you must obtain a good salary, as you seem the principal actress and equestrian.'

Bianca told him frankly how she was situated with the manager; that she had received more advantageous offers from other quarters, but that being in debt to Mr Simpson she could not get free.

Conrad was extremely indignant. Every moment he felt a stronger interest in the young girl so strangely thrown on his humanity. He told her how much he had been pleased with her acting, and asked if she had no desire to take a higher walk in her profession.

It is the peculiarity of strong characters to know their own wishes. Bianca's embarrassment left her, as she candidly and frankly spoke to her friend of her position. She relied on him instinctively.

'I feel,' said she, 'capable of doing better things. I love the profession, but I would like to have better things to say, not be condemned to utter the trash of last night; but I have no books, no means of getting instruction; I desire beyond all things to enter a regular theatre, no matter in how humble a capacity. I would work upwards. I can speak English now, and I feel I could make my way.'

'I thank you,' said Conrad, 'for speaking to me as a friend, for thinking of me as one; I will try to merit your confidence. I am obliged to go on northward to-day, but I shall return this way in a month, when I will see you again. I will in the meanwhile write to a friend about you. I will not lose sight of you till something is settled. You shall hear from me soon. Clear off all your scores with Simpson, and give him notice, but make no fresh engagement till you have seen me.'

Conrad was about to give her a sufficient sum to allow her to work up her arrears of salary; but suddenly recollecting that he had not yet paid a visit to the bank, he was obliged to stop his speech in some confusion. He shortly after took his leave; but in less than an hour after his departure, Bianca received a parcel, containing a copy of Shakespeare in one large volume, and a note enclosing 5*l*. The note was as follows.

Dear Bianca,

I send you a trifle to free you from Simpson; the book you must study for my sake, and tell me about it when I return; till then think of me as your sincere friend

Conrad Percy.

CHAPTER XVI

THERE are moments in the experience of most people, which come unthought of, unlooked for, bringing a gush of deep joy that is like pain in its intensity—it is almost a *pang* of ecstacy. Such a moment was it to Bianca, when she opened Conrad's parcel and read the note it contained. What now to her was hunger or privation; she had received a talisman against all evil, that it should not come nigh her. The whole day passed in a feverish delight; and if, when with so little human prospect of meeting him, she had been devoted to the idea of Conrad, it may be judged whether she were not now confirmed in her allegiance to it for life and death! She expected no return, she thought of none, her own sentiment was so engrossing, so all-absorbing, that it left no room for considering whether Conrad returned her love or not. With the deep humility of a true passion, she did not venture to aspire to being beloved as she herself loved. He was a bright particular star,* so far above her. She only desired to be allowed to worship him without repulse.

At the end of the week she signified to Mr Simpson that she intended to quit his company. The worthy copier of Buonaparte was put into a royally Buonapartean rage, and found some difficulty in expressing himself adequately to his ideas of his character, and the occasion. At first he turned a glance he intended for annihilation, upon her; and then folding his arms, he desired her, with a sarcastic tone, to repeat what she had just been saying.

'I said,' replied Bianca, 'that Mr Percy has promised to get me an engagement at a regular theatre, and that I wish to leave your company so soon as I shall have worked out the money you have advanced to me.'

'So! it's all well, very well,' said Mr Simpson; 'you cannot suppose you are necessary to me in any way, because you are not, the least in the world. It is for yourself I speak: to be near me, to learn maxims of your art, to hear what I say on the profession, was a great advantage to a young beginner like you, and I did think you appreciated it. I had better hopes of you, Bianca; but

now to leave me in this shabby way for a regular theatre is what
I did not expect; but all are alike—it is interest, and not art, that
moves men; for the sake of a pitiful increase of salary, you can
leave me, when you might go down to posterity as my favourite
pupil!'

'But then posterity might say you half starved me, and took
advantage of my necessities to drive the hardest bargains; so it is
as well for your fame that I should go whilst there *is* life in me.
How much have you advanced me?'

After a few further expressions of majestic displeasure, Mr
Simpson descended to business. Mr Simpson was not a dishonest
man, at least he would not have allowed that he was; but he
piqued himself on being a sharp 'man of business' and driving a
'keen bargain'. Under the extenuating name of 'business', there
lies a debatable ground between honesty and roguery, amenable
to its own laws of morality, and understanding no other.

After much grumbling at the shabbiness of Mr Percy, in
stealing away one of his troop, Mr Simpson, with the sulky look
of a much-injured man, agreed to give Bianca a written release
for that day five weeks, which was just a fortnight longer than he
had any real claim to her services for the money he had advanced.

Bianca was too happy in her own mind to raise objections to
any thing. On her way home she invested a shilling of her small
capital in paper, pens, ink, and sealing-wax, and was far more
particular in the choice of them than if they had been articles of
dress. Her first care was to arrange their small room, to make it
look its best; then she dressed herself with as much *recherche*★ as
her means allowed, and that was not much; but it was a woman's
instinct to make herself look as well as possible, for the presence
of her lover, and she felt as if she were going to approach Conrad.
Her mother was knitting placidly in her arm-chair, beside the
fire. *Her past* was erased from her memory; and she had forgotten
all the burning passionate love of her youth, with all the evil it
had wrought her, and was utterly unconscious that her child was
even now, for the first time, setting her foot on that enchanted
ground, there to wander in wildernesses that have no way, and
without a hand to guide her! Though a complete wreck from
what she had been, Bianca's mother still retained traces of loveli-
ness—her figure was noble and commanding; but her imbecility

had given an expression of aged childhood to her faded face; her magnificent eyes had lost their speculation, and gazed around with a stupid vacillating look, seeming to take note of nothing. She was dressed in a black stuff gown, with a white handkerchief round her throat; her hair, which was quite grey, was confined under a muslin head-dress, which Bianca had great skill in fashioning.

Bianca sat at the table under the window, her face buried in her hands; all the burning emotions, with which her heart was full, were unable to furnish her with a form of expression; and she was, besides, in such an intoxication of feeling, that she was carried away in dreamy beatitude, and could make no adequate effort to rouse herself even to the task in hand. Every word Conrad had spoken, every look and tone recurred to her, and the thrill of emotion when he had touched her hand to say farewell, all came back again and again; her whole nature was unlocked, and all the imaginative passionateness of her age and nature, was loosened from the torpid unconsciousness of girlhood, like a torrent which had been frozen at its fountain by the blaze of the summer sun. There sat her mother, like a presence from the world of passion, to warn her against the perilous adventure towards which she was turning; but what availed it? What power had Bianca to profit by the monition? She had already come under the influence of the Enchanted Land, and must follow her fate. She had no longer the power to guide herself, if she had even retained the wish to return. At last she lifted her head, and dipping one of the pens in ink, began to write; but here a most mortifying difficulty presented itself; she had forgotten till now that she could hardly write a word, and all her exaltation of feeling was about to end in the pitiful production of a few cramped, straggling, and almost illegible lines. Under any circumstance the letter would have been difficult; now it was all but impossible. However, Bianca was not one to give up any thing so near her heart, and after spoiling four of her sheets of gilt-edged paper, she contrived by dint of printing the letters she found difficulty in writing, and looking out for the words she had to spell in her Shakespeare, at last to produce, if not a finished specimen of caligraphy, a reasonably legible and entirely original looking letter. It was very brief; she was surprised to find how little she really had to say; and when she had thanked him for his presents, and told him her arrangement with Mr Simpson, she found all the rest must of its nature remain unutterable for her; so, out of all patience with what had cost her so much pains and labour, and which bore no likeness to the glowing thoughts which filled her heart when she sat down to write, she folded her letter with tolerable neatness, and having directed and sealed it to the best of her ability, she put on her bonnet and took it to the post, and returned home full of anxiety, lest amongst the many hundred other letters, her precious venture should happen to be precisely the one overlooked, or lost, or mis-sent. Then she tormented herself as to whether she had addressed it rightly,— and finally, her memory, to comfort her, suggested all the rumours she had ever heard of mails being overturned, and post-bags lost or stolen. However, it duly arrived, and was placed on Conrad's breakfast-table the next morning. 'Upon my honour I did not think the girl could write so well; that is not at all a vulgar letter, is it?' said he, tossing it to his companion.

'Ah, from your young *protégée*! I say, Conrad, don't turn her head, poor little thing; and, if I might turn Mentor, I should say, don't play the fool yourself. These sort of adventures are the devil for seducing one into mischief one never intended.'

'No fear of that,' replied Conrad, gravely; 'and besides, my governor will have to recommend her—he has some theatrical connexion, and I shall turn the matter over to him. I must write to the old boy to-day, and it will be something to fill up my letter; he dearly loves what he calls the romance of real life.'

Conrad did write, and the result was, that before her engagement with Mr Simpson terminated, Bianca received another letter from Conrad, enclosing a few lines, recommending her to the notice of the manager of the Theatre Royal in a neighbouring town. But, alas! nothing of the same kind is twice perfect. Conrad's letter told her he could not return through M——, and that he did not know when he should see her again; but he gave his address, and told her to write freely to him whenever she needed anything. Bianca wept bitterly; she had been counting the days in the hope of his return, and she felt a chill disappointment at his speaking so calmly of the uncertainty of ever seeing her again. However, she wiped her eyes, and comforted herself with thinking of all the improvement she would have made when next they met.

She made a journey and carried her letter to the manager, and found him a cold, hard, dry man of business, without the least enthusiasm for the profession, but a keen judge of what was likely to take with an audience; a quick eye for the capabilities of his actors, but with no more feeling for them, no more sympathy either with their personal needs, or any aspirations they might happen to have for perfecting themselves in their art, than any of the stage properties or decorations might have had. If an actor showed available talent, and worked well, he retained him—so long as he was useful. He paid well where he was obliged, and screwed down every one who was not in a position to compel better terms. He had, moreover, the character of being very profligate in his conduct towards women; and several very bad stories were whispered about his heartless conduct towards young women who had belonged to his company. Such was the worthy master to whom Bianca was recommended.

She knocked at the door of his room with a trembling hand, and was bid to come in, by a tall, portly, rather good-looking man, who was swinging back in a chair, before which stood a table covered with green baize, and strewn with letters and papers. As Bianca advanced he looked at her with an air of deliberate insolent criticism, like a man who considered himself a connoisseur in female charms.

Bianca, without speaking, presented her letter.

'So!' said he, tossing it down after he had read it, 'you desire to enter a regular theatre, it seems. How long have you been with Mr Simpson, and what sort of business have you been accustomed to?'

Bianca replied in as few words as possible, for she felt excessively annoyed at the impertinent familiarity of his look and manner.

'Can you recite any thing to give me an idea of your talent? Can you repeat one of Calista's speeches,* for example?'

Bianca was obliged to confess she could not.

'Well, then, is there no passage in some of the plays you have acted?'

'They are such trash, at the best,' said Bianca, 'that any passage separated from the scene would sound sheer nonsense; but I think I could repeat some bits out of Shakespeare.'

'That will serve excellently well. Begin anywhere you like, for I have not much time to spare.'

Bianca, with some trepidation, and a feeling of shame, as if she were revealing her heart's secret, began to repeat the soliloquy of Helena, in 'All's Well That Ends Well.' It was the only passage she could think of at the moment, and the manager was impatient.

She repeated it with so much delicacy and tenderness that the manager was taken by surprise.

'Come,' said he, when she had finished, 'if you do as well as that always, you will be sure to get on; but you have a great deal to learn, and nearly all the women's places are filled up; but, as you come recommended by an old friend, I don't like to refuse you. I cannot flatter you that you are worth much at present; but, however, if you like to agree for eighteen shillings a week, to act in any thing you may be put to, why I will see if I can find something for you to do. But, remember, there is to be no picking and choosing, or grumbling; you are to act any thing you may be wanted for, and you must not expect to be put into leading parts at first.'

Bianca expressed her willingness to accede to this arrangement; and, after a few further remarks, the manager dismissed her, with an intimation that he would send her a part to study, and let her know when the piece was called for rehearsal.

Bianca had now obtained her wish; she was engaged at a regular theatre, but she did not feel so elated as she had anticipated; in her dreams she had overlooked all the wide desert of subordinate drudgery she would have to traverse; she had grown accustomed to being the first person in Mr Simpson's company, and she felt a discouraging chill, for a short time, at finding herself at the very bottom of the ladder, and feeling herself dwarfed, as it were, to nothingness, standing beside the immense task her ambition had prompted. But her spirit soon rallied; and she made a solemn resolution that no difficulty should present itself to which she would not oppose at least as much resolution and patience as should be necessary to combat it; that she would turn aside from no drudgery, take offence at no professional humiliation, but keep her eye steadily fixed on her own purpose; and that purpose was to rise to a leading rank in her profession.

When it came to the point, she was very sorry to leave Mr Simpson, who, in the main, was a reasonably worthy man, though he had so pitilessly screwed her down in the article of salary; still she might have been with many worse people. He was sorry to part with her, for he had a regard for her, quite independent of her usefulness to him.

'Well, good bye, Bianca,' said he, when she took leave of him. 'I wish you well; and if this theatre scheme does not answer, remember, you can come back to us. You are high-minded, like all young people; but if you get a fall, and wish to come back, you can.'

Bianca thanked him, and they parted on cordial terms.

CHAPTER XVII

'THE Prince of Darkness is a gentleman,' and therefore we do not believe he ever made the noted saying attributed to him, that 'It is better to reign in hell than serve in heaven.' No gentleman would have thought such a thing; only some poor, tenacious, low-bred individual, who feared to have the shine of his own little rushlight eclipsed, if he ventured into better lighted society, and therefore cultivated the dusk, *pour se faire valoir.*★ Satan has been slandered, he never adorned himself with such a piece of pinchbeck sublimity. Still we are free to confess, that it is trying to human vanity to emerge from a scene of small triumphs, from the village where one may have been Cæsar, to take a place in the awkward squad of raw recruits, and submit to be drilled, and caned, and disciplined, with hope of making oneself a regular soldier—of becoming, not a commander-in-chief, but only one in a regiment where there are a thousand as good as ourselves— and being able to believe, that, though we may not be distinguishable to the naked eye of indifference, still we have been made partakers of a better order of things. A person who can submit thus to efface himself, must have something really valuable in him, and the probability is he will come to shine on his own account some day; but that is the accident, not the element, of his aspirations. To become better, to become excellent, is what he seeks—the rest is as God pleases.

Bianca had the strength to be capable of this. She had long been the first person in Mr Simpson's company, and now she had to find herself less than insignificant. No one taking the smallest interest in her, all the good places filled up, she was reduced to being a brick in a wall—just preventing an unsightly gap, that any one else could have filled just as well. The first part sent to her was that of a pert chamber-maid in a little after-piece; it did not consist of more than two dozen lines, and for sense and meaning it fell far below any of her circus parts. However, she learned it, and determined to make the best of it.

But when she went to rehearsal, she found herself like a child in a strange school. Nobody condescended to take any notice of her. Some of the performers looked at her with supercilious contempt; the women whispered and tittered together, and laughed maliciously at her mistakes in the stage business. The man with whom she had her scene, swore at her for spoiling one of his points, by looking the wrong way at a curtain. None had the good nature to give her any available directions. Some of the men looked boldly and insolently at her, and in a manner that made Bianca strongly disposed to resent it on the instant. She felt degraded and insulted, and thought with regret of good Mr Simpson, and the rough good-will of her old companions; and she missed the beautiful horses dreadfully; none of the people about her seemed half such Christians! She went home miserable enough from this her first rehearsal in a regular theatre, and a Theatre Royal into the bargain. Men are naturally, and from instinct, in a state of mutual war with each other; go into what society one will, we shall find the ranks serried against us, unless we take with us influence to cause a place to open for us, or strength to force one for ourselves: for it is the latent power that lies within us, to obtain what we desire by force, if need be,—the being able to fight for ourselves,—which alone gets us any respect in the world. No mildness, nor amiability, nor goodness will stand us in any stead, unless the power to make ourselves *felt* and *feared* in an extremity, makes itself apparent through all the beautiful sky-blue haze of amiable qualities. Bianca had no place as yet; but she intended to make one.

At night, however, she met with a glorious compensation, which made all the annoyance of the morning as dust in the balance. The leading actor of the day, the head of the profession, was then fulfilling an engagement in the theatre; this happened to be one of his nights. The play was 'King Lear'. Bianca stationed herself at one of the sides. She had never seen real acting before. If she had felt a love for her profession when she had only a vague instinct of its capabilities, what wonder that she became passionate when she beheld it in one of its most superb manifestations! She stood like one entranced, leaning against one of the side scenes; she felt a new life awakened within her; but all feeling about herself, all thought of herself, was absorbed in the awe and reverence with which she regarded this revelation of the invisible powers of art. It was a glimpse of the supernatural; she was baffled in her attempt to comprehend it; her powers of body and mind gave way under the intense excitement; she sank on the ground and leaned her head against one of the scenes, half-drowned in a flood of passionate tears that welled up from the deepest depths of her soul—such as can be only called from their source by the Divine soul shining into our hearts, and giving us a glimpse of ineffable things that no man may utter. An ocean, cloven to its depths, seemed revealed for an instant before her eyes, and she sank like a weed upon the brink of what she dared not gaze on. Her tears brought her back to her mortality, and relieved her from the oppressed and overwrought state which, if it had continued, must have brought on serious illness. We are girt round with weakness, and this very weakness is the refuge and defence of humanity, as well as its limitation.

The actor, who had been the means of thus rousing her, had to pass in one scene close beside her, and he was startled at the expression of her countenance;—a priestess listening to an oracle would have had a similar look. He addressed her, but she could not reply. He had the soul of an artist, and could recognise the spirit that was stirring within her. He was obliged to leave her, to enter on the scene. But this man, who dedicated his whole life to the art, felt that, in the dumb admiration of this young, unformed girl, he had received the highest homage that had ever been paid him; and he felt, too, that to have had the privilege of kindling that young spirit, by revealing to her the first glimpse of excellence, was a transcendant reward for the life-long toil he had dedicated to his art.

After the curtain fell, he looked to see if she were still there; and going up to her, laid his hand on her shoulder, and said, gently:

'You, too, have greatness in your heart; let nothing discourage you in your course.'

Bianca did not attempt to reply, but she seized a corner of his dress, and raised it reverently to her lips, and withdrew.

'Who is that striking-looking girl?' he inquired of the man who had played Edgar, and who just then came by.

'I don't know; some body St Leger picked up in the circus, I heard; he has always an eye for good-looking subs. I never saw her before to-day, so I suppose she is a fresh importation.'

'He has shown his judgment,' said the other, coldly; 'she will make a noise in the world some of these days, or I am much mistaken.'

Whenever our feelings have been at all exalted for a little while, we are sure to be thrown down to earth again with a rude shock;—we have dreamed that we were flying, and we awake falling. Bianca had to dress for her part in the farce; the emotions of the last few hours had completely driven it from her memory, she was in a sort of waking sleep, and until she found herself before the curtain, she never discovered that she could not say one word!

'I have forgotten all!' said she, in a voice of dismay to the man who was acting the part of a fine gentleman's gentleman.

'Confound you, for a fool,' replied the man; 'you will spoil my point. You were to coquet me;—your first word is that it is a long time since you saw me.'

'Oh-h!' said Bianca, making a desperate effort, and a dim glimmering of her part came to her. In the circus she had often been obliged to improvise dialogues, of which the situations only had been indicated, and this stood her in good stead now; luckily, she recollected her companion's point, and gave him besides an opportunity of making another, so that his alarmed dignity was composed.

'You got out of that devilish well, let me tell you,' said he, when they came off; 'but I would not advise you to play any more of those tricks—they won't answer.'

The next night there was no great play, Bianca had not her attention distracted from her own business, and she found one place was more like another than she had imagined. But evening after evening, so long as his engagement lasted, she stood in her old place, drinking in every word, and look, and movement of the great actor, until her whole soul was filled and saturated with noble conceptions.

The last evening that he acted, after the curtain dropped, he went up to Bianca and said kindly—'My good young lady, I should much like to befriend you; you have that about you I like to see in young beginners, and you will be heard of some of these days if you persevere. But you have a great deal to do, and much to learn, and many bad habits to unlearn. It will take you at least five years before you have mastered the mechanical part of your art, and all your life long you will find work before you; but for at least five years you must drudge—you have strength and patience, and let no difficulties make you distrust your aspirations,—they are the voice of God, you must have faith in them. When you are fit to be removed, you shall find a friend in me. I am old enough to be your father, therefore let me give you one caution,—on *no* pretence entangle yourself with obligations to the manager; endure any hardships, but accept no benefits from him. Will you promise me this?'

'Indeed I will,' said Bianca, gratefully, 'and without asking *why* you say so.'

'There's a good girl,' said the actor; 'it will be some months before I am here again, and now let me see what progress you will have made.' He shook hands with her kindly and cordially, and Bianca went home feeling so strong and proud, that difficulties were things she could not believe in—she felt sure of achieving all things!

CHAPTER XVIII

WHEN Alice and Bryant had returned all their visits, and attended the requisite dinner-parties and evening-parties, the time at length arrived when they might sit down in peace in their own house, as Alice hoped, and lead the life she had so often sighed for, beside a being older, wiser, and better than herself, who would love her as much as her heart desired, and be her guide in all things.

The home of which Alice had now become mistress, was a large, handsome, old-fashioned, country house, situated in a fine park-like enclosure, about a mile and half from the nearest town, but not a trace of its smoke could be seen under the shade of the fine old trees, which were thickly planted around. The entrance to the house was up a wide carriage-drive, planted on each side with chestnut-trees. The house itself was picturesque-looking, of dark red brick with stone copings, presenting a long façade of gable ends, nearly covered by a luxuriant growth of ivy; it had once upon a time been moated, but that unwholesome piece of feudal state had long since been filled up and converted into flower-beds. Within, the house still retained its old-fashioned rambling aspect, long galleries, odd passages, and rooms stuck in all manner of bewildering places; but whilst the distinctive character of the house had been retained, all the innovations of modern comfort had been carefully and judiciously introduced under the auspices of Mrs Lauriston; the contrast between the close-fitting windows; the patent grates, and commodious furniture, with the wild rambling look of the building, was quaint and pleasant. Beautiful hot-houses and a conservatory, filled with choice plants, had been erected by Bryant to please his sister; and although the establishment was on a much more unpretending footing than Matching Park, still Raven Hall (as Bryant's place was called) had a remarkably pleasing and auspicious aspect.

To outward eyes Alice had not a care or a sorrow, and she herself fancied that she was going to be perfectly happy. Bryant was deeply attached to his young wife, but he was not a demonstrative man; his sister had never cared for any expressions of attachment, and therefore, he had not acquired the habit of using

them; but Alice had a gentle and loving nature; to her, kind
words from those she loved, were of far more value than kind
deeds, an idiosyncrasy common amongst women and children.

Bryant had weighty business concerns on his mind; the temporary interruption caused by his marriage, had induced an
accumulation of urgent affairs, which now occupied a more than
ordinary share of his time and attention, so that when they
subsided into the ordinary routine of domestic life, Alice was left
very much to herself; the daily guidance and sympathy, from
which she had anticipated so much comfort, by no means occurred to Bryant as either necessary or desirable: he had never
been used to any thing but the decided, unwavering, manners of
his sister, and would almost as soon have thought of regulating
the amount of her food, as of giving Alice any sort of counsel
about the employment of her time. He desired that she should be
happy, and enjoy herself, provided the latter did not imply that
he should be expected to visit a great deal, or to see people who
were not connected with his business; otherwise, she might do
what she liked, go where she liked, and spend as much money as
ever she pleased. But what Alice asked was sympathy and guidance; she did not care for indulgence.

One of her earliest fears in her married life, was lest she should
not acquit herself well in her housekeeping. She was haunted
with the dread that she should not make Bryant so comfortable
as his sister had done, and also, lest she should spend more money
than had sufficed during the dynasty of her sister-in-law.

'My dear Bryant,' said Alice, one morning, in a deprecating
tone, as Bryant, with his letters in hand, was preparing to depart,
'have you five minutes to look over my housekeeping-book for
the last month? I am afraid you will think I have spent a great
deal, but I could not manage better.'

'Why need I look at the book?' replied Bryant. 'I am very busy
this morning. Can you not add up a simple row of figures, and
tell me how much money you want?'

'But I should like to know whether you approve of what I have
done; and to be sure that you do not think me more extravagant
than your sister used to be.'

'My darling! do not be fantastic. What does it signify whether
you spend a pound more or less in the week, if you are comfort-

able? I have never refused you money yet, why, therefore, do you persist in quoting my sister, as if she had been a first wife? It is childish, all this. I have plenty of book-keeping at the works, and do not wish to have the house-book on my hands besides. How much do you want, that I may bring it at dinner time? Will fifty pounds do?'

'Oh yes, the half of that. But tell me, have I vexed you?'

'Oh dear, no. How can you think so?'

'But *do* you love me?' persisted Alice, half crying.

'Why Alice, what *is* the matter? What can I have done to make you doubt it? Are you ill?' said he, anxiously. 'Come, tell me, what is the matter; is it because I refused to add up your sums for you? Come, do not be a baby—give me the book, and let me see.' He good-humouredly resumed his seat and drew to the table. 'Why, you keep your accounts beautifully, Alice! and they are added right to a fraction; there is no need for me to go over them. Now let me make a memorandum of how much you want.'

'But have I spent more than Margaret used to do?'

'You know best, my love; but I really cannot stay to enter on the chapter of Margaret's economy; my time is too precious, and too short. I shall be in to dinner as usual. You had better take a drive this fine morning.'

He once more took up his hat, gave Alice a hasty kiss, and mounted his horse, which had been waiting for ten minutes. He put it to the gallop, and was out of sight almost directly. Alice looked after him with tearful eyes. 'He never turned his head,' sighed she. 'It is the first time he ever omitted to look back at me. What can I have done?'

She sat down listlessly to practise some new music; but the thought of Bryant's coldness recurred again to her mind, and she finally burst into tears. She had the comfort of shedding them all without remonstrance; and after she had made herself sufficiently miserable, by thinking over every possible and impossible cause of annoyance which she might have given, she became more calm. But she was destined to endure a real disappointment. A short note was brought to her from Bryant, telling her not to wait dinner, as he should not be home, having missed some parties on business by a few minutes, whom he had now to meet elsewhere.

Alice felt a twinge of conscience, to think that the ten minutes she had detained him in the morning had been the cause of this *contretemps*.

She remained alone until late in the evening, and when Bryant at length arrived, he looked harassed and weary. Alice placed his slippers, and made the tea, which had been brought in an hour before.

'Why, Alice, how could you be so foolish as to wait for me so long?' said he; 'another time, always dine or drink tea as the case may be, without waiting for me. I am very uncertain, and am often detained when I least expect it. You will have your house completely upset if you depend on my return at stated hours.'

'I should prefer going without dinner and tea altogether, to having them without you,' said Alice.

'That is talking nonsense,' replied Bryant: 'it is only foolish people who do not conform to necessary circumstances.'

He relapsed into silence, and regarded the fire with an air of gloomy thought.

'You are very silent,' said Alice, at length, trying to speak cheerfully, 'have you nothing to tell me?'

'No, nothing at all—I have been seeing people and talking all day, until I am quite weary.'

After another long pause, during which he seemed to have become utterly unconscious of her presence, he suddenly said:

'Alice, you are looking very pale; you had better go to bed; I must sit up for some hours yet. I have brought home some accounts that must be gone into to-night.'

'And you so wearied!' cried Alice, sympathetically. 'Cannot I help you at all, write down from your dictation? Let me at least sit beside you; I will not speak a word.'

'No, love, no, I must be alone; good night.'

He lighted her candle, and opened the door for her; and almost before it closed, he had become absorbed in a heap of perplexed-looking papers. The next morning he was up early, and ready to depart before Alice was dressed; he called to wish her good bye, but before she could reach the hall-door, he was almost out of sight.

Alice was perplexed and miserable for the whole day, and could not get rid of the fancy that he was displeased with her for detaining him on the previous morning. Bryant returned to dinner, but his presence brought little comfort to Alice; he continued silent and reserved; never speaking, except to reply to a question, and then evidently with unwillingness. Poor Alice had three days of silence, perplexity, and tears; which last, however, she had the good taste to keep entirely for her own private solace; but she was beginning to look pale and very miserable, when on the fourth day Bryant came home a different man! He was lively, talkative, cheerful, and it seemed as if a heavy cloud had been dispersed from his aspect. He observed for the first time, on looking at Alice during dinner, how changed she seemed.

'My dear Alice,' said he, when they were alone, 'has any thing distressed you? Have you heard any bad news? Tell me what is the matter,' continued he, tenderly.

'There is nothing the matter now, dear Bryant,' said Alice, trying in vain to restrain her tears; 'but you have been so gloomy and silent of late, that I feared you were displeased with me, and did not love me as formerly.'

'My dear child, why will you take up with such fancies! You have had a narrow escape from something that would have been really distressing! For the last few days I have felt great anxiety about some accounts which had arrived from our Iron Works in Silesia, and I feared my presence there would have been required. It would have been impossible to take you along with me, and I must have left you for, perhaps, some months. Happily, this morning we have received fresh advices, and all may be arranged without me. Whenever you see me silent as I have been, you must not think me unkind. Be sure that I always love you. Whenever you vex me (which I do not believe is in your power), I will tell you. Trust me, Alice; and never doubt my affection, because I do not make a demonstration of it. I have many things to harass me; I am very sorry any thing disagreeable should result to you from them, but you love me well enough to bear with me; and will you not do so without making yourself miserable, and me also? for it is very distressing to me to think I have given you pain.'

'But I wish you would tell me what annoys you, and let me share it,' replied Alice; 'any anxiety would be preferable to the fear I have suffered the last few days, lest I had displeased you.'

'My darling! you could not share the worries of business with
me. I cannot speak of matters at the time they are pressing on my
mind;—no, my love, there is nothing for it but your kind
forbearance. I know it must annoy you; but I feel very grateful
for your sympathy, though I may not seem to notice it. Now, kiss
me, and promise that you will never needlessly torment yourself
again.'

Alice gave the kiss and the promise; but it was beyond her
power to keep it. Although this explanation seemed, at the time,
as if it must comprehend in itself all future misapprehensions that
could possibly arise, still, on every succeeding period of gloom or
reserve there seemed a speciality, which prevented the self-tor-
menting Alice from deriving any comfort from this compendious
assurance.

CHAPTER XIX

MRS HELMSBY had never been to visit her daughter, although Alice had now been married more than six months. Alice had divined Bryant's dislike to his mother-in-law, although he had carefully abstained from saying any thing disrespectful. However, it was a duty that could not in decency be deferred any longer; accordingly Bryant told Alice that he thought she ought to write and invite her mother to spend a month with them, now that the country was looking so beautiful. The letter was accordingly written, and a gracious acceptance returned. Mrs Helmsby was to arrive early in the following week, and Bryant had arranged to leave home to transact some indispensable business. It was earlier than he had intended to go; but he would thereby shorten his own maternal penance, and avoid leaving Alice alone. Alice was rather glad of this arrangement, as it relieved her from the embarrassment she always felt when her mother and her husband were in presence; and, much as she was disposed to think Bryant always in the right, she rejoiced extremely at the prospect of seeing her mother, and receiving her in her own house. Nothing in this world ever occurs exactly as we plan it. Mrs Helmsby caught a severe cold, by imprudently going out to do some shopping on an extremely wet and cold day; and on the day she ought to have set off for Raven Hall she was confined to her bed. She grew so much worse, that Alice was sent for. Bryant accompanied her, and for three weeks she remained beside her mother, uncertain whether she would live or die. At length a slight change for the better took place, and Bryant insisted on her coming home with Alice. She never completely rallied, but lingered on until the beginning of winter, and then died.

Her death caused a blank in the existence of Alice, which could hardly have been expected from the uncongenial nature of their characters. But it was the loss of a daily solicitude, an object which employed her whole time, and took her thoughts away from herself and her own sensations. After the first natural grief had subsided, a weight of depression fell on Alice, which no effort could shake off. Her husband was at this time necessarily much absent, and did not remark it; he was, besides, so much accustomed to his wife's 'fancifulness', as he called it, that he had come to consider it as a tax, which he had to pay for her many excellent and charming qualities. He was essentially a practical matter-of-fact man, and had no conception of the morbid sinking of heart and deadly sadness which so easily beset imaginative temperaments, whose owners are not subject to the stern tonic of the *necessity* to work. Alice sank under the weight of a golden leisure, which she had not the energy adequately to employ. Worldly prosperity is a much greater drain upon our energies than the most severe adversity; there is no spring, no elasticity; it is like walking through life upon a Turkey carpet. Large and noble faculties are required to make a wise use of worldly prosperity; there is little stimulus in, and no excitement beyond, what the individual can furnish for himself; his days are rounded with security, and softly cushioned against all the harsh realities of life.

To the outward eye the contrast between the lot of the half-sisters is painfully glaring. The one, surrounded with all that makes life pleasing, and the precious possession of a strong enduring affection to give a value to all things.

The other, struggling with poverty, leading a life of hard labour, with the prospect of the workhouse if sickness or accident should disable her; suffering all this for no fault of her own, but inheriting it in consequence of the wayward, impetuous, ungoverned conduct of her parents, who had rushed upon responsibilities which they were not prepared to fulfil; with no one's affection to feed and stimulate her with words and looks of sympathy; alone with her own lot, to wrestle with it as she may; a helpless mother dependent upon her exertions, none to guide or counsel—none to care whether she should stand or fall.

But 'a man's *life* does not consist in the abundance of things which he possesses.' We could none of us live, if we had not some hope, into which we may open the actual *present*. If our *life* were really no more than there is made manifest in the passing day—in the things that occur, the small details by which one day is carried into the next—it would be such a poor mean affair, that no one would have courage to live out half his days. But the most prosaic amongst us, unconsciously idealise it. 'The things which are *seen*, are not made from those which do appear,'—and although nothing may distil from the unseen well of life within us, except common place days filled with ordinary business—still we instinctively feel that *they* are not our *life*: there is an ideal possibility of some latent power within them, which gives them a value beyond what they actually achieve. Every action we do, means more than it says;—it is the symbol of some thought, some hope, some effort. If we were built up in our daily life, and all glazed over to the smooth compactness of surface into which our actions are set each in its own place—meaning neither more nor less than the mechanical result of the concurrence of certain pitiful necessities—the spirit of life would be stifled out of us;—we should become dead jars of clay, instead of aspiring, palpitating, living human souls. No matter how mean or trivial may be the occupations which are appointed to us,—we can work at them with courage and perseverance, so long as we do not feel condemned to them as the 'be all and the end all', the *realisation* of our *life*,—so long as there is a side on which we may escape from that which is seen and definite, into that which is unseen and infinite. It is the being condemned to live with those who lead mechanical lives—lives without significance—who see in the daily routine of household business, in the daily occupation of going to the mill, the counting-house, and the different works of life, nothing but modes of filling up days and weeks, called in the aggregate *life*,—without an idea of looking round—much less *beyond*,—it is *this* which drives passionate souls mad; but if there be one opening through which the air from the everlasting universe of things may breathe upon us, we can feel strong and cheerful—no matter how bare of material comforts our lot may be.

This was Bianca's supreme blessing, which rendered all the hardships of her lot as dust on the balance. Alice, on the contrary, was hemmed in by people who cared for none of these things. She had not confidence enough in her own yearnings to make a way for herself; she did not sufficiently believe in her own aspirations to incur the comment, and censure, and want of sympathy of those around her; she endeavoured, instead, to make herself like to them, to feel satisfied with what satisfied them; she was haunted by a dull sense of self-reproach, she was divided against herself, weak, helpless, and dissatisfied. She was naturally religious,—had a deep sentiment of reverence and dependence, and might therefore have taken refuge in religion; but even that had been rendered so mechanical, that she saw no beauty in it that she should desire it;—she believed as she had been taught, because she was too timid to doubt the penalties which she had been told attached to disbelief; but her heart obstinately refused its sympathy, it remained cold and unimpressed. The mysteries of religion, as made visible in books of theology, are rendered frigid and mechanical; men are forbidden to believe any thing, or to hope any thing, but what is already written. The future life is mapped out as definitely as the life which now is; orthodox monotony has attempted to strip even death of its mystery, by dogmatising on the realities which are to succeed it. The mephitic atmosphere of scepticism, is a relief from this;—we at least breathe more freely. We rush out into the wilderness, to obtain at least the liberty of wandering without meeting on every hand straight narrow paths, hedged in by sharply asserted limits; to feel ourselves free to indulge in our own hopes and fears without dictation.

Why do men so earnestly seek after pleasure, as it is called? It is because they, for the time, get into a certain idealised element. They go to dinners, balls, *soirées*, dramatic entertainments, with a certain *hope*; they know not for a certainty who or what they will meet with. A preparation—an incantation has been made to bring them together, and they go to seek they know not what.

CHAPTER XX

TIME passed on, without any remarkable occurrence. Bianca continued her humble course; small parts were cast to her in every thing that chanced to be played,—tragedy, comedy, farce, melodrame; she did the best she could with them, and had even begun to attract the approbation of the regular *habitués* of the theatre, who marked her as a painstaking, promising young actress. Her companions took little notice of her; she was not popular; for the women could not disguise the fact that she was strikingly handsome, and they could find no handle against her character, so that their malicious feelings were in a state of very painful suppression. Bianca was not nearly so comfortable as in the circus. True, old Simpson was violent in his temper, and very hard and mean in all his money matters; but then he took a cordial interest in every individual of his troop; he rejoiced when they got any applause, and felt so much real sympathy with all they did, that it was quite a comfort to act under his eye. He took a real pride in their success, and, except where money was in question, he showed much consideration and kind-heartedness for them. He was a real artist in his line, and no attempt at excellence was unappreciated by him. In the theatre, on the contrary, all was dull and in routine; any sort of enthusiasm for the profession was unknown, and would have been laughed at, had any one shown it. None of the actors had any ambition, nor any desire for excellence; they acted with a certain business-like completeness, and were content to be thought not worse than average provincial actors. The manager seldom was seen; he never addressed a word of encouragement to any of them; he looked to getting as much out of them as he could, and the actors looked to giving as little as it was possible. Neither party considered their profession as an art to be reverently cultivated,—only a means of getting a livelihood. No wonder that Bianca felt in an ungenial atmosphere!

One night she acted the part of a young madcap page with much grace and spirit, and gained great applause. As she was passing up to the dressing-room, she met the manager, who was staring at one of the side scenes.

'I tell you what,' said he, catching hold of her hand, 'you have acted devilish well to-night; you are a deucedly clever girl, and worth all the company put together. I'll see you put into better business soon.'

Some one came up at that moment, and he dropped her hand suddenly, and appeared as if he were giving her some common directions.

Bianca went up stairs, wondering whether she was dreaming, or what such a sudden insight into her merits might portend. From that day the manager contrived to be constantly in her way, as she was either leaving the theatre after rehearsal, or going home after the performance in the evening; and always addressed some flattery to her. She found herself in the enjoyment of many little privileges which, however, did not seem to be known by the rest of the company; the treasurer alone seemed in the secret, for he told her one day mysteriously, 'that she had only to ask the manager for what she liked, and she would be sure to get it, she was such a favourite, though he could not show his partiality openly'. This speech rather perplexed Bianca, who, without too well knowing why, had taken a great antipathy to Mr St Leger, which was the name in which the manager was pleased to rejoice. The young creature, who filled a place a step above Bianca in the company, and who had hitherto treated her with supercilious contempt, suddenly began to make advances to her acquaintance; but it was evidently against the grain, and much suppressed bitterness and dislike were apparent through the veil of cordiality she assumed. Many hints and half speeches reached Bianca's ears, which she could not comprehend, and she could get no reply when she requested an explanation beyond a contemptuous smile, and an 'Oh, every body can see what you are about.' It was like fighting with shadows; there was evidently a mystery going on, and Bianca found her position materially altered without her being able to say in what it consisted. Every body seemed to have become afraid of vexing her, and yet there was an undefined insolence and maliciousness, which she felt, though she could not have made any tangible accusation against any one. This was worse than being overlooked as a nobody; but Bianca was too full of her own projects, and too much engrossed in her endeavours to study and improve herself, to have much attention to waste on green-room politics. She was as completely a being apart from the other actors, as if she had lived in another world; there was nothing in common between her and them, except belonging to the same company. There had been a continuance of dreadfully wet and stormy weather, and Bianca not being very warmly clad, had caught a terrible cold and influenza, which was the more provoking, as it came at a time when she was studying the best part that had yet been cast for her, in a new play which was to be brought out the following week. She had dragged herself one morning to rehearsal, and when there she fainted from exhaustion. Mr St Leger, who was in his own room, soon heard of what had happened, and came in a fuss of humanity to insist on her going home immediately; he made her swallow a glass of the particular Madeira which he kept in his own room, and told her not to think of coming to the theatre again till she was quite well.

Bianca was astonished at so much consideration; but as, at the present moment, she was quite unequal to going through the rehearsal, she followed his injunction and went home, very much troubled to know what she was to do for her week's salary, which she knew she could not earn, and what would become of her if she were fined for missing the rehearsals; and, above all, anxious about her appearance the following Monday in her new part. She was so little beforehand with the world, that a week's illness would, in her present circumstances, embarrass her seriously. She had always enjoyed such robust health, that this was her first serious indisposition, and, like all people to whom illness is strange, she fancied herself worse than she even was. But whilst, depressed by gloomy forebodings, she was sitting, in the afternoon, over her small fire, a note was brought in from the treasurer, saying, that Mr St Leger had directed him to tell her that her attendance at the theatre, either for rehearsal or performance, was dispensed with till Monday night, when it was hoped she would have recovered her strength, and be well up in her new part; that she need not be uneasy about her illness, as her salary would be paid as usual. This note was the best medicine Bianca could have received, and she began to think Mr St Leger must be a much better man than she had taken him for. On Monday night she was nearly well, and quite able to act. She was surprised to find an elegant new dress prepared for her part; for though the piece had been announced with 'entirely new dresses and decorations', yet she did not expect to find them descending to her own share. But no woman is ever displeased at a piece of finery; and even Bianca, with all her high aspirations, dressed herself with the satisfaction that might be fancied in a peacock finding his new tail in all its glory, after a dreary moulting. She was in capital spirits, and acted extremely well; the house was full, and she had a success which reminded her of the old times at the circus. She went home highly elated, and began to fancy she had already begun to rise.

She was crossing a bridge that lay between the theatre and her lodgings, when she perceived a female leaning over, and looking intently into the river. It was the young actress we have mentioned, as cultivating her acquaintance.

'Why, Miss Douglas!' cried Bianca, 'what are you doing here, at this time of night, and in this pouring rain?'

'What is that to *you?*' said the other, sharply. 'Go about your own business; it is my turn to be here to-night—perhaps it will be yours before long;' and she turned away, and leaned again over the low wall.

'But, Harriet, I am *sure* there is something wrong with you; nobody who could help it would be standing here to-night. If you are in any trouble, let me help you.'

'You!' cried the other, impatiently; 'no; I hate the sight of you; the only comfort is, that you will be as miserable as I am before long—your triumph won't be long. Now go your ways, for I want neither you, nor any thing you can do. I hate you. That's plain enough, is it not? and you are the cause of my being here.'

Bianca thought she was going out of her mind; she again attempted to soothe her and persuade her to go home; but she remained sullenly silent. At length she said, passionately—

'I thought the street was free, at any rate, but it seems I am to be tormented everywhere. I have no home; I was turned out of my lodging this morning, and dismissed from the theatre on Saturday. I went to St Leger to-night, to beg for money to buy a piece of bread—I have not eaten all day—and he refused, and ordered me to leave the place. As I was stealing off, I saw you, in your new dress, going on the scene, and I heard them applaud you. Do you wonder now that I hate you? I came here. I did not know whether to go on the street, or fling myself in here. But now you may tell that man, when he is poisoning you with his kisses, and his flattery, that you saw the last of me. These are my last words in this world!'

She made a sudden spring, and would have plunged over, had not Bianca caught hold of her, and held her firmly.

'You will come home with me, to-night, Harriet,' said she, quietly, but resolutely, 'and to-morrow we will consider what is to be done; but, come along with me now.'

The excitement which had nerved the poor girl gave way, and she burst into a fit of tears. Bianca did not loose her hold till they were at the door of her lodgings.

'My mother will be asleep, so we must not awaken her,' said she, as they went up stairs. There was a small but bright fire shining in the grate, and a table with a loaf of bread, a jug of milk, and some oatmeal stood before it.

'Oh, how comfortable you are,' cried Harriet, shivering with wet and cold.

'It is better than being out of doors,' replied Bianca. 'But now take off your wet things, and wrap yourself in this old cloak, whilst I make the milk hot. There, come close to the fire, and try to get a little warm.'

Bianca busied herself over the supper, whilst her companion crouched over the blaze, and looked with curious gaze round the room.

'It is like a palace,' said she, enviously. 'How do you make it so comfortable?'

'There is nothing in it,' said Bianca, cheerfully. 'But now eat this before you talk any more,' at the same time handing by far the larger share of the steaming milk porridge. They both ate their portion heartily.

Miss Douglas, indeed, had tasted nothing but a glass of gin that day.

When they had finished, Bianca said, 'Now, Harriet, tell me the meaning of all you were saying on the bridge. How have I injured you?'

'I do not hate you now,' replied Harriet, 'but you had better have left me where you found me. I am comfortable now, but I shall be as badly off as ever to-morrow, and all would have been over by this time. My curse on that villain, for he is one!'

'Come, come,' said Bianca, 'we are not in the last act yet—something will turn up for you.'

'It does not matter much,' replied the other, gloomily, 'he has ruined me, body and soul; but if I live, I will be revenged on him. It's no good telling you a long story, which has nothing new in it; take care of yourself, Bianca, for he has his eye on you, and he is a heartless scoundrel, with no more feeling or honour, than that shoe. All his kindness to you is a mere pretence; don't let yourself be taken in by it; he is a villain, and the worst of villains, and I wish I had died before I had seen him.'

Bianca tried to soothe her, but she shook her head, and said, 'It is no good your trying to put me in spirits, I try to stand it out to myself; but sitting here beside you, I feel, and know I am degraded; I have no pleasure in thinking of myself,' and she again began to weep bitterly.

She was a very handsome girl, with large blue eyes, which had a bold enticing look, and a fine lazy-looking figure. Her fair hair fell dishevelled over her face and neck; altogether, there was a desolate *abandon* about her, as she leaned over the fire, which contrasted singularly with the severe *retenue*★ and composure of Bianca's appearance. 'Come,' said she, 'let us come to bed now, and to-morrow, I think, I have a scheme that will answer; but we must be careful not to disturb my mother. You must be content with part of a bed for to-night, to-morrow we will make some arrangement.'

The next morning Bianca was, as usual, up betimes, and had the room in order before either her guest or her mother awoke. After breakfast she said, 'Now I will tell you my plan. I think my old circus manager, Simpson, would engage you—he is in town. I will go with you before rehearsal, and there is an attic in this house you might have very cheap, and you might come and sit here by our fire whenever you like.'

'Well, I don't know but that might suit me very well; but do you really mean that I may come and sit in your clean bright room? Well, you *are* a good soul, and deserve all the luck you will get.'

They found Mr Simpson in all his glory, meditating on a 'Roman Triumph',★ which he intended to bring out in a style of surpassing splendour. He was very glad to see Bianca, and listened very graciously to her proposal about her companion.

'I would rather have had *you* back,' said he; 'but it will sound well in the bills to say, "From the Theatre Royal, at great expense", though I shall only give her ten shillings a-week all the same.'

This business settled, Bianca had to hurry to rehearsal. She was in a state of pleasant excitement at her success, and felt no sort of misgiving about herself, or any thing else under the sun.

After rehearsal was over, a message was brought that Mr St Leger desired to see her in his private room. A significant laugh went round amongst those who were within hearing. Bianca took no notice, but obeyed the message, and found herself face to face with the manager, who was sitting at a table, on which stood a decanter of wine and some glasses. He had dressed himself with elaborate care; his hair was curled and perfumed, a large diamond-stud glittered in his glossy, black satin stock; he had altogether a flashy supercilious *roué* look, as of a man accustomed to look on all women only as so many speculations for a *bonne fortune,* and to decide on their claims to personal charms as he would have done on the points of a horse.

Bianca felt excessively annoyed at the impertinent scrutiny of his half-closed eye as she entered; but she stood silent till he spoke and expressed a hope that she was quite recovered.

'You look pale still,' continued he, 'and your complexion is not so brilliantly transparent as it was; but a little rest will bring all round. I cannot afford you to lose any of your charms. I shall not let you exert yourself till you are quite right again.'

This might be all very friendly, but Bianca did not feel it to be so; her face crimsoned at his impertinence, and she haughtily replied:

'I was told you wished to speak to me on business.'

'So I do; so I do; but sit down, sit down,' and he drew a chair into line a few paces from his own.

Bianca moved it so as to face him, and sat down opposite. He poured out a glass of wine, and handed it to her.

'I never take wine, thank you,' said she; 'and shall be glad to hear why you sent for me, as I wish to go home.'

Mr Montague St Leger was rather disconcerted at this straight-forward manner of keeping to a point. He began to flatter her on her capabilities as an actress, and to expatiate on his good-will towards her, and his desire to push her on in the profession, and to hint that he had great things in view for her; but all the while there seemed something behind which he was wishing to say; he had endeavoured to edge his chair nearer to her, but she had removed in the same proportion, and seemed to wait so impassively till he should declare the purpose for which he had summoned her, that he was constrained, contrary to all his tactics, to be explicit. He offered her the business of the principal actress in the company, who was about to retire, and a salary of three pounds a week; but coupled with conditions, insinuated, rather than distinctly expressed, which roused Bianca to a pitch of indignation that deprived her of all powers of speech. She rose, and, with a look of scorn and loathing, the most intense, flashing from her face, darted from the room, leaving Mr Montague St Leger singularly mortified and crestfallen at the issue of his King Ahasuerus-like designs;* but the sorest point was the unmistakeable expression of Bianca's look. He had been accustomed to consider himself irresistible, and Bianca's look of detestation galled him to the quick. He swore to be revenged.

'Confound the jade,' said he to his confidant, the treasurer, who entered shortly after; 'her virtue shall cost her something. She shall find what it is to insult *me*. I trust to you to make her know herself; torment her life out, do any thing—short of actually driving her from the theatre.'

'You may trust it to me,' replied the other. 'I have a few scores of my own to settle with her ladyship.'

CHAPTER XXI

AFTER that occurrence, Bianca found her position become almost intolerable.

That same evening, when she went to performance, she found some strange rumour had got afloat concerning her. Every one looked strange at her; the women whispered together, and refused to speak to her; the men made insolent jests within her hearing, evidently intended to apply to her. She was treated like one lying under an interdict.

The malice of her companions was not confined to behind the scenes. In the stage business, every little act of malice that could tend to baffle her play, and throw her into confusion, was pitilessly committed; nothing was omitted that could make her appear to disadvantage. The most malicious reports were circulated about her, with an industry which, considering her humble position in the company, was rather surprising. No one, except the lame old prompter, ever said a kind word to her, but all professed to believe her an abandoned character.

Bianca armed herself with a proud patience. She did not need to be told who was the enemy who had done all this. She made no complaint or remark, but gave up going into the green-room, and stood at the sides to await her turn of going on.

One evening, as she stood shivering in the cold draught that swept from all sides, in a low thin dress, waiting for the beginning of a scene with her stage 'lover', the old prompter passed. He stopped a moment, looking compassionately at her, and said in a low, hurried voice: 'Keep up a good spirit of your own, and don't let yourself be worried into doing wrong, and you will have the best of it yet. Go on as you have begun, and you will rise over their heads before long; the folks here are malicious, but they are not fools, and not one of them believes all that is said of you; only you have vexed somebody, and they think to please him by tormenting you.'

People must be drowning before they know the value of a straw, and none who have not been in Bianca's position, can know the strength and comfort she found in those few words. To discover that she did not stand alone in this systematic, petty persecution, but that one person, at least, felt sympathy with her, gave her all the courage she needed, and she felt herself able to endure cheerfully, as well as proudly.

But something of more practical importance was in store for her. On the Saturday following her interview with the manager, when she went to draw her salary, she was told, to her great dismay, that she was *fined* for her *unexplained* absences the previous week! In vain she pleaded the note she had received; the treasurer declared that no partiality could be shown, that he had written without sufficient authority, and that she might appeal to the manager if she chose; but, in the meanwhile, must submit to the forfeit she had incurred.

Bianca retired in silence; she would not give the curious and malignant bystanders the satisfaction of seeing her complain; but she was none the less in despair as to how she was to wear through the ensuing week. Her heart turned sick at the horrible consciousness thus forced upon her, that if, from any accident, she were to be unable to wrestle with the iron necessities of each never-failing day as it arose, she and her mother must be crushed under their heavy, steady, unslackening steps. She stood with nothing but her own hands between herself and starvation, and they seemed very feeble to ward it off. A feeling of fright and despair, such as she had never known, seized on her. But her soul was too indomitable for such a mood to last long; she felt, instinctively, that she had no choice but to go on, looking neither to the right road, nor the left; and she had an innate conviction, that in one way or other, she should not be mastered by her difficulties. She had no idea that there was anything heroic in this calm bravery; it seemed to her the simplest necessity laid upon her—she could not have told how or why—but a necessity from which there was no appeal, to do the thing that seemed right, and trust courageously for the consequences. She had a childlike indifference to the future. It never occurred to her that it was 'prudent', or 'well', or 'expedient', to do a questionable action to-day, because it might prove to be convenient to-morrow. She had no idea of *secondary* motives, and therefore never got bewildered in the haze and mist that streams up from the small details of every day as it arises and passes away. She was eminently *single-minded* in all her ways, without the least consciousness that there was anything excellent in it. There is a species of stupidity in real greatness which can neither see nor comprehend the subtleties and prudent foresight of worldly cleverness.

Something good generally arises for us at a time we most need it, and least expect it, and to Bianca it came in the guise of a letter from Conrad. This would have sufficed to carry her through much heavier troubles than those she was fighting with.

It was before the days of the penny-post had dawned—but Conrad had been thoughtful enough to pay the postage. It was only a few lines of inquiry and encouragement, and telling her, that he had met her friend the actor, the previous evening, who was speaking of a very promising young actress he had met with at the——theatre; and, on inquiry, it had proved to be his *protégée*, Bianca. Conrad expressed great satisfaction at hearing such a good account of her, and desired her to apply to him in any difficulty or need.

The letter was kindly and delicately worded, and Bianca was in a maze of happiness and tremulous emotion. She went to the theatre that night fenced round with a deep sense of joy that no stranger could mar; she acted with the precious letter lying like a talisman on her heart—she looked almost superhumanly lovely. Her complexion suffused with a radiant glow that made rouge needless, and her lustrous eyes seemed to shine through a soft atmosphere of joy. It is certain that nothing makes a woman look so beautiful as the internal consciousness that her love matters are going on happily; and, on the other hand, nothing brings worn, haggard looks so quickly as an annoyance from the one she loves.

Mr Montague St Leger passed Bianca as she was waiting to go on—he was quite startled at her looks. It was no longer with him a lazy inclination to obtain possession of her, but a fierce cruel determination to let nothing stop him. 'It must be ambition and hunger to bring her to terms,' said he to himself; 'she has no friends, as far as I can learn—she will never hold out long.' Bianca caught sight of him, and shuddered with disgust, as if a toad had touched her. It seemed to her to be sacrilege against Conrad even to have met his looks.

It never crossed her mind to tell Conrad her trials and difficulties, but she addressed herself to him as to her guardian angel—the

one who had been sent to stand beside her in her deepest need.
'If I ever achieve any thing in my profession,' she wrote, 'it will
be my faith in you that has strengthened me, and the desire not
to be unworthy of your goodness, that will have kept me from all
evil. Wicked things are said and done in the world, and we must
endure them as we can—but believe always that I would sooner
die than become any thing I should not, be or do any thing
unbecoming one whom you have befriended.'

After she had written and sent her letter, she felt tranquil. The
only point in which the malicious reports afloat about her in the
green-room affected her was, the fear lest through some of the 'stars'
who were constantly coming down, they should reach the ears of
either Conrad, or her friend the actor; and now it seemed to her
she had provided against that; she had *told* him that she would not
prove unworthy, and she felt as if he *must* believe her. For would
not *she* have believed his word, even though an angel from
Heaven had testified to the contrary!

Time passed on, and the season of the——theatre came to a
close; the company were, however, to remove to a neighbouring
town, until the period for re-opening their own theatre returned.

Bianca's mother had been gradually failing, though nothing
beyond great debility and increased helplessness seemed to ail
her, and Bianca hoped that the change of air would do her good.
As soon as they reached the town, her first care was to find an airy
lodging somewhat out of the town, although it gave her a long
walk to the theatre; but her mother did not derive the benefit she
had hoped; she became weaker every day, and Bianca had difficulty in leaving her even for her necessary attendance at the
theatre. Her mother seemed uneasy when any stranger came near
her, and could not bear Bianca to leave her sight; so that although
she hired a nurse, it did little towards relieving her anxiety or her
toil, for she was obliged to get up many times in the night to give
her mother drink and medicine; her own rest was completely
broken, and she had scarcely strength for her daily business. One
morning, about a week after entering the town, Bianca ventured
to request permission to absent herself from the next day's
rehearsal, mentioning at the same time the state in which her
mother was; she did not like doing this, but she had no alternative. She received the required permission, and an intimation that

she had only her own obstinacy to thank that she did not obtain more indulgences.

At the end of the week she was *discharged* from the theatre! She had no appeal, for her engagement only ran from week to week.

Stunned and in despair she turned away, there seemed now no outlet through which she might escape. Arrived at home she flung herself on her knees, but no words came from her lips. She was conscious of only one hope, and that was that her mother might die, before things came to the worst.

That same evening after dinner, as Mr St Leger and his friend the treasurer were sitting over their wine, he said,

'So you gave Bianca her dismissal; how did she take it?'

'Oh, seemed very cut, I promise you, in spite of her pride. I don't know what in the name of fortune she will do now.'

'Ah! ah!' replied the other, with a low chuckling laugh, 'I fancy she will be more tractable in a day or two; but we must leave her alone, and let it work awhile. If the old woman is so bad, she will do for her, what she would not to save herself from starving; her spirit will not help her here.'

CHAPTER XXII

'THEE had better go to the door, there is Alice Bryant in her carriage. May be she does not want to alight this wet day.'

This was said by Mr Hodgson, the principal chemist and druggist of——, and whose speech betrayed him a Quaker.*

'So thy mother is no better,' said he, turning to a tall, pale young woman, and taking an empty medicine bottle from her hand. 'Well, I tell thee she should live well, or else my medicine will do little good. There, give her arrowroot whenever she will take it, and the bark as before. I have no time to take thy money to day, so we will never mind it.——Good morning to thee, Alice Bryant; this is not a day for a delicate plant like thee to venture out.'

The girl who had been speaking to Mr Hodgson, sighed and looked at the rich satin mantle, lined with fur, of the new comer, and at the carriage waiting for her, and then took up the packet of arrowroot which the good-natured Quaker had given her.

'Thou wilt come and say if thy mother is worse to-night,' said he, as she was leaving the shop.

'I thank you much,' replied the girl, in a voice of singular sweetness.

Alice looked up, and was struck with the noble expression of her face, though it was then thin and pale, and it seemed as if care had eaten all the youthfulness of it away.

'Who is that remarkable looking girl?' asked she.

'I wish I could get any one to be interested in her,' replied Mr Hodgson, 'for I believe her to be a good and deserving girl; but she is an actress out of work, and somehow all the ladies I have mentioned her to seem to think she is not good enough to be helped. I wish thee would do something for her, for her mother is dying, and she is just worn out with care and nursing, besides being hungered, as thee may see by her face.'

'Poor thing!' said Alice; 'I will certainly do something for her. I could do more if she were any thing else, but Mr Bryant has a great objection to those sort of people. She is starving, you say. How came she to lose her situation in the theatre?'

'She could not nurse her mother and do play-acting both. Pleasure hardens the heart, and the theatre manager turned her away, to starve or do worse.'

'What is her name, and where does she live? I will visit her myself before I go home.'

'She is called "BIANCA"; rather a curious name, but she has no other as far as I can learn; and she lives at Shaw's Fold, nearly half a mile from here.'

Alice, having made her purchases, and regained her carriage, ordered it to drive to 'Shaw's Fold'. On the way she began to feel rather nervous at the strong step she was taking in going to see an ACTRESS: and to reassure herself, repeated, a dozen times, that Mr Hodgson, *a Quaker*, would not have recommended her, had she not been a deserving object. But then he had also owned, that no other ladies to whom he had mentioned her had interested themselves, and this rang in her ears. She would have given the world for a precedent, to have quoted to her husband, and to herself! She would have been thankful for the presence of her sister-in-law, either to have encouraged her, or to have turned the balance effectually against her undertaking. The excessive dread of blame, which was the leading feature in her character, destroyed all unity or comfort in her own mind; it made all her actions timid and limping, and paralysed all energy and spontaneity. Once assured by an authority she deemed competent that a course was right, she could have gone to martyrdom for it; but she could do nothing without a sanction. This gave, perhaps a delicacy, and what is called a feminineness to her character, but it made her negative and useless; which, however, most men seem to regard as the peculiar type of womanly perfection.

Her reveries and misgivings were, however, interrupted by the stopping of the carriage, and the footman, who touched his hat at the window, saying, 'This is Shaw's Fold, ma'am, who shall I ask for?'

'Ask for a young person called Bianca, who has a sick mother.'

Shaw's Fold was a row of cottages, standing a little off the road, with strips of somewhat dilapidated gardens before them. The palings were broken, and the gates mostly off their hinges. A crowd of children came running from all directions to stare at the 'grand lady'; and several untidy looking women, some with babies, and some with their arms rolled in their aprons, came to their doors to hear what was wanted.

Alice did not at all like the sensation she was making, and was half tempted to give up her errand and return home, when the footman returned with intelligence, that the young woman did not live anywhere there; but that a young woman, who worked in the theatre, and had a sick mother, lived at the 'Little Fold', the first lane past the turnpike. Thither Alice ordered them to proceed. The road down the lane was very bad; evidently used only by carts, which had left deep ruts in the stiff clay, which threatened an overturn every moment to the carriage. However, no such catastrophe occurred; and it stopped in safety before a small whitewashed cottage, where Bianca actually lived.

A fat, coarse, but good-natured-looking woman, was standing within, over a washing tub, her hair in loose strings falling from under a cap, and her red shining elbows splashed with soap-suds; the place was filled with the steam, and Alice nearly fell over a large black pan, which had just been lifted off the fire. She ceased her work and dropped a curtsey as Alice entered. 'Indeed, ma'am,' said she, in reply to her inquiry, 'I am main glad any lady is good enough to come to see after the poor creature; she is just the quietest, most industrious, pleasant-spoken lass I would wish to see; she tends that old lady night and day, and fairly pines herself with hunger to get things for her. I am sure I am pitiful to see her. I'll go first to show you the way. Here be a good lady come to see you,' said she, pushing open the door of a small room at the head of the steep, creaking stairs; 'take care, ma'am, that is just an awkward spot.'

Alice entered the room and saw Bianca on her knees, trying to support her mother, who was suffering from a distressing cough and difficulty of breathing.

'Here,' said the woman, kindly, 'let me help you, my arms are stronger than yours,' and she lifted the sick woman and placed the pillow to prop her up. 'Ah, well a-day, the poor old lady sinks fast; I fear you won't have her long,' continued she, in a condoling tone. Women of that class are like children; they love to say anything to make an impression.

Bianca looked still more pale and emaciated than when Alice had seen her in the shop; her eyes were flat and haggard, and sunk in her head, and all her features sharp and pinched. Alice was little in the habit of paying these sort of visits, and felt some confusion in accounting for her presence.

'Mr Hodgson told me your mother was ill, and I came to ask if she needed anything,' said she.

'You are very good,' said Bianca. 'I need nothing myself, but if I had only some wine for my mother—Mr Hodgson says she must live well, and I have not the means to get every thing.'

It was the same deep, soft voice, which had before struck Alice.

'You shall have it,' replied she, 'and any thing else you require.'

Alice had the heart of a true gentlewoman; her manner to Bianca was precisely that in which she would have addressed the grandest lady of her acquaintance; she did not feel that conferring a benefit gave her a right to be either patronising, or to ask impertinent questions.

'I will come again and see you to-morrow, if you will allow me,' said she.

'God sent you to me at my worst need,' replied Bianca, whose heart bounded at the refined and gentle tone of kindness of her unknown sister. We are unable to say whether it was the force *du sang** which influenced them, but certainly those two women felt drawn to each other more strongly than actual circumstances could explain. Alice did not remain longer; but when she reached the kitchen, she inquired of the woman what she thought her lodgers most needed.

'Well then, ma'am, if you ask me I must say that it is just every thing; for the poor things are fairly lost; they have pawned every thing, and when the lass goes out, I have to lend her my bonnet and shawl, for it is weeks since she had her own. She does a little sewing when she can get it, but it is earning a dead penny.'

Alice gave a trifle to the woman, recommended her lodgers to her kindness, and drove home full of benevolent schemes. She had got something to interest her and occupy her, and, in spite of her sympathy, felt in better spirits than she had done for weeks; for the time being she was delivered from the black cloud of ennui which had weighed upon her like a fog. Arrived at home, she looked out from her store-room a lavish supply of those things she deemed most acceptable, and with the assistance of the housekeeper, packed a large basket with nourishing delicacies and more substantial food—wine was not forgotten. From her own wardrobe Alice supplied a warm cloak, and everything she could imagine needful in the way of clothing; she took a childish delight in making her present as complete as possible; she had not experienced so much pleasure for a long time, and was quite impatient till the servants' dinner was over, that she might despatch the footman on horseback with the important basket. Alice was very rich and very charitable; she gave a great deal away to the poor, but was too fastidious to have any taste for beggars and common-place poor people; all her sympathies, however, were excited for the poetical-looking Bianca, and for her deep need borne with so much austere dignity—*c'était faire au même temps le bien publique et privé.*★ That which made for Alice a morning's distraction and an agreeable excitement, was to Bianca life from the dead.

CHAPTER XXIII

THE acquaintance, thus begun, did not cease; not a day passed, in which Alice did not either visit her *protégée*, or send an ample supply of all she could imagine useful or acceptable. In her conversations with Bianca she became conscious that she found a sympathy with all that was lying hidden in her own heart; an echo, as it were, of her own early dreams and aspirations, but which had been *froissé** and trodden down under the common-place wisdom and heavy trivialities with which, from her cradle, she had been surrounded. There was a calm, clear judgment in Bianca, a broad, practical way of viewing things and stripping them of the atmosphere which distorted them; and Alice, with the gentle docility of heart which made her so interesting, began to cling to the young actress, and lean upon her with that keen appreciation of what was good and strong, which a consciousness of her own vacillation and timidity made instinctive in her nature. The frank humility with which she recognised it, made her inexpressibly touching and graceful.

Bianca was precisely the friend Alice needed, and Bianca was fascinated by the feminine grace and gentleness which her own mode of life had completely prevented her either seeing or cultivating.

The pleasure Alice felt in this intercourse, gave her courage to bear the sarcastic amazement of her sister-in-law, at her enthusiasm for a strolling actress. Alice had written to her husband an account of Bianca and her mother, but in the calm, guarded manner which was necessary to meet his taste; and when he gave her his sanction, 'to see that the poor things wanted nothing', he was far from suspecting the degree of intercourse springing up between his wife and the poor actress. Mrs Lauriston wrote him a sensible letter, to warn him of the mischief; but as he happened to dislike the tone of it, he contented himself with desiring Alice, in his next letter, to recollect she was in a conspicuous position, and to be careful not to be imposed on by unworthy objects, as any ridicule she incurred would fall on him. Alice, with the keen sensitiveness of a sister-in-law, directly suspected what had happened, and was only the more determined to justify herself in taking her own way.

Bianca's mother grew every day worse, and weaker. She hardly seemed conscious of her daughter's presence, and sank gradually and gently from the life-in-death, which had so long been her lot, into the entire unbroken insensibility of DEATH.

Her departure was not perceptible. Bianca, who stood beside her bed, administering some nourishment, did not perceive when she drew her last breath; she was startled by one strange flash of intelligence in her eyes, and then it seemed as if she fell off to sleep.

Bianca fell beside the bed. The mistress of the house fortunately entered, and she was removed to the other room, but she remained many hours in a most distressing state; all her strength had been overstretched, and all her nerves were unstrung. Calm, self-governed, as she generally was, she had lost all control of herself, and a violent nervous crisis was the result. A messenger, who had been despatched to Alice, now returned, accompanied by her, and every thing that kindness could suggest was done. Alice stood over her like a pitying angel, and did not leave her the whole day; but it was not a sorrow any sympathy could mitigate. The death of her mother broke the only tie that bound her to the world—she no longer belonged to any one. In the intervals of that terrible day, when she was able to think calmly for a moment, a horrible fright seized on her soul as she felt herself standing utterly detached both from the world on which she stood, and the unknown world whence she came forth. To her disordered fancy it seemed as if a breath of wind would carry her away from the face of the earth, and whirl her she knew not whither. A sense of the vast loneliness in which she stood, terrified her. She felt like a child whom its companions leave alone in a strange place; and she filled the air with screams.

Alice, in great distress, sent for her own medical man, who by large doses of laudanum succeeded in stupifying her, but gave orders that she should not be left alone for an instant; and Alice sent one of her servants to sit up with her, and also gave orders for the funeral.

For several days Bianca remained in alternations of stupor and violent excitement. She was not allowed to go into the room where her mother lay; but on the morning of the funeral, her ear caught the sound made in removing the coffin. She sprang out of bed, and, flinging herself on her knees, began to recite the prayers for the dead; then, rising reverently, kissed the coffin, and was removed in a state of insensibility to her bed. She had no more violent convulsions, but it was many days before she was able to leave her room.

Alice was an angel of kindness during Bianca's illness, and as soon as she was able to move, brought her to her own house for change of scene; which was a piece of real heroism, all things considered.

'You shall stay here with me, dear Bianca,' said Alice, 'and feel quite at home till we find some plan for you. These two rooms are your own; they open out of each other, and I have amused myself by trying to make them comfortable for you.'

Bianca felt very grateful; but the feeling that it was all voluntary kindness, and that she had no hold on the love of any human being, made the sense of her loneliness feel heavy on her heart. Her eye was caught by a portrait over the mantel-piece.

'Tell me who is that?' she said, eagerly.

'That is an old portrait of my father when he was a very young man,' replied Alice; 'it is very badly painted, though it was done in Italy, where he resided some time.'

'How very strange!' said Bianca, going up to look at it more closely, 'what was your father's name?'

'Helmsby—Phillip Helmsby,' replied Alice, rather surprised.

Bianca recognised its likeness to a small miniature her mother had always worn in her bosom, and which she knew was the portrait of her father; at this moment of utter desolation she was not alone in the world; her first impulse was to fling her arms round the neck of Alice and call her 'sister', but the door opened and the footman announced that 'Mrs Burrel was in her carriage at the door, and requested to speak to Mrs Bryant for an instant, as she had no time to alight.'

Alice flew down stairs without noticing Bianca's agitation. Whilst she was away, Bianca took time to reflect. She felt instinctively that Alice, with all her amiability, all the kindness she had shown her, would be embarrassed if she knew their relationship. Bianca knew the timid conscientious character of

Alice, and she knew that she would struggle to be all she ought, whilst the *gêne** of finding a relation in such a questionable social position would destroy all the comfort of their relationship; she had pity on her sister's weakness, and though her whole soul was overflowing with love and tenderness, she resolutely determined to quell the mighty 'hunger of her heart' for natural affection, and to keep the secret to herself for the present at least.

She stood gazing at the portrait, her heart filled with ineffable yearning; the tears streamed down her thin cheeks as she thought of the desolate abandonment to which she had been consigned, one phase of her existence blotted out before she had seen the day.

Both men and women embark in love or friendship, as if it were all pleasure—an agreeable exercise of the emotions. They use eloquent and passionate persuasion to obtain the influence and affection they desire, but hardly one has an idea of the solemn covenant they take upon themselves. When their vanity and self are gratified by success, they grow weary, and the love they have gained becomes a charge to them. A real affection is a heavy responsibility to accept; it is a solemn trust, and one that neither man nor woman can lightly undertake. That one who dares to say to another, 'Give me thy *heart*', ought to prepare himself, not by yielding headlong to passionate emotions, but by self-government and self-devotion, by stability and constancy of heart, to become strong enough to bear the weight of another existence attached to his own, and to take without shrinking all the consequences of his engagement: either man or woman who embarks in 'an enterprise of passion', without counting the cost, may escape human judgment, which does not legislate for such things, but they commit the most grievous sin of which the soul of man is capable. The most precious things are desecrated and degraded to pleasures, with a cowardly sensualism that enervates the heart. Till men can recognise the *responsibilities* of the affection they accept, there will be no honour, nor strength, nor stability in them. Love and friendship are not *amusements*, they are solemn covenants; and woe to those who seek to extract the pleasure whilst they ignore the duties.

Bianca was still gazing on the face of her father's portrait when Alice returned. 'What has happened, dear Bianca, that has so moved you?' she asked.

'I was thinking how very happy you are to have known a father; it must be like an incarnation of the love of God, revealed to yourself with a sweet individuality in which none other can partake.'

'But do not you remember your father?' said Alice.

'No, no,' said Bianca, bitterly; 'I know not whether he was ever aware of my existence. I am an illegitimate child; he had forsaken my mother before I was born. She had never loved but him, and became the wreck you knew her—all her passion was thrown back upon her soul, and her whole life was laid waste by the overflowing flood. I am thrown solitary on the world, below the mark of shame, to be saved or lost, as it may chance. Oh, you are very happy to have known a father!'

Alice was rather scandalised at this frank avowal, and only hoped it would never be known either to her husband or her sister-in-law, as it would make it still more difficult for her to justify the choice of a *protégée*. Mrs Lauriston being a perfect dragon of virtue, she would not, had it depended on her, have allowed the bearers of a *bar-sinister*★ to come within the pale of Christian salvation;—they seemed in her eyes a species of monster which ought hardly to be admitted into the world, and certainly never allowed to rise higher than scullions or servants of all work to those legitimately born!

In less than a week Bianca had reason to rejoice in her resolution. One evening a letter was brought, that had been forwarded from her old lodgings; it was from Mr Montague St Leger himself, and written in a most elaborately respectful style, stating that a great actor from London was to appear the following evening, and that his principal actress was suddenly taken ill, and that unless Bianca would consent to supply her place at this short warning, he must close his theatre and forfeit his expensive engagement with Mr——. 'Will you,' he said, in conclusion, 'be at rehearsal tomorrow morning at eleven o'clock, and can you be up in the part of Mrs Haller★ by night? In case you have entered into no other arrangements, I shall be glad to offer you an engagement for the next month, to take the leading female parts, at a salary of two pounds a-week; the first week to be paid in advance, and to begin from to-day.'

Like the sound of a trumpet to a war-horse, was this letter to Bianca; all trace of the languor of indisposition vanished instantly. She started up to find Alice, who just then entered the room.

'What good news have you heard, that you look so radiant?' she asked.

'Read there,' replied Bianca; 'and yet, though it is good in one sense, it has a strong alloy, you see. I must leave you suddenly.'

'Oh, Bianca!' cried Alice, 'surely, surely you will not return to that dreadful way of life! I was in hopes you had forsaken it for ever. I had all sorts of plans for you. I wrote to a friend of mine, telling her about you; and here is a letter I have just received, offering to take you as her nursery governess, at twenty pounds a year, and then I could always have seen you, and you could have spent all your holidays with me!'

'Dear, kind friend!' said Bianca, taking her hand, caressingly; 'you have been my guardian angel; without you I must have been either dead or mad by this time. I owe you an immensity of obligation, which I can only pay by loving you with all my heart and soul. Any *possible* desire you expressed about me, I would kill myself to perform; but you cannot change my nature, I must be what I am. The stage is to me a *passion*, as well as a profession; I can work in no other direction; I should become worthless and miserable; all my faculties would prey upon myself, and I should even be wicked and mischievous, and God knows how bad, if I were placed in any other position. You don't know what it is to be devoted to an art; it possesses one like a demon; it is a sacred necessity laid upon me, which I cannot help obeying. Do not think me obstinate or ungrateful. Besides, what else am I fit for? The place of a nursery governess would not suit me; and even if your friend were generous enough to try me, she would not be able to persist in the questionable course of keeping an ex-actress about her young children. No, no, I must realise myself in my own way, or not at all. I am already *flétrie*★ in the eyes of all the quiet, gentle, still-life people amongst whom you dwell.'

'But,' said Alice, impatiently, 'I cannot let you go so soon—I care for you, as I never cared for any one—you do me so much good—I feel a better person since I knew you. Why need you leave me?'

'Dear Alice (let me call you so), be assured that I love you more than I dare express; none but a *sister* could feel for you, as I do.

When I have raised myself in my profession, and have made myself a place in society, I will come back to you; then, perhaps, our intercourse may be renewed; but at present, there is a gulf between us; situated as you are, you cannot continue to see me, and I do not wish it. If I succeed, be assured you shall hear of my success; meanwhile, let me continue to love you, and whatever blame or questioning your kindness to me may subject you to from your own circle, be strong enough not to regret it. You have acted most generously by me, and I will never disgrace you.'

'And when must you go?' said Alice, wiping her eyes, though in spite of herself, she was rather relieved from an indescribable embarrassment, by the calm decided manner in which Bianca broke their future intercourse.

'I must be at rehearsal to-morrow by eleven, so I shall leave you directly after breakfast, that I may have time to fix myself in some sort of lodgings: I should not like to go straight to the theatre from here.'

'John, the coachman, lets two rooms in his house; I know if you went there, I should hear of you constantly, and see you, too, sometimes, and you would not seem to be gone quite away from me,' said Alice.

'That would suit me well, if it could be arranged,' replied Bianca; 'and you will come and see me act, will you not?' continued she, coaxingly. 'I want you to see what I can do. This is the first chance I ever had; luckily, I know my part for to-morrow; but I will send you word when to come. I should like you to see me in a good part.'

The next morning, Bianca engaged the two rooms in John the coachman's house, and Alice undertook to have all her things removed, and arranged, whilst she was at rehearsal. She spent the whole morning in contriving to surprise Bianca; and when the latter returned, she found a stand of beautiful flowers in the window, pictures on the walls, books in a small book-case from Alice's own bedroom, and every corner showing traces of the labour of love, that had been so minutely at work. Alice was waiting to receive her. 'I could not let you come to a solitary home,' said she. 'Now come and look how you like what I have done. I shall come and see you very often, remember.'

'As often as you are allowed,' said Bianca, mournfully; 'for you are not a free woman: but absent, or present, I shall love you equally. It is a new chapter in my life that is commencing, and you have helped me over the roughest part of my way. God will bless you for it.'

CHAPTER XXIV

THE morning after Bianca's departure, Alice received a letter from her husband, to say that he would be at home that same day for an early dinner, and that he would be accompanied by Mr Conrad Percy, the son of his old friend.

Alice's first thought was, to rejoice that Bianca was safely out of the way, for she felt, in an instant, the dislike her husband would have to coming in contact with such a questionable style of acquaintance. Alice was good, kind, affectionate, and devoted in an eminent degree, but she was utterly destitute of moral courage. She had an intense horror of being *blamed*. Her husband's approaching return made her think of Bianca with fear, and she almost wished her whole acquaintance and connexion with her could be blotted out. Not that her *own* feelings were changed, but she had begun to look on the matter with his eyes. Then she began to think anxiously on what she should order for dinner; and whether her house and household would suit the fastidious taste of a Londoner. She had always heard Bryant speak with great respect of Mr Percy, senior, and incidentally of the style in which he lived, and the perfect order of his household. Alice fancied that Mr Conrad Percy, his son, would be a milder emanation of the same perfections.

Conrad's father was a distinguished barrister, in great practice, with a handsome private fortune of his own; he was a hard, rigid, tyrannical man; he talked a great deal about justice and mercy, 'and love to his species', but he never gave any of the 'species' within his reach any peace, unless they conformed in all things to his will; he preferred giving assistance to those who needed it, in words, rather than any thing else; but his worst enemies were obliged to admit, that he always uttered very beautiful sentiments, in a very beautiful tone of voice. His wife had been many years dead, and Conrad was an only child. After leaving college, his father had him at home to live with him; to be his companion, he said, when liberated from business; but, in reality, not to let him go from under his immediate influence.

His son was his born subject, and could not give notice, like his servants, when they could stand being worried no longer. He gave him a handsome allowance, but kept him strictly dependant upon him. Conrad was studying for the bar (after a fashion), but he had no genius for hard work, and having the prospect of an ample fortune, there was not the spur of necessity upon him, which seems the only condition under which men can achieve any study in this world. He had become a refined, dreamy, imaginative young man; his health was not strong, so that he did not feel his situation so irksome as it would have been to many others; he had a passionate desire to travel, which, however, his father would by no means indulge. It was a severe attack of illness, threatening consumption, that induced his father to consent to his going into the country along with his friend Bryant. The physicians had recommended Naples, but he would hear of nothing out of England.

There is something absolutely intoxicating in the sight of the country, to one who has been confined to a sick room in a town; there is no pleasure in existence equal to it; it is worth being ill to enjoy it. Conrad felt the freedom of getting completely away from his father's control, and gave himself up to a dreamy luxurious stillness of enjoyment. There was a mysterious beauty in the thick leafy trees, the rich green of the leaves and meadows, the soft freshness of the air, and the little gleams of scenery standing here and there, like pictures, out of the wide landscape. Nothing like passionate emotion had ever been aroused in his nature; but it was slumbering, nigh to wakening, in dreams, vague aspirations, and sentiments without shape or object. He was in the calm that precedes the breaking up of the elements. Bryant talked little; he was thinking of his business, and their journey was performed almost in silence. They arrived about four o'clock; Alice was at the door to welcome them almost before the footman had opened it. She was too glad to see her husband, to have much thought for Conrad, though she certainly felt relieved, when she saw an elegant gentle-looking young man, who, in spite of an air of fashion, did not seem as if he would be very critical on her house-keeping, or perceive how inferior she was to her sister-in-law.

Dinner was ready when they arrived, and after a hasty toilet the travellers sat down. There was much for Alice to hear and tell, and she was glad of the presence of another to shelter her whilst she told the history of her *protégée*, and where she had installed her.

'Well, my dear,' said Bryant, when she had finished, 'you know I never object to your amusing yourself, but another time I wish you would pick up your *protégées* in a less questionable line of life. I have an intense dislike to actresses, and all that sort of thing, and should not wish you to become a lady patroness of them. I don't blame you for what you have done, my love,' added he, seeing Alice blush painfully. 'This Miss, whatever is her name, seems an inoffensive young woman of her class, and you can take a box for her benefit and all that, but now she is gone back to her old way of life, let her gently down—that is all I mean, and now let us talk of something else. You must amuse my friend here as well as you can, for I shall be full of business for some days. You had better take a drive to my sister's and show him the place, and then perhaps she will suggest some plan for to-morrow.'

At this moment the head manager of the Works was announced. Alice finished the grapes on her plate, and then rose from table. She felt hurt and discomposed; what her husband had said about Bianca had jarred upon her feelings, and his reference to his sister was enough to ruffle any woman—it was such an instinctive preference of her opinion to his wife's. He did not intend to worry her the least in the world, but men are very clumsy and obtuse in all the complicated and delicate matters of female jealousy.

Whilst she was chewing the cud of her discontent, Bryant entered, followed by Conrad.

'Here, my dear!' he cried, 'I come to install Conrad under your care, for I must be off to the Works with Blick. I have brought something for you too, which I had better give you whilst I think of it.'

He left the room, and shortly returned with a superb India shawl.

'There!' said he, flinging it gallantly over her shoulders, 'I hope you will like it. You once said you wished for one; this was the handsomest I could find. I cannot say I think it pretty, but perhaps you will see more beauty in it than I do.'

'Oh, how superb!' exclaimed Alice, 'and how good of you to recollect what I said so long ago; but I wish you admired it, I should wear it with so much more pleasure then.'

'Nonsense!' replied her husband, 'do not be so childish; if you like it, that is quite enough; and see, when you go to my sister take her this scarf, it will not do to kill her with envy of your Cashmere all at once. Now, good bye, Blick is waiting for me.'

'You will be home to tea?' said Alice.

'No, indeed, I shall not; I shall be engaged in the counting-house till late, so do not even sit up for me—I shall be so uncertain.'

Poor Alice! even the possession of a real Cashmere shawl did not comfort her for being left by her husband, and so immediately after a long absence, to plunge into business. She began to torment herself to discover a reason; first fancied that she had displeased him about Bianca—and then, that he had become indifferent to her. If she had been alone she would have indulged herself in a peaceable fit of crying; but as Conrad was there, she was obliged to postpone it till another time.

Conrad began to find the atmosphere of the house very oppressive, and to wonder what on earth he should do with himself. Alice, by way of conversation, began to express an interest in his health, and to hope it would improve in their fine air; but Conrad had no taste for settling either his own ailment or other people's, and he asked her to give him some music. Alice immediately opened the piano, and played a few slight airs with much delicacy and feeling, but without any pretension to being a fine performer.

'I wish I might invite Bianca,' she exclaimed at last; 'she sings so beautifully, not like any one else I ever heard.'

'Bianca!' cried Conrad, who was lounging at the window; 'what Bianca is that?'

'The young actress I was speaking of at dinner.'

'Oh, I did not catch the name, and am ashamed to say I was not attending, but tell me about her now; if she be the person I mean, she has a mad mother whom she supports.'

'She is the same,' replied Alice; 'and is she not charming? I am so glad to find somebody who feels an interest in her, and to whom I can talk about her. Mr Bryant has such a prejudice against professional people; they seem so unsubstantial to men of business.'

'Tell me all about her,' said Conrad, seating himself beside her work-table, 'and I will wind this silk for you the while.'

Alice soon told him all she knew about Bianca.

'Will you take me to go and see her to-morrow?' said he.

'Why,' said Alice, 'you see I don't know whether Mr Bryant would like me to go; but I will ask him.' And then Alice began to wonder what any of her acquaintance would think, if they should call and find her *tête-à-tête* with a handsome young man; and the bare thought of all they might say, made her feel very uncomfortable.

'What an intensely disagreeable woman!' thought Conrad, wondering at the sudden stiffness of her manner; 'but it is impossible to get on with these provincial people.'

'I should like to go to see her act to-night,' said he, aloud, 'if it will not interfere with your hours.'

'Oh, not in the least,' replied Alice. 'I will order tea directly, as I shall be very glad to hear from you how she succeeds. Poor thing, what a deplorable way of life for her! Is it not? Do you not think it degrading for a woman? I wonder government will allow it!'

Conrad thought any thing would be better than the decent stagnation in which she seemed to live. He did not say so; but made his escape as soon as possible from a *tête-à-tête*, which he felt insupportable.

CHAPTER XXV

BIANCA had often figured to herself the possibility of Conrad's coming unexpectedly into the theatre, and appearing before her, as he had done on that memorable night at the circus; in fact, she lived in the vague hope of seeing him any day; but, on this particular night, she had no fancy or presentiment of what was actually taking place; which shows, that in spite of animal magnetism, every thing befalls us when we least expect it. The play was *Romeo and Juliet*; it was a character with which she could identify herself completely; it was a fine conception, perfectly worked out, for it was not acting, it was her own heart and life she was embodying, and it was to Conrad that all the passionate burning love was dedicated. *He* was the only Romeo she saw—the actor on the stage was only the masque, the lay figure of him whom she addressed. Conrad, all the time, entirely unconscious of this, was sitting, wonderstruck with her genius and beauty. He had become madly in love with her before the end of the first act; and, by the time the curtain fell, he felt almost in despair of ever inducing such a being to listen to him. He was intensely jealous of every man in the theatre, fancying that any one of them might be a favoured lover; in particular, he felt as if he must dash out the brains of a young officer with moustaches, in the same box with him, who was most vigorous in his applause; and who, he fancied, interchanged intelligent glances with her at some of the most tender passages. It was with the utmost difficulty he refrained from insulting him, when he heard him turn to his companion, and say, 'Faith, I'd have no objection to be Romeo to that girl!'

Conrad did not dare, much as he wished, to send a message to her dressing-room, but went home like a man walking in his sleep. He could scarcely answer Alice's questions on his return; but replied, in the most absent manner, at complete cross purposes, refused all refreshment, and very soon requested permission to retire to his own room.

Alice fancied she must have offended him in some way, and began to examine all she had either said or done; but the only conclusion she could come to was, that he was a very strange young man, and that Londoners were always so conceited, and found nothing good enough for them when they came into the country.

'Well, Conrad, how were you pleased last night? What do you intend to do with yourself to-day?' asked Bryant, the next morning, at breakfast. 'I hope you slept well, and found all comfortable.'

Conrad coloured and started; he thought there was a hidden sarcasm in Bryant's speech, for he had not slept at all, but been walking up and down his room nearly the whole night, and he feared his steps must have been heard. Bryant was reading his letters, and did not look up. Alice was pouring out the coffee, and thinking that the new footman did not clean the silver so well as his predecessor. Conrad ate nothing, and thought Bryant would never go. At length, having ascertained that he had finished his third cup, he put his letters together, inquired at what hour dinner would be ready, and told Conrad that if he chose to ride, there was a horse at his service, unless he preferred going with Alice to call on his sister; and then kissing his wife's forehead, with the air of a man not thinking of what he was doing, he left the room. Shortly afterwards he passed by the window, where Alice had stationed herself to watch him, but he did not look up. Alice turned away with tears in her soft eyes— she felt very lonely, and as if she were of no value to any body.

Conrad sat pinching the ears of Alice's Italian greyhound, to cover his want of confidence to propose that they should go and see Bianca.

'We had better set out soon, as we have some distance to go,' said Alice at length.

'Yes,' said Conrad eagerly, 'or we shall not find her before she goes to rehearsal.'

'Whom? My sister-in-law?' said Alice. 'I was speaking of her; Bianca lives close by, but I fear Mr Bryant would hardly like our calling. He seemed quite impatient this morning when I began to mention her.'

Conrad was in despair. 'You forget,' said he, 'that I am an old friend, and have a right to congratulate her, and perhaps she would not like to receive me if I went alone.'

'I don't know what to say,' began Alice.

'My dear Mrs Bryant,' interrupted Conrad, nearly twisting the dog's ear off as he spoke, which shrieked dismally and ran to his mistress—'I *must* see Bianca. It is only common courtesy in me to call. If you do not like to accompany me, tell me where she lives, and I will go alone, and you can call for me on your way to Mr Bryant's sister.' He spoke quickly, and almost angrily.

'But there is plenty of time,' said Alice, somewhat surprised, 'I will write her a little note if you will wait a few moments; and there is a book I want to send her, perhaps you will take it.'

Conrad felt ashamed of his warmth, muttered something about the uncertainty of his stay, and whilst Alice went to her writing-table, lounged about the room, took up some of the books from a book society, read the names of the members pasted at the beginning, pulled about the ornaments on the chimney-piece, and thought she would never have done.

'Here is the London newspaper,' said Alice. Conrad took it, and read it, wrong side upwards, for a few moments, and then put it down.

At last Alice finished writing her note; then she read it over, putting in all the stops and the dots that had been omitted; folded, directed, and sealed it. Conrad watched each process with a sort of patient desperation. At length, when he felt that another moment would drive him mad, she gave him the note and the book, but was again going to delay to wrap it in paper.

'Oh, pray let me have it as it is,' cried poor Conrad; 'I cannot bear to carry things muffled up in paper.'

He had still to listen to minute directions for finding his way, and at last narrowly escaped having the footman sent to show him the house. At length he was free. Until he was fairly out of sight, he walked like one pursued; but, as he drew near to where Bianca lived, his steps slackened. His heart beat so violently he could scarcely breathe; his veins seemed filled with lead; he walked several times past the house before he could summon courage to knock; and he was only driven to it at last, by the thought that, if she had to go to rehearsal, he should lose the opportunity altogether.

Bianca was sitting in her neat room, occupied in mantua-making a dress for *Lady Macbeth*, which she had to play that same evening.

A set of zinc ornaments, and a glaring diadem for the queen's costume, were on the table; a stage mantle of crimson velvet, trimmed with gold tinsel, hung on the wall beside the window. Had she known, she would have almost foregone seeing Conrad at all, sooner than have been found by him with these environments. No one could have a keener perception than herself of the tinsel tawdry reality of all stage effects, and no one could loathe the details of her profession more than she did. It required all her imagination and enthusiasm for her art, to carry her through the coarse, gaudy, glaring, accessories. Her own appearance was in singular contrast. She was dressed in a white morning robe, which crossed over the bust, and a purple merino apron marked her round and slender waist (both were the gift of Alice); her luxuriant hair was all gathered in a large knot at the back of her head. She was standing before a glass and trying on the head-dress, when the woman of the house opened the door to say that 'a gentleman was inquiring for her.' She had barely time to take it off when Conrad stood before her! He began at least three sentences without finishing one; his voice died in his throat, and he literally had lost the power to speak intelligibly. Bianca, on her side, was equally discomposed; her face and neck were suffused with crimson—the veins in her neck and temples throbbed almost to bursting, the room swam before her eyes, and she grasped the back of a chair that stood near to keep herself from falling. At length, by a violent effort, she composed herself, and desired him to be seated; and busied herself in sweeping away the work which was encumbering the table into a large work-basket.

'I have brought this note, madam, from Mrs Bryant; I would not have ventured to intrude without her sanction,' said Conrad, at length, hardly knowing what he was saying, and speaking from the very extremity of his embarrassment in the most formal manner.

Bianca felt a sharp pang of disappointment. 'Oh, she sent you!' said she, haughtily.

'Yes—no—I requested—I did not know whether I might venture—' stammered Conrad, 'in short, how could I dare expect that you would receive me—but you are displeased—I wished—I thought—'

'Oh! not displeased,' said Bianca; 'but I felt pained that—'
She hesitated, in her turn.

'Bianca!' cried Conrad, madly, '*are* you glad to see me, or have
you quite forgotten me? I could not help coming to you; tell me,
have I done wrong—will you not speak to me—are you angry?'

'No,' said Bianca, and tears she could not control, fell from her
eyes, through the long fringes that covered them.

Conrad, hardly conscious of what he did, left his chair, and
knelt beside her. The same thought and feeling were in the heart
of both; the barrier between them melted like ice; they themselves hardly knew the words that passed between them; but they
knew that their hearts and souls were fused into one; they were
both wrapped in one intense feeling of content and happiness.

How long they were together, neither knew, until they were
interrupted by the arrival of Bryant's servant, who came to
inquire whether Mr Conrad Percy was there, as his master was
waiting dinner for him. Both started in dismay, when they heard
his voice.

'Heavens!' cried Conrad, 'I have kept Mrs Bryant waiting all
the morning to take me to pay a visit. I was to be back in half an
hour. What am I to say to her?'

'And Heavens!' cried Bianca, 'what is to become of me? I have
missed rehearsal, and not a bit of my dress is ready for to-night!'

But instead of seeming distressed at their lapse from all propriety, they both laughed; for they felt themselves armed against
any sort of evil that could befal them, either now or ever.

CHAPTER XXVI

FOR a whole month, Conrad and Bianca were undisturbed in their dream of happiness; no cloud or shadow rose between them. They saw each other every day; sometimes they walked together; sometimes he sat with her in her lodgings; till the country people, and the people of the house, and the people at the theatre, all had their own version of the phenomenon. Bryant and Alice were the only two persons in the neighbourhood who had not heard of the scandal, except the parties most nearly concerned, Conrad and Bianca themselves. But if 'thrice is he armed who hath his quarrel just',* seven times are those armed against scandal who have no idea they are giving rise to it. To both Bianca and Conrad, it seemed the most natural thing in the world to be together every instant of time they could command; the only strange thing was to separate at all. Luckily for Bianca, she was now so indispensable at the theatre, that neither manager, treasurer, nor underlings, dared to say any thing likely to vex her. She was treated outwardly with the most profound respect.

'It is a comfort,' said Mr Montague St Leger one day, 'to see that the "icicle of Dian's temple"* has melted at last, like other mortal frost work,—and what airs the minx used to give herself!'

'Well,' rejoined his companion (Bianca's old enemy, the treasurer)

> 'It soothes the awkward squad of the rejected
> To find how very badly she's selected.'*

'If she had tried she could not have found a more insignificant, ordinary fellow than this young puppy.'

'I wonder if he intends to marry her,' said Mr St Leger.

'She is quite capable of trying to take him in,' replied the other. 'Who is he at all, do you know? it would be only right to give his friends a hint of what he is after.'

'So it would,' rejoined Mr Montague, setting his stock. 'Find out about him, and let us send a letter "from an unknown friend", to spoil my lady's ambitious game.'

'Oh, I'll soon find out all about him, never fear.—Ah, my dear girl, how late you are!' said he, suddenly breaking off, and addressing Bianca who just then entered, in the most coaxing tone. 'We are all waiting for you, but you are quite a sultana, and have your own way completely.'

Bianca gave a contemptuous shrug, and without deigning a reply, began her business.

Two days after the above conversation, old Mr Percy found amongst his letters one couched in most ominous language, warning him to lose no time in saving his son from the snares of an artful woman of loose reputation, an actress, with whom he was completely infatuated, and who was seducing him into every species of vice and extravagance.

Every body professes not to pay any attention to anonymous letters, but notwithstanding they always infuse an unpleasant degree of suspicion. The old gentleman first poohed and pshawed, and declared that writers of anonymous letters ought to be ducked in a pond and horsewhipped—declared to himself that he did not believe a word of it; but in the course of the morning he found himself thinking that he would be all the better for a little country air, and that as he should have to write to Bryant, about a certain case that Bryant had put into his hands, he had much better see him: it would save writing, and be more satisfactory. The result was, that the next day the old gentleman made his appearance at Bryant's house, about an hour before dinner.

Fathers should never risk their welcome by going unexpectedly to see their children who are out on a visit. It is ten chances to one but that their dutiful offspring have fallen into some sort of pleasant mischief, and don't care to be disturbed; and this, without any imputation on their filial piety—it is merely a sense of incongruity. Things that, at the moment before, looked quite right and natural, assume a quite other aspect in the paternal atmosphere. The most innocent, respectable life in the world, takes, as every body knows, a very questionable, shabby-virtuous air, when recorded in a court of justice;—much like the aspect of articles in a pawn-shop, which, no matter how good they may be, always lose the halo of respectability which made them shine in their original sphere.

Alice was alone when Mr Percy arrived. He seemed to her a very nice, mild old gentleman, far more agreeable than his son, and she soon found herself talking away to him with great interest. In the midst of all manner of compliments and honeyed speeches the old gentleman had, without seeming to question her, drawn from Alice a great deal more than Alice knew she was communicating; indeed, a great deal more than Alice knew herself. But knowledge is not knowledge, except to those who can use it; it is a dead stone, unless they have the secret to strike fire from it.

'He goes out fishing, and walks a great deal,' said Alice. 'He says his physicians ordered him to take a great deal of exercise. And then he discovered some old college companion in the neighbourhood, and has been there a good deal. We do not see much of him in the house. I fear he has had rather a stupid visit on the whole. The theatre seems the only amusement he cares much for.'

'Have you a good company here?' asked Mr Percy, negligently.

'I don't know, we so seldom go. There is one young actress, whom Conrad thinks very clever. She is a very respectable young woman, and he made us go, a large party, to see her one night.—Are actresses ever received in society in London?' asked Alice, innocently; but she received no reply, for Bryant, at that moment, came in; and shortly afterwards, Conrad returned, punctual for once, to dinner. His heart misgave him when he found his father had arrived. All his castles in the air—all his dreams of happiness, from being bright rose-coloured clouds, became thick, dark, and portentous of nothing but storm and tempest. The instant he saw his father's face he felt instinctively that he had been making a great fool of himself, and that his father would have no sympathy or mercy on him. Nevertheless, nothing could be more a model of paternal manners to a grown-up son, than the candid *bonhomie* with which the old gentleman greeted him; though, to be sure, he did not know that at that very moment there was a letter lying for him at home, which had passed him on the road, to request his sanction to this 'dear son' Conrad's marrying Bianca, and bringing her home to keep house for them,—or it would have ruffled his temper, politic as he was.

During dinner, Conrad talked a great deal, meditating all the while how he should make his escape to Bianca. He dwelt much on the old college friend whom he had discovered—whom, by the way, he had seen once for a quarter of an hour, and who had all the credit of having his company during his frequent absence and unpunctual returns. It was a great relief to him when, after Alice had withdrawn, his father began to engage Bryant in a professional discussion of the Chancery suit; he was stealing off, when he was called back.

'What do you intend to do with yourself to-night? Bryant and I will soon have finished our business, and I want some talk with you.'

'I thought of going to the theatre, sir,' said Conrad, biting his lip.

'Well, I don't mind if I go with you, and perhaps our lovely hostess will honour us with her presence; but do not go out of the way, for I want you.'

Conrad flew to Bianca with much the sort of feeling that a bird might return to its nest, knowing it had been marked by a mischievous school-boy. However, as his father must see Bianca some time, it was as well he should see her to the best advantage.

The old man easily contrived to learn all the particulars about Bianca from Alice. He was really charmed with her acting; and, on the whole, thought that his son might have done a more wonderful thing than fall in love with her. The next morning he brought matters to a crisis, by requesting his son to take a walk with him. They proceeded in silence for some time; at length, looking at him sideways, he said, abruptly,

'Well, what have you got to say to me?'

Conrad felt as if a pistol had been discharged in his ear, but after a minute he replied,

'I wrote you a letter, sir, yesterday.'

'Ah, well, I shall find it when I get home. Tell me what was in it.'

Who is there that, when a child at school, has not known what it is to go up with a carefully conned lesson barely balanced in the memory, and have it all driven away by the abrupt jerk with which the book has been taken! Poor Conrad could not say one word.

'Well?' said his father; 'come, come, out with it; a bird in the air whispered to me about some little actress down here; what is it all? You have made a fool of yourself, I suppose, and want me to help you out.'

Relieved by the tone in which his father spoke, and finding the ground already broken, Conrad, as briefly as he could related the whole history of his acquaintance with Bianca, from the time of his first meeting up to the present, and concluded by expressing his determination to marry her.

His father listened patiently enough; it was an interesting story, he had quite made up his own mind what to do, and so there was no need of going into a passion; and the game was in his own hands, for his son had no money.

'Well,' said he, when Conrad was silent, 'I do not reproach you; young men will be young men, and must all sow their wild oats. I wish my son to look on me as a friend,' continued he, sentimentally; 'I shall prove myself such. You have done all that can be expected; you have asked my sanction to marry this girl, which of course I shall not give, so she must be content with your honourable intentions. Hark you, Conrad, marriage is a young man's great card in life, and I am not going to let you throw your chance away. You will be in love with a dozen women yet, and as you are not a Turk, you cannot marry them all; so don't want to be a romantic fool and mortgage your liberty for the first that comes in your way. I will forgive you any folly but a foolish marriage. I am not going to have the family disgraced. If you are so desperate, persuade her to go abroad with you, get your folly over, and come back in your senses. But I give you fair warning, that if you marry her, you shall never see my face again, nor have one farthing to keep you from starving; and you know,' added he, in a sharp distinct whisper, and his small keen eyes gleaming as he spoke, 'that what I say, I shall not fail to do.'

Conrad knew perfectly well that his father could not forgive an offence if he would; that his smiling, oily, pleasant-looking, deadly malice, was never to be extirpated when it had once taken root; but though young men are great fools, yet they have a sort of loyalty that prevents their understanding the possibility of deliberate villainy. He dropped his father's arm, and drawing himself up to his full height, he said in a tone as determined as his father's had been:

'I will *not* ask Bianca to be my mistress; it is more than I deserve if she consents to be my wife. If you turn me out of doors, I will seek some means of earning a livelihood, and will ask Bianca to wait till I can support her; and now you have my decision. I am your own son, and you know that I shall keep *my* word, as you will yours.'

The young man was not nearly so cool as his father; his face was flushed, his eyes sparkled, and he concluded with an indignant snort as he strode away. The old man looked after him, shrugged his shoulders, and, putting his hands behind him, walked quietly on. His whole desire in life was, that his son should make a noble alliance, and he was not going to be thwarted in his only wish by the head-strong Quixotism of a youth. At the end of about a quarter of an hour, he retraced his steps towards the house. The wily old man had determined on what he would do. He first ascertained that his son was *not* with Bianca, and then he despatched his own servant with the following billet:

'The father of Conrad requests Mademoiselle Bianca to give him a private interview. It is necessary that it should be quite unknown to his son, as it nearly concerns his interest.'

Poor Bianca was thrown into a state of dreadful perturbation by this portentous note; but returned a verbal answer, and in less than a quarter of an hour Conrad's redoubted father stood before her.

At first Bianca was struck with the smiling blandness of his appearance, which looked, at first sight, like the finest benevolence. To her, Conrad's father was the epitome of all that was grand and heroic.

The old man, accustomed to read faces, saw at once the sort of line he must take. His favourite maxim was, that it is the height of ability to induce people to do right things from wrong motives; but when it suited him, he was equally apt in taking advantage of their best qualities.

He took her hand in the most paternal manner, and gently seating her beside him on the sofa, began a long speech with 'My dear young lady,' and went on with many compliments to her superior understanding and so forth, to tell her that if his son Conrad married her, he would cut him off with a shilling and his malediction! he made a great fuss about his grey hairs; and concluded by appealing to her generosity not to take advantage of his son's rashness and inexperience, but to *refuse him*, which she would find more to her own advantage. It was a very well put together speech, and must have been very moving, for at the conclusion of it, poor Bianca was crying bitterly, whether at its eloquence or at the prospect of giving up Conrad, the reader must judge. The old gentleman also went on to say, with much delicacy and circumlocution, that though there was a prejudice in favour of legal marriage when there were estates, and titles, and noble families concerned,—the absolute necessity of it was lessened when (as in Bianca's case) there was no one but herself in question. This of course could only have been done to try her: such a paternal, excellent old gentleman could never have contemplated his son taking a mistress to keep him out of other mischief, till such time as he had a suitable marriage ready for him. Of course, it was only to see what her principles were like when he hinted that, in his son's peculiar circumstances, she might generously become his companion, and trust to his honour, disinterestedness, delicacy, and a great many more cardinal virtues; though we are bound to say that he did hesitate a little in this last proposal, because he fancied she might get too much influence over him, and he did not feel it would be quite safe to trust his son with her at all. There were advantages and there were disadvantages, and the cautious old gentleman was fairly balanced between them. Meanwhile, poor Bianca, with her face buried in the sofa cushion, was sobbing bitterly. At last she raised her head, and said in a tolerably steady voice.

'I will not be the ruin of one who has been my saviour. I owe every thing to your son. I will not marry him against your consent, if he asks and entreats ever so much, or if I die for it.'

'There is a brave young woman!' said the old man. 'I thank you for your words. You promise me this? You shall have no cause to regret it, or to find me ungrateful. You are very prudent, and you shall find me your friend. I will retire now, relying on your *promise*.'

'You may,' replied Bianca, almost contemptuously.

After his departure Bianca endeavoured to collect her thoughts, to determine on the course she should take. Whilst she loathed the old man for the selfishness and grossness—the heart-lessness with which he would have tempted her to sacrifice herself and her good fame—she still felt that he had a right to object to his son's throwing away all his prospects for the sake of an obscure country actress, without even a name or a relation. She felt keenly the distance of social position between herself and Conrad. Whilst she was bitterly musing, Conrad entered. For some moments they neither of them spoke; at last Conrad, maddened by the sight of Bianca's tears, began in the most pathetic and earnest manner to entreat her there and then to unite her destiny with his and marry him, to prevent the poss-ibility of his father separating them. He told her all that had passed between them in the morning, and concluded by again passion-ately conjuring her to marry him at once, and run the risk of all that his father could or would do.

Bianca recovered all her firmness whilst Conrad was speaking; she had loved Conrad when it seemed altogether hopeless that she would ever see him again in this world; he had not only come back, but had loved her as devotedly and passionately as even her heart could desire. To a true woman, the being loved by the object she has chosen, is the one matter of importance, all other things are secondary considerations; and Bianca having con-quered what to her was as the kingdom of Heaven, was not likely to doubt that all other difficulties would be smoothed in due time; she was so happy and satisfied with being beloved, that even the impending separation could not altogether depress her. Her love was too much a part of her own soul to depend on the accidents of sight, and presence; and besides, he was with her *now*, and she felt very courageous.

'Conrad,' said she, putting one arm round his neck as he knelt before her, 'you must be ruled in this by me. For the present you must yield to your father's will and go abroad. You have always desired to travel. I am not your equal. Your father has every right to object to your making such a match; a sixth-rate actress in a provincial town, a girl without friends, whom nobody knows, almost without a country. I am not fit to be your wife; every one would say the same; he has a right to refuse his consent to such a match; I am of his opinion, and I refuse *mine* also. I will not marry you. Hear me to the end,' said she, as he made an impetuous movement to dash away from her, 'hear me to the end, my Conrad; travel for three years, and *then* come back to me; by that time I shall have worked my way in my profession, and in the world's eye have become more your equal. Then I shall at least have proved myself worthy of you. I believe that God has given me what is called genius. I have power in me to become all I desire; I must prove it and work it out. To you my whole soul is given—you have been the guiding star of my life—you will be its crown and glory. To you I dedicate my life; I am yours whenever you claim me. Your father will then have no right to withhold his consent; but go *now*, dear Conrad, we must both *earn* our blessedness. I *am* yours; you are my god, my religion, my whole life is yours. You have been the one thought of my heart since the day I first saw you; and it is not likely I shall change, now that I possess the priceless treasure of your love.'

Bianca spoke firmly and passionately, and she looked like an inspired sybil. Her eyes were full of ineffable tenderness; she was so filled with hope and conscious power, that she did not see the gulf of separation that was beneath her feet. Conrad could perceive nothing else. He raved, and wept, and reproached; all that the most distracted and passionate love could urge, in the way of persuasion, to make her change her resolution, and marry him in despite of his father, the devil, and all hindrance, were quite in vain.

'Three years, Conrad—I ask only three years; come back and claim me then, and I will have made myself worthy of being your wife, and the world shall not say you are flinging yourself away.'

'Three years, Bianca!' said Conrad, bitterly. 'You know not what you are saying; in three years we shall not be what we are now. I have a presentiment of evil. Marry me NOW, and bind me to you, body and soul, for life. I will work for you, starve for you, love you to all eternity—my whole being is saturated with love for you. Bianca, do not send me away into the wilderness. I cannot answer for the chances and changes that may come upon either of us;—this is a crisis in my life. Bianca, let me stay with you—let me live or die with you. We know not how we may both change, if separated.'

He knelt to her, kissed her feet, and used every passionate entreaty; but to Bianca, when she once saw that a certain course

was *right*, it became a moral necessity to pursue it; she did not feel
to have the option of leaving it;—as he became more desperate,
she grew more calm.

'Hear me, Conrad,' said she, at last; 'I swear to you solemnly,
that I will consider myself as your betrothed wife, before Heaven,
and nothing but your own will can dissolve my oath.'

'You promise,' said Conrad, 'that you will never give me up,
till I give you up, and that will never be till the elements fall
asunder;' and then, taking a signet ring from his finger, he put it
upon her hand. 'Promise me, too, that you always wear this, and
never use it, except to me;—and now give me something of yours.'

'I have not an ornament in the world,' said Bianca, 'except
stage trumpery.'

'Give me this, then,' said he, untying a little blue handkerchief
she wore round her throat—he kissed it, and put it next his heart.
Whilst he was in this somewhat calmer mood, Bianca persuaded
him to depart. They settled that they were to see each other once
more, to take a last leave; but Conrad's father was much too wily
to lose the advantage he had gained.

He saw by his son's look of despair and misery, that Bianca had
kept her promise; he resolved not to risk the failure of her
courage in a last interview. He pretended a sudden call home,
and that very night, without well knowing how it had happened,
Conrad found himself travelling with his father towards London.
In three days he was on his way to Italy. Bianca remained at
home, stunned, and suffering all the reaction of her firmness and
courage; but still she had a secret happiness, a source of life
hidden in her soul, which prevented her from being overwhelmed even with the dead desolate feeling of absence. Conrad
loved her, and she belonged to him; and so long as she possessed
that consciousness, nothing could make her very miserable, and
even her suffering was better than any happiness she had formerly
known; then she had the consciousness of her purpose to employ
all her energy; she was working now for Conrad's sake. She
wrote to him constantly, and had an ever flowing stream of letters
from him, so full of burning love that it is some wonder they did
not set fire to the post bag.

About a fortnight after Conrad's departure, Bianca's friend the
old actor came down, to play a series of his best characters,

previous to taking a farewell of the stage. He was as much her friend as ever, and was wonderstruck at the progress she had made. For Bianca, his coming was about the best thing that could have happened, for it roused her energies and stimulated her intellect, and thus prevented her falling into a state of dreamy emotion.

As to Alice, she often sent Bianca kind presents of any thing she fancied would be useful, and once or twice called to see her; but she was too afraid of vexing her husband to keep up much intercourse with her, and Bianca had too much tact to embarrass her by putting herself in her sister's way.

CHAPTER XXVII

THE engagement of Bianca's friend, the actor, came to a close. He had been much pleased with her. At first he felt almost tempted to take her with him to London, and obtain an engagement for her there at once; but a little consideration induced him to change his mind. Bianca was so patient, so unconscious of the extent of her own powers, so earnest in her endeavours to learn, without any idea of showing off herself in anything she did; in short, possessed so many sterling qualities, which enhanced the value of her genius (qualities, indeed, without which genius cannot 'have its perfect work'), that he determined to leave her to mature her powers in obscurity a little while longer. 'She will learn all the better,' muttered he, 'for not being hampered with the expectations which a promising first appearance always entails; and she will not get warped or mystified by dwelling in the heated atmosphere of her own reputation. She will take all the more permanent rank, and take it at once, when she does appear.' Thus thinking, and thus saying, he still determined to place her more pleasantly, and not to leave her to the tender mercies of Mr Montague St Leger. He was on the point of proceeding to Bath, and a few lines from him produced a reply from the manager, offering a very eligible engagement for Bianca. The letter came the last morning of his stay in——, and putting it in his pocket, he walked towards the theatre to meet Bianca, on her return from rehearsal.

'You must invite me to walk home with you, my dear young lady,' said he, as he met her; 'for I want to have a long talk to you about a great many things. You can spare me an hour, can you not?'

Bianca was almost overcome by this honour, as she considered it, and could hardly find confidence to say how glad she felt.

They walked in silence till they reached the small house where Bianca lodged. It was not her poor little room, that she felt ashamed of showing him, for she would have experienced just the same awe and reverence had it been a palace. The benevolent old actor, who felt towards her as if she were a daughter of his own, was much pleased as he glanced round the room at the modesty and propriety of the arrangements; it was what he had hoped, what he had expected to find.

'Ah, ah, you are beginning your library betimes; what books have we here,' said he, going up to a set of mahogany shelves (Conrad's present), which hung against the wall. 'Shakespeare, of course,—and a good edition; and some of our old dramatists; Hazlitt's Essays; Schlegel's Lectures. How did you get hold of those German translations from Schiller and Goethe?* Your friend has a good judgment,' said he, glancing on the fly leaf of a volume he had taken down, and which opened at 'Conrad to Bianca'. He fixed his eye upon her face, and in a second he had a clue to all that had surprised him in her conduct. He took her hand kindly, and said, 'You must consider me as if I were your father; tell me, are you engaged to that young man?'

'Yes,' replied Bianca, steadily.

'Come, tell me about it. You will not prosper the worse for my knowing, and you may trust my discretion,' added he, smiling kindly; 'tell me your history from the beginning. I feel curious to know the elements that have made you what you are.'

'I will tell you any thing you wish to hear,' replied Bianca; 'but there is nothing to interest any one but myself, and only that, because it is to myself it has occurred.'

'There, there, that will do for a nice little prologue: now begin, for the coach goes at three o'clock, and I must not miss it; so begin, like a good girl.'

With a little hesitation at first, but gaining confidence as she proceeded, Bianca in a quiet, straightforward way, gave her friend the history of her life since coming to England, concealing nothing, not even her belief that she had discovered her half-sister, and her reasons for not claiming her relationship. Of Conrad, she spoke modestly and naturally; she was proud of belonging to him, and did not feel that there was any shame in avowing it; it was the strong rock and safeguard of her whole life; she had dwelt under the shadow of it, and it had kept her from all evil; it was the only life of which she had to tell, and she felt a pleasure in speaking of it.

If all women were not brought up in such unnatural traditions of what is 'feminine' and 'maiden like', and 'sensitively delicate', they would not feel it a bounden obligation to tell lies, and deny an honest lawful affection for a lover. But they are crushed down under so many generations of arbitrary rules for the regulation of their manners and conversation; they are from their cradle embedded in such a composite of fictitiously-tinted virtues, and artificial qualities, that even the best and strongest amongst them are not conscious that the physiology of their minds is as warped by the traditions of feminine decorum, as that of their persons is by the stiff corsets which, until very recently, were *de rigueur* for preventing them 'growing out of shape'. Bianca had been left to nature and chance, and nobody had ever taught her propriety; and that is the only apology we can make to those who consider her candour rather too strong.

'Well, you are a very good girl, and a brave girl, and I come back to all my prophecies about you.—You will be a great woman yet, whether I live to see it or not. I like you for trusting me with all the truth, instead of shuffling, and trying to mystify me with modesty. You have given me a real respect for you, and now,' continued the actor, taking a pinch of snuff out of a superb gold box, 'let us settle a little what you are to do. I could take you with me to London, and get you an engagement there fast enough, and you would make noise there, but I do not think it would be a good thing for you to be embarrassed with the care of a reputation before you are come to the full perfection and maturity of your powers. You must consider your genius as a sacred deposit intrusted to you, to devote to the manifestation of your art, and not for the glorification of yourself; it is of much more importance that you should become perfected, than that all the theatres of the world should see and applaud you as a tenth muse. You are strong and patient, and can *afford* to wait. Your work is with you, and the reward before you; but the work is of infinitely more importance than the reward—let *that* follow in its own season. I look to you with a hopefulness I cannot express in words. You have a higher task before you than merely to make a reputation for yourself. You must not only take the head of your profession, but you must make that profession what it has never been made yet. There are wonderful and glorious resources in our art, and they have never been recognised nor developed; it has never risen to be considered more than an amusement. In mechanical and industrial ages, all the fine arts are apt to be looked on as merely amusing, or at best ornamental. But our art has never, in any age, been made honourable. This actor, and the other actor, have been "ornaments to their profession", and all that; but none have ever loved it for its own sake, and dedicated their lives and powers to its honour, instead of to their own. The stage has had glorious actors, but the art has had no priests; all have wanted to be better than their profession, instead of reverencing it beyond all earthly things. How then should it ever become more than a toy, a vanity? I believe you have it in you to raise it from its meretricious degraded state. It needs to be purified from the sensualism that has defaced it, before it can assume its legitimate rank. This is the idea I would have you keep before your eyes—it is worth dedicating a life for—any one can work from a personal motive, but few have faith enough in an idea to give themselves for it.'

'I hardly understand you,' said Bianca; 'I can conceive no higher motive, or more ennobling, than the desire to become worthy of one we love. I love my profession; I would grudge no labour to perfect myself in it, I would change it for no other in the world. But if there had been no one to whom, in my soul, I might dedicate my efforts, for whose approval I strained every nerve, I could not have worked. I could not work from a mere personal motive—it needed something to take me out of myself to induce me to aspire to excellence. I do not desire success for my own sake: but the motive *you* set before me, does not touch me—does not inspire me; I do not even *feel* what you mean.'

The actor shook his head and sighed.

'Well,' said he, 'we must have patience; go on from any motive you will, it will grow higher and nobler in time; your soul will need a stronger support ere long than the approbation or even the love of any human being. The time will come when you will think on my words. When you discover (as you surely will) that you yourself are of a nature infinitely higher and worthier than him on whom you are lavishing all the passionate treasures of your strong noble soul;—when you discover that the one object to whom you have dedicated yourself—in whom you desired to lose yourself—whom you have made your god upon earth— shrinks in cowardly fear from your entire and perfect devotion, and dare not accept your offering, but reels and staggers under the burden of your perfect love—is wearied and frightened at the very entireness with which you give up your whole soul to him—and you are left lying, fallen, and crushed under the ruin of your hopes;—then in your desolation will arise a conviction of a nobler and purer motive. You will cease to seek the vain stimulant of passionate emotion; you will feel a higher spirit aroused within you. Art will reveal itself to you in all its wonderful majesty, and you will be nobly consoled. You will see that *it* alone is worthy of the dedication of a life time; you will give yourself to it in spirit and in truth; you will feel the glory of being its priestess, and interpreter of its mysteries; you will feel then that the responsibility of genius was not laid on you, that you might lavish it on an individual for the gratification of your own emotions, any more than that you might spend it on your own glorification, to make yourself a name upon the earth. You are consecrated to act a certain part, and must give yourself with your whole soul to the work appointed you. In vain will you make idols, and try to give yourself to them; they will break when you trust to them in your need. But alas! alas! through how much suffering will you not have to pass, before you believe this! I had hoped you would be led by an easier path; but excellence can be perfected by suffering alone.'

He paused. Bianca, awed by his tone of solemn adjuration, remained silent awhile; at length she said, timidly.

'Oh, if you only knew the strength and the comfort the spirit of love gives to a woman, it is that alone which can move her. It has been my own salvation; what but that has kept me from evil? It is that alone which has led me on, which has given me any sort of worth I possess.'

'It will not lead you to the *end*,' replied the other; 'you are trying to compress the god within you, to place it in a shrine of clay, and you will be broken up by it. But, meanwhile, go on as well as you can, I do not desire to make you suffer before your time. My words sound ominous and fearful *now*; the day will come when you will find strong consolation in them. However, I have not settled the immediate business I came for; read this letter, and tell me are you disposed to close with the offer?'

'Oh! how am I to thank you sufficiently?' said Bianca, gratefully, 'this is so exactly the thing suited to me. I feel what you say of London, and I would not desire an engagement there if I could obtain one. I care for perfecting myself in my art more than for any praise or credit. Oh! to be able to realise the idea of which *you* gave me a glimpse when I beheld you acting for the first time! to enter into that world, which as it were lies unseen around us, and bring out thence the thoughts and conceptions that are hidden there, and force them into a visible shape, a bodily expression, I would consent to dwell in darkness my whole life. Let *me* be nothing for ever, if I may only once give shape to those unutterable mysteries which at times seem as if they would cleave my very soul in sunder, with their dumb ineffectual strivings to become manifest. There are moments, when it seems as if I must become *mad*, I feel so incapable to give them shape and utterance; as if it needed that I, myself, should be broken to pieces like a jar of clay, that all which is blindly stirring within me may find way. I feel so weak, and my desires so indefinite; what I want to realise I can nowhere see or grasp, and yet it lies around me like a strong spirit, in whose presence I stand, though I see it not, and I sink down baffled, and weak, and paralysed. I can grasp nothing; I can do nothing,—that which I clutch at so blindly is "high, and I cannot attain unto it!" At those times it seems as if there were nothing but death for me. Oh!' cried she, springing wildly from her chair, and tossing her arms, 'why do you speak to me as if I could do any thing; why do you speak vain words! I do nothing, I can do nothing; I grind my life out, but it will not take the shapes that haunt me: weakness lies like lead upon my soul. Oh, if you knew! if you knew!' said she, sinking on her seat once more, and covering her face, whilst the tears poured like rain through her fingers.

'Ah!' said the actor, deeply moved, 'who that has striven, does *not* know these things? It is out of struggles like these that any achievement must come, conquered and carried captive from the realms of madness and darkness. We must take our reason as well as our life in our hand, and be ready to lose both, if we would desire to attain to that which is invisible. Does the thought of Conrad give you strength at such times as these?'

'No,' replied Bianca, 'I never think of him then, and I have never felt inclined to talk to him of these things;—it is in all my *human* difficulties that the thought of him strengthens me.'

'Well,' said the actor, rising, 'love him as long as you can, and as well as you can. Love is the first strong impulse that moves the soul to aught that is good or great, by taking us out of our-selves;—but it is not the "be all and the end all";—however, I say to you go on; you are of the right order. Do not let yourself be wearied or discouraged; I shall be seeing you again soon, and we will speak more of these things;—it strengthens and comforts me to know you thus. Do not forget to write by to-night's post—I shall quite look forward to acting with you. Now, farewell.'

He kissed her broad forehead, and she heard his footsteps descending the stairs, before she was conscious that he had departed, and then it seemed to her as if she had been cold and thankless in her acknowledgements, and she felt blank and lone-ly—she felt as if she had been suddenly thrown down to the earth after enjoying the converse of an angel, and for the remainder of the day all around her seemed coarse and cold. However, she did as he had desired, and closed with the offer from the Bath theatre, and arranged to join the company after the following week. She also addressed a few lines to her friend the actor, and felt happier after she had expressed the feelings with which his kindness had filled her heart.

Mr Montague St Leger was bitterly chagrined to find that his intended victim was not only escaping from him, but making a move upwards in the world; he would have given the world to find a pretext for preventing her departure; but her engagement was closed. He did not venture to see her; she drew the remain-der of her salary, and lost sight of Mr Montague St Leger for ever!

CHAPTER XXVIII

BIANCA remained nearly the whole of the ensuing three years a regular member of the Bath company; when the theatre was closed she obtained engagements in other towns; her reputation gradually extended, and she became a great favourite. Her old friend had given her one or two introductions, but she made valuable friends for herself, and was received into very respectable society. These were the most important years of her life; she was laying the firm foundation of her future fame; so that when the season of her great success arrived, it was not a sudden and wonderful stroke of good luck, but the legitimate harvest of patient toil. She might possibly have become too self-reliant, too much self-concentrated, had not her efforts been consecrated to a purpose out of herself; it was not fame for *herself*, it was not success for her own sake, that she sought; it was to make herself worthy of Conrad; all her worldly aims centered in him; and this kept her free from any morbid anxiety about her own reputation. She continued what she had been in more obscure circumstances, calm, steady-purposed, and single-minded. When she first entered Mr Simpson's establishment she had only a blind instinct of *doing her best*, and this had grown into a second nature; she did not recognise it as a principle, for she had never been taught to articulate her morality in portable aphorisms, like so many moral cordials, to be administered to her virtues when they seemed drooping. 'The world's foundations deep' are cast on the imperishable granite rocks; but they lie down far out of sight—it is always *very poor land* where the granite comes to the surface. People who are constantly thinking of their principles, and making an audible appeal to them in all they do, lead generally very barren lives: they seldom possess a rich organisation, or a powerful vitality.

Bianca never did *less* than her best; and that was her one rule of action. She had a strong purpose, which saturated her whole life, even to her lightest thoughts and most casual actions.

As to Conrad, the account of him is less satisfactory; for the first six months, he wrote regularly to Bianca, the most desperate and passionate epistles that ever were written since the days of Abelard and Eloïse.* By imperceptible degrees they became less frequent, more reasonable, and less ardent; but Bianca loved too intensely, and was too much engrossed by her own passion, to perceive this change.

'Had he not sworn his love a thousand times?' was the thought that stilled all misgivings: besides, the idea of blaming him never once occurred to her; whatever he said or did became right in her eyes, because it came from him. She loved him with all the passionate concentratedness of her nature. Not one human being in a thousand can bear the weight of the entire and perfect love of another. At first it is very flattering to all the finest vanities of humanity; but after a very little time the burden becomes intolerable, and there is an aggravating sense of responsibility under which the spontaneity of the weaker affection is crushed down. The consecration of an entire existence can be sustained only at the expense of an entire existence surrendered in return: if the return be in any wise less perfect and complete, the heart staggers and bends under the priceless burden; and in the end, by a mere impulse of self-preservation, the object on whom it has been bestowed casts it down, to be trodden under foot or perish by the way, so that he at least may be relieved from it.

In general, both men and women are too much inclined to consider LOVE as a mere amusement; to take it up lightly, under the impression that gratified feeling will be sufficient to carry them to the end; but it is far otherwise. Whoever accepts the gift of an entire and true affection contracts a weighty responsibility.

When Conrad left England he felt little inclination to visit great cities, or to enter much into society. For some months he travelled through the Tyrol, Switzerland, and the north of Italy, making long excursions on foot, and writing to Bianca glowing and poetical descriptions of all he saw and felt. After he had been absent about six months he came to Milan, and he chanced to go to the opera the first night of his arrival. A young singer made her *début* that same evening in one of the minor parts, and he was struck by her real or fancied likeness to Bianca; she was very beautiful, and soon had crowds of adorers; Conrad could not long flatter himself that he was only taken by her resemblance to another; he fell in love with her on her own account, and succeeded in making her his mistress. He still cared for Bianca more than for any one else in the world, but she had ceased to be his sole object; he continued to write to her, but more rarely, and assumed in his letters a mysterious tone of melancholy. In order to engage her sympathy and prevent complaints of his neglect, he talked a great deal of the weight and misery of separation, and the small chance there was of their being reunited for long years; all which, to poor Bianca, who did not know the real state of matters, sounded very moving, and she exerted herself to comfort and reassure him; above all, she filled her letters with the most touching assurances of her own unchangeable affection.

After a while Conrad made the mortifying discovery that his Italian was by no means faithful to him—that she had, in fact, a noble army of martyrs to her charms, to whom from time to time she shewed much mercy. He peremptorily broke off the connexion in disgust; he contrived also just at that time to fall ill of a fever, and he had a long and tedious convalescence. His old tenderness for Bianca revived, and he wrote to her in his old strain, entreating her never to doubt him, but to bear with his moods, and reassuring her against all his apparent coldness, past or future.

Bianca never *had* doubted him; and with this letter to refer to, no future conduct of his could cause her misgivings.

Conrad's father had determined to keep him at a distance until he was quite cured of his infatuation, and therefore turned a deaf ear to all his entreaties to be recalled to England, on the plea of illness; he suggested to his son that as he had taken a disgust to the law, and given up all idea of reading for it, he should enter the Austrian service for a few years. This suited Conrad's fancy, and a commission was obtained for him. He had a vague hope that thereby he might become independent, and obtain Bianca, without waiting for the celebrity by which she was to earn the problematical consent of his father. Had he been as firm of purpose as Bianca, this would have been quite practicable; but his affection had already ceased to be perfect and entire. Then, too, he fell into all the irregularities and dissipations that beset unoccupied young men with a handsome allowance. In proportion as he became more worldly and *blasé*, his ideas about women became coarser and more rigid; and after the fashion of that style of men, he expected them to do all the virtue going in the world, in spite of their own individual efforts to thwart it in all the women they came near. His experience of continental theatres and their *coulisses*★ gave him a great disgust to every thing connected with the stage. He did not actually break off his engagement with Bianca, but he allowed it gradually to fall into abeyance. He expected that, in the course of nature, Bianca would receive other offers, and that, tired of waiting for an uncertainty, weaned by time and absence from her attachment to him, she would dispose of herself, and save a formal rupture; he even wrote to give her a delicate hint, that, much as it might cost him to renounce his right to her love, still his own prospects were so precarious, his father so obdurate, &c., &c., &c. that, although he loved her more than ever, still, if she could find any one who would make her happy, he would stifle all selfish feelings, and love her as a brother; and concluded his letter by a touching picture of the solitary life of exile he was leading for her sake.

Bianca did not at all understand this kind of generosity; the very idea that it was possible for any power on earth to dissolve her connexion with Conrad, was too terrible to think upon. She wept bitterly; the picture of his loneliness and exile touched her kind heart to the quick, and prevented any suspicion of his estrangement. She set all down to his generous delicacy, in not wishing to bind her to an indefinite engagement, and returned a passionate refusal to accept her liberation; at which he shrugged his shoulders, as he read it over a eigar.

Thus was the state of affairs, when one day Bianca was surprised by a visit from her old friend the actor, who, journeying southward, had made a *détour* of some distance, to see how his *protégée* went on.

'I am come to Bath for no other earthly reason but to see you act to-night! Do not I love you very much?—and could any lover of five-and-twenty do more?' cried he, gaily, as he entered.

'You do not take me at all by surprise,' cried she, springing up to meet him. 'Nothing you could do in the way of kindness would astonish me.'

'Well, and how do they treat you here, eh?' said he, seating himself; 'and do you feel strong enough to take a first-class rank in London? but I shall see that to-night, so there is no need to ask you now. How does Conrad go on?'

'His father continues as much opposed as ever; all my hopes depend on my success in obtaining an engagement at one of the great theatres in London—he has not been in England since I saw you.'

Her old friend looked at her steadily for a moment, then took a pinch of snuff. 'You have been a good girl, and a patient one, and you will have your reward. You have lost nothing; you have played for the great game, and that does not bring a quick return, but a lasting one.'

'I can still wait,' replied Bianca, 'a little longer now will be nothing—one can always *go on*; it is the beginning that needs resolution.'

'Well, well, I shall see to-night, and now you are to come back and dine with me. I ordered a nice little dinner to be ready early; and you must tell me all that has happened since we parted.'

At night, after the play, the old man took her hand, and said,

'You are up to the mark; we must get you an engagement in London. You have made good use of your time, and I am quite satisfied with you. I have a piece of news to tell you to-morrow. Good night, now.'

Bianca went home very happy; she seemed to have come suddenly in sight of the realization of all her hopes.

The next morning early, her good genius arrived; he had a letter in his hand.

'There,' said he, 'write at once to——, of Covent Garden,* state what you want him to do, and enclose this letter from me. I think it will help your business. Now, what will you give me for my news?'

'Tell me first, and perhaps—but we shall see.'

'Well then, the father of your friend Conrad is seriously ill. It is very unlikely that at his age he should recover, so I do not suppose he will stand in your way much longer. And what is more, his medical man told me that he had ordered his son to be sent for from Germany, or wherever he may be.'

'How long is this ago?' said Bianca, eagerly; 'he has never written me word.'

'Perhaps not,' replied the other, drily; 'he is such an affectionate son that he can think of nothing else—but I should say that
he had been in England for the last fortnight.'

'I do not believe it—I will not believe it!' said Bianca.

'Well, my dear, you know best. I have given you my authority,
and I have given you my conclusions from the same. My advice
to you, is, that you keep yourself quiet, and let the first thing he
hears of you be an immense triumph; do not let him *find* you
where he *left* you. I take quite as much interest in your success,
as if you were a child of my own; but you must let yourself be
guided by me; when you women get hold of a love affair, you
make that your business, and the most important things which
concern your real interest, you make your play; but you are all
alike.'

'What would you have me do?' said Bianca, impatiently.

'Just this,—make no attempt to communicate with him, press
on your business in London, and do not see him till after you
have made your *début*. You will need all your energies, and if *he*
comes in your way I know how it will be; you will be taken up
with him, and let every thing else go to the devil.'

After a few more words, Bianca promised to follow his advice,
and he left her clinging with intense eagerness to the idea that her
success in London would dissipate the last obstacle between
herself and Conrad, and concentrating all her energies to bring it
to pass.

The information given to Bianca was quite correct. Conrad
actually was in England. He had not written to Bianca, though,
to do him justice, it had several times struck him that he ought to
do so; but, on his arrival, he found his father extremely ill, and
he had quite enough to occupy him, and keep him from doing
anything he had no particular inclination for. About a fortnight
after his return, his father died; and then he pacified his conscience by thinking that after he had arranged his affairs a little,
he would go down to Bath, and take Bianca by surprise.

Bianca all this while was in a suppressed fever with anxiety.

Her worldly affairs, however, went on smoothly enough.

The manager sent a prompt and polite answer to her application, offering to give her at once an opportunity of making her
début, and an engagement to the end of the season if she suc-

ceeded. So far, all was well, and having, with some difficulty, induced her present manager to release her from the remainder of her engagement with him, Bianca started for London, to throw all her hopes upon the cast.

There was a great deal of preliminary worry to be gone through, and several vexatious delays, before everything was fairly *en train* for her appearance. She had chosen Juliet for her first appearance, chiefly, if we are to tell the truth, because she believed it was a play of good omen to her. It was in that part Conrad had seen her, four years ago.

Her old friend was indefatigable. He made her rehearse with him in her own lodgings; gave her every instruction that his genius or judgement could suggest; he had set his heart on her success, and was living his own career over again in her.

Bianca exaggerated to herself the audience before whom she was to appear, and, as the night drew near, felt great trepidation.

'My dear child,' said her friend, 'you have been a very good girl, indeed; very docile in listening to instruction; and now I tell you, that you exceed every thing I had conceived of the part— you are the woman for whom the stage has long waited; whom I desired, but never hoped to see; and now I shall die satisfied. Only be true to yourself; have no fear, for that is beneath you.'

The eventful night at length actually arrived, and Bianca's anxieties centred in one thought—'Would Conrad be in the theatre?' If he were in London he could not be ignorant of her presence, for her appearance had been underlined, in immense letters of every colour, all over London; those who ran could not avoid reading of the 'immense attraction', held forth that night by the theatre of Covent Garden!

The curtain drew up! the play began. She was received with immense applause, and called before the curtain at the end of the first act. The enthusiasm went on increasing to the end, when it seemed to exceed all bounds; bouquets, bracelets, wreaths, every possible missile of admiration were flung at her in profusion. Her old friend met her at the side as she came off trembling, exhausted, and sick at heart.

'My dear girl,' said he, warmly, 'let me thank you for the happiness you have given me this night!'

'Let me go home,' was all the reply he received.

'But, my darling child, you will change your dress first?'

'No, no, no; for pity's sake let me go home—I cannot remain here,' said she, vehemently.

Tenderly, as if she had been a child, he lifted her into his own carriage, which was waiting. He had no difficulty in divining the cause of her suffering—*Conrad had not been present!* He did not speak to her during their course, nor did he attempt to enter the house with her. He pressed her hand affectionately, saying, 'I shall look in upon you some time to-morrow.—Poor girl, poor girl,' muttered he, as he drove away, 'I see how it is going to be! Why will women give in to a *grande passion*, and make themselves miserable; if they did but know it, there is not a man amongst us all who deserves it!'

CHAPTER XXIX

WHEN Bianca's maid entered the bed-room she was startled to see her mistress extended at full length on the floor. Her exclamation roused Bianca, who immediately arose and in a quiet voice desired her to take away those bouquets, and then to undress her.

'I shall just go and put them into water, Miss Bianca, for I never saw such beauties; they are all hot-house flowers, and will set off the drawing-room beautifully.'

'Do what you like with them, only do not let me see them again; throw them down any where, and attend to me, I am not going to wait all night till you have attended to your own fancies.'

The attendant knew Bianca's humour, and began without reply to disencumber her of her stage dress. Bianca did not mean to be unkind when she spoke thus hastily, but the great strain on her energies, day after day, made her irritable; she was often harsh in her manner, and required much patient forbearance; but the woman really loved Bianca, and supported these spurts of temper in silence, never attempting to justify herself; and this patience won more on Bianca than if she had received a signal service. Gentleness and forbearance are never wasted except on cold and *égoiste* natures, who receive all things as their due, and never give but what is of scrupulous measure and temperament, looking with a stony composure to ascertain 'what ought to be expected'; who carefully watch their sensibilities to prevent their boiling over, and who shrink from acting on an impulse because they 'know not to what it might lead them'. Surely, people might as well go to the devil in a fit of enthusiasm as stand petrified into a pillar of salt, for him to come and fetch them, to the great deliverance of the place they have kept in barrenness. People like Bianca love those who bear with them; and to those who love, much is forgiven. People in general are ready to pardon any sin that does not seem as if it arose from want of feeling.

The next morning Bianca's maid entered laden with news-papers and letters of congratulation. Bianca appeared asleep, but opened her eyes as the light streamed through the curtains.

'Well, Margaret, what letters?'

'Oh, a great plenty, Miss Bianca, and I hope they will please you,' said the woman, drawing aside the window-blind.

Bianca looked hastily over the outside of the letters, but none were directed in *his* hand. She then seized a newspaper, not to look at the notice of her own appearance, but in the vague hope of seeing something about *him*. In the account of fashionable occurrences she found amongst many other equally choice pieces of information, that Viscount Melton had been 'entertaining a select party of guests at his seat in Staffordshire'; and in the next paragraph she saw it recorded that Conrad Percy, Esq., returned the day before from Melton Hall, where he had been staying on a visit to Lord Melton.

When people are in an uncertainty about a friend's affection, they catch eagerly at any straw, and try to believe it a firm rock. When those we love have grieved us, or given cause to doubt them, we seize thankfully on the shadow of an excuse, for laying the blame on ourselves. The more we love them, the more passionately do we feel the need to forgive them.

Bianca began immediately to fancy she had been unjust to Conrad, and she was so glad to find he had not been in town that she forgot to reflect how emphatically her own appearance had been announced in all the journals.

There seems to be two separate individuals in our own single embodiment, and sometimes it would be laughable, if it were not sad, to see the pains that one half takes to persuade the other, of something which it desires to find true; but the infidel half is always stronger than the believing one; and we are made very miserable and uneasy by this inner contention.

The day passed slowly over; Conrad did not come, and fevered and weary, she went to the theatre in the evening.

At the end of the first act, she returned to her dressing-room. A note had just arrived; it contained but one line,

'May I see you after the play? I will be waiting for you.

CONRAD.

Bianca went through the remainder of the play as if she had been inspired. HE was present, and it was at his feet she was laying her success. She had worked for long years in the hope of making herself worthy of him before all the world. And this night was, to her, the dedication of herself and her work to him, for whom she had toiled. She rejoiced now, that he had not seen her whilst any doubt hung over her success; it was not an *attempt* she wished to offer to him, but an approved and perfected work. She had been stamped with public success, and now she felt greedy of applause, that she might have her triumph so much the more splendid to fling at his feet. She recollected that night at the circus, when he first witnessed her efforts; she was then only anxious about what he would think of her; but now she had become a finished artist; she knew her art, and was conscious of her own mastery over it; she did not now feel anxious for his praise or admiration for what she was doing, she only desired him to sit like a God above her, that she might lay her gifts upon his altar.

When the curtain fell, she flew upstairs to her dressing-room; but her agitation was so violent, that she could hardly support herself whilst Margaret changed her dress. She trembled so much, that she nearly fell in attempting to descend the stairs.

Good God! men suffer more on the threshold of a long desired happiness, than if they were entering a torture-chamber.

At the stage door Conrad was standing negligently, and looking with a mixture of contempt and curiosity at all that was passing; his head was turned, and he did not perceive Bianca till she was close beside him. He saw she was agitated, and, without speaking a word, lifted her into the carriage, and followed her himself. He, too, was moved at the sight of one he had once so much loved; but he was not prepared for the passionate emotion with which Bianca, suffocated with sobs, flung herself on his breast. He was embarrassed, and almost frightened at the sight of such strong emotion; he had nothing within his own soul to meet it, and he was oppressed with it. Still he caressed her tenderly; but he felt awkward, and feared lest she should discover how much less fervent his feelings were than hers. But his vanity was soothed, and that enabled him to go through a scene which, on its own merits, was very wearisome. 'Half the men in London would envy me, if they saw me;'—and this reflection gave a fictitious value to his position. When a man has once got over his passion for a woman, he finds her demonstrations of attachment very irksome; if they proceeded from the most indifferent woman in the world they would please him better, because there would be at least something open—he is not *sure*, beforehand, that she may not prove the yet unseen queen of his soul: but a woman whom he has once passionately loved and forgotten, has neither hope nor mystery remaining for him; she is a discovered enigma. No matter what noble or precious qualities lie within her—he has explored them, and found they cannot enrich *him*; there is no more to hope, or expect, or discover. Bianca had just one chance of regaining Conrad, and but one, and that she flung away within the first hour of their meeting. Her position was so changed, her whole nature was so matured and developed, within the four years of their separation, that she was, in fact, a new creature. Had there been the least uncertainty, the least difficulty, the least appearance of indifference, Conrad might have been stimulated into a desire to regain his empire over this brilliant creature; but when she flung herself upon him, and let him see so clearly that she was still the same Bianca as of old, that same Bianca of whom he had become weary, and that her affection was as glowing and overpowering as ever, the faint spark was quenched which might have become a flame, and he felt something like displeasure at her, for being more constant than himself. However, he began to express all the admiration he felt for her acting, and to foretell all sorts of glories for her. 'You surpassed all my expectations, Bianca, and realised all that could be embodied in a dramatic Muse. What other actresses may have been in their generation I know not—but you make all who behold you very thankful that they live in this.'

'Oh!' cried Bianca, impatiently, 'do not praise me, *you*—other people can say all they think about my genius, it is for you I have laboured—it is for you I have endeavoured to make myself of some value, to make myself worthy of you. Of what worth is my genius to me except that! Only tell me that you do not despise it, that you love me as you did when last we parted, that is all I care to know. The praise I get from others is for you to put your feet upon—it kills me to be *praised* by you.'

Conrad never liked to give pain. He could do cruel things when his own comfort or inclination were at stake, but he had not nerve enough to give pain before his own eyes; he had, to do him justice, a fund of good-nature. He felt worried to see people suffer, and therefore he did his best now, to say and do all that was expected from him. If she had only shown one tithe of the passion she manifested, it would have been a much easier task; but now he felt all enterprise or enthusiasm choked out of him by her vehemence. Men are beasts of prey in their souls; they desire or value nothing but what they conquer with difficulty, or some sort of violence; and they require to find an antagonising resistance.

When they arrived at Bianca's residence he entered along with her. She had become calmer, and they got on more pleasantly together. There was much to hear and to tell on both sides—he felt really interested in her progress, for it was in some sort the work of his own hands. She gave the history of her life since they parted with great spirit, and it amused him much more than her love. He also had to tell her about himself, and his own doings; but, as might be expected, with great modifications. He entered warmly into all her plans and prospects, and expressed the most zealous anxiety to serve her—in which he was quite sincere; and they talked with all the intimacy of earlier days, but still her eyes hung restlessly and inquiringly upon him. She was thirsting for some definite expression of love, and there was an innate honesty, or perverseness, or devilry in him, which hindered him speaking the desired word. He would really have been very glad to pacify her, but he could not find it in his heart. At half-past eleven he rose to go, saying it would not be right to let her keep him longer; but promised she should either see or hear from him on the morrow.

When the door closed behind him it jarred on Bianca's inmost soul. She felt baffled and disappointed, though the charm of Conrad's presence still lingered round her like a perfume, making her believe, even in spite of herself, that she *must* be happy; she sat for some moments stupified, and gazed with a bewildered look round the room, as if it were impossible this strange blank could remain. 'Nothing, *nothing*, is it all nothing?' she cried, at last, in a tone of such desolation, that it must have wrung the heart if any had heard it. She leaned her head on the table, and a gush of tears, heavy and passionate as a tropical shower, relieved her oppressed heart. Her sobbings gradually subsided, and she arose calm, and even hopeful. 'He does not love me as I would have him,' said she to herself, 'but, surely, now that I have made myself worthy of him, it will not be difficult to win him. Men cannot stand absence like women—he is not to blame.'

CHAPTER XXX

BIANCA'S popularity kept at its high-tide—every phase that worldly prosperity could assume seemed presented to her; a magnificent engagement, praise in prose and verse, until the very flowers of speech drooped and faded under the warmth of flattery. Lovers of every grade presented themselves in squadrons, and she had more invitations to balls, soirées, dinners, déjeuners,* and réunions, of every kind, than she could have attended in a dozen years; for no sooner was it satisfactorily asserted that not the shadow of a shade rested on her 'perfect respectability', than people began without fear to do their share towards rewarding so much virtue, by lighting it up with their 'countenance'. Her personal manners, and extreme agreeableness in conversation, kept up the prepossession in her favour, and gave her a *succès*, as marked in its way, as that she had achieved in her profession; she remained to the end of the season, a lion of the first magnitude.

All this, if it did not revive Conrad's passion, at least stimulated his vanity, and effectually checked any thought he might have entertained about breaking off their engagement. She was so beautiful, and so devoted to him, that he could not help feeling a sort of tenderness for her.

It was really very flattering to find a woman like that, keeping up her attachment to him, through years of absence, much neglect, and (although she never suspected it) infidelities of every kind. Still, LOVE is too grand in its own nature—too divine, no matter how it may be debased, to be kept alive entirely by gratified vanity: it will neither be bribed nor compelled.

Conrad's ideas of the female character had become much changed during his residence abroad, and Bianca was no longer the kind of woman who captivated his imagination. He had become thoroughly disgusted with all that was theatrical, or had a tinge of display in women. He had lived both in Vienna and Paris, and had seen the 'French-novel style of women', as he called them, in every phase and variety, till he was thoroughly wearied, and took up extremely strict ideas of the simplicity, timid innocence, and shrinking delicacy, that ought to be found in women; he had a dove-like ideal, which he thought perfection, and the only woman who would have had a chance of touching his heart, would have been some white-robed vestal whom he should only have been allowed to see at a distance, and who would have had the grace to shrink back with alarmed modesty, had he attempted a nearer approach. The nearest realisation he had ever seen of his present ideas of womanhood, was at a flower-show, a few days after he saw Bianca. A young Quakeress was walking with a stout and stupid-looking old gentleman, who seemed to be her father; any other relationship would have disgusted Conrad's fastidious taste, for he had a notion that women ought only to appear in public with their fathers or their husbands—and this lovely creature, in her delicate bonnet, and shadow-coloured gown, with her complexion of the softest and faintest red and white, and her large timid blue eyes, which sank under his ardent gaze, was decidedly with her father. She had, also, a sweet voice, like the whisper of a breeze; although the only words he caught were 'My father, let us go home.' And the stout old gentleman, roused from his abstraction, perceived, and cast a furious glance at the dashing looking Conrad, who had not then sacrificed his Austrian moustaches, and hastily carried off his daughter to a sober chocolate-coloured chariot, drawn by a single fat black horse, which drove gently off, leaving Conrad perfectly entranced with admiration at the modesty of English women, and the prudent guard kept over them by English fathers. 'Ah,' said he, to his friend Lord Melton, who just then rejoined him, 'if women did but know how much men admire the delicate timidity which makes them look like a half-opened rose, they surely would never give in to that audacious confidence which can meet a man's eye without blushing.'

'And all women are positively to be made after the likeness of your fancy—to please *you!* well, I call that modest and reasonable.

> 'Concluding in my hours of glee,
> This world was only made for me.'

'I went to see Bianca last night; now she seems to me much more like an ideal woman than any little undeveloped girl blushing amid her lilies and roses. What a noble look and presence has

Bianca! something in her voice and manner announces *reality*. What she utters seems only the shadowing forth of what lies within in greater perfection. I would give the world to be presented to her.'

'If you will come along with me now, I am going to see her, and will introduce you; but I thought you had always kept clear of actresses.'

'I have a great dislike to all green-room associates, I dislike intensely what you call "actress women"; but when I see strong genius bearing that indescribable impress of being a genuine utterance from *within*, and not a mere artistic display for the sake of personal honour and glory, I can honour it even though it takes the guise of an actress exercising her profession. But how do you come to know her? you are the first man I have asked who pretends to claim any sort of acquaintance; she might have dropped from the skies for what any one seems to know about her.'

'I got acquainted with her by a singular accident many years ago, and knew her well before I went abroad; all the people who are now applauding her as the last eighth wonder that has come to pass, are only coming round to what I thought of her when she was in a fifth rate position at a provincial theatre; she is a very wonderful woman, and I have the highest respect for her.'

'I am half afraid of destroying the impression she has produced already, by seeing her more nearly.'

'You need not be,' said Conrad; 'you will admire her more in private than on the stage, and you may take it as a compliment that I offer to present you, for I feel as jealous what men come near her as if she were my—sister.'

Lord Melton and Conrad had become acquainted abroad, and had renewed their intimacy since his return; he was about thirty, and had only recently come to his title; he was extremely handsome, with large dark blue eyes, and a remarkably sweet expression of countenance, in spite of a shade of *hauteur* in his manners which at first sight seemed to contradict it. He was a man of very fine character, and a thorough gentleman, which is the highest praise that can be given to a man, for it takes the perfection of many excellencies to make one. He had great reverence for women, and was never heard in his life to say a harsh or a coxcomical thing about them; he was a keen judge both of men and things, and quite as fastidious in his notions as Conrad, though much more candid and charitable in his opinions.

Bianca was alone when they entered; the flash of pleasure that passed over her face and kindled her eyes, as she saw Conrad, did not escape Lord Melton, and did not strike him in the sisterly light which she had been represented in by Conrad. She received him with frank cordiality, and Conrad felt flattered by the impression she evidently produced on his friend, for whose judgment he had a great respect. It had a good result for Bianca, it increased her value in his eyes, and for several days after he treated her with some return of his old manners. If Bianca had possessed a spark of coquetry she would have got on much better, for men are so soon wearied of any thing like tenderness—and of all men Conrad could the least stand being too well treated; he had that perverted love of power which takes the shape of cruelty; he liked to tyrannise over Bianca, to make her suffer; he liked to feel that whilst other men were worshipping and flattering her, he could make her days dark or bright by the alternations of his humour; and he liked to enjoy this power in secret, for he was careful never to compromise himself in the eyes of the world by his attendance on her. Though there were a dozen reports flying about that she was engaged to one person or another, Conrad was never talked about; any superior intimacy was all set down to the score of his being an old friend who had helped her in her career many years before. What his ultimate intentions were perhaps he did not know exactly himself; he was extremely jealous of every man who came near her, and was as arbitrary in the behaviour he exacted from her towards all aspirants to her favour as if he had been her most ardent lover. Like all men who have been lax in their own conduct, he had most rigid ideas of what women ought to be; and Bianca, who had taken care of herself all her life, and had a frank decided manner of bearing herself and expressing her own opinions, was constantly warring against the ideal female standard which he was constantly preaching up to her—being most unreasonably dissatisfied because she continued to be—*herself*!

Her friend the old actor frequently came to her, but it so happened that he always missed Conrad, although he had a great desire to see him. Perhaps Bianca had some share in this, for she did not like any other visitor when Conrad was with her; he, on his side, was extremely glad whenever any one came in to break the *tête-à-tête*. However, one day, soon after Lord Melton's visit, the actor and Conrad met at Bianca's house, and took an intense antipathy to each other. Conrad professed to have an engagement, shortened his visit, and went away with a look Bianca well knew when he was displeased—leaving Bianca very *distrait* and miserable.

'My dear Bianca,' said the old man, kindly but gravely, 'that man will break your heart; it is of no use your trying to make a hero of him, for he is not one, and never will be one, and you will only break yourself against the iceberg of his self-love; he has no idea of any thing higher than himself; he has no notion of any excellence but what pleases him; *self*, with him, is "the first, last, midst, and without end" of earthly things, and as you are not conformed to his image, you will have no comfort with him. I do not deny that he has been of great service to you, that he has in some things behaved very well—but you must have the courage to break with him, or he will work you ill. He does *not* love you, and he is capable of holding you on and on to an indefinite engagement, and leaving you at last when it suits him. It has been my profession always to read indications of character, and I tell you that unless you assert yourself, you will be broken in pieces and trodden under foot by that man; you are standing in a false position with him.'

'Oh, indeed you are judging him harshly—you do not know him,' cried Bianca; 'I am too *exigeante*—I know I am not what he requires a woman to be; but that is my fault for coming short, not his for having a high standard, and he tries to serve me in all practical things. Oh, he is very good;—it is you who do not know him.'

'Bah!' said her friend—'I suppose women came into the world under an engagement to talk a certain amount of nonsense before they die. You are just as great a fool as any woman I ever knew; I will never talk to you again; you must take your own way;—but come! if you are going to the theatre I will take you.'

The next time Bianca saw Conrad, the first words he uttered were—'My dear Bianca, I wish you to get rid of that actor friend of yours—I dislike him extremely; and, considering my objection to being mixed up with your stage people, I think you might keep him at a distance. If my wishes have any weight, you will cease to receive him.'

'But, Conrad, consider how much I owe to him—what a friend he is to me. I am sorry you do not like him, but I shall not give him up; you are unreasonable to ask such a thing.'

'Unreasonable to ask you to cease to receive a man who annoys me! but I see, my opinion has little influence when opposed to your own headstrong ideas. I say no more, except that I do not choose to be exposed to meeting this actor whenever I come.'

Other visitors came in, and put a stop to further words. Conrad did not recover his temper, and Bianca was for once thoroughly provoked at the arrogant and overbearing tone he had assumed; she was far too much attached to her old friend to think of even appearing to yield to Conrad's demand, and she did not condescend to make the least concession, but left him to recover his temper at his leisure. After about a week's sulkiness he came round to his normal state; and finding that there really were some limits to his power, he behaved rather better to Bianca till the end of the season.

CHAPTER XXXI

THE season in London had come to an end. Bianca, and every body, went their several ways to follow their private devices.— Bianca went down into the country to fulfil several provincial engagements. Conrad, as his father's executor, had still much business on hand. Amongst other things he had to see Mr Bryant; with whom, in later years, his father had become associated in many speculations. 'What an odd coincidence,' thought he, 'that almost the first visit I have to pay, after meeting Bianca again, should be to the very place where I first fell in love with her; and the very last place in the world I would willingly revisit. My recollection of those Bryants is unmitigated stupidity.' Nevertheless, he wrote a highly polite letter to Bryant, to tell him that he would come to him for a couple of days. Alice and Bryant were at breakfast when the letters came in. Alice had only a few casual correspondents, and felt little interest in the post-bag.

'There, Alice!' said Bryant, handing her one of his letters—'it is from young Percy, who was here a few years ago. You cannot have forgotten him, for he fell in love, or some mischief, with that actress *protégée* of yours. He will be wiser by this time, it is to be hoped. You see he talks of coming down for a couple of days, and we must be civil to him.'

'Dear! how very tiresome,' said Alice, 'I wanted to go for a fortnight to the sea-side. Your sister will be quite vexed if I disappoint her.'

'Well, my dear, it cannot be helped,' replied her husband; 'he is coming on business, but, if he feels inclined to stay for a little shooting, we must invite him; and, once for all, I wish you to be civil to him.'

'I don't think he will care much for that,' said Alice. 'I think he was, without exception, the most disagreeable young man I ever remember to have seen; he used hardly to speak to me; and then, he always seemed to think nothing was good enough for him. I think I will invite Mrs Frank Greville and her daughter for two or three days. She is a young lady who finds no young man a bore, and then the civility will have been paid, and I shall be glad to have it over. Two disagreeable things transacted together.'

'Just as you please, my dear,' said Bryant, who was now deep in a letter from St Petersburg, about iron rails; 'only it is a pity you seem to find every thing disagreeable you have to do. I wish you could take an interest in something. I think it must be because you do not employ yourself enough—you should walk out more. But I must be off,' continued he, gathering up his letters. 'I have an appointment at ten o'clock. What time do you dine? But no matter, do not wait for me. I know I cannot spare the time to come to dinner.'

'But,' said Alice, discontentedly, as he was leaving the room, 'am not I to see you all day?'

'I fear not; I am so harassed with business—if there were thirty-six hours to the day I should have too little time for the engagements I must complete.'

When Alice was left alone, the tears filled her eyes: she had learned not to let her husband see them, but not to restrain them. 'I am nothing to him,' said she, bitterly; 'nothing compared to his business. If I were dead to-morrow he would never miss me, except perhaps when he had a dinner-party. I am of use to no one, and not a creature cares for me. Bryant could make me so happy if he cared for me ever so little, or if I could do any thing that would please him.'

After indulging herself in these meditations a little, she began to water her plants, and then walked round her drawing-room, to see that all the ornaments and *bijouterie** were rightly arranged; then she had an interview with her housekeeper, and gave her orders, and regulated her accounts; after that she wrote a note, in a beautiful delicate hand, on perfumed paper, to her sister-in-law, to tell her that a dreadfully disagreeable visitor was coming, which would prevent her joining them at Blackpool; after which, she wrote another note to Mrs Greville, inviting her and her daughter to come and stay a few days, adding that they were expecting to see 'a friend of her husband's, a young officer in the Austrian service'. This she knew would secure them both, and she began to be in better heart about the next week's prospect. After she had despatched her letters to the post, as the day was wet, and she could not go out of doors, and no visitor could be expected, she sat down to work at a large ottoman, which had been long on hand; then she practised for a little while some music she had just received, and read *Ernest Maltravers*,* then recently published, and thought that she was much in the situation of Valerie de St Ventadour, although her husband bore not the smallest resemblance. She was interrupted during its progress by the unexpected arrival of Bryant, who had been suddenly called to Liverpool on business, which would possibly detain him for two days. After the excitement of preparing his portmanteau, giving him a hasty luncheon, and seeing him depart, had subsided, she had nothing further to break the monotony of her day. She finished her novel, and, wearied in heart and depressed in spirit, she retired to rest.

Such was the average manner in which Alice passed her days. Her husband lived in a world apart; he loved her more than any thing else in the world; but he was engrossed in arduous business undertakings, which tasked all his energies;—he had no leisure to be a companion to his wife, or to provide her either with occupation or amusement. Any thing she might express a desire to have, he would procure without regard to trouble or expense; but he would never think of it himself. When they were together, he was invariably kind and affectionate, but often abstracted and silent;—the quiet, calm manners, which had at first attracted Alice towards him, became, at length, mysterious and repellent to her; she grew afraid of him, and timid in the expression of her affection; she desired only to discover in what she might please him, whilst he was only anxious that she should amuse herself, and make herself happy her own way. Constantly occupied himself with affairs of deep importance, he had no idea of the weight of *ennui* which was eating out the life of Alice. He was not in the least insensible to Alice's demonstrations of affection, although it was not in his nature to be demonstrative himself; and he sometimes wished his wife to be a little less sensitive and romantic. Above all, if he had been in the least practically aware of the intense mischief of *idleness*, he would hardly have taken the questionable step of inviting a dashing, unoccupied young man, very little younger than his wife, to come and spend even two days under his roof.

If Alice had fallen into the hands of a man who could have attended to her, or if she had possessed a friend who could have obtained a salutary influence over her, she might have become an exquisite character. She had that peculiar quality in women, to receive in perfection the impression designed for them by a mind superior to their own. She would have become all that a superior man could have desired for a companion; she would have reproduced his thoughts and aspirations with a grace beyond his imaginings; she would have been himself, 'in finer clay'. Depending upon him, taking her whole being from him, she would have loved him with a devotedness, the graceful clinging tenderness of which would have prevented any shade of passionateness or sense of violence. She had not it in her to stand *alone*. She was destitute of the strong internal energy which might have supplied the absence of external support,—and she drooped like a delicate plant, weighed down under a treasure of precious fruit, which, for want of due tending, might never come to perfection, but would fall away in unripened promise. Although she had so little active energy, yet she had an immense power of passive resistance to all influences that did not come in the guise of something superior to herself. Nothing coarse, sordid, or vulgar, could touch the indestructible refinement which was the leading quality in her character. As to her *principles*, she had been all her life educated and thrown amongst highly moral and respectable people; but no motive fit to actuate a rational being had ever been presented to her. She had a vague, poetical sense of religion, but no notion of any practical influence from it. What she heard preached in church was too vague and too prosaic to take any sort of hold on her daily life. She had never dreamed of transgressing any of the conventional rules of society, which, to her, were synonymous with virtue and propriety;—the idea of questioning them had never occurred to her. She had a morbid conscientiousness, which made her painfully anxious to do right, without ever feeling satisfied with any of her own actions; but she had not a single strong abiding principle of right or wrong to govern her as by a moral necessity, from which there could be no appeal. She had the instinct of looking to those around her, to know what she ought to do—to her husband especially, who constantly gave her the baffling reply—'Do just whatever you think best!' Such was the aspect of her life and character, at the time circumstances brought Conrad on his second visit.

It was splendid weather, towards the latter end of the month of September, when Mrs Greville and her daughter drove up the avenue to 'Raven Hall', and were received in the hall by Alice with much cordiality.

Mrs Greville was quite the finest lady of Alice's acquaintance, who had, therefore, invited her as the fittest pendant to the very fine gentleman she fancied Conrad to be; indeed, she was very thankful to have any one whom she thought Mrs Greville might feel an interest in meeting, for Mrs Greville had an inordinate desire to know people who moved in rather better circles than she did herself; in short, to rise in society was her ruling passion. She was the wife of the proprietor of extensive glass-works, about ten miles from Alice's neighbourhood; and they lived in great style at an ancient family seat, which had formerly belonged to a noble family, but had been bought some years previously by Mr Greville, along with a good deal of the adjoining land. Mrs Greville was in great hopes that now they had bought an estate, they would come to be received amongst the county families, with whom she cherished an acquaintance, which was somewhat languishing, in spite of her zeal. She was many years older than Alice, cold and repulsive in her general manners, extremely haughty, and not at all handsome; but she dressed with great taste, was well informed, and decidedly clever, and could be very agreeable indeed when she thought it worth her while; she was insatiable after amusement, and every thing or person that could in any way contribute to it was unscrupulously placed in requisition, and cultivated just so far as either chanced to promote it; but none could ever flatter themselves that they obtained the smallest hold on her sympathies. She rather considered it a condescension to visit Alice; but then she lived in a beautiful house, and it was a nice place to bring her friends to when they came to visit her, and Alice was so very elegant-looking, that it gave a good impression of her general acquaintances, when she produced her at her most select dinner parties. Her daughter, Miss Rosina, was a pretty, stylish-looking girl, who had been fashionably educated and finished at a Parisian school, which entitled her to be a leader amongst her own set. Her mother intended her to marry extremely well, by which she understood some one above her in rank, for she always said she 'thought family of so much more importance in these days than fortune, which she supposed every body possessed who chose'.

These ladies arrived and were consigned to their dressing-rooms, some time before Conrad made his appearance; he had grown much handsomer and more manly-looking than when Alice had last seen him. Also, he wore a magnificent pair of moustaches, and he had a firm self-possessed suavity of manner which was extremely prepossessing; he addressed Alice with a frank and yet respectful friendliness, which at once dissipated all her prejudices against him.

Alice always appeared to the greatest advantage when at the head of her table, which is just the position that tries a woman's manners more than any other. Conrad was extremely struck by the grace with which she presided, and the taste which was evident in all her arrangements. Her unpretentious, quiet manner, also struck him forcibly, contrasted as it was with the elaborate self-consequence of the other two ladies; Mrs Greville he disliked intensely the first instant he saw her, and the young lady was far too self-confident, too dashing, and too much disposed to flirt, to meet his views of what was becoming in women: however, she thought him extremely charming, and was very well pleased to find no other young ladies present; for she naturally considered that her mother and Mrs Bryant counted for nothing, and took to him as her lawful prey: there were one or two other gentlemen present, but she did not consider them worth her attention. 'What an exquisite creature!' said Conrad to himself, gazing after Alice, as she quitted the dining-room, 'she looks like a swan amongst crows.'

There was a party in the evening, which went off rather heavily. Mrs Greville did not consider any of them quite entitled to be treated with her agreeable phase, and, therefore sat in what she considered aristocratic dignity and indifference, seasoned occasionally with a little impertinence. Her daughter flirted in the most *prononcé** manner with Conrad, proud of having such a stylish cavalier attached to her side; but Conrad chose to consider himself as in the service of his hostess, and exerted himself most zealously to aid Alice to amuse a set of people, who had no notion of amusing themselves. There was a little music, and some singing; Miss Greville favoured the company with an elaborate specimen of brilliant fingering and execution, and she sang too, on request, with the air of a person who had earned a reputation. All this was very wearying to Conrad; but he was repaid by the pleasure of watching the quiet grace with which Alice moved through these unelastic and unstimulating elements. 'She realises my idea of an English lady,' said he, as he lay down that night.

The next day, they were to go to a dinner-party, and in the morning they were to drive to see some ruins; it certainly was, in itself, a very stupid visit; but Conrad felt it a gleam from Eden, and he thanked Bryant many times, for allowing him to see thoroughly English life, and expressed himself so warmly that Bryant cordially invited him to come to see them whenever he liked, and to consider that there would be always a bed at his service.

Bryant had been much pleased with the young man, —in the executor business between them Conrad had shown great business talent, and so much deference to Bryant, that his good opinion might be a little bribed; but there had been a great friendship between himself and the father, which he felt quite disposed to continue to the son.

CHAPTER XXXII

THE first news Bianca heard, when she came up to town to fulfil her engagement for the ensuing season, was the death of her old friend, the actor, who had expired after a short illness at the house of a friend, with whom he was on a visit. It was a great sorrow to Bianca, who regarded him almost as a father. He left her, by his will, his furnished house at Brompton, and a considerable legacy in money. All the goods of this life seemed to be showered on Bianca at once; and the one thing she once hoped they would be the means of obtaining for her, seemed further off than ever.

When Conrad came up to London, she was struck with the change in his behaviour: he seemed to have taken an intense dislike to every thing she did; he found fault with her attachment to her profession; found fault with her for conversing in company; objected to her manners, as independent and unfeminine; in short, was as harsh and disagreeable as the terms on which he stood with her gave him the right to be. One day, when she complained of his want of common politeness, he replied, 'My dear Bianca, I speak to you, as if you were my wife; there are no grounds of mere politeness between us; what I say to you is for your good, and you would do more wisely to profit by it, than to carp at the mere manner.' Above all, he was jealous and annoyed at the legacy which had been left her; that the old actor was dead, and would never offend him more, was hardly sufficient atonement; he quarrelled bitterly with Bianca, because she took up her abode in the pleasant house that had become her own. 'Fancy ALICE flaunting in a legacy left her by an actor!' he ejaculated to himself. 'What a difference between the two women!'

Lord Melton became Bianca's constant visitor; every day he grew more and more attracted towards her; he was somewhat puzzled as to the terms on which Conrad stood with her, for the latter had not mentioned his engagement to him; but he never for one moment surmised aught derogatory to her honour: he saw several things he could not explain, but he had firm confidence that she had a satisfactory reason for all she did. Each time that he was in her presence, strengthened the empire she had acquired over him. She on her side, admired him extremely; she had a profound respect for his judgment and opinion; his gentle delicate kindness, which was shown in a thousand unobtrusive ways, won greatly upon her, and she felt him a refuge from Conrad's harshness and caprice: but with all that, she never dreamed of loving him, or thought that he cared for her, except as a companionable friend, but went on rejoicing in his society, without thinking of the pain she was preparing for him. One day he came to her, grave, pre-occupied, and evidently out of spirits; after various attempts to cheer him, she said, 'What is the matter with you? you are grown like Conrad to-day—do not grow moody—but tell me what is vexing you?'

'I am very miserable,' said he, 'and that always renders people disagreeable; will you let me ask you one question, and not think me impertinent—so much of my happiness depends on your answer. Will you tell me the terms you are on with Conrad? what *right* has *he* to be as disagreeable as I have made myself this morning? Are you engaged to him?'

'Oh!' said Bianca, with an expression of pain, 'do not try to change the position in which you and I are together; you are the friend I most value in the world. I cannot tell you the source of comfort your friendship and society are to me. You may, per-haps, not think it a compliment, but indeed, I can give you no higher praise,—I always feel with you, as if you were my *mother*; you are so gentle, so delicate, so little *exigeant*, and I feel such a perfect confidence towards you; it will deeply grieve me, if I have deceived or misled you, with regard to my sentiments, and I shall suffer bitterly, if our intercourse is broken up; but you have a perfect right to ask the question, and an equal right to receive an explicit reply. I *am* engaged to Conrad—and was so before he went abroad: he has grown cold and estranged of late; but he has never expressed a desire to be released; as you were his friend, I thought you were aware of it, or I would have told you before.'

'And you, Bianca? do *you* wish to be released?'

'No!' replied Bianca, with an accent that instantly destroyed all hope in Lord Melton's breast.

'Then I have no further business here,' said he, in a voice of deep mortification. 'I thank you for your frankness.'

'Oh, do not leave me in displeasure!' said Bianca, as he was rising to go. 'What have I done to forfeit your friendship? Have I ceased to deserve that you should continue to me as you always have been? I grieve to give you pain; and you know not how thankfully I have treasured you as my best and most valued friend. Be generous—I cannot let you go away from me. If you knew all I am suffering, you would feel revenged for any ill I have unconsciously inflicted.'

Tears filled Bianca's eyes as she spoke, and there was a tone of profound sadness in her words which touched Lord Melton to the heart; and made him think he had been most unjust, selfish, and unkind, ever to have thought of himself, or desired any return from her.

'I know,' said he, in a subdued manner, 'there is nothing in me to deserve you should love me for it; I ought to be satisfied, and feel honoured by the high place you accord me in your regard. Do with me whatever you will, only do not banish me from your presence, nor deprive me of the intimacy I have enjoyed;—let me be your friend—let me be of service or comfort to you, and I will ask no more;—tell me that you are not angry with me, that what has passed will make no difference in your feelings to me?'

'If I were to tell you all I feel for you at this moment,' said Bianca, half smiling, 'you would build all sorts of wild thoughts upon it. I shall hold you very fast now that I have been so near losing you.'

Bianca's servant entered and whispered something.

'I must send you away now,' said she, 'for the Greek dress for my new part is come, and I shall be deep in stage millinery and finery for the rest of the morning; I dare not neglect it. You do not know how much dress has do to with our success.'

'Will you not let me see it,' said Lord Melton, pleadingly, 'and then I shall know that I am reinstated.'

'Well, if you really wish to stay, you may, but I give you notice it will be very stupid work for you.—You can tell Madame Michaud to come in,' said she to the servant.

'I think a passion for dress must be in the primeval formation of a woman's mind, as a geologist would express it,' said she, laughing. 'How do you do, Madame Michaud—how have you succeeded?'

Madame, with many *minauderies*,* unpacked and held up a superb Greek costume.

'Oh, how gorgeous!' exclaimed Bianca;—'madame, you are a woman of genius; if I make an impression in this part, half of it will be owing to you!'

'That is not a correct cap,' said Lord Melton; 'it is very pretty for a fancy dress, but it is not a real country cap.'

'Pardonnez, monsieur,' said madame, deeply offended.

'I have one I brought from Scio at home, that would be much better. Will you let me send it you?' said Lord Melton.

'I shall be too glad of it; I don't like this one myself, but I shall put it on now, to judge of the effect.'

She returned in full costume, looking radiantly lovely.

'Have you a dagger amongst your treasures,' said she.

'Yes, but I will not give it you. I am horridly superstitious.'

'It is not one of my superstitions,' said Bianca; 'and yet I have so many, that I ought to respect those of other people. I think it is very unlucky to give hair; but a dagger is quite an exceptional thing. But now you must go in earnest, I am really going to be busy. You will return soon,' said she, holding his hand as he was departing, and looking fixedly at him.

'*Very* soon,' replied he, with meaning. 'Do not fear me, you shall find me all you would have me.'

He had not long departed, and the milliner was still there, taking directions for another stage dress, when Conrad came.

'Is not that a glorious costume?' cried she, spreading it before him.

'You know how much I dislike seeing the insignia of your profession. The effects are well enough, but I cannot endure to see them in process; you know how completely they are opposed to my taste, and you might have the delicacy to keep them out of my way.'

Poor Bianca looked terribly mortified: she had hoped that Conrad would have admired her in the Greek dress; it was for him alone she wished to look well.

'I ought to have remembered you did not like women's finery,' said she, submissively, and hastened to banish both the milliner and the dress, and all the paraphernalia that had got scattered about; and then came and seated herself, half timidly, beside Conrad, who had the grace to feel a little ashamed of his splenetic humour.

'I am a great brute to you sometimes, Bianca, and you are very patient with me. I do not deserve it—you are a great deal too good for me.'

This was quite true; but Bianca did not believe it. She would thankfully have endured a much worse ill-humour for the sake of such an *amende*★ to make up for it. Conrad continued much kinder and more agreeable to the end of the visit, than he had been for a long time. At last he said: 'I have engaged myself to dine with two friends of mine from Paris. Were you not saying something once about wishing to act in Paris, if a company could be got together? I will make inquiries, if you like, to-day; they will be able to give a good opinion as to your probable success.'

'Oh, how very kind you are!' said Bianca. 'If you do not dislike it, I have it much at heart to go to Paris; but I would be governed by you.'

'Well, I will speak to my friends, at any rate, and then we can talk further; but I must go now.'

He took a very affectionate leave of her, and left her happier than she had been for many days.

Several days passed, and she saw nothing of him. She fancied he was engaged with his friends, and tried to be patient; but it was very hard work. At last, one morning, a letter from him was put into her hand.

CHAPTER XXXIII

BIANCA opened the note with a trembling hand, read it eagerly, and then flung it with a passionate gesture on the floor. Poor Bianca! the note was not what she had hoped for. The perfume of love was not upon it; there was not the glowing out-pouring of a heart to which utterance was an imperious necessity, and yet not expressing, but only giving indication of, the passionate depths within; instead of this, there was kindness, and friendly interest; a letter no third party could judge of, for the eye of one deeply loving could alone perceive all that was wanting. One line in particular maddened her; it was at the end, 'Dear Bianca; be calm and wise: it is all you need, to be perfect.'

'Calm and wise,' echoed she, bitterly; 'how should I become so? how should any woman be so without a strong and noble heart on which her poor beating, passionate soul may fling itself and find rest? how should one thrown back upon herself be calm and wise?'

At this instant Lord Melton entered; she had been so engrossed that she had not noticed his knock. Her flushed and agitated face told him at once that something was wrong, but her habitual control of manner did not forsake her. She welcomed him cordially, and began to converse on indifferent subjects; but her eyes, in spite of herself, kept filling with tears, and there was a touch of bitterness in all she said—a deeper meaning than her words conveyed. Lord Melton was pained to the very soul to see her thus suffering, but he thought it best to take no notice, except by that touching sympathy of manner, that genuine *manly* kindness, for which a woman, at such times, is so grateful. At length he rose to depart, without having obtained any sort of insight into what was grieving her.

'Oh, no, do not go yet,' said Bianca, entreatingly; 'you do me so much good; sit still and talk on to me. I am not myself very amusing this morning, so it's the more charity in you to stay.'

'Tell me then, Bianca,' said he, seating himself beside her on the sofa, 'what it is that is distressing you. I cannot endure to see you suffer; if I am indiscreet, say so, but do not be displeased with me.'

'Nothing new,' said Bianca; 'nothing but what to you would sound very trivial. I have been worried by a letter this morning, it only came just before you arrived, and I had not recovered myself.'

Lord Melton's eyes fell, at this instant, on the crushed letter which had got itself pushed under the table; he knew it was in Conrad's handwriting, and a pang of jealousy shot through his heart.

'Conrad has vexed you,' said he, quickly; 'what has he done?'

'It is a letter about my acting in Paris; he has been taking a great deal of trouble to make inquiries, and get me proper introductions; he has been very kind, but it is not always kindness alone that one requires.'

'No,' said Lord Melton, earnestly; 'there are times when kindness pains more than any ill-treatment. When we get kindness, where we looked for love, it is a desolate thing.'

Bianca did not reply, but she looked up at Melton, and the tears streamed heavily over her face.

'Oh, Bianca, you are wasting all the treasures of your soul on a dream—on a delusion. Conrad is not the sort of man for you to love, he will never satisfy your tender and passionate nature. If he had it in him to make you happy I could resign you to him; for I *love* you, Bianca, and to see you happy would satisfy me. I know it by the misery it gives me to see you suffer. Oh, Bianca, let me love you, let me be your near, dear, friend; command me any way, and let me serve you. But I cannot endure to see you suffer thus.'

'You *are* my friend,' replied Bianca, 'my near, dear, friend, I rely on your affection; it is egotistic to draw, as I do, such strength and comfort from your friendship, from your *love*, for it well deserves that name, and to give you so little in return; but you are the one being on whose firm strength and prudence I rely. It is to *you* I instinctively look, in all my difficulties; *you* to whom I turn in all my troubles. You see,' said she, smiling mournfully, 'it is the old story from the beginning—the one devoted, and the other exacting; living on your offerings, exhaling your love—and glad of it. But I am of no good to you. I feel humbled before you. You are great and magnanimous, and, believe me, I know your worth. Bear with me, continue near me. What would become of me if *you* were to forsake me?'

'Oh, Bianca, you are very merciless. But I will stay beside you, I will never leave you till I see you happy. Command me in any way; I am yours,—body and soul. You do not love me; still, let me feel that I am necessary to you in any way. Let me *serve* you, and that is all the return I ask. Let me feel that *my* being is mixed with yours; in some way, however distant, that my life has not been in vain for you. The day when your happiness will be complete without me, when I can no longer be of use to you, this life will be closed on me for ever; all I live for will have departed from it. Bianca! the consciousness that I can serve you is almost a compensation for your love. You must love as I do, before you can know the blessing it is to give one's life to the one we love. You have been frank and noble, you have used no juggling and coquetry with me. By Heaven! I believe it only makes me love you more madly to see the love you feel for another; it makes you more grand in my eyes. And yet, if I see you WITH him—though you spare my feelings in every way—oh! then I am filled with rage and dumb anguish. I *hate* him, and feel that I could kill him. It is only when he is absent, and I am alone with you, enjoying your dear confidence, possessing your friendship, that I can forgive you for loving him. But here, as I am now, at this moment, I ask no more. I feel that no one else can love you as I do; and that is a consciousness none can take from me.'

Bianca's tears were falling fast. 'Do not make me feel guilty, my dear friend,' said she, taking his hand in both of hers; 'do not sacrifice yourself to one who so little deserves it of you; and yet, God knows, if you were to leave me, nothing could compensate for your loss. I cannot help the past, I cannot recall it; you are every thing a woman could desire; I am a weak, self-willed, passionate woman, whom you might well despise; but I cannot blot out my life. Before I knew you, Conrad was the star of my hope. Listen to me, and I will tell you all. *He* was the secret of my attaining to my present position; it was for *him* I worked, and for him that I aspired; when I was a young, friendless girl, *he* stood beside me in my deepest need. Providence, Destiny, or what you will, threw him in my way; he befriended me when I had no other friend, and it is owing to him that I am not a degraded outcast; he helped me to a position in which I could work my own way; he was my benefactor; he gave me books, and showed me the mine of precious things that lies in them. As a young man he showed a noble and generous interest in my fate, and placed me in a regular theatre, where I might rise to a higher grade in my profession; do you wonder that I loved him? Do you wonder that he filled my heart and soul? I have lived, and grown in my affection for him, till it has become a part of myself. It has been a talisman keeping me from all evil; it has been the secret of my strength. As a young man, of one or two-and-twenty, when I was in a very humble position, shortly after I had entered the regular theatre—fairly started on my career, but had made no way—he would have braved his father's anger, and would have married me. He loved me madly; but, alas! I fear, more from opposition, and the excitement of circumstances, than from a true passion. No matter, *I loved him*, as you love me. I was not what I am now. I felt a consciousness of power within me, but I had achieved nothing; and it would have been suicide in him, dependent as he was on his father, a student in his profession, to have thrown himself away on a sixth-rate actress, however promising she might be. I *refused* him—he knew *why*—he knew my love, for of *that* I made no secret. I told him that I would work my way; and that then, if he pleased, he might claim me. He went abroad, and I remained at home, to work my way up to him. We did not meet again for four years. At first he wrote me letters full of passionate love, but at last they ceased. He gave a prudent reason—that they led to no results, and only unsettled him. He had become prudent, and thought passion a very childish thing. Time passed on, I made a provincial reputation, which is never worth much; but I felt that I had, in some degree, mastered my art, and was fit to appear before a London audience. I came, and succeeded—he was not in the house! From the theatre,—from those deafening applauses, the wreaths, the acclamations when I was called before the curtain, the summit of my life's endeavours,—I came home. Oh, that night! Well, I can suffer nothing worse. I have felt the worst a human being can endure, and—live. I am convinced people never died under the torture: pain kept them alive. I left the theatre, the instant I came off. I could not have remained a moment—I was crushed and suffocated. I came home and flung myself, in my stage dress, just as I was, on the ground; not weeping, but my very heart crumbling away with dry agony—there I lay, all my sorrow crushed down into my soul—so deep, no words nor tears could reach it. After a while, I know not how long, my maid came in laden with the bouquets that had been thrown to me. I rose quite calm and let her undress me. I suppose I must have slept, for I remember nothing, till I saw her at my bedside the next morning, with a heap of newspapers and letters, full of congratulations and praises. I had achieved success—but what was I to do with it? I had never wished it for myself, and to be *alone* at the moment of one's triumph, is more bitter than to be left desolate in one's sorrow. When I got up—I had visitors all day. Nothing but flattery and praise. My despair was in my soul, and had left no traces of its entrance. So I was complimented on my equanimity. They little knew the fearful ballast that kept me down! At night I was to act again. Strange as it may seem, I was the better for it; I felt as if my profession would not be ungrateful for all the life-blood I had spent upon it.

'That night, when I came off the stage, I found in my dressing-room a note from *him*, asking if he might see me after the play. The distance between our hearts was greater than any that had ever been between our circumstances. *I*, who desired to fling myself into his arms, saying, "There, take all my success, all my genius, it is all for *you*—I have worked and succeeded for *you* alone"—felt all my gifts thrown back upon my heart! When I entered the carriage I found him waiting at the door, and he sprang in after me. Oh, how often had I pictured to myself that moment—looked for it, toiled for it—it had been to me a "star hanging in darkest night";—and now I had attained it. He to whom I had given my whole soul was beside me, paying me compliments, saying the most beautiful and graceful things, and in the sweetest voice;—but oh! no genuine tone, not one true word! My god, whom I had adored, had vanished on the moment of becoming visible! Even the friend of my early days was no longer to be discerned;—a gay, graceful man of the world was at my feet! I felt that I had again to subdue him, and I determined I would accomplish it. But, alas! an after-game of love is harder even than an after-game of reputation. I fear I have not succeeded. There is no more to tell you—what I have suffered in hope, fear, and anxiety, is not to be known. I cannot tell what I expect. I am hard, *exigeante*, variable—my temper is failing under this daily torture—he neither comes on nor goes off; he is jealous if I show any attention to others, but I remember his love of old and cannot be satisfied with his homage now. Oh,' said she, shivering with misery, 'I cannot live thus—I must know my fate—I must know his real feelings—I must know the best and the worst. Dear friend, in you, and your clear judgment, I trust to save me from myself. See Conrad, talk to him of me—note his words, his looks, his tones. *You* will not be deceived. Tell me, on your honour, all that passes. If he be trifling with me, I can and will be free from him. I have staked too much, and am worth too much, to flatter his vanity. Let me know how I stand in regard to him; in you I shall have no self-deception to fear. You *will* do this,' said she, beseechingly. '*You* will not abandon me, now that I feel sinking?'

She looked so utterly broken and wretched, the touching tone of her voice altogether unmanned him. At that instant, when no disguise remained, under which hope for himself could linger, he felt that he loved her more madly than ever, and could dedicate his life to watching over her. He rose from the sofa, and walked up and down the room. At last, mastering his emotion by a strong effort, he went up to Bianca, who sat gazing vacantly before her.

'I will do all that you bid me,' said he, in a husky voice. 'I will see Conrad to-day. You shall know all.'

'Dear, faithful friend!' murmured Bianca, raising his hand to her parched lips; 'God bless you, for all your goodness to me.'

He pressed her hand violently to his heart, and abruptly quitted the room.

VOLUME TWO

CHAPTER I

LORD MELTON, on leaving Bianca's presence, mounted his horse, and rode towards the Park to meditate a little on the singular commission he had accepted, and to get, if possible, a little composure into his soul.

He did not exactly hope to find Conrad fickle, for he loved Bianca too truly not to desire her happiness beyond all things; but he could not get rid of his human nature sufficiently, to endure any one to do her happiness but himself. With all his loyalty and generosity, he found he had undertaken a task much harder than he had imagined, whilst stimulated by the presence of Bianca, and the sight of her tears. He would have been thankful for an excuse to quarrel with Conrad, and felt for a few minutes as if he could have shot him with great satisfaction; but instead of that he was obliged to go in search of him, speak civilly, and invite him to dinner!—a trial to have ruffled the torpid well-broken nature of any saint, and Lord Melton had never felt so un-saintlike as at that moment. He was savage at himself for having accepted a position of so little dignity; his wounded love for Bianca, his wounded love for himself, his jealousy of Conrad and indignation at his conduct to Bianca, all combined to produce (we are sorry to record so unheroic a fact) a dreadful fit of ill humour—unmitigated by the slightest gleam of self-complacency from the countenance of any of the virtuous motives which had incited him to the undertaking; indeed, for the time being, they were pleased to buffet and torment him, as if they had been so many devils.

With all this, however, he remained firm in his resolution to perform all that Bianca had required; the consciousness that it was for her sake, and at her request, was the only thought that soothed his irritated mind. He was not up to encountering Conrad just then, however; so, turning his horse's head, he put it into a gallop, and never stopped until he found himself near

Wandsworth Common. Violent exercise is the finest thing in the
world for calming mental irritation. Melton felt all the better for
his ride, and returned to town at a more tranquil speed.

On his way home, he called at his club, it being about the hour
when Conrad was usually there. Melton had the comfort of
finding that he was engaged for dinner; and though he agreed to
dine with Melton the day after, still there was a respite.

How was it with Bianca all this day?

For a short time after Lord Melton's departure she felt happier
and more tranquil than she had been for many days; she had
implicit trust in Melton, and she hoped, she knew what, from his
intervention. She was relieved by having found a faithful friend
to whom she could confide her secret heart; the comfort of having
talked over the wearing anxiety which was eating out her soul, to
one who so well understood and sympathised with her, was
inexpressible; and she did not reflect on the horrible pain she had
inflicted on that noble and disinterested nature. Her own feelings
engrossed her; and she could not help pressing heavily on the love
which had flung itself under her feet, to make her way easier.

But this mood did not last long; the intense weariness, and yet
ever shifting restlessness of her sick soul, hindered her from
seeing any thing in the same light long together. She seemed to
herself to be weltering as it were in a quicksand, where she could
find nothing on which to rest her foot; she was worn out with
baffled efforts to find the solution of her misery; her energies
were stagnant; all manner of wild fancies, and fantastic resolves,
exhaled from her dull, senseless heart, and she had no power to
grasp at or grapple with them.

She had no rational expectation of seeing Conrad that day, and
yet she listened to every footstep on the stairs, to every knock at
the door, till she was in a fever of excitement and expectation.
She had ordered herself to be denied to all but Conrad—should
he call—so there was nothing to break in on the monotony of her
day. She attempted to write some letters, but after a few lines
sprang up from the table in a paroxysm of impatience; she sat for
a few minutes with her hands tightly strained within each other,
then starting up, she walked with hurried steps to and fro the
apartment; sharp groans were the only articulation for the agony

of her soul, as she writhed convulsively, like a crushed worm on the couch. 'I *cannot* endure this,' she cried at last, in a quivering tone; 'what *have* I done, what *have* I done, that it should be laid on me?'

In a little while, the paroxysm passed—the tension of the muscles relaxed. A volume of Shakspeare (the same given her years ago by Conrad) caught her eye; on reaching it from the table, it fell, and some flowers dropped out; they were the bouquet he had flung her that night at the circus. The recollection of all he had been to her in those days, all his boyish generosity and delicacy, hardened now into manhood and worldly wisdom, came upon her; his once passionate love, old words of tenderness and endearment, all came back on her parched and burning heart; but it was like those poor shipwrecked wretches, who, dying of thirst, endeavour to assuage it with the salt-sea-water, at the cost of madness. A violent fit of convulsive weeping, which seemed as if it would tear her frame to pieces, followed, and relieved, or rather exhausted her. She fell into a deep heavy slumber, which lasted till her attendant entered to tell her that the carriage was at the door to take her to the theatre.

'Why did you let me sleep so long?' said she, hastily starting up. 'Is it not very late?'

'All in good time; but indeed, and indeed, Miss Bianca,' said the woman, who had been her attendant many years, and who loved her as a child, 'you look more fit to be buried than to go to the play; and then that great party afterwards, you are not fit for it, indeed; do send back word to the party at least, and say you are not well.'

'I wish any body would bury me,' said Bianca, 'and then I could be quiet; what is that you have brought? Tea? put some salvolatile in it.'

'I don't see how you are to get through your work to-night, except by a miracle; you have not eaten this blessed day, since morning; you will just kill yourself.'

'Oh, you will see I shall get through very well, people do not die so easily. Here, whilst I am at the theatre, send and get this prescription made up, and have it ready when the play is over.'

When Bianca reached the theatre she found it much later than she imagined; the orchestra were in their places, and she had to dress in great haste. The necessity for exertion brought back all her energy; as her dressing proceeded her spirits returned, and she was herself once more, or rather she forgot herself in her part. Her character on this evening was a very arduous one, and never had she acted with so much energy; all the passion that was consuming her she poured into her part, and her triumph was immense; the house was nearly brought down with applause; all her private grief was for the moment swept away by the maddening excitement. An actress must in her very essence be of a quick, passionate, and above all, of a mobile temperament; the energy within her must lend itself easily to all forms and expressions; it must not remain locked up in one mode of manifestation. Bianca was emphatically born for an actress, and this stood her in stead now. The play gave a vent to all the unutterable emotions that had been tearing her heart all day; the leaden weight of deferred hope and sickening expectation was melted off, and went to give an intense and passionate meaning to her acting which, perhaps, it had never had before. When at the close of the piece she was called before the curtain, she was in great bodily exhaustion certainly; but, for the time being, not a trace remained of all the dark clouds which had overcast her soul.

Her attendant brought her some refreshment, before she prepared for the *soirée*. Lord Melton was waiting for her in the carriage,—he had been in the theatre; and if he had been in love with her in the morning, he was still more madly enamoured to-night; she seemed to him little less than divine.

An actress's triumph is certainly made visible and tangible, is brought home to her senses in a vivid manner that no other profession admits of; her influence may be short-lived, but it is an infatuation whilst it lasts; and to feel that she is exercising 'sovereign sway and masterdom' over a whole assembly, wielding their souls as she chooses, producing what emotions she will, playing upon them as upon some curious instrument, is like being possessed of a magician's power; the fruits of her successes are all paid into her hand, she, as it were, receives ready money for her genius. True, there is rarely fame for her; she leaves no trace behind of what she has been, she has her portion of goods in *this* world; but then that present moment is well filled up, and it is only in sorrow and disappointment that one clings to the future. Bianca was by no means insensible of her own power; she saw the effect she had produced on Melton, and she enjoyed it; besides, it seemed a good omen to her heart.

'I could not,' said he, as they drove along, 'do your bidding to-day; he was engaged—I shall see him to-morrow. Oh, Bianca! Bianca!' exclaimed he, passionately, 'who can resist your will? You can subdue all men's souls to you. What hope can I have that he is insensible to you? Oh, forgive me, forgive me! You are so good, and I am so miserable; but when I see you radiant and triumphant, I feel thrown to such an infinite distance from you. I could not stay in the theatre to-night; I could not bear to see you. I was killed to think that I could make myself nothing to you, whilst you are the world to me—high as heaven. Bianca! you must be a *man* before you can know the madness of loving in vain.'

'You men have so many distractions by way of compensation,' said Bianca;—'but see, we are arrived—are we late or early? I cannot stay above an hour, I am so weary. Will you see that the carriage comes round?'

There was an immense crush on the staircase, and it seemed a vain attempt to make their way in that direction. 'Come this way,' said Lord Melton, 'we can get to the drawing-rooms through here; I know the house well.' He crossed the hall, and lifting a *portière*,* he led Bianca into a small room fitted up as a tent; two or three card tables were laid out, and the centre was filled to the roof by a stand of costly plants, which surrounded a small fountain. No one was to be seen as they entered.

'Let us rest here a little while,' said Bianca, 'it will not be so pleasant when we get up stairs, and if there be such a thing as a glass of water within reach, I should be thankful for it.'

'Wait here, then, until I return, and I will forage for you.'

'You shall find me here,' replied she, seating herself; 'only don't be gone long—it is not worth taking any trouble about.'

A few minutes after his departure, Bianca heard the sound of voices approaching in the opposite direction. Her heart stood still, as she fancied she distinguished that of Conrad amongst them.

'I tell you, my good fellow, that Bianca has not arrived yet; I have just been through the drawing-rooms. It was a long play to-night; and when she gets here, it will be an hour before she can make her way up stairs, so possess your soul in patience, and sit down to a game of *écarté*;★ there will be ample time before she appears.'

'The *Satirist* says that you are about to marry her—I beg pardon, that she intends to marry you. Is that a truth, *par hasard?*'★

'God forbid!' said Conrad, in an annoyed tone—'it is a report I thank none of my friends for repeating. No, I leave her to Melton; a man with a coronet, and fifteen thousand a year, may afford to marry a fancy wife,—to season the dull and decorous respectability of his position. I feel tempted to no such eccentricity; I should have spoken long since, if I had had any serious intentions.'

'You might have spoken fast enough; but would she have responded, is the question,' said another voice; 'and what may be the fault which your fastidious excellency finds with the charming Bianca?'

'I have no idea of marrying at all at present,' said Conrad, in a piqued tone; 'and when I do marry, I shall choose to have a wife all to myself, and not one whose heart is case-hardened, by having stood a siege from every man about town who has chosen to address her honourably or dishonourably.'

'Aye, it would be curious to calculate the number of stage kisses she had received,' said another; 'how many would you guess them at?'

'Come, come, that is not fair,' said some one, good-naturedly, 'no one ever perceived the least levity of behaviour in her. I never heard even a whisper to her disadvantage.'

'The Bianca is a very good girl,' said Conrad, 'but she is the last woman in the world I would marry. I would as soon take Van Amburgh's half-tamed tigress,★ as a grand high tragedy woman for my wife. Besides, I have a horror of all professional women. There ought to be a law to keep women from getting their own living: there are men enough in the world to work. Women ought to be taken care of, and kept in retirement; they have no qualities which fit them to struggle with the world.'

'Every body knows you to be *tant soit peu*★ oriental in your notions,' replied the voice of the young man who had first spoken, 'and the fair Bianca would not be exactly a promising subject to begin with. *Pour moi,*★ I like a woman with a dash of the devil in her, and able to fight for herself. I would marry the Bianca to-morrow if she would have me.'

'Bravo!' cried Conrad, 'I will tell her so. She will be here by this time, I should think. Let us go.'

The voices ceased; Bianca remained stunned, stupified—she felt turned to stone. Shortly afterwards Lord Melton returned.

'I hope I have not quite tired out your patience,' said he; 'but, good God! Bianca, what has happened?' he cried, shocked at the sight of her rigid and bloodless countenance.

'Nothing, nothing,' said she, in a quiet voice. 'I have only been overhearing what was not intended for me.' She took a glass of water from his hand and drank the whole of it. 'Now let us go up stairs.'

'You are not fit for it, Bianca. Let me take you home. I can call the carriage in an instant, if you wish it.'

'No, no, I tell you, I am quite able to go through my business; only, do you keep close beside me, and do not leave me.'

'But, Bianca, you are ill, you are frightfully pale, there is something terrible in your looks.'

'Is there?' said she, indifferently; 'then the people will feel quite sure that I have taken off my rouge, and think that it does not suit me to go without—come along.'

He led her across the tent-room to the door on the other side. A slight shudder passed through her when she looked at the spot where the conversation had passed a few minutes previously. A card-table was breaking up as they went by, and the people gazed curiously at her.

'That was the Bianca,' said one, when they were gone. 'She does not look nearly so well off the stage as I should have expected.'

'Oh,' replied another, 'they are always so painted, one cannot tell what they are really like.'

'The terrible look' Lord Melton had remarked, passed away before they reached the drawing-room, and nothing but the most ordinary and placid expression remained.

Conrad and his friends had grouped themselves in the doorway to await her coming.

With the most friendly *empressement*, Conrad advanced to her. 'How *very* late you are,' said he, 'I began to fear you would not come. Will you let me present one of my friends to you; he is an ardent worshipper of yours, and a very good fellow beside—MR MARCHMONT, you may present your homage.'

The good-looking young man who belonged to this name, bowed to her; and Bianca recognised his voice when he spoke, as that of the young man who had deprecated the insolent remark of one of his companions. Nothing could be more captivating than the manners of Bianca; nothing exaggerated or overstrained; it was perfectly natural and well-bred; but marked with a peculiar air of kindness and conciliation. A crowd of people soon came round her, and she talked to every one, and smiled and bowed to every one to whom it was needful; but Lord Melton saw the absent look of her eyes, which her smile never illuminated. Every one seemed to do his possible, to say the best possible things. Bianca, who did not in general excel in this species of light skirmish, seemed that evening inspired, and was brilliant enough to have established a dozen reputations.

'You would hardly suppose, to look at her, that she was an actress,' whispered the young man who had been presented by Conrad.

'But she *is* one, nevertheless,' said Conrad.

At length the crowd began to disperse, and Bianca rose to go; Conrad pressed forward to offer his arm, but she had already accepted that of Lord Melton. Conrad, however, followed her to the carriage, and seemed extremely anxious about the adjustment of her shawl, expressing great solicitude about her exposure to the night air. This last incident, was the crowning drop in poor Bianca's cup that night; but she wished him good night in a steady voice, and then fell back fainting in her carriage.

CHAPTER II

EARLY the next morning, Lord Melton received the following note from Bianca. It was scarcely legible:

DEAR KIND FRIEND,

I am better this morning, but dreadfully weak. I cannot see even you, for I must get myself up for to-night; it is a new play, and there is no help for it. Take no more trouble about what I requested yesterday. I know all I need to know.

What a blessing it is we cannot be defrauded out of death; that is a rest that will not fail us. God bless you.

BIANCA.

Lord Melton guessed every thing, and was ashamed of himself to find that his secret feeling was a flash of gladness; he did all he could to suppress it; but there it was in spite of him, for he felt convinced that the real live Conrad was not his rival; that he was only a phantom dressed by Bianca's imagination, which must fade 'into the light of common day',* and he loved Bianca deeply enough to have patience; he could have waited seven years, like Jacob, and found them as seven days* now that for the first time he had a hope for himself. He forgot, meanwhile, how poor Bianca was suffering; but our own personality sits closer to us than any other feeling; no generosity can enable us to get rid of it; our 'self-negation' is at best but a generous fiction, by means of which we try to love some neighbour better than ourselves; but it will not do; when that neighbour comes into collision with our self, our feelings take part with our self directly; we can love those who combine with us, and enhance our self by reflection, but we cannot feel any genuine complacency for those who cross it. Lord Melton felt in a much better temper with Bianca than he had done the day before.

The day passed dreamily away; he did nothing, and was surprised to find it dinner-time so soon. Every thing stood precisely as it did on the previous day, and yet every thing was changed for him. At the same hour the day before he had nearly killed his horse by galloping it, in a frenzy of love, spite, and desperation;

now, he felt quite up to being glad to see the very man he had wanted to shoot yesterday! Really we are all fine creatures, to be immortal! we ought to be shut up in glass tubes to show the variations of the atmosphere, and so turn our fantastic nature to some purpose!

Dinner passed without much conversation; it is too good a thing to be talked over, and is, besides, a trifling with one's digestion,—the greatest blessing under heaven!

They were alone after dinner; Conrad luxuriously thrown back in a large chair, had lighted a cigar, and, half-closing his eyes, was watching the curling smoke in a state of dreamy beatitude. Melton was smoking too, but pacing restlessly up and down the room.

'Melton!' cried Conrad, disturbed by his companion's movements, 'you are as bad as a wild beast in a cage; and even a tiger is too much of a Christian not to lie still after his dinner. What *are* you in such a peripatetic reverie about? did you quarrel with the fair Bianca last night?'

'Why do you suppose that?' asked Melton, coldly.

'Come, come; every body can see that you are her favoured cavalier, and are the only one who gets a chance of even quarrelling with her, for she plays the discreet princess to a miracle.'

'I have a great respect for Bianca,' rejoined Melton, 'and I do not like—in short, it has always seemed to me a hard case, that professional women should be liable to be pressed as subjects for all manner of idle discourse and speculation.'

'Is she not a free topic—is she not a public character? If we may not speak of an actress, Heaven have mercy on our tongues! What *may* we speak about?' said Conrad, in unfeigned astonishment. 'But I can quite understand your feeling—that is the worst of having a public character for a Dulcinea,* there's no having her all to oneself; the *éclat* that surrounds her is piquant to one's vanity, it is urged on by glare and gas-light, the flourish of drums and trumpets, and the acclamations of the select members of the pit and gallery; and when one penetrates to the goddess, one finds the atmosphere round her in a fog with the sighs of a hundred hopeless passions. The broad fact of her virtue may be firm as adamant, but, for my own part, I would prefer a woman who has been less tried!'

'Do you speak from your heart?' said Lord Melton.

'Certainly,' replied Conrad; 'and now do sit down, for I want to talk to you since we are on the subject. I have the highest respect for the Bianca, whom I have known ever since she was a child. She was my *protégée*; and, as a young man, I was passionately in love with her. It was a mad adoration; I should have ruined myself for her,—if she would have let me,—have braved my father's anger, and married her outright; but she was very generous, as the phrase is; or, rather, she had common sense, for she refused me, confessing, at the same time, that she loved me; and, I believe in my heart, she did. She was full of dreams of distinction in her profession, and promised, if ever she entered on her heritage of glory, to bestow it on me. We parted, I to go abroad, while she remained to drudge at home. But she is one of those obstinate constant ones, who cannot be estranged by absence. We used to write very moving letters to each other for a long while. But though a woman's love may subsist on letters, a man needs more substantial diet; and, besides, she was too vehement; there was no keeping up with her. A salamander would have been scorched by her letters. Her sun put my fire out; a phenomenon, true in morals as in physics. Travelling about from country to country does not tend to make a man constant. In short, my passion for the fair Bianca died a natural death. I still retained a sincere friendship for her, but that is not much. When she appeared in London I was not in the house; but she made a hit, and I went the next night; and really it was superb! and exceeded every thing I expected. It did not make me in love, but in vanity with her; and, by Heaven! I was dreadfully embarrassed to find her so constant. However, I renewed my homage to her. But a passion once extinguished '*ne renaît jamais dans la même place ni pour la même personne*',* as I need not tell you; and we have had nothing but squabbles, and I am tired to death. When I came here to-day, I determined, if I had an opportunity, to open my mind to you. The truth is, I want to get out of it; for, at present, I am neither one thing nor another with her.'

Lord Melton was struck dumb at this unexpected and undesired confidence. His first impulse was to laugh at his own whimsical position; but he was obliged to say something, so he asked—'Do you then dislike Bianca?'

'Far from it,' cried Conrad, 'I have a real respect for her, and would serve her in any way I could; but I cannot be in love with her. I like being in her company, I like talking to her, *mais cela suffit.** Of late years I have got a real horror of professional women. I never would marry an *artiste* of any grade. A woman who makes her mind public, or exhibits herself in any way, no matter how it may be dignified by the title of art, seems to me little better than a woman of a nameless class. I am more jealous of the mind than of the body; and, to me, there is something revolting in the notion of a woman who professes to love and belong to you alone, going and printing the secrets of her inmost heart, the most sacred workings of her soul, for the benefit of all who can pay for them. What is the value of a woman whom every one who chooses may know as much about as you do yourself? The stage is still worse, for that is publishing both mind and body too. Every body may go to the theatre to see an actress, and may pass whatever gross comments on her they will; she has no protection, is open to every species of proposal, and that is not precisely the line of life from which one would choose one's wife. You know I am not straight-laced, but in the matter of matrimony one's respectability is at stake; it is the ground in which one hopes to take root and flourish, and the profession of an actress or an authoress is not the most promising for one's credit; besides they have been too much accustomed to admiration to be able to do without it, or to be satisfied with the mere approbation of a husband. Since I got entangled again with Bianca, I have been thinking a great deal on this subject, and feel very strongly.'

'Then do you mean to asperse Bianca's character?' asked Lord Melton, fiercely.

'By no means,' rejoined Conrad, 'I am speaking of professional women. It is Bianca's misfortune that she is one. I dare say half the men about town could testify to her perfect virtue, respectability, and insensibility, and all that; but I am not in love with her, and therefore my theory and practice are for once in wonderful harmony.'

Lord Melton had hardly been able to contain his rage during this ineffable harangue. 'Why then,' he said, bitterly, 'do you join the chorus of applause that greets her every night, if you despise her for her profession?'

'Pardon me,' replied Conrad, shrugging his shoulders; 'what should we do with theatres and actresses?—we were speaking of matrimony, and I told you my opinion. I would use all my influence to support Bianca; I would stand by her through any attack that might be made on her; I would be her staunch partisan (as I always have been); I would be her steady friend; but that has nothing to do with loving and marrying. I could not love a professional woman, and I would cut my right hand off sooner than marry one; they are all very well in their way, but no wife or daughter of mine should ever, with my consent, form an acquaintance with actress, artist, singer, or musician.'

'Would you then make them Pariahs?'

'No, other people may not be so particular, and the world is wide enough for them; besides, what do women of that sort care for quiet domestic life, such as we all dream of when we marry, no matter what Don Giovannis* we may have been in our bachelor days. It is all very fine talking about liberality and all that, but a professional life ruins a woman as a woman. They all of them follow their profession, not from any high love of art, but to gain their living, and that takes the shine out of any ideal or poetry that might invest their art; they do not believe what they profess to set forth, they do it for a piece of silver and a morsel of bread, and get out of it as soon as they can. Then, consider the fierce passions that are aroused, the envy, the jealousy, the stimulated vanity, the self-love, susceptible almost to insanity; and for what purpose do they pay this fearful price?—To amuse a few hundred lazy people for a couple of hours, who go to see them, not to have any great or high thoughts stirred within them, for one-half of them don't even understand the good things that are said; but to have their *ennui* gently stimulated, or because they don't know what else to do with their evening; and the life and soul of a woman is to be melted down to minister to the caprices of a parcel of people who have a contempt in their heart for the very thing they go and applaud. Can such a mode of life be any thing but a degradation to the women engaged in it?'

'Because the mass of people in the world are stupid, and blind, and coarse, I do not see how that degrades the individuals who make it their business to endeavour to refine and cultivate them,' said Lord Melton.

'First-rate people are, and always will be, first-rate,' said Conrad, 'no matter what their profession; but as regards the stage, of which we are more particularly speaking, the gain is not worth the expenditure of body and soul it requires; people are not to be taught virtue in earnest by seeing virtue in play; they go to be amused, and don't thank you to be any thing else; and I have too strong a feeling about women to desire to see them sacrificed to any such hopeless notions. Men may stand it better, but what is it that professional life does for women? Take Bianca, if you will, as a specimen, she is one of the best, and what has been its effect? it has unsexed her, made her neither a man nor a woman. A public life must deteriorate women; they are thrown on the naked world, to have to deal, like us men, with all its bad realities; they lose all the beautiful ideal of their nature, all that is gentle, helpless, and confiding; they are obliged of necessity to keep a keen eye to their own interest, and, having no inherent force or strength, they are reduced to cunning; their intercourse with others becomes a matter of interest and calculation; they may, and many of them no doubt do, keep virtuous in the broad sense of the term; but, in their dealings with men, they use their sex as a weapon; they play with the passions of men to some degree like courtesans; they use the charms of their persons to carry their purposes; they may have no intention to realise illicit hopes, but whilst a man is not quite hopeless, he will exert himself with a zeal, which, if he were quite sure nothing was intended, would be circumscribed by a very wooden horizon. The soft plastic virtues which are the charm of a woman, are all lost—and how can it be otherwise? Look what a professional career is. It is a life that turns men into tigers—a state of war and fierce struggle; a man must be ready to tread down every obstacle, even if that obstacle were his best friend; he must know no friends, nothing but patrons or rivals;—every nerve strained to the full to work his way forwards to fame and distinction, unless he have, along with that, a fierce and fiery will, an indomitable perseverance, and a stern energy that, as it were, makes him nerved with iron and sinewed with brass, he will be trodden under foot;—it is a state of war without bloodshed; and what ought women to have in common with such a career as that? They have not physical strength for a hand to hand fight; they are incapable of any concentration of energy, or drudgery of hard work; the best results they produce are graceful failures; their beauty lies in falling short, rather than achieving. A woman's work cannot be judged on the basis of its real merit, like that of men; consequently, it never is; there is always a gallant fiction which guides the judgment. All that a professional woman achieves, then, at such a grievous cost of all that is charming in her nature, is only to do what a man would have done much better. The intrinsic value of a woman's work out of her own sphere is nothing, and what are the qualities developed to make up for it? She has got to a knowledge of evil, for she has had to fight against it—to put it aside (if indeed she *have* put it aside); the bloom and charm of her innocence is gone; she has gained a dogmatic, harsh, self-sufficing vanity, which she calls principle; she strides and stalks through life, neither one thing nor another; she has neither the softness of a woman, nor the firm, well-proportioned principle of a man; from her contact with actual things, she is slightly masculine in her views, but the *woman* spoils their completeness; she cannot attain, at least she does not attain, to manly prudence and grasp of intellect. She is a bat in the human species; when she loves, she loves like a man, and yet expects to be adored as a woman—the good gods deliver us from all such.'

'And this,' said Melton, sarcastically, when Conrad paused, out of breath, 'is the inner side of the flattery with which you deify the successful artistes who minister to your pleasures; this is your secret opinion of the women, who, like so many roses, are crushed and exhaled, to produce scarcely one drop of perfume! It is lucky none of them hear you, or we should have the rest of the season turned into a desert. The nymphs of the ballet would be strangling themselves in their garlands; and as to her Majesty's female servants, the singers and actresses, they would be throwing up their engagements at a minute's warning, and Lord Byron's "Curse of Darkness"* would fall on all pleasant things! Try this fresh claret, and tell me, in sober earnest, what women ought to be, and to do, to meet your notions of female perfection. What is the birthright of excellence they lose in making use of the talents Providence may have given them?'

'The sort of woman I dream of for my wife, is, in all respects, the reverse of Bianca,' said Conrad, gravely. 'A rational, though inferior intelligence, to understand me and help me in my pursuits; clinging to me for help, looking to me for guidance; a gentle, graceful timidity keeping down all display of her talents, a sense of propriety keeping her from all eccentric originality, either of thought or deed, her purity and delicacy of mind keeping her from all evil, rather as a matter of exquisite taste, than from any idea of the coarse realities of things, right and wrong. She would shrink from evil instinctively; and it is your pleasure to keep her fragile, graceful nature from being too rudely tried;— you *know* she has no strength, therefore you preserve her carefully from all danger. There is something inexpressibly touching in a true woman's helplessness, her graceful prejudices, and aversion to every thing that is too *prononcée*; she is the softened reflex of her husband's opinions—she does nothing too well. For the woman, whom alone I could love, would be too delicate to desire to attract admiration by her accomplishments; she would be religious, because she could not help it, but she would be alike removed from philosophic doubt or enthusiastic bigotry. A woman ought to have too much taste to be either a sceptic or a saint. Quietly at anchor by her own fire-side, gentle, low-voiced, loving, confiding—such is MY ideal of a woman and a wife; and certainly a professional woman would not be likely to realise it.'

'Bravo,' cried Melton, 'you paint well, upon my honour. I must take a glass of wine to recover from such a vision of exquisite helplessness. Your taste seems a mixture of Oriental notions and European customs. I agree with you, however, that wise guidance is precisely the one thing needed by women, and precisely the thing they seldomest obtain. Women fall very unluckily into the world: they have all sorts of precious qualities and capabilities lying within them, which they know not how to use aright, and it is their misfortune that in dealing with them, *secondary* motives are alone appealed to. Women are put under plenty of conventional restraint, there is plenty of punishment in store if they go astray, but no broad principle is ever given on which they may take their stand; arbitrary enactments, no matter how surrounded by a *chevaux-de-frise* of social excommunication, unless they recommend themselves to the heart and conscience as *in themselves* right and true, will fall down like houses of cards at the first breath of a strong temptation. Women from their birth are kept from that knowledge which contact with the actual things of life alone can give; they are placed in a state of pupillage; and how, I ask you, do men fulfil the task they have arrogated to themselves of laying down the law for women? All women feel their weakness, and wise guidance and government is what they all yearn after. I question whether a woman ever took a lover without a hope to find in him the one who would guide her and lead her into all that it was right and desirable she should become—the one being on whom she might implicitly rely. And what is it that they find, with their incomplete maturity, their undeveloped capabilities, their crude imaginings, vehement feelings, and blind aspirations after something better and stronger than themselves? Poor broken, fluttering things that they are! with indications of whatever is pure, lovely, and of good report, yet without the strength or knowledge to educe meaning and order from all the precious things crushed together and fermenting within them, they *do* need guidance—they call for it earnestly and passionately, and what *is* the guidance they find?—an appeal to their sense of *gracefulness!*—the standard of right and wrong offered to them is the approbation of us men; all their virtues and qualities are degraded into *charms*; no higher motive is ever suggested to them than that of being agreeable to us; they are to be flavoured with virtues and tinctured with accomplishments, just up to the point to meet the taste of the day, but never with the intent to strengthen their own hearts and souls. A woman is a rational being, with reasonable soul and human flesh subsisting, and yet she is never educated for her own sake, to enable her to lead her own life better; her qualities and talents are not considered sacred personalities, but are modified, like the feet of Chinese women, to meet an arbitrary taste. What is the most stringent caution ever offered to young women to lead their life by? It is, "Do not do so and so, do not say so and so, before MEN, they do not admire it." When it was the question about giving women education—"Men do not like learning in women", was the grand argument used. Men are allowed to examine into their religious opinions, to be philosophers, to be sceptics, to be no religion at all, if they please; but has it not been said a million times, "No man would permit his *wife* to be an infidel,"—not because it is a bad thing for her, personally, but because "religion in a woman looks so lovely." And yet a woman has a soul of her own to be saved; but she is never appealed to on *that* ground;—she is exhorted to be modest, "because modesty is her great charm",—and as to female virtue, that is legislated for on the score of its social convenience; and though there is no end to the fine things that have been said in compliment to it, yet they all resolve themselves into that. Then their gentleness and softness are "so lovely", and are preached up in all the books written with the purport of teaching the women of England their duty—and no other motive is ever given. It no doubt is highly desirable that women should be all these things; but what I complain of is, the all–pervading sensualism which runs through the education and legislation men have provided for women. If women were machines, were in very deed our property, then, indeed, all this might answer; but they are *not*, and there is no possibility of educating them up to the point of being conveniently fascinating, and then stopping short;—they have higher qualities existing in them, and unless those qualities are appealed to, you cannot hold them, or influence them; they are *living souls*, and you cannot dogmatise to a *life*, nor cut it out according to pattern.'

'Well, but my dear fellow,' interrupted Conrad, 'the women who follow their own devices, and insist on being strong-minded women, are deucedly disagreeable; and they always end by making fools of themselves.'

'Those women who have strong qualities, decided tastes, aspirations after higher and better modes of life, possessing genius, in short, have no vent for their energy; the vitality that is in them has no adequate mode of manifestation, unless they have a definite profession. If they are in private life, all their energy is flung back upon them; it becomes overlaid with *ennui*, and they sink into apparent indolence and quietness, but a diseased action goes on within—they are restless, discontented, having so much more energy than they can employ; greedy after excitement, no matter of what kind, their talents and their life are fretted away together. In private life, their soul's energy has no outlet but love—love, or religion—and *that* never comes till afterwards; so they throw themselves headlong into a *grande passion*, and go to the devil, if the devil stands in their way. It is a fearful responsibility to have to deal with such women; and your rules of taste are hardly likely to prove rules of life to such fiery natures, in such emergencies. They require a *living principle*, by which they may guide themselves aright. For, depend upon it, to such as these, it is a very small matter to be judged by men's judgment. They have an instinct for right and truth, and nothing but being taught and guided to perceive aright that which "*really is*", can control their passionate wayward nature. Rules and decorums, and the "three thousand punctualities", fall from them like "green withes". A man is never embarrassed by any qualities he may possess; he has always a legitimate channel for their employment.'

'And so have women,' cried Conrad; 'there is always plenty for them to do. Let them find out some man wiser and better than themselves, and make themselves into a beautiful reflex of his best qualities. It would be far better, and more becoming, in a woman, to do this, than to set up, on her own basis, as a superior, independent being. Let her be agreeable and good tempered, and make his life happier. What can she desire better? It is no good, my dear fellow, your going on in this way about the rights of women; in the long run, people always get as much as they deserve; and if women are so ill-treated, as you say they are, it is just because they do not induce any thing better; any way, they were never intended to go blazing about with distracted reputations, as authoresses, actresses, and what not. No good ever came of it yet; they are neither happier, nor more respected for it. If they admired a higher order of character, in men, I suppose men would have to improve themselves to meet the demand accordingly. So what is the good of talking, and wanting to make women disagreeable?'

'It puts me out of all patience,' cried Melton, 'to hear of nothing but the "becoming", and the "agreeable"; there are qualities, even in women, of infinitely more importance. To be "agreeable", is *not* before all things necessary, even in a woman: they never were intended to lead a purely *relative* life; and, until they cease to be educated with a sole view to what men admire, they will never be any better than they are. We require virtue, and strength, and truth, and reality, from women; grace and agreeableness are secondary qualities. I can tolerate a woman with real genius and qualifications for it, following a profession, because, to a degree, it gives her a personal and independent existence.

The objections you raise are accidental, not essential; and I believe in the possibility of finding women who pursue art, for the love of art, and not for the glorification of themselves. What, however, can be worse than the present order of things? As things now stand, in what does the delectable state of "refinement, helpless confiding-delicacy" and all the trash in which women are educated *end?* If a woman has not a family, or a profession, to occupy her time, she either takes to drinking, or intriguing, or to playing the deuce in some way, and all to deaden and distract the *ennui* that eats into her vitality,—vitality which she has never been taught, adequately, to employ; and to which, in the end, Acteon-like,* she falls a prey. Your ideal of a woman would not stand the wear and tear of real life. Weakness is *not* grace, for that requires well-controlled strength. Women have an inner life as real as that of man, as full of struggles and griefs; if they are to be kept from evil, they must have as strong a law of right and wrong to control them; they must not have their moral sense palled and tampered with by *conserves* of morality, or a gospel according to *gracefulness*; there is only ONE law of what is really right, for men or for women, and no second motive, no sense of decorum, will stand either man or woman in stead in the hour of trial. A sense of propriety cannot swallow up temptation. I am not a stickler for the "rights of women", if by those you mean becoming a soldier, or a lawyer, or a member of Parliament. The rights they really do want, though they cannot so well articulate them, is to have a sense of right or wrong inculcated for its own sake, and not to have the life choked out of them by having the decorums and "the becoming" eternally substituted for it—not to have their lives and souls frittered into a shape to meet the notion of a "truly feminine character", but to be allowed to grow up freely, and to have their natural characters developed as God made them. But come, let us go and refresh ourselves by seeing Bianca. We shall be in time for the last two acts. She is a a noble creature, if ever there was one!'

'With all my heart,' said Conrad; 'only, if you had intended to go and see her, you might have followed the considerate example of the old country parson, who shortened his sermon, because, as he told his parishioners, there was to be a bull-bait in the afternoon, and he thought they might like to go!'

CHAPTER III

THE next morning Lord Melton went to see Bianca. He found her just returned from rehearsal, lying pale and exhausted on the sofa. He was pained to the soul by the haggard, wretched expression of her face. She looked older by several years than the last time he saw her. She half rose as he approached, and said,

'You are the only person I wanted to see. Sit down and talk to me; I am wretchedly tired; indeed I am always weary now; but we have just had a three hours' rehearsal, so there is some excuse this time. Were you in the theatre last night? I did not see you.'

'I went late; Conrad was dining with me, and we got into rather a warm discussion. The curtain was just up for the fourth act when we arrived. In that last scene with your children you were very grand; it was like being struck with lightning. I can give you no idea of the sensation you produced on me—you touched a chord that had never been stirred within me before. What a mother you would make!'

'Ah!' said Bianca, smiling, 'depend upon it, a woman has only half her soul developed until she is a mother. No matter how clever or full of genius she may be, there are within her depths of passionate tenderness, strength, and devotedness; instincts, wisdom, which can only be unsealed in her for her children. I felt *that*, last night. I could only imagine what it would be; but I felt there was a secret I could not fathom—a depth of holy mystery into which I could not descend. I have had parts with scenes about children in them before, but I never felt so passionately affected as I was last night.'

'I could not look round,' said Lord Melton, 'but from the dead silence, I should fancy all the house was as much affected as I was myself. Do you like the play as a whole? The papers speak well of it.'

'My own part in it is very strong, and the situations are very effective, but the dialogue is not equal to it; and besides, it was written expressly for me, and that is reversing the order of things. The actor should be made for the play, not the play for the actor, for it then always has more or less the air of being made to a pattern; and when the author has his eye always on the peculiar capabilities of the actor for whom it is designed, he does not and cannot go freely and fearlessly abroad into the wide region of human nature—he never gets off the stage. His work has always an air of the special and temporary, not of the broad, eternal, though ever moving, depths of humanity; the emotions and passions are all more or less stage properties, as much as the dresses and decorations; and therefore I prefer plays which have been written without any special reference to my capabilities.'

'What is the sort of character you like acting the best?'

'I never played Queen Katherine in "Henry the Eighth",* and I have a fancy I could do it well; and if I were a *man*, I should enjoy playing "Hamlet". Oh, you do not know, you cannot imagine, the bitterness of heart, the intense envy I have felt in former years, when a grand play has been put on, and I have felt no hope, no prospect, of getting beyond my own little part of two dozen lines! Oh, the maddening mortifications I have had to devour! I used to beg to have some of the copying of the theatre, it eked out my salary; and you may fancy what it was to have to write out words that burned my heart, and feel all I had it in me to do with them if they had been cast for me. I used to think I should be at the summit of my desires if I might attain the privilege of choosing my own characters. Alas, and alas!'

'Well,' said Lord Melton, 'there is no doubt that it is a privilege, and one that you must rejoice in having gained; power and position are valuable to those who can use them, but they are means not ends; and you are worthy to possess them, for you use them to noble aims and not to your own aggrandisement and glorification.'

'Ah,' replied Bianca, bitterly, '*power* is not what a woman asks—it does not lessen her sufferings, or make her happier.'

'Would you desire to be without sorrow or sufferings,' said Lord Melton, gently; 'and is making yourself happy precisely the highest thing to be aimed at? "Happiness" as "our being's end and aim," has always seemed to me a most "lame and impotent conclusion" for such a noble and mysterious drama as the life of even the most insignificant of God's creatures. As much of it as falls out for us incidentally, we are of course glad to possess; but to make it a distinct and recognised aim, to convert our life's pilgrimage into "a search after happiness", seems to me drivelling—to the last point of paralytic imbecility. What is *life* in its very essence but the *power to struggle?* All the happiness I can conceive a noble rational creature aspiring after, is the privilege of not being taken at a disadvantage; of having the free use of all his faculties: not to be confined or cramped in his efforts, not be weltering and struggling like a strong swimmer in an eddying current, nor embarrassed by being divided against himself, but free to wrestle erect and manful against all the difficulties that beset him. I do not, my dear friend, believe in any state of happiness in which we may sit down quiescent, till we go off into a state of coma; that would be a life-in-death, thickening our souls and stupifying our hearts, till there would remain hardly a step between us and death, as far as any spiritual manifestation went. No, no: believe me, that to possess our souls entire, not to get them warped or crippled by any dispensation that befals; to be able to solve the problem of whatever pain or sorrow we may be called on to endure, and so bring light out of darkness, strength out of weakness; is all that a noble or heroic soul would feel disposed to pray for. To be able to take patiently not only the external accidents and casualties of life, but even the still harder-to-be-endured consequences of our own actions, brings far more real comfort, more tranquillity of soul, than all the panting aspirations after some undefined conjunction of things under which we expect to live in perfect felicity to the "end of a long life", as nursery fairy tales say.'

'Ay, ay,' replied Bianca, mournfully, 'what you say is heroic and manly, and capable of strengthening the soul of those already at ease; but when we are suffering, when more seems laid upon us than we are able to bear, when our very lips are white with the agony within us—at such a time, we can only feel the quivering of our nature, we can only hear the groans that articulate it. However, we need not endure for ever, that is one comfort.'

'My dear, dear friend,' replied Melton, 'I must not have you weak. You must not be faithless to yourself; you are too richly freighted with precious gifts, recklessly to make shipwreck. You are not your own; you have a task to do in this world, and if you neglect it, you will not be guiltless. I am not ignorant of the heavy blow that has fallen on you; but a merely personal grief is no excuse for your abandoning the post in which you are placed,—for neglecting the work to which you are sent.'

'You speak to me, as if I were a *man*,' said Bianca, bitterly: 'what use has a woman for all her gifts, what object has she in all her work, but to centre them in some strong and loving heart; and if she finds not *that*, she has neither gifts nor wisdom. If my "gifts", as you call them, do not seem precious in the sight of him for whose sake I have toiled and aspired,—and in some degree achieved,—of what further use are they to *me?* They have failed me in my need, and are worthless. They have not only failed to win me the love of the only human being from whom I ever cared to win it, but they have actually hindered me, have been the real obstacles which have turned him away from me; and now I hate them, I despise them,—and, like faithless servants, cast them behind me. Do not speak to me of them,—what have they brought but wretchedness and humiliation, masked in success and adulation! You see me here before you, a scorned and rejected woman, knowing myself to be so. I heard from his own lips that he despises me, for the very faculties which have been consecrated to him in my inmost soul; and do you think that, after such a revelation, all the shoutings, and applaudings, and bouquets, which greet me nightly, will not sound in my ears like the acclamations of a mob at the sight of a man in the pillory,—or the execution of a felon, if you will. No doubt we are all equally considered by them—a spectacle, and nothing more?'

'You are speaking bitterly, Bianca; and what is more, you do not in your heart *believe* what you are saying. As an utterance of pain and impatience, it may pass, but it must not be recorded as the deliberate expression of your belief. The opinion of a hundred Conrads, the selfish sensualism which would degrade the race of women down to a mere standard of taste,—considering them, and their gifts and virtues, of value only in so far as they are pleasant and graceful in his eyes, and the eyes of men generally,—cannot make that true which is essentially false. Gifts like yours were bestowed for something better than to make the possessor desirable in the eyes of any individual, no matter how exalted, or fascinating, or excellent he may be. Conrad does not happen to admire women of a marked character, or of distinguished talent; but that does not make them worthless, nor does it alter the fact that you are a woman of genius, of strong energetic character, devoted to an art which has never yet been developed in its highest and noblest capabilities, but has always had the misfortune to be looked upon rather as a vehicle for the manifestation of personal capabilities, and for the acquirement of personal credit, than pursued as ART, containing an Idea and significance far beyond the casual success or talent of its votaries, which are very secondary. That they devote themselves honestly, and with a single-minded purpose, to make manifest, as far as in them lies, the soul, the *Idea* that lies hidden in their art,—to be articulated in the laws and forms of their profession,—and, making it visible to the eyes of men, make it also honourable;—this I conceive to be the true end for which men are endowed. I conceive further, that every man who has received a special power to work in any mode of art (no matter what), has a responsibility not to be evaded,—and he is bound to persevere and work on, through good success and bad success, through evil report and good report, and can be released by nothing but death. If he be a true artist, one whose soul is really filled with living fire from the altar of the Eternal,—if he be a true spirit, and not an earth-vapour,—he *will* go on, *will* endure to the end; and no matter how faint and weary he may feel, ready even to lie down and die by the way,—still he will not desist, he will not lose his faith: he will find strength at his utmost need, and he will go on, struggling to give form and utterance to the Divine idea that lies in the ART of which he is the priest, grappling with the undefined and mysterious, yet all-pervading, spirit, and compelling it to make itself visible to those who have no skill to seize on it for themselves. But this can only be achieved by those who are pure in heart,—free from double motives or selfish desires for their own credit, and with whom it is the *Work* that is ever present, and not the *Reward*. They who have this high calling dare not stay their hand on account of any insult to themselves: they are marked for a higher service, and to them it is a small matter to be judged of men's judgment,—they are bound to magnify their Work, and make it honourable. The motive that has been influencing you, dear friend, although beautiful and devoted in its aspect, has still been all too low, too entirely personal to be worthy of you. It is now taken away from you; it may be that this is to teach you to go on in a higher and nobler spirit—to endure, as seeing that which is invisible. It has been necessary that you should suffer this also, and I feel convinced that you will not fail.'

Bianca had buried her face in the sofa pillow during this speech, and did not immediately reply. At length she said in a broken voice,

'One's own misery sticks so close to one, it is all *within*; whilst what you say, though strong and true, seems to lie abroad on the outside. Your words ought to give me strength, but they do not touch me; I feel so weak and wretched, that I can believe in nothing else. No, no, you must give me time—it is from time alone, and not from any efforts of my own, that I hope to live down this sorrow. The strong hours will conquer it.'

'I am content to have you say this,' replied Lord Melton. 'I hope all things for you. Do you think that I am on a bed of roses all this time? Oh, Bianca! would that I might bear your sorrow for you. It is horrible for me to see you suffer thus!'

'You must forgive me that too,' said Bianca, smiling sadly, and passing her hand down his face. 'Misery makes us press very heavily on those who approach us to support our fainting steps. I do not deserve your friendship, but you do me good. What should I be at this instant without you? But now you must go away, for I dare not talk any more. Shall you look in at the theatre to-night?'

'I will try to do so, if only for half an hour; but I am not sure that I can.'

'Remember,' said she, holding his hand, 'that I shall be acting for you. You must not quarrel with me for any motive that will carry me through, and I would do much for the sake of pleasing you. Now, farewell.'

CHAPTER IV

BIANCA was not long in deciding on the line of conduct she should adopt towards Conrad, nor in following it out when she had once made up her mind. After Lord Melton had quitted the room, she lay still for a few minutes, and then, with a composure that surprised herself, she went to her writing-table which stood in the window, wrote a rapid note, directed, sealed it, and despatched it to the post with a sort of cheerful alacrity; and when it was gone, felt really pleased, at last that she stood no longer in a false position. She went to the theatre at night in a feverish excitement of spirits, which she fancied a resolute composure; acted extremely well, and thought she had risen superior to her weakness; but when called before the curtain, she recognised Conrad in the stage-box, and all her equanimity was gone. Indignation, bitter scorn of herself, helpless, passionate love, swept like a tempest through her soul, leaving her a struggling wreck. She went home almost mad; but with a wild hope lurking in her heart, that Conrad, touched by her note, had been unable to break with her, and had come there to let her understand that he would not forego his claim, nor accept his freedom. She imagined she should find him waiting for her at home, to tell her how she had misjudged him, and how little he desired to be set free. 'Any one here?' she inquired, hurriedly, as she sprang from the carriage.

'No, madam,' was the reply.

'Any letter come?'

'Nothing at all, madam, since you went out—except Lord Melton's man with some grapes and flowers; but no letter or note of any sort.'

Bianca's heart sank dead within her, and she flung herself on the sofa in a fit of passionate weeping. Then she began to hope for the morrow. Conrad had not been home—had not received her note—she should hear from him on the morrow. The certainty that some explanation, some words of frankness and affection, must be wrung from him by what she had written, almost comforted her, and prevented her feeling the desolate hopelessness of her position.

On Conrad's return home from two balls and a *soirée*, at which he made his appearance after the theatre, he perceived Bianca's note on the table amongst a heap of other letters. He opened it the last, with a feeling of annoyance and dread; he expected a reproach for his absence and neglect. He found the following words.

DEAR CONRAD,

I overheard a conversation not intended for me on Thursday evening, in the tent-room at Mrs Bingham's party. Why have you not been more frank with me? Why leave me to ascertain your feelings by a mere accident? It was not well of you to do so, and I deserved better at your hands. You have suffered much needless annoyance; had I known that you felt me an entanglement, disavowed by your feelings, and disowned by your judgment, you might have been free long since. However, it remains for me to set you at liberty now from any claim I may have upon you on the score of our engagement, and you are honourably free henceforth. But the generosity and kindness with which you have befriended me can never be effaced,—they lie in the safe keeping of the past, and can suffer no change. If I have wearied you with my affection, forgive me; it was all the return I could make. God forbid I should be a clog or a weariness to you.

In conclusion, I have one favour to beg at your hands. As I am obliged to continue on the spot till the termination of my engagement, will you refrain from attempting to see me, or from throwing yourself in my way. Believe me, it is from no anger or resentment that I ask this, but that I may be able to keep the composure necessary to my work. No bitterness or unkindness lurks in this request. God bless you, Conrad, for ever and ever.

                                                    BIANCA.

Conrad was not nearly so delighted as might have been expected, at reading this note. He had been taken at his word unawares, and we hardly any of us recognise our wishes when we see them suddenly realised. However, he was a man of the world, and knew that his present fit of relenting would pass away, and that the release offered to him must be accepted now, or never, as there would be no getting out of a renewal. The next morning, as Bianca was at breakfast, she received a note, the handwriting of which made her heart stand still.

'Any one waiting?' she inquired.

'No, ma'am; Mr Conrad Percy's servant brought it, and said there was no answer.'

She allowed the note to lie several minutes before she had courage to open it. When she did so, the whole paper swam before her eyes, and it was some time before she could decypher a word; at length she read as follows:

Bianca! you desire me not to seek you, and, therefore, I do violence to the impulse which prompts me to come to you. God knows the pang your note has given me. You are dearer to me than you believe, than I believed myself. With my whole soul I respect and admire you; and even those casual words you overheard must have told you the consideration in which I held you personally, the bitterness of them was for your profession. But whenever or wherever you might have heard me speak of you—the high respect and regard in which I have always held you, would have been always marked—do me that justice at least.

I have shrunk from an explanation with you in a way that was cowardly, and that I do not justify; but pardon me if I say that it was the ungoverned passionateness of your nature which made me shrink from a scene likely to prove equally painful to you and to myself. If you are suffering at this moment, believe me, Bianca, you are not suffering alone; my very soul is torn by the severance of the ties that have bound us, but I believe it is wiser to accept a present suffering than to entail a future and more lasting one upon ourselves. We are not suited for each other. I look to the end; and this alone enables me to resist coming to throw myself at your feet, and entreating you to forget all that has disturbed us. You are quite right, and show your usual firmness in desiring that for the present we should not meet, and therefore I feel that I am fulfilling your wishes when I depart for Paris to-night; afterwards, I shall perhaps proceed to the south of France and Spain, and at all events shall not return to England for some months. Now, Bianca, farewell. Dear—very dear—will you and your welfare ever be to me. Do not fancy this letter harsh or unfeeling; my tears drop on the paper while I sign this—

CONRAD.

Whilst reading the letter, Bianca was at times in doubt whether Conrad really intended to give her up after all, but the conclusion banished all hope, and she sat like one turned to stone; not thinking, not feeling, but utterly stupified. After awhile, she became conscious of a sense of freedom and certainty, an absence of the gnawing restlessness—the weary alternations of hope and despair, which had so long harassed her; and for a few hours she felt better and more at ease. But when our grief is one that sinks deep into our souls, although we feel it at first comparatively little, 'bear it wonderfully well' as nurses say, yet the pain that has first stunned us, at last awakens us, and never sleeps more. The whole of that day passed over pretty well; Bianca employed herself resolutely, and called up a sort of scornful indignation to her support. A truly great soul never feels so surely convinced of its own worth, as at the moment of undeserved humiliation; Bianca felt that she had deserved better at the hands of Conrad. But she still loved him with the whole force of her nature, and the need of *forgiving* him lay in her soul. A truly loving heart can find no solace in anger. The dreary weariness of a love without hope began to press heavily upon her; there remained nothing more for her to do, nothing but to sit down to *endure*. She heard accidentally of Conrad's departure, and that only seemed to add another leaden weight to her heavy life. She struggled courageously to keep up to her work, and she did it. None who saw her acting night after night with so much tenderness and passion, could guess the frightful collapse that ensued. The condition in which she spent the intermediate time was horrible. The agony of her soul produced spasms of real bodily pain. She was astonished at the misery which had befallen her; it seemed too great for any one to endure it and live. There is suffering so vivid, so infinite in its aspect, that the sufferer cannot believe that it is in very deed laid upon him to endure it. He looks upon it as some terrific jest of fate, not intended to be carried out;—and when it flashes upon him that there *is* this affliction really existing in all its tragic, stern, rock-like reality, filling with its hard dark presence the whole length and breadth of his horizon, crushing him down so that he can feel nothing else, can discern nothing else before, behind, or on all sides of him—he believes it can never pass away, but will always continue then as now: for the torture of the present is too intense to leave strength for hope,—for any thing but the weary wondering how nature can endure so much and not loose her hold on life. At times Bianca rallied, and the paroxyms of intense anguish faded into a stupified calm, to rouse her again to suffer with renewed intensity, till she could realise the awful description of wretches in everlasting torment, 'they gnawed their tongues for anguish'. Then with all this there was the damning self-contempt, the consciousness of the unavailing helplessness of her misery,—of a stern originality to *her* alone,—to the rest of the world a common tale of no meaning. She struggled on, however, during the month that remained of her engagement; at the end of that time she was in such a deplorable state of weakness and prostration, that her servant called in a medical man. Lord Melton, who had been out of town on business, was terrified on his return to see the ravages four weeks had made in Bianca. She had fallen into a torpid melancholy, and now that the necessity of rousing herself to appear at the theatre was over, she seemed like a curious piece of mechanism, which has run itself down and stopped. She had become utterly indifferent to all that passed around her, and could be roused by nothing; she scarcely noticed Lord Melton on his return.

'I do not disguise from you, my lord,' said the physician, 'that although there is no organic disease, there is such an alarming debility and general prostration that the worst results may follow. Medicine can do little for her; there ought to be a complete change of scene. If she has any friends they should be sent for, the sight of them might act upon her beneficially. It is a moral influence alone that can be of any benefit; medicine can do nothing, for there is no specific disease to act upon.'

'Then you recommend change of air?' said Lord Melton.

'Most assuredly,' was the reply; 'she should be taken to the sea-side; but anywhere would do, provided the change be complete. She must be removed immediately, or I will not answer for the consequences.'

'How long has she been in this dangerous state?' asked Lord Melton. 'She was not so when I left town a fortnight ago.'

'She has broken down all at once,' said the physician. 'I saw her the last night she played, and I never witnessed a more admirable performance.'

Bianca had no friends, no relatives in the world. Admired, flattered, successful as she had been, she had yet no hold on society, no *home*; she was alone, but for her confidential servant, in her deepest need; she belonged to nobody; the reed to which she had clung had broken in her grasp and drifted away, leaving her to sink in the deep waters that were overwhelming her soul.

Lord Melton was inexpressibly touched by the loneliness and abandonment in which he saw her. The passionateness of a lover seemed to merge itself in the thoughtful tenderness of a brother.

After considering awhile he wrote to his only sister, who lived in Devonshire, telling her all the facts of the case so far as he could without compromising Bianca's secret, and begging her to come and fetch her to stay with her for a little at Willersdale Park.

CHAPTER V

LADY VERNON (Lord Melton's sister) was a widow, and many years older than himself. Left with a handsome jointure, and possessing an estate in her own right, she had, besides, as much to occupy her time and thoughts as any woman need desire. She was a large, tall, majestic-looking woman, with the remains of great personal beauty. She was rather peremptory and decided in her manners, but kind, conscientious, and enlightened in her ideas. She had lost all her children in their childhood, which gave a touch of sadness to her character, and softened what would have been otherwise too firm and unbending. (Neither men nor women are good for anything who have not been well broken up by suffering.) She was intensely proud, and a great stickler for family honours and genealogies; was learned in the heraldic natural history of all the species of lions, bears, griffins, stags, talbots, wiverns, and every kind of bird, beast, or impossibility which figures on the 'coat armours', as Sir Symond d'Ewes* calls them, of all the nobility and more important gentry in England. She had the greatest possible respect for ancient descent. She lived in a dignified retirement at her seat of Willersdale Park, seldom coming up to town, but giving her whole attention to the management of her tenantry.

The house was an extremely ill-favoured red-brick building, in the Dutch style, of the time of William and Mary, but it had a sober substantial look withal; her equipage and establishment were in keeping with it.

She had no taste for actresses; they were entirely out of her line. Certainly there were instances of some of them marrying amongst the nobility, but it was not a precedent she at all admired, and she was much afraid lest her brother should be induced to follow it.

When she received her brother's letter, she was at first much put out of the way, but his reliance on the innate goodness of her character was not disappointed. She did not feel at all tempted to receive an actress as an inmate of her staid respectable abode; but on the other hand, she was touched at the picture of Bianca's lonely and mournful position. She quickly made up her mind, and actually arrived in London before her brother had begun to calculate on an answer to his letter.

'My dearest Margaret,' cried he, 'this is kind and good and worthy of you; it is all I could have desired. If you only knew how much I love you for it!'

'Well, well,' said his sister, 'I am an old woman, and I did not know what scandalous stories might be set going about the poor young thing, if you were the only person seen much about her, so I thought I had better come myself and give my personal sanction to her.'

'Poor girl, she is too ill to be sensible of it,' said Lord Melton, hardly able to repress a smile at his sister's idea of sanctioning an illness; 'but you are good and considerate all the same.'

'The character of a young woman in her position is so soon whispered away, and nobody believes in brotherly love in these days,' said Lady Vernon. 'I am not going to take *you* back with me,' continued she, 'I dare say you would like to go well enough; but I shall not have you; if you are very good, I may perhaps invite you down on a visit while she stays; but I am not too sure that I shall.'

It had never struck Lord Melton that he was not to accompany Bianca; he had quite settled in his own mind how delightful it would be to continue near her, to watch over her, and he felt terribly disappointed; however, it would not do to contradict his sister, so he submitted, though not with the best grace.

'When do you think she will be ready to travel?' asked Lady Vernon, again.

'The sooner, the better, the physician said.'

'Well then, the day after to-morrow, let it be; I want to get home again; the noise of these streets does not suit me at all. And now, if you are ready, we will go and see the poor thing.'

On the day named, Bianca was removed in Lady Vernon's carriage, by easy journeys, towards Willersdale Park; and Lord Melton undertook to arrange the business affairs, which her sudden illness had rendered her unable herself to see to.

On arriving, Bianca was installed by Lady Vernon in two pleasant rooms, opening out of each other, looking on the garden, and commanding a pleasant view of the country beyond.

In less than a week, the total change of scene, the pure air, and perfect quiet, had wrought such a change for the better, that she was able to walk in the garden, and to be taking long drives every day. She was still very silent, but the deep gloom that had hung over her seemed lessened. She was able occasionally to rouse herself to reply to Lady Vernon, and to notice what was passing around. At the end of a month she was like one recovering from a deep stupor, and coming back gradually to the use of her faculties. She did not again relapse into her former black melancholy; but continued steadily to regain strength and cheerfulness—at least outwardly. She was not yet up to any sort of occupation; and Lady Vernon wisely and kindly left it to time, to perfect her recovery.

One day, rather earlier than usual, when Bianca descended to the library, which was Lady Vernon's usual sitting-room, she found her sitting before a table covered with work-boxes, prettily bound books, pictures, and trinkets of various kinds.

'Are you about to open a bazaar?' asked Bianca, in some surprise.

'Oh no, my dear, these are the prizes for my school; the girls go home to-morrow, and we are to have a grand examination this afternoon before the prizes are distributed; do you feel at all inclined to assist at it? We shall have a sort of feast afterwards; do you think you are strong enough?'

'I feel as if I should like to go very much,' said Bianca, 'but what school is it?—they cannot be poor children for whom such beautiful prizes are intended.'

'No,' said Lady Vernon, 'they belong to a class which, to my thinking, needs thoroughly educating a great deal more than the children of the actual poor. They are girls born in a more pretentious sphere of life, in the odour of gentility, but without sufficient means to get a thorough education, or to be perfectly comfortable in their attempts to keep up what they fancy to be the proper appearances of the condition in life to which they are pleased to consider themselves as belonging. Half-educated, full of vain notions, and leading a life of painful effort and pretence to appear richer and genteeler, than is, to say the least, *spontaneous* to their position, these girls are vain, useless, trifling, and what to my mind is worse than all the rest, irredeemably *vulgar,* for ingrained vulgarity cannot exist without being symptomatic of many graver faults of character. I am not speaking of any conventionalisms of etiquette and external manner; what I mean, is a deep-seated pretentiousness to a better appearance in every way than they have any intention or power to realise, but one still striven after, for the sole purpose of making other people *think* this, that, or the other—which is not a fact, but only meant to be thought one. The poor things have nothing to go upon, no reality of any sort about them, except their vanity; and where any reverse happens by the death of their parents, misfortunes in business, or what not, such as deprives them of their means of living, shoals of these young women are thrown on the world utterly incapable of work, and, whether they are "ashamed" or not, "to *beg*" is very unprofitable! No habits of discipline or self-denial have been given to them, and what are they to do? They have not the virtue to hang themselves out of the road, but go,—hundreds of them,—to a far worse destruction both of body and soul.'

'Well, and your school,' said Bianca, seeing that the good lady had talked herself out of breath.

'I am coming to that,' said Lady Vernon; 'I like to begin at the beginning. On one side of the park there was a spacious house and large garden, which happening to be vacant, I fitted up for a school about ten years ago, and put at the head of it a woman for whom I have a thorough respect, and who had been regularly educated to the business of tuition, and had not taken it up as an amateur means of getting a living. The parents of the girls pay fifteen pounds a-year, for I don't want it to be a charity school, and they also supply them with clothes. For this sum the girls are boarded and thoroughly educated. First, we begin with all useful things, such as writing, arithmetic, grammar, and so forth; they are then initiated in all the mysteries of "plain work", as it is called, and are taught to make their own dresses: for it is perfectly dreadful the sums that young women spend at their mantuamaker's. When they are tolerably skilful in practical matters, then those who have any taste for accomplishments may learn them; but if they take them up, they are to learn *thoroughly*, and not a mere smattering. They are taught professionally, so that if needs be, they may either teach again or employ them as a means of earning a livelihood. Those who show any taste, are instructed in the art of wood-engraving, etching, designing patterns for embroiderers; there is another branch I have lately thought of, that of designing for calico printers; it has not come to much yet, but it is quite feasible, and all of them may be followed by young women in their own houses,—a great advantage. If any wish to learn music or singing, they are taught, but it is on the condition that they are to learn thoroughly and severely; so that, if they are cast on their own resources, there is something for them to fall back upon. The masters I select and pay myself, and I know them all to be competent and conscientious. Some of the departments are filled by girls who were formerly pupils in the establishment. It is not so much what they learn, after all, that is the most valuable—it is the habit which is burnt into them of being in earnest, of doing *thoroughly* all they profess to do; *that* is a principle which will enable them to go through life, and is the beginning, middle, and end of wisdom. With young girls, of course, a good deal goes by fashion; that I cannot help; but at least the prevailing notion in the school is, that it is disgraceful to put *words* for *things*. They dress all alike, and wear white in summer and black in winter; for I wish them to get modest and becoming notions of dress, and they cannot go very far wrong so long as they keep to those two colours. Of course I have entirely my own way with the girls, I make that a stipulation, so I have no sort of plague with the parents. Well, my dear, it is only a mite, to be sure, but I have the comfort of knowing that a few, at least, of the rising generation, are turned out thoroughly taught and with good notions of industry; and my hope is, that they will prove a little leaven leavening a great mass of idleness, folly, and frivolity, with sentiments befitting responsible and rational creatures. Girls, in general, get a smattering of all sorts of knowledge, but they are not taught that these lessons mean something,—they are not impressed with the imperative necessity of having their life guided by strong principle; they subside into helplessness and idleness: harmless they may be, so long as no evil presents itself, but they are at the mercy of the first strong temptation that offers.'

'Do you make them go to church?' asked Bianca.

'Yes,' said Lady Vernon, 'I let them go regularly enough; but it is not the vague instruction they hear there that will do them good or harm. I am an old-fashioned church-woman myself, but people must get the principles they can lead their lives by elsewhere than from the pulpit in these days; nobody can make much of the sermons preached there.'

'I should like to go with you very much,' said Bianca, 'if you will take me. When do you start?'

'After luncheon—and here it comes!—but, my dear, I don't want to trepan you; and so I give you fair warning it will be a long affair.'

'Oh, I feel quite up to it,' said Bianca.

As soon as luncheon was despatched, the carriage came round, and they speedily arrived at a pleasant, old-fashioned family house, with a large walled garden at the back, and in the front a lawn, sheltered from the road by several fine old trees. The number of girls was about five-and-twenty, of different ages. They were remarkable only for an extreme composure of manner, and a quiet, earnest look, which pleased Bianca much.

'They are very lady-like in their appearance,' whispered she.

'I don't think they consider much about how they look,' said Lady Vernon, 'and that may be the reason!'

Their proficiency was examined into by Lady Vernon, who also inspected the work they had done during the half year, and the prizes were distributed, though all received something in the shape of a reward. Afterwards, Bianca was introduced to the mistress—a lady about forty years of age—not at all clever-looking, but with a firm, decided, and yet benevolent expression of face, that looked as if she were quite competent to keep all who were under her control up to the mark.

Then followed the 'feast', which Lady Vernon had provided, and a pleasant chattering evening ensued. There was a good deal of music;—one of the girls, a dark-eyed, passionate-looking girl of about sixteen, attracted Bianca's notice. She was the principal musician of the school.

'You care a great deal for music?' said she to her.

'Yes,' replied the girl; 'I should like to go to Italy and learn to sing. I care for music more than anything else in the world, and I never heard any to satisfy me, except once in a dream.'

'And what do you want to do with your music, when you have learned?'

'I do not know; I have only thought yet that I desire to go to Italy, and to hear as much music as ever I can. Do you sing?' asked she. 'I wish you would let me hear you.'

'Well,' said Bianca, good-naturedly, 'what must I sing? I am very fond of this "Mass" of Haydn's; I will see if I can find something from it.'

Bianca had very little voice—but she had all an Italian's feeling for music, and had, besides, been obliged to study it, in some degree. She threw into it the same intellect and passionate earnestness that marked her acting, so that they who once heard her, rarely forgot her. She felt quite pleased to be able to give the girl pleasure, and sat down and sang every thing she could recollect, for more than an hour.

'Ah! that is something like the singing of my dream?' said the girl, with glistening eyes.

'Only I hope, my dear, for the credit of your musical angel, that it had a better voice,' said Bianca, tapping her cheek.

But now Lady Vernon's carriage, which had been standing a long time, could be kept no longer, and there was a general breaking up.

'You are not much fatigued, I hope,' said Lady Vernon, as they drove home.

'Oh no, it has done me a great deal of good,' said Bianca. 'I have really enjoyed myself. What are you going to do with that girl who played so well?'

'I don't know,' said Lady Vernon; 'she is the first we have had with any decided musical talent, and I hardly know what to do with it. Music is apt to be such a dangerous endowment for women.'

'But, my dear lady, dangerous or not dangerous, that girl has real genius, and she will become a singer. It is of no use rebelling against Providence; rather let me add my mite towards your good work. Let her go to the Academy when she has finished with you, and I will undertake to see after her.'

'My dear soul,' said Lady Vernon, 'you are very good—very good, indeed; but we will hope better things. I should be very sorry, indeed, to bring one of my girls out as a professional singer. I don't like such people.'

'Well,' said Bianca, laughing, 'promise me at least, that if circumstances prove too strong for you, and you change your views, that you will make me useful. How long has your school been established? It must be a very expensive affair.'

'Well, so it is,' replied her ladyship. 'I have only had it working for ten years. Before then, I used to mess away my funds with helping *protégées*, who, do what I would, always kept falling from lowest deeps, to lower depths of helplessness; or, in subscribing to this, that, or the other society—things I took no real interest in; and I began at last to consider that with all my income, I ought to produce a better result than I was doing; and that I had a responsibility laid upon me, which I was not adequately discharging. About this time, the case of a family which had moved in rather genteel circles was left, by the death of the father, in utter destitution; without money, without any well-to-do relations to help them, and without the necessary energy to help themselves; the girls were ignorant and pretty-looking; educated enough to pass muster in a drawing-room, but utterly incompetent to take any sort of situation; they were not even fit for ladies'-maids; they could not thread a needle—they were useless. Still the poor things could not starve, so I had them to stay a little while with me, and got my maid to teach them to do needlework; and I tried to get them into orderly habits; and then I succeeded in finding for one of them a situation, something between that of a nursery governess and a *bonne*; and I also got the others placed in some light employment, where they might have made a respectable livelihood. But to earn one's own living requires something more than mere needing it; it requires discipline, patience, and self-denial. These girls were not bad, by any means; but they had been accustomed to idleness, to visiting, to flirting, and having their own way in all things; they had no strong principles to control them. I encouraged them all I could, and with very moderate perseverance, they might have done well: but before six months were over, one had eloped with an old lover, who took her "under his protection", as it is called; and the other, a short time afterwards, went on the streets: she was persuaded to try her fortune as a singer at one of the singing saloons, and her downward course was short enough, poor girl! This is one instance out of a hundred similar ones. *Protégées* always bring dissatisfaction; it is like meddling with fire-works— it is a thousand chances if they do not explode and burn your fingers; and so I began to think I would for the future have nothing more to do with such vexatious speculations, but that if I could do something for the *class* of girls to which my luckless *protégées* belonged, it would lessen the *supply* of cases of distress; and that it would be far better to turn out a few thoroughly-taught, well-principled young women, than to melt away my substance in affording a rickety assistance to those whom nothing would ever enable to walk alone. A case of great distress always stimulates somebody's sensibilities; anything very palpable always does; but the need of help and instruction before matters come to extremities is not so striking, so every body must work at what seems to them most desirable. I never in my heart took cordially to all that "society" work, and I am quite sure now, that it was very well for me that I got out of it. I have found something at which I can work heartily; I believe that I am doing at least a *mite* of usefulness; and so people must do as well as they can in this world.'

'You have a real vocation for education,' said Bianca, laughing, 'it is a pity you were not born a governess.'

'No, my dear, I could not have had my present influence, or have carried out my plans so much as I do, if my bread had depended on my teaching. As "Lady Vernon" I am quite independent, and my "ladyship" gives me a vast weight with the fathers and mothers I want to persuade. My dear child, you don't know all the difficulties I met with before my school was set to work; the false pride, the pretentiousness, the vulgarity—to say nothing of any thing else, that I have had to tame and smooth down—it would take a day to tell you about: however, it only showed me the necessity of what I was striving to do, and made me more determined to go on. People have a fancy, that a certain class of virtues, called the common principles of morality, are indigenous, in all but very poor people. Now, this is a great mistake. They need a vast deal of cultivation,—certainly a misty tradition concerning picking and stealing, and the necessity of young females being modest and virtuous, pervades all decent society; but nobody seems to know how much goes to make up these qualities of honesty and virtue. They are not to be improvised in a moment, neither do they come as a matter of course, the moment there is a call for them; and yet an immense number

of the young women who move in a respectable sphere have no
more guiding principles of actions taught them, than if they were
so many cats. When any emergency arises, and there is any stress
to prove what is really in their hearts, it is no wonder so many
extraordinary lapses occur in persons, who had, in their prosperity, seemed of correct and unexceptionable conduct. There is
a great fuss about giving women a negative purity of mind, but
there is no care taken to give them any strong *antiseptic* qualities,
whereby they may *resist* evil. But what a prosing I have given
you! and how sleepy you must be!'

'No,' said Bianca, 'I take great interest in the subject. I have
been thinking that if it had not been for my good old priest at
Birmingham,—what would have become of me? Really I owe a
great deal to a few strong and very definite exhortations he once
gave me, when I was quite a girl, and placed in circumstances
which brought a deal of evil under my eyes. One word spoken
in season often helps us in after times, when those who spoke it
have long since forgotten it.'

'Very true,' said Lady Vernon; 'but now let us go to bed, you
have sat up much too late. By the way, Melton comes here
to-morrow; he will only remain a few days.'

'I shall be very glad to see him again,' said Bianca, as she went
up stairs.

The next morning Lord Melton arrived. He had thought his
sister's invitation a long time in coming; but he was quite pacified
when he saw the improvement in Bianca's appearance. She was
quite well enough now to be amused, and to bear company. Lady
Vernon gave several parties; they were an entirely different style
of people to any Bianca had ever seen—country gentry, who did
not often go up to London.

Lord Melton was Bianca's constant companion. Lady Vernon
was often engaged with her own private affairs, so they were a
good deal alone together. He read to her, rode out with her on
horseback, took long walks with her; and every thing in the
shape of books, or music, or new caricatures that he fancied could
amuse her, was brought down for her. To Bianca, Lord Melton
was a dear and valued brother; to Lord Melton, Bianca became
every day an object of deeper and stronger attachment, and he
was not at all satisfied with the calm regard she accorded to him:

still he was willing to 'bide his time', and carefully refrained from overstepping, by any undue warmth of manner, the friendly relation into which she had accepted him; and as there was no rival to dispute with him Bianca's undivided attention, he made himself tolerably contented. At first his visits did not exceed a few days each time, but they gradually became longer, till at last Willersdale Park seemed to have become his natural home.

CHAPTER VI

ONE evening after tea, as the ladies were sitting at work round the lamp, Lord Melton took up a book that had arrived that day from town, and volunteered to read aloud to them.

It chanced to be a novel which had just come out with a great success, as a highly moral book: one of the Reviews said of it, '*Une mère en permettrait la lecture à sa fille.*'*

After reading and skipping and looking on to the end, he at length flung down the book, exclaiming,

'Upon my honour, I can stand this no longer. How can you both sit there so patiently, to listen to such twaddle of rose-coloured imitation-virtue. You know well enough that human nature utterly renounces all affinity with nine-tenths of the stuff that is put into books to pass for high morality. It is just one more roll to the monster ball of vague opinions, which is ever accumulating and filling up the world. There you sit, both of you calling yourselves sensible women, yet neither of you ever lifting your voice to protest against all the nonsense specially consecrated to the description of the virtues proper to your sex. The devil is the father of lies, and I wish he would fly away with all his children, instead of leaving them to run wild over the world; but he is without natural affection, or else this thing would not be here.'

As he spoke, he jerked the unlucky book to the other end of the room, narrowly escaping the destruction of a choice vase of Indian china, and actually dislodging a glass of flowers which stood beside it.

'Oh, my precious china!' cried Lady Vernon. 'Maurice, Maurice, another time do make a virtuous demonstration at your own risk, and not amongst my frail treasures. Only think what mischief you might have done!'

'Luckily for us all,' replied her brother, 'there is a broad margin to the possibilities of this world, and nothing is so bad or so good as it ought logically to be. I might have broken your china, but I did not, so there is no harm done. Forgive the shock I have caused to your feminine susceptibilities. It has calmed my zeal.'

'I am glad to hear it,' replied Lady Vernon, laughing; 'and perhaps you will descend from the heights of declamation to the special details of what you wish Bianca and myself to do.'

'In the first place, I would have you both enter your own protests against those opinions which are taken up by society on different points, but which nobody means, nobody believes, and nobody thinks of practising. Shrugging your shoulders, and saying, *sotto voce*, 'I don't agree, though it won't do to say so,' is not sufficient; society, civilised society, is enamelled in cant. Every pore is stopped, and a thick veneer of MAKE BELIEVE is spread over every thing. What a talk for instance there is just now about the condition of women; and how much do you think can come out of all that is said, sung, and written upon the subject? It is quite deplorable, and I thank God every time I say my prayers that He did not make me a woman to be given over to patent moralists.'

'There is no making us profit by them, that is one comfort,' said Bianca.

'Allah Akbar! God is great and nature is powerful, or else the world would be in a sad case,' replied Lord Melton. 'Stifle Nature, endeavour to muffle her in sententious rose-coloured phrases as much as you will, every now and then she asserts her own reality, "*avec explosion*", as the French dramatists say,—to the great relief of the social system.'

'Grand explosions of nature are not at all safe transactions,' rejoined Lady Vernon. 'Can you suggest no quieter method of regenerating society in general, and the condition of women in particular? I agree with you to the very extent as to the rose-coloured sort of morality generally imputed to them and exacted from them, but they should not be taught to laugh at that till they have learned something better.'

'But,' said Lord Melton, 'what is radically *false*, can give no strength. Women have a great deal of modesty, delicacy, and feminine refinement, but they are not taught the principles from which these ought to spring as natural fruits. Certain qualities are praised, but it is like children who make a garden by sticking full-blown flowers into the ground and expecting them to keep their bloom. Those who instruct them do not go to the real principle which shall teach them to discern right from wrong, nor give them any strong truths by which to guide their steps amongst the temptations and delusions which beset them; therefore we find that all the talk they have heard about "graceful modesty" and "female delicacy", does not enable them to stand against the stern reality of a strong temptation. Propriety cannot swallow up passion.'

'A rabid fit of truth-telling seems to have taken possession of you,' said his sister, 'and you have taken possession of that easy vantage-ground of general declamation, which all objectors and theoretical reformers find such a pleasant dwelling place; but come out of it for once, and if you can suggest any practical thing that women can do to mend themselves, I, as a woman, will thank you most gratefully. Women would be only too thankful for wise guidance, and it is precisely what they do not get.'

'Nay,' said Lord Melton, 'I can suggest no compendious system of morals like the receipts in the "Housekeepers' Manual",—the spirit must be renovated before the details can be amended. Was it not in the Sandwich Islands that Captain Cook was invited to a grand banquet, at which the chief, by way of doing him honour, first masticated all the choice morsels, and then transferred them to his guest all ready for swallowing. That is the sort of way in which women's minds are fed. They are kept in a state of perpetual childishness,—not *childhood*—that is a graceful and natural state. Women out-grow childhood without attaining a developed and matured nature. I know an immense number of women, of one sort or other, and hardly one of them seems to have attained the practical sense of a school-boy. Their personal gifts and graces developed, they learn the art of society, they obtain power and influence over men in right of their fascinations, but they have no foundation of a real knowledge of things to back their empire. Whenever it happens that, instead of talking, they have to take a practical step for themselves, they have nothing to go upon; and, in earning their experience, it is ten chances to one but they ruin their reputation.'

'Women, in general, have no settled occupation,' said Bianca, looking up. 'Those who have families, have, indeed, a legitimate employment, enough to employ all their energies. Those women, too, who have to gain their own living, have their hands pretty full. But, with these exceptions, women lead a life of nonentity, so far as the *real value* of their occupation goes. All they do is to pass away the time, and it is of little real consequence whether it be done or let alone. Look, for instance, at the great body of unmarried women, in the middle classes—they spend their days in the same kind of trifling that slaves in the East amuse themselves with, till some one comes to put them into a harem. They want an object, they want a strong purpose, they want an adequate employment,—in exchange for a precious life. Days, months, years of perfect leisure run by, and leave nothing but a sediment of *ennui*: and at length they have all vitality choked out of them. This is the true evil of the condition of women. The need of some sort of a stimulant becomes, at last, an imperative necessity—it is the cry of their expiring souls, an impulse of self-preservation; they possess unsatisfied, unemployed powers of mind—a strong vitality of nature, that must consume them, unless an adequate, legitimate employment be provided for them. They must find something that is *worth* being done; voluntary employment will not stave off the evil. The very possession of existence inspires a desire for activity, and it is melancholy to see the blind vague efforts women make to be useful; they do their various things, not as an imperative duty, but because they have "plenty of time", and play at being Lady Bountifuls and lady patronesses to poor people, to get rid of their own weariness. I do not set myself up as an example of what women in general should be, but this one blessing I have had to counter-balance the many questionable items in my position, I have had a definite employment all my life: when I rose in the morning my work lay before me, and I had a clear, definite channel in which all my energies might flow. I was without social position, I had no friends, no respectability; often wanted food. I had to struggle with vexations in my daily life enough to break any one's heart, in daily contact with most undesirable environments; but with all this I was kept clear of ENNUI, which eats like a leprosy into the life of women. I was leading a life of my own, and was able to acquire a full control over my own faculties; and I have always had a sense of freedom, of enjoyment of my existence, which has rendered all my vexations easy to be borne. I would not, I tell you again, wish the generality of women to resemble me. I have had too much struggling: I am become in some degree hard and

coarse from my contact with the harsh realities of life; but I *do* say
that the idea of my life has been true. I have had work to do, and
I have done it. I have had a purpose, and have endeavoured to
work it out; and I say that if you could furnish women with a
definite object, or address motives in them fit to animate rational
beings, you would have a race of wives and daughters far different
from those which now flourish in your drawing-rooms; the
quality of their nature would be elevated; they would be able to
aid men in any noble object by noble thoughts, by self-denial, by
real sympathy and fellowship of heart, nor would they, as is the
case too often now, aid a cause by merely pressing their vanity
into the service of their charity, and think they have done all that
is needed when they have raised a few pounds by dedicating their
amusements to an object of charity, to give it a zest, and make
them fancy it some new thing.'

'But, my dear Bianca,' said Lady Vernon, 'you are like Melton,
keeping to safe generalities. How, in the present state of society,
are women to be employed? They cannot all work for their
bread, and what is there for them to do? Women's employments
are so limited.'

'I told you,' replied Bianca, 'that there was no compendious
receipt to improve the condition of women; their present position has been of gradual growth, and has all the disadvantages of
a transition state. They used to be subordinate to men in every
sense; they were household servants—*bond-women*, in short: they
are now become ornamental appendages, and enjoy a sort of
fictitious existence and consideration; language, as somebody
said, "has been mystified for the use of women", and a whole set
of elegant virtues has been invented for their special adorn-
ment—an improvement I grant, but not enough: not REAL
enough to govern wisely their frail, passionate, wayward nature,
or to meet the height and depth of their necessities.'

'Well,' said Lord Melton, 'I have listened to you both, as in
duty bound, seeing you both belong to the class of the patients,
but I think there is too much talk going on for much good to
come out of it, and my idea would be that in the present stage of
the business all the woman of England should be shut up in what
Catholics call "RETREAT":—they should be alone, and have
nothing to do but to sit down and consider what it is they

have been taught all their lives, how much of it they really believe, and how much of it they have ever practised; they should have to consider what is a real matter of conscience, and what only a matter of convention; they should have to examine themselves truly as to what it is they really love, and what are the things they REALLY hate, and what, candidly speaking, they care nothing at all about. Of course they would not be expected to reveal the result of these considerations, it should all be for their own private satisfaction. It would be some time before they *could* be sincere with themselves,—before they could strip off all the moral flannel-waistcoats, steel-collars, and go-carts, in which they have walked all the days of their life; but they would be able do it in time. They should have no books; neither should they have pen, ink, or paper to write diaries or confessions with; four bare walls should be all they had to see; if you chose to be rigorous, a diet of bread and water might be added. They should come out thence, and begin their life anew; their actual occupation might not be materially changed, but the spirit in which they would pursue it would be different: the face of society would be renewed, for the very well-spring and fountain would have been cleansed. I believe with that great man, who said—"*Reality and perfection are the same thing.*" '

'I see only one objection,' said Lady Vernon. 'One half of your fair penitents would hang themselves in despair of making any thing out of the *chiffonnage*,★ to which their life had been reduced.'

'Those who have not strength, or grasp of principle strong enough, to enable them to amend their ways when they perceive their errors, and to conduct themselves in a way worthy the possessors of that solemn reality called *Life*, and of their high calling in being modes of God's manifestation upon earth, ought to depart to Hades—the region of ineffectualities.'

'Good Heaven!' said Lady Vernon, looking at her watch; 'it is nearly two o'clock,—to bed! to bed! to bed!'

CHAPTER VII

BIANCA remained three months an inmate with Lady Vernon, recovering both her bodily health and her moral strength after the painful shock which had so nearly destroyed her. The first symptom of her returning energy was a desire to return to the fatigue and excitement of her old way of life. She began to re-act against the repose and elegant employments around her. Letters of business, which had followed her from London and been thrown aside in disgust and helplessness, now began to claim her attention. She felt the need of something to do, and made arrangements for visiting several of the chief provincial towns. A few days after the conversation recorded in the last chapter, she announced, at breakfast, her intention of leaving Willersdale Park that day week.

'Nonsense, my dear, nonsense,' said Lady Vernon; 'I am not going to part with you; and where do you want to go to? and what do you want to go for? I cannot understand such a sudden freak at all, and you will just stay peaceably where you are until you get quite well.—Why, Melton,' said she to her brother, who just then entered the room, 'what do you think, here is Bianca talking of going away next week! It is quite out of the question.'

Lord Melton felt a very disagreeable shock when he heard his sister's abrupt announcement; he had all along known that Bianca could not stay with his sister for ever; but he had put off thinking of the evil day, and now it had come on him unawares. He could not at once say any thing, but his change of countenance was not lost on Bianca, who felt the more how needful it was for her to get away.

'I must indeed leave you, my kind friends,' said she; 'I am not yet able to lead a life of quiet and ease for long together—it is the vice of my nature. I have been on the stretch and struggle all my life, and I cannot subside at once into respectable and still life; so you must let me go now. I will, if possible, return to you at Christmas—if you will take in such a vagabond again?'

'Ah, you miss the excitement you have been accustomed to; and excitement is such a bad thing, when it is the staple of life,' said Lady Vernon. 'My dear girl, how can you give yourself up to it? With all your superiority, and fine perceptions of what is refined and beautiful, how can you tolerate such coarse excitement and such a glaring trashy mode of existence? I am speaking to you now, in my right of being an old woman, and you will forgive me for saying that it strikes me as the only shade in your character!'

'It is the shadow of the substance, my dear Lady Vernon, and you could not change it without changing my character altogether. You forget that I am a vagabond born, and with as clear a vocation for being an ACTRESS, as any of the saints of old had for being martyrs—I could have done nothing else in the world. I needed to have all the restless energy worked out of me. If I had been born in a respectable sphere of life, I should have infallibly gone to the devil, and brought shame and confusion on my peaceable kindred. My natural tendencies would all have been violently crushed down. I should have found no opening for my energies in the smoothly-compacted surface of female existence. God gave me my talents, such as they are, and I should have been possessed as by a demon, if I had not been able to give free scope to them. I am not so good as you think me, by any means; and if I am worth any thing, it is the real hard work I have had to go through, which has made me so.'

'That may sound very well,' replied Lady Vernon, 'but when one thinks of the *sort* of work it is on which you have spent your life, one can feel no respect for it. I am not speaking of you individually, but of your way of life, which is altogether worthless, and unworthy of any immortal being. Your whole life is spent in dressing yourself up, and pretending to be that which you are not. Oh, I wish I could say any thing to induce you to give up that mode of life which is so especially dreadful when followed by a woman—nothing shall make me believe you like it.'

'We all live in our own meridian,' said Bianca; 'and can see only our own horizon. You cannot think how strange all you are saying sounds to my ears. You will laugh, when I tell you that I have often wondered how women, who were *not* actresses, contrived to pass their time; what they could find to do when they had their whole day free from any large occupation,—no

rehearsal for three hours in the morning, no long performance in
the evening,—to say nothing of hard study between the times. I
can see quite well the sort of look my life bears to you, but to *me*
it has quite another aspect. So far from despising it, I am passionately fond of it. I do not deny that I enjoy my success, but I have
a higher aim; I hope to elevate my profession into one of the fine
arts,—to see it ennobled, and freed from the meretricious degradation into which it has sunk. I see all that might be made of it. Any
thing considered merely as an amusement becomes despicable.
But the stage requires so much from its professors; it so takes their
life and soul, their very life-blood, that it ought to have higher
capabilities and nobler tendencies than merely to serve as a
vehicle to amuse the *ennui*, or to occupy the idleness of an
audience. I do not scruple to confess to you that the applause I
receive is sweet, and that I should find it very hard to live without
it; it is the seal and token that I have produced the effect I aimed
at. You do not know what you say, when you speak of it as
coarse excitement merely. You do not know the sense of power
there is in seeing hundreds of men and women congregated
together, and to know that I can make all that assembled
multitude laugh, weep, or experience any emotion I please to
excite:—there is positive intoxication in it, and I would not
change that *real* power to become a queen, and have to work my
will through the cumbrous machinery of a government. I act
directly upon my subjects, and the EFFECT follows instantly upon
my effort. I *see* all I produce; and I cannot express to you the zest,
the intoxication, the delirious enjoyment of a successful performance; it gives a sense of *power,* that for the time elevates one above
mortality. It does not last, certainly. I have sunk down weary and
fainting after this fierce excitement. Then there is the depression
of having constantly before me an ideal I cannot attain, and of
knowing that those who applaud so vehemently, do so only
because they do not discern it as I must. All I have achieved looks
as nothing beside that which I am striving to attain: but it is out
of my very discouragement that I have learned knowledge which
triumph cannot give; it is out of my hours of blackness and
despondency that I have learned my secrets, and have risen again
for the struggle. Strength comes out of weakness left by the
fatigues of labour. Give up my profession!—no! not if it were in

ten times worse repute than it is: so much the more need would there be to redeem it. My dearest Lady Vernon, you can talk better than I, but come and see me ACT, and then I will make you feel more respect for my profession; any way, it is my destiny to be an actress, and I must work it out.'

'Well, go then, Bianca,' said Lord Melton, sadly; 'go now, but come back to us when you are wearied; the glory that dazzles you will soon disappear—art, for its own sake, never satisfied a woman's heart yet.'

'And that is the reason women have generally achieved so little,' replied Bianca; 'they do not serve their art with that singleness of mind and oneness of purpose which all art requires—it is jealous, and admits no rival. For me, I have now no second thought to divide my devotion, and henceforth I belong altogether to my work.'

She felt sorry she had spoken so warmly, when she saw the cloud that settled over Lord Melton's countenance. He was deeply pained by her last words, and after a pause, he said:

'Whilst you are following your destiny in your own way, I shall carry out a project I have long entertained—I shall travel in the East, to see Jerusalem, Thebes, the Pyramids, and "the Zodiac's brazen mysteries".'

Bianca now flinched in her turn. 'Ah!' said she, with a slight shudder, 'I hate the word "*travel*", it has cost me so much. Am I to lose you, too?'

'You are like all women,' said Lord Melton, pettishly; 'you care for nothing until it is taken away from you. When I am three thousand miles out of your reach, you will perhaps think of me with kindness; any way, the experiment is worth trying.'

So saying, he quitted the room.

Bianca fancied it was only a spasm of temper, that would soon pass away; but the cloud drew darker. There was nothing to lay hold of, nothing to complain of, but the distance increased every day between them; he was kind as ever, but there was a grave, polite, displeasure visible through all; he avoided all private conversation with her, and whenever they chanced to be alone, he evaded all her attempts to come to an understanding.

The day Bianca had fixed for her departure arrived, they were together for a moment after breakfast.

'Maurice,' said she, hastily, 'why are you displeased?—tell me what I have done. I cannot bear to depart thus; let us be friends.'

'Friends, certainly, we *are* friends,' replied Lord Melton, gravely, taking no notice of the hand she had stretched out to him. 'You may rely upon me ever, as you would upon your own brother.'

'But why are you so changed, so cold? It kills me to think that I have displeased you.'

'Bianca, it is of no use trying to cool down a volcano and make it a comfortable drawing-room fire. You know it is *not* as a *brother* that I have cared for you; it is mere trifling to talk as you do. I cannot afford to consume my life in a fruitless passion; these last three months have been very pleasant, too pleasant, and I tell you frankly that I am going away in the hope of forgetting you. I have ceased to have any hope of winning you. You would not have left us thus, without saying any thing to me of your arrangements, had you not——'

Lady Vernon entered before he could finish his sentence; the carriage came to the door, and there remained nothing but the bustle of departure. Bianca departed more depressed and melancholy than she had believed any thing could ever make her again.

Lord Melton kept his word and made immediate preparations for his departure, but he was detained more than a month before they were complete. During the whole of this time Bianca did not hear from him; she only knew from his sister's letters that he had left the Park and gone up to London. She felt very uneasy, but on the whole thought it best to let things take their course. One morning she received the following note:

'DEAR FRIEND,—I was very cross the morning you went away. I was a great brute, but I could not help it;—forgive me. I go on board in an hour, and purpose remaining absent a twelvemonth. If I die in that time, there will be an end of all that concerns me. If I forget you, there will be an end of my unfortunate love; but if I live, I expect to come back in the same mind, and I shall try my fortune with you once more. When you write to me, do not fancy that I am vexed or sulky. I care for you just as I have always done, and you know how that is; so do not go vexing yourself about me, but be a good girl and take care of yourself. Write to me very often; you know I am your affectionate brother by your own confession, if I am nothing else, and I expect to be treated accordingly.

MELTON.

Bianca felt very glad when she received this letter; she fancied it was because Lord Melton had become more reasonable.

Lady Vernon wrote to her frequently, and she was soon too busy to have time for fanciful speculations.

CHAPTER VIII

Letter from Bianca to Lord Melton.

DEAR FRIEND,—I have been a long time in writing to you. I have a great deal to tell you; so much, that I fear it will never all get said. I have been working very hard, and found it, at first, sad up-hill work, after the idle, pleasant life I had led so long. Whether it was that I had begun to look at things through your sister's eyes, or whether I had grown accustomed to better things, I do not know; but the fact was, that I nearly took a disgust to all the theatrical accessories, amongst which I had been living all my life. Every thing connected with the stage looked coarser than it had ever done before. Do not rejoice in the confession, for I have been too hard at work to have leisure for the cultivation of my susceptibilities, and they have died a natural death.

I am now in the place where I first entered regularly on my profession; the scene of the first struggles, the hopes, the heavenly brightness of my life. I cannot express to you the horrible complication of emotions with which I found myself here once more. I did not think that I had been such a weak fool!—"past *is* past, and gone is gone"—I am content that it should be so. Any thing that actually *is*, ranks higher than the most beautiful hopes that ever "gilded the eastern horizon"! No, no, facts, realities, no matter how stern, are the only things I would ever desire to hold by; and so I have no regret for my past dreams—I *once* believed in them, NOW I have proved them to be only dreams: "*non regionam di lor*".* But all this is not what I was going to tell you. The old company to which I formerly belonged is all dispersed. Mr Montague St Leger, and all his glory, have passed away. It is an entire new set of people, except the old prompter, who once spoke a kind word to me when nobody else did; and it has been a real pleasure to me to see him again. I might be his daughter, the old man is so proud of my success, and that he prophesied it. He was so much affected on the first night of my appearance here, that he could not go on with his duty, and a substitute had to be found for the remainder of the evening. But neither is all this what I really wanted to say to you. I go on chattering, as children make a noise in the dark, to keep themselves from being frightened. Well, then—I have seen Conrad! I met him in the street, quite accidentally. I did not even know that he was in England. You may fancy I was horribly startled. He was calm, formal, and polite. God knows what I was. I came home after it, stunned, shattered, miserable to the last degree. I had seen with my own eyes, I had realised, the fact of his supreme indifference for me. I was like a criminal long left under sentence of death, who fancies he has become reconciled to his fate and weaned from life, but when suddenly brought out to suffer, finds that the cold definite reality passes all understanding. There is no hope in a reality; it is what it is, and there is no escape from it. My dear friend, I, too, have gazed on the face of a reality that has turned all my passion to stone.

A few days after the rencontre I went to pay a visit to Mrs Bryant, who befriended me once when I much needed a friend. I was ushered into the drawing-room, and there I found Conrad again! Things, in this world, seem to move in a cycle; things, people, circumstances, all come round again into their old position, and yet the result is so different. Five years ago I was here, acting at the same theatre, playing the self-same characters, Alice was my friend, Conrad was on a visit there, all the circumstances were similar, and yet how changed in their significance!

Alice received me kindly; was, I am convinced, glad in her heart to see me; but there was a constraint in her manner, evidently a fear lest any one should call and find an *actress* sitting there. Conrad assumed a quite different manner to what I have ever noticed in him before, a contemptuous, supercilious polite-ness, as if all women of my class were established in a species of recognised degradation. Fleury, the French actor, mentions in his memoirs, that the men of fashion in the old régime never condescended to say MADAME to a Bourgeoise, or a woman in a shop, but addressed them as "*Ma'me*" so and so,—a delicate shade of impertinence, that proved them masters in the art. Conrad's manner to me was in *that* style. Alice asked me to dine with her one day next week, when her husband would be out of town. I happened to glance in an opposite mirror, and caught a look of Conrad's, which I knew well of old; it is a look he has when a proposition is made which he dislikes. I refused on the plea of having no time; Alice easily accepted it, and soon after I took my leave, and came away depressed in heart. Alice herself cannot vex or alienate me, but I can see that our intercourse will cease. I know how easily she is influenced by those around her. I know so well the mischief and danger of her position, and I know, too, that I should be a good companion for her.

You will wonder why I plague you with a long history about a woman whom you never saw, and who would not interest you if you had. Alice is my HALF SISTER: her father was my father also, but I am illegitimate, and never knew him; he had abandoned my mother and become a respectable man before I saw the light. Alice is ignorant of this. I was careful not to tell her when I was a poor, unknown, almost starving girl; for I saw then (in spite of my affection and gratitude for her) her extreme timidity, and the utter absence of all moral courage in her character. Her conscientiousness would have made her desire to treat me as a sister, and her horror of all blame or scandal would have taken away all comfort from the relationship. I determined that I would keep silence until I had made for myself such a position in the world as would prevent my being considered a disgrace to a respectable connexion. I did not even tell Conrad of this relationship; I had hoped that during this visit I might have made myself known to her, and claimed her for my sister. I cannot tell you how full of love my heart is towards her. Now I see that it can never be; it is another illusion gone, another hope passed away in unripe blessedness;—let it go, I yield it up; no sin of my own has made me an outcast, and I have done all that lies in me for the atonement of the error that first caused it. I speak to you calmly, but I have shed bitter tears; it seemed to me such an innocent desire, one that I might have knelt down and begged God to grant. I have succeeded in my ambition; but all by which I had hoped to sanctify that ambition, to give to it value and sweetness, has been thwarted, and what good shall my life now do me? Dear friend, dear friend, do not think me ungrateful to you, nor unmindful of all you have done for me; but I am traversing a path where all my pleasant things have been laid waste. I have no heart left to form new hopes. I am contented that things should be as they are. I would not desire to change them now that I see their nature. I can say no more than this,—I must sit desolate for a while, and then perhaps I shall gain strength to go on less wearily. But why should I plague you with all this, except that you are my friend, that you are patient with me and love me, and are better to me than I deserve.

Your faithful friend and sister,
BIANCA.

CHAPTER IX

'MY dear Bryant,' cried Alice, as soon as they were seated at dinner (the day of Bianca's visit), 'I had quite an adventure this morning. Who do you think has been here?'

'Perhaps the Emperor of China? if you insist upon my guessing; but I think you had better tell me, instead of driving me pitilessly out into the wilds of conjecture—WHO has been here? I ask you with an emphasis that would touch the heart of a sphinx!'

'Well then,' replied Alice, 'as I am made of "penetrable stuff", I will tell you; but I do not promise that you shall consider it a "pleasing fact". Bianca, the celebrated actress, has been to see me! I little dreamed when she was my *protégée* years ago, that she would come to be a woman of distinction. She was looking extremely well, and much handsomer than formerly; she came in her carriage, and was dressed beautifully. She said she took advantage of being in the neighbourhood, to call and thank me for my past kindness to her.'

Bryant looked rather grave. 'That is all very well for once, my dear: it might be very grateful and all that, to call and show you that she had prospered in the world, and to let you see that she had a carriage of her own; but now that both those objects are attained, I do not wish you to renew your acquaintance with her. I should much more dislike your knowing her now that she is become a noted person, than when she was struggling in obscurity. Professional people live in a world of their own; and it is very undesirable that they should be introduced into the private circles of the middle classes: it tends to destroy that sobriety and balance of conduct which makes their peculiar virtue, without introducing at the same time the abilities, and powers of pleasing, which are the redeeming qualities of the other class. I have a singular objection to meeting with authors, actors, artists, or professional people of any sort; except in the peculiar exercise of their vocation, which I am willing to pay for. There may be respectable people amongst them, but they are not sufficient to give a colouring to the class; and as a class, there is a want of stamina about them: they have no precision or business-like habits, the absence of which leaves an opening for faults with very ugly names; and persons whose profession it is to amuse others, and make themselves pleasing, cannot in the nature of things expect to take a very high position. Men cannot feel reverence or respect for those who aspire to amuse them.'

'Well!' cried Conrad, laughing, 'I have always observed that heavy, sententious, stupid persons, seem to entertain a species of contempt for those who possess the lighter gifts of being enter-taining; but I never heard it made into a theory before. To leave that part of the question, however, let me ask you, whether you consider that the province of those who profess the fine arts, is only to amuse? Do you think that they have gained the real end of their labour when they are paid for what they do? and do you consider the production of works of art to be a mere mode of earning a living?'

'This is an industrial country,' said Bryant; 'the great mass of sympathy and intellect takes a practical direction—a direction that we understand; we have no real knowledge of art, no real instinct or genuine aspiration after it; and I should say, that in our hearts we do not respect, love, or honour fine art in any of its manifestations, as we do that which is scientific or practical. To the Italians, to the French even, music and pictures are neces-saries of life; to us English, they only take the guise of ornament, or convenience—of superfluity, in short. That being the case, we naturally do not feel drawn to the society of artists; we have nothing in common with them—we do not admire them; neither do we feel disposed to introduce to the society of our wives and daughters, a parcel of actors, artists, musicians, and so forth, who have no stake in society, who have little to lose, whose capital is all invested in themselves and their two hands, and who have, therefore, naturally cultivated themselves far beyond what we practical men have had a chance of doing, and are capable of throwing us into the shade in our own houses, whilst they show that they despise us. Let them keep their places, and let us keep ours!'

'But do you allow nothing for the civilising influence of men of cultivated intellect amongst you?' said Conrad.

'Railroads will do more,' replied Bryant; 'every people must work out its civilisation in its own way. Love of the fine arts is *not* our speciality,—we do not know a good thing from a bad one, unless we are told; and the pretence we make about it has a bad effect on our character. There is such a pressure of competition, and so much enterprise in all departments of industry, that all the energies of English people are absorbed and worked out in that direction. Show a man of mechanical genius, in the manufacturing classes, the finest statue that ever was made—his first question will be, "Was it made by hand?" and his next thought would be, to invent a MACHINE, to produce something like it by a mechanical process; he would see nothing in it which might not be obtained by a machine.'

'Perhaps,' said Conrad, 'that may explain how, whilst the *results* produced by the energies of the commercial classes seem stupendous, like the works of demi-gods the people themselves are absolutely unendurable—they are, in general, real barbarians, savage men.'

'What would you have?' said Bryant, shrugging his shoulders; 'they do the work of the world, and real labour was never yet made to look beautiful; we are engaged all day at the full stretch with our nerves, sinews, brains, strained to the utmost tension; and do you think we have either strength or time to spend in trying to move along gracefully? We, who have to grapple with realities, grow stern and rude as the elements in which we work; we have to produce the substance out of which refinement, civilisation, the very country itself, have to come forth. It is not our fault if the fine arts, and the artists who produce them, seem small and trivial beside the immense interests with which we have to deal, and the materials with which we have to work.'

'But,' said Conrad, 'do you not think that this movement for the encouragement of art and diffusion of universal taste, will have a softening and fertilising influence on the rudeness of the industrial classes in this country?'

'It will be only an acquired taste,' replied Bryant: 'but, perhaps, like our hot-house fruit, it may have a finer flavour than in the countries where it is indigenous. It is not a movement in which I take the least interest myself,—but whatever is genuine in it will go on,—and all the talking in the world will not keep the rest alive. We shall see what comes of it in the end; but in the mean time, I have remained here talking a great deal too long. So good bye to you both. What are you going to do this afternoon?'

'Mrs Bryant talked of taking me to a party,' said Conrad.

'Ah! that will be well. You had better take the carriage. If I can, I will join you in the evening'; and, with a nod to Alice and Conrad, Bryant left the room.

'I have promised to take Mrs Lathom some ferns; she has none, will you come with me to the conservatory to cut them?' said Alice.

Conrad did not need asking twice; he rose with alacrity, and joyfully followed her.

'Do you,' said he, as they walked along, 'share in Bryant's indifference to the fine arts? I should say not; every thing around you announces a cultivated taste.'

'Ah!' said Alice, 'I inherit from my father a passionate love for pictures; he had a fine collection, but they were all dispersed when he died, and I have felt as if I had been all my life banished from my natural home, and forced to live in a strange place where I could not feel *at home*. I was very young when those pictures were sent away; there were some statues and busts, too; and yet I remember them so well. I dream of them at night; and whenever I hear of heaven, I instinctively think of my father's house full of pictures and beautiful objects, and hope to be restored to it. I have tried to paint, myself; but though my whole heart seems melting with a love for an idea of some ineffable picture I never saw, yet I have no control of hand, and what I have produced are such blurred and patched daubs, that I have given up the practice. You see I am surrounded with every thing that a woman can desire, and yet I feel shut up in prison; I can get to hear and see nothing that my heart cares for. I hardly know what it is that I do thirst to hear and see; I say pictures, because these are the only things that ever expressed to me what I feel I need; but there are many other things besides them; it is not the actual pictures that I desire, but what they seem to mean and utter that I want to hear. If I might travel, I should find it; but Bryant cannot leave home, except on hurried business-journeys, and cannot take me with him; so I only go to the sea-side in summer. The sea makes me happy, when I can go by myself, away from every body, and look into the clouds after the sun has set. What I want to see and know so much, seems then within my reach.'

'Whose dwelling is the light of setting suns,'*

said Conrad, half to himself, as he listened eagerly to all she said.

'Ah! where does that come from?' said Alice, turning quickly to him.

'Do you not know the poem?' said Conrad. 'I will read it to you when we go in. I have that volume of Wordsworth in my portmanteau; have you never read him?'

'No,' replied Alice.

'Well, I am almost grateful to you,' replied Conrad, 'for now I shall have the great pleasure of showing you for the first time two poems that have a mysterious influence upon me, and stir my soul to its foundations as no other words ever did. They work on me like a spell; if they take the same hold upon you, there will be a bond between us beyond relationship; they never fade; their effect now is as strong as when I read them first a thousand times ago.'

'I will not be an instant in cutting the ferns,' said Alice, 'and then we will go back and hear them before we set off. Is not that branch of fern a miracle of beauty and grace? to me ferns always seem to have a supernatural look.'

'Will you give me one?' said Conrad.

'What would you do with it?' asked Alice. 'You could not carry it to London with you, and I cannot find in my heart to let it get broken and die. I could almost as soon let a young child come to harm; no, no, let the poor things stay here in their appointed home: but you may carry these, and take care you do not break them; and now let us go back to the house, I am impatient to hear these poems.'

As soon as they returned, Conrad fetched the volume containing 'Lines on Revisiting Tintern Abbey', and Alice seated herself at her embroidery by the window. Conrad had a finely-toned voice, and he had the gift of reading remarkably well, but they were qualities quite lost on Alice at the present moment, so entirely was she penetrated by the poem; it was as if the voice of the heart of nature had syllabled itself, and made her own yearnings articulate. She sat with her face concealed from Conrad; tears, in which no pain mingled, coursed each other down her cheeks, and were the only utterance of the feelings that had been roused.

'Now,' said he, after a pause, 'let me read you the other poem I mentioned, the "Ode on Immortality".'

'No, not now; I could hear nothing that would break the impression of the other; and, besides, the carriage will be here immediately.'

She rose and left the room. Conrad was half dissatisfied at her manner, which he thought betokened too much indifference.

'How could she go on with her worsted work, when she was listening to such words of inspiration!' thought he, moving almost unconsciously to the frame where she had been seated. Bending over her work, he saw that it was quite wetted with her tears, which shone like dew-drops on the half-finished flowers.

'Ah!' cried he, with enthusiasm, 'how beautiful she is in all things!—with what exquisite modesty she concealed her emotion—how infinitely more touching is the general coldness of her manner, than all the passionate sensibility of other women! Bianca would not have shrunk from letting me see her tears, and she would have told me all she felt; I should never have had the delight of surprising her thoughts thus!'

He pressed his lips with enthusiasm on the embroidery: in which act he was almost surprised by Alice, as she opened the door, looking as lady-like and calm as if no emotion had ever ruffled her fair brow, or soft, star-like eyes. Conrad thought her exquisite, and she was dressed, too, exactly according to his taste. She wore a white chip bonnet, of a shape that suited the style of her face; the Cashmere shawl he remembered of old over a dress of delicate rich-coloured silk.

'Are you quite ready?' said she, smiling; 'the carriage is come round, and we are rather late, but we shall have a lovely drive.'

He assisted her into the carriage, and seated himself opposite to her. For some time they neither of them spoke. He was watching her, without seeming to look at her, and she was still filled with the thoughts awakened by the poem.

'I owe you so much more than I can ever express,' said she, at last. 'Will you lend me that book?—or, what will be better, will you, when you go back to town, get me all his poems?—they will be like a new life to me.'

'I am surprised you never met with them before,' said Conrad.

'We have no library worth any thing in this neighbourhood; and I know so little, that I cannot direct my own reading. I wish you would tell me some more books to get; I feel that I waste my time sadly, and I do not know what to do.'

'Would you not find it worth while to subscribe to some good London library, and have the books sent down to you?'

'Bryant would think it waste of money,' said Alice. 'We have a Book Society; but no books are ordered in that I care to read.'

'You have a great deal of time to yourself,' said Conrad. 'In what do you employ yourself all day?'

'I hardly know,' replied Alice. 'I have nothing to do that seems worth doing. I am depressed under a constant sense of waste, a vague consciousness that I am always doing wrong, and yet I can find out nothing that I ought to do. I need some one to direct me and guide me. Bryant is all day at his business, and is so engrossed in it, that I have scarcely any of his company, and he wants to rest when he is at home. I used to think that I should be so happy, if I might have all my time to improve myself, and spend as I like; but now that I have it, I do not know what to do with it. My whole life is one cloud, and I have a sense of responsibility which I can neither adequately discharge, nor deliver myself from. I have nothing to look forward to. When I get up in the morning, I know all that is likely to happen before night; one day is like another, and the weight of life that lies upon me is intolerable. If I had children, it would be different, I should have something to live for; as it is, I am of use to nobody. I did not like saying so at dinner time, it would have looked like contradicting Bryant; but the only companion I ever felt really to get good from was Bianca;—she was with me a little while some years ago, and she seemed to know so well all I needed, and said such wise things, without seeming to think them wise, that I felt stronger and better whilst she was with me, than I ever did before;—but you heard the objection Bryant expressed to her. I dare not ask him to let me see her again.'

'Believe me,' said Conrad, gently, 'she is not the kind of companion you ought to have. Bianca is a wonderful woman, but she is in a position that must, of necessity, demoralise the essence of all that is feminine and womanly in her nature;—she is too coarse, too strong, too passionate—you could not feel any real sympathy with her; and when a woman has once dwelt beneath the brazen glare of popularity, her beauty and value as a woman is destroyed, and the intrinsic worth of what she does to compensate for it, is more than doubtful. I should grieve much to see you disturbing the pure, gentle current of your life, by admitting a woman like Bianca into your privacy.'

'Do you know much of her of late?' asked Alice.

'A great deal,' replied Conrad, gravely. 'Do you remember the mad passion I conceived for her when I came here for the first time years ago?—it ended in an engagement, which was still subsisting when I was here last. After I had seen you, I felt that Bianca was not a woman with whom I could spend my life; and I broke off the engagement irrevocably. You have far higher qualities as a woman than Bianca, with all her brilliancy. I feel myself a purer and a better man since I have known you; and you have raised the whole sex in my eyes, since in you, I have seen realised the qualities I dreamed of as most excellent in woman.' Conrad uttered this in a calm, firm, almost austere manner, which took away all tinge of flattery or gallantry.

Any further conversation was, however, prevented by their arrival at 'Fairy Hill', the residence of Mrs Lathom.

Mrs Lathom set up to be a 'superior woman'. Conrad had hardly patience to endure the supercilious coldness and pretentiousness of her manner, which she considered the extreme of all that was elegant. He was indignant at the tone of deep-seated superiority she assumed towards Alice; to Conrad himself, she intended to be very gracious; but it was like the atmosphere of a state drawing-room in November, with its fire not thoroughly lighted. A few friends had been assembled to meet him; but they sat stiff and silent on the superb gilded chairs. There was not sufficient geniality to animate the dead weight of elegant upholstery that filled the whole room. It stood in all the hard unassimilated individuality of its native warehouse, and seemed as if it never would feel itself at home. Every thing in the room—the pier-glasses, the marble slabs, the marqueterie tables with their gilded feet, the sumptuous carpet, the satin curtains, the gold paper and gilded ceiling—all impressed on the beholder an unmitigated sense of wasted money: there was no geniality to make it forgotten.

A solemn whist-table in one corner, a few books of engravings in miraculously splendid bindings, and a few faintly warbled songs from one or two young ladies, were the only aids the victims found to pass through the dreary evening. What conversation there was, passed in a low tone between neighbours; all that Conrad could hear was of the most bald, insipid description. To Conrad, fresh from London society, and the conversational fireworks flashing about there, it seemed marvellous how human beings could exist in such a stagnant region; and yet all the people, taken individually, were sensible, educated persons, only they did not possess the art of being sociable.

Conrad sat down to whist and lost a few sovereigns whilst sighing for eleven o'clock. A sumptuous supper at length seemed to rouse the guests into something like vitality. Mr Lathom handed a portly-looking lady in black velvet and point lace to the seat beside him, at the bottom of the table; and a stout, grave, pale gentleman in spectacles, seated himself beside Mrs Lathom at the top; every one else found their place as they could. Conrad got beside Alice, and sat down much astonished at the profusion of every thing he saw before him; but when people have dined early, and have been bored without intermission for a long evening, a good supper is not a disagreeable diversion, and Conrad, though he denounced it as a barbarism, found himself submitting to it with much complacency. Bryant came in just as they were sitting down. There was a little talk at supper, but it was exclusively either political or commercial, and very uninteresting to Conrad, who could take no part in it.

'Is this the average of your society?' said he, in a low voice, to Alice.

'As far as amusement goes, yes,' replied Alice; 'but some of the gentlemen are very clever, and very agreeable when you can talk to them, but it is not the fashion here to talk much to women; they naturally have more to say to each other, being all in business together.'

'And the women?' said Conrad.

'Oh, that one sitting beside Mr Lathom is a very nice woman, very kind-hearted and genial; but I am not intimate with any of them; they think so much of being "select" in their society, but I would be very thankful for somebody nice, no matter what set they were in. How different Bianca looked to all the women here!'

'That is not a fair comparison,' said he; 'Bianca has cultivated all her personal gifts and graces to the utmost; it is her profession; but she would not have had the grace to spend a long, stupid evening patiently as you have done, and yet you are qualified to mingle in any set, however intellectual or refined.'

'What a luxury it must be,' cried Alice, 'to have the *entrée* to London society, to meet really clever people, and hear witty speeches, and things worth listening to!'

'Every patch of ground looks greener than the one we stand upon,' said Conrad, laughing. 'I am going back to London to-morrow, and yet I consider those who have the privilege of coming to see you whenever they like are much more to be envied than I am!—But are we never going away? I long to be home in your drawing-room, to rest my eyes after all the gilding they have seen to-night; I have been trying to calculate how many sovereigns must have been melted down to cover that room!—people should in decency disguise their money a little. But do let us go. Bryant wants a cigar, I can see.'

Alice rose; her example was followed by the rest, and the company dispersed generally.

CHAPTER X

IF people only would believe it, wishing is just the most insanely dangerous pastime a rational being can indulge in! forethought, plans, schemes, are generally in the end, however successful they may seem, nothing more than elaborate folly, in which it would have been much happier for the parties had they been disappointed. Good King David, the father of a wise son, and himself a very politic man in his way, used to say emphatically: 'In vain do they rise up early, and late take rest, and eat the bread of carefulness';*—and the sailor-song says quaintly enough—

> For Providence will have its way,
> Let men do as they will!

Men would have fewer troubles, if they took less pains to bring them upon themselves. Their greatest plagues generally result from their success in some scheme on which they have specially set their heart.

All this moralising is *à propos* to something that Bryant considered, at the time, a great stroke of good fortune.

The night after they returned from the party at Mrs Lathom's, and the gentlemen were smoking their cigars together after Alice had retired, Conrad, who did not too well know what to talk about, negligently asked Bryant, what he thought would be a good investment for a few thousand pounds. He had not thought of the subject the moment before. Bryant caught at the suggestion; it would suit his schemes just then remarkably well to have a little additional advanced; and if he could induce Conrad to connect himself as a sleeping partner with his house, it would be a good thing for him, and not a bad one for Conrad, as he considered the result secure. He began to sound Conrad on the subject. Conrad, who would cheerfully have risked, not a part of his fortune alone, but the whole of it, for a chance of getting a hold on the family, listened eagerly to the proposal, and departed the next morning, promising to think of it,—and fully resolved to close with any terms, thinking thereby that he would be able to see Alice again and again. Bryant, Conrad, and Alice, when they heard of it, all fancied in their hearts that they must have been wearing 'a wishing cap', so extremely propitious did the plan appear. The realisation of it seemed to progress equally well; the details, all arranging themselves, had fitted into each other without any drawback or hindrance; it rose like the building of Solomon's temple, in which no noise of workmen or hammers was heard. Really, if men did but know it, the desire of their own hearts ought to make them afraid!

Conrad came down again in a fortnight. He had shaved off his moustaches—they looked a phenomenon in the circle where he wished to be domesticated, and he was anxious to get rid of every thing incongruous, and to look as much as possible like an English man of business. It was settled that he was to remain a few weeks with the Bryants, to get some knowledge of affairs, whilst the details of the partnership were arranged. In the course of these few weeks a great deal that no one thought of went on below the quiet, dreamy, prosaic surface of their every-day life.

Bryant took a real affection for Conrad; thought him an upright, intelligent, generous fellow, with great talents for business, if they were cultivated. Alice was not aware of the hold Conrad was gaining over her; her whole life was brightened up; she became sensible of thoughts and energies which had never stirred in her before. She employed herself with a zeal and interest she had never before felt in any of her occupations. It had become a matter of course to look to Conrad as a companion, to turn to him instinctively for counsel and approbation in all she did. His taste, his opinions, moulded hers. He directed her reading, he read to her, and all she did or said found a gentle echo in him. She had never been so happy in her life. Nor had she ever been so charming. She seemed, for the first time, to be placed in a congenial atmosphere, and all her graces and virtues expanded in its kindly warmth. To Bryant, Alice was gentle and loving as ever. His coldness and distraction did not annoy her now. She did not feel them; her own happy cheerfulness was diffused, like a sunny light, on all within her influence.

Conrad's love and veneration for Alice knew no bounds; every day increased her empire over him; the more he loved her, the more carefully he buried it within his most secret heart. To live in the light of her looks, to be near her, to hear her speak, was all he asked. He would not have sullied the gentle purity of her soul by a word that an angel might not have heard, nor have startled her by a tone or look of passion. He loved her with every fibre of his nature. All the best and purest feelings of his soul were called forth. Every baser passion seemed subdued and purified. For the time, he felt satisfied and content to add to the comfort of her daily existence, and asked no return; wished for nothing, except to remain near her, and watch over her, like a guardian angel. He could not feel any sense of guilt, for he had never been sensible before of so many generous and noble impulses. He really loved her, and love ennobles all it touches. 'It makes the reptile equal to the god.' So things went on. 'But all this world contains holds in perfection but a little moment.' Excellency cannot be stereotyped—it must be maintained by the struggle and strong grasp of life alone. Left to itself it loses its shape and glorious beauty, and fades and falls away into corruption and dissolution.

There was to be a grand dinner-party. Conrad had been talking of going back to town, but he remained for it. He had begun to think that he ought to go—that he could not live there all his life; that he must go away; for this thought alone had disturbed the blessed tranquillity in which he had been so long dwelling. But it was settled he was to remain till after the dinner-party. It was the morning of the day: Alice was arranging flowers, and busying herself in putting out her drawing-room ornaments, and arranging the room as it was to be. She moved about in her delicate-coloured morning dress like a gentle Naiad.* Conrad was lying on one of the sofas, pretending to read; but, in reality, watching her as she flitted gracefully to and fro. She arranged her lamps, put out her best cushions, and filled a large alabaster basket with flowers. She was very much absorbed in her employment, and did not perceive the intense expression of Conrad's eyes.

'You perceive I have followed your taste in the lamp—I took the one you admired. Now come here and tell me how you like the effect of the room; I think it is very pretty as you look through those folding-doors.'

'You do all things well!' said Conrad, with involuntary energy.

Then, confused at his own warmth, he walked into the inner room, and pretended to be altering the position of the lamp; but he scarcely knew what he was about, and lifting it awkwardly, the heavy lamp overbalanced in his hands and fell to the ground with a terrible crash.

'What is it?' cried Alice, running in dismay at the sound. 'My beautiful new lamp! and the oil is all over the carpet!' She began hastily to pick up the broken glass, but put her hand down heedlessly on a large jagged piece, which cut it severely. She uttered a slight shriek at the pain, and Conrad in great agitation lifted her upon a sofa, for she had turned sick and pale at the sight of the blood. Conrad examined her hand and pressed it to his lips; it seemed to him like sacrilege to let any of the precious drops be lost.

'Give me some water,' said Alice, faintly. He threw out the flowers she had so carefully arranged, and brought the vase to her; she drank a little, and he sprinkled her face and neck.

'It is nothing; I shall be better soon—do not be frightened.'

'Oh, Alice! you are hurt—you are dreadfully hurt, and all through my fault,' cried Conrad, in despair. He washed the wound and bound it skilfully up: the perspiration stood on his forehead, and his face was as pale as the handkerchief with which he had staunched the wound. When he had finished, he shuddered and buried his head in the sofa pillow beside her.

'Poor dear Conrad, how I have frightened you,' said Alice; but Conrad did not speak; he seemed under the influence of violent emotion beyond his control, and the couch shook with the sobs that burst from his bosom.

'Conrad, Conrad!' said Alice, wildly, 'tell me what is the matter. Are you hurt?—are you ill?' and she attempted to lift his head with her soft white hand. Conrad started at her touch and looked up. She was terrified at the expression of his countenance; his lips were still marked with blood, traces of tears were on his cheeks, and his eyes were pale and almost extinct.

'Speak to me, Conrad—one word—tell me what has come to you that you look thus?'

'I love you, Alice!' said he, in a low hard whisper; and with a look of passion and despair, such as no woman could misinterpret, he rose and left the room.

CHAPTER XI

IN spite of all the occurrences of the morning, the dinner-party came to pass at its appointed time. Alice was standing in the drawing-room, ready to receive her guests, looking a little paler than usual—but that might arise from her accident, for her hand was very painful; the bandage was covered with black ribbon, and she was obliged to rest it in a sling. The carpet showed evident tokens of the misadventure, and it was quite a topic of conversation for the time before dinner.

'Lamps are a great source of anxiety,' said one lady, pathetically. 'I have been tormented to death with them; they always took the opportunity of either falling down, or going out, or beginning to smoke, when I had company, though they burned beautifully at other times; they might have known and done it on purpose. But now I keep a footman to attend expressly to them, and I take no anxiety about them. If any thing goes wrong, it is a comfort to have somebody to blame for it.'

Others recited their various plagues and experiences: it seemed a universal ground of sympathy. Conrad did not make his appearance until just as dinner was announced. Alice felt him come in, although she did not look towards him. He kept at the opposite end of the room; but in the general movement of sitting down to table, he found himself placed nearly close beside her, divided from her only by his companion and her right-hand neighbour, who had brought her in to dinner. She was dressed in black velvet high to the throat, without any ornament except a pair of pearl bracelets, her husband's gift when they were married, and which she had put on as a sort of talisman this day. So much in this world goes on from habit, goes on because it has been once set going. Alice sat at the head of her table, went through all the customary duties of her place, spoke and answered, mechanically, words of course, and yet she was conscious of nothing that was going on; none of the company, with *one* exception, saw any thing peculiar in her manner; she was very quiet and silent—but seldom spoke. She never looked towards Conrad, and he once only addressed her to say—'May I give you some wine?'

She took it, but did not raise her eyes beneath the one glance he turned upon her. The evening passed over like most other evenings after a well-conducted dinner-party, where the guests are all highly respectable, but by no means stimulating company. There was coffee handed round to the ladies, and after coffee they had a little music. Some of the dowagers held a privy council of gossip amongst themselves; while the younger ladies sat about and looked at books and engravings, and were harmlessly *ennuyé*, until the gentlemen re-appeared, which they did just as it was time to depart. The carriages were announced, the owners entered them, and were driven away, and the whole affair was at an end.

As soon as the last guest had departed, Bryant ordered candles to his private-business room, desiring his wife not to sit up for him, as he had his evening letters to read, and should probably be up late. Alice was once more alone, sitting on the couch in the inner drawing-room. What she was thinking about it would be hard to say; she did not know it herself; she was stunned with the declaration and the occurrences of the morning. How long she had remained sitting there she knew not, when she was roused by Conrad, who entered, looking pale, miserable, and desperate.

'Alice!' said he, 'Alice, you must let me speak to you for five minutes, now all those dreadful people are gone. It is the last time. I am going away to-morrow, and I cannot leave you thus. Come up stairs to your own sitting-room; we shall be interrupted here; you must hear what I have to say. Alice, do not make me desperate, do not make me more wretched than I am. I thought this evening would be eternal. For pity's sake do not hesitate:— what have I done to deserve that you should not trust me? Alice! you must hear me, you shall hear me, I demand it as a right: I have that to say which you must listen to, and I cannot speak here.'

The servants were, in fact, beginning to extinguish the lights; Alice feared his agitated manner would attract their notice.

'What have you to say?' said she, hurriedly. 'For God's sake, consider what you are about; you will be seen—you will be heard—go away now.'

'Will you let me see you alone for five minutes, in your own sitting-room? Alice! I am desperate, I am capable of any extravagence; do not drive me beside myself; you *must* hear me. I deserve better at your hands than this.'

Alice trembled violently, and half made a gesture to rise, and then drew back. The servant entered the room where they were together.

'Mrs Bryant,' said Conrad, in a formal tone, 'will you look out the drawing you promised to give me; I go away so early to-morrow there will be no time then.'

To escape the eyes of the servant, Alice rose. At the door of her sitting-room she stood for a moment irresolute, but women of her character have an instinct to do whatever seems decidedly expected from them. She went in and stood beside the fire-place, almost insensible from agitation. Conrad had lost all his power of utterance. He leaned against the mantel-piece, not daring to raise his eyes to her. The emotion of each rose to a point of agony.

'Alice!' said Conrad, in a choking voice, 'I wished to ask—I could not go away without—Alice!' cried he, impetuously, all the pent-up passion of his soul finding its way like a lava torrent; 'Alice! I love you—my whole soul is yours. I have no life but you. You are my god—my religion—my life. I love you. Do not send me away from you; my whole soul is devoted to you. I have lived in your shadow—in the sound of your dear voice; you have been like a blessed angel to me; all I know of goodness or purity is from you. Alice, I love you. Do not send me away from you, I cannot go—I will not go—I must stay beside you. There is no world—no life—no place but in your presence. Alice, Alice, tell me not to go away, let me stay—let me live as your slave, I will never speak one word to you that a blessed angel might not hear. I ask nothing—I desire nothing, only let me stay—let me be under the same roof with you. I have controlled myself—I intended to go away in silence, but I have no power to go, the torture has forced me to utterance; let me stay and I will be dumb. Alice, Alice, be merciful. Ever since I saw you I have loved you, and have I not been silent? It was to be near you, to have the right of approaching you, that I embarked with Bryant. I ask nothing but to remain beside you: once living in your dear presence, I cannot leave it; why must I go away? Why are you banishing me? I am mad, and you have driven me mad. My whole life centres in you. I will not go away; let me stay, and I will never offend you more. I thought to fly to save myself from perdition, but I am lost, I am lost, let me stay!' He uttered this frantic appeal with a rapidity and energy that made it almost inarticulate.

'Conrad! Conrad!' said Alice, 'what words are these? For pity's sake hush, I must not hear them. You must go. You will not be so wretched long. We are both very wrong. Go; you must go, and not return. Oh, why did you ever come!' cried she, in an accent of despair.

'Alice, it is the only life I have ever known; this last month, this last precious month, would have been cheaply bought with an eternity of pain. If I had not loved you, I should not have known life;—it has been the only thing I ever did that was worth coming into the world for. I love you; I will pay the penalty, if it be death or madness. Oh, I rejoice in suffering for you. I ask no return from you; I ask only not to be driven from your presence.'

Alice had never witnessed strong passionate emotion. All her life her soul had been athirst for words of love; all the words he uttered found an echo in her own soul; and she was obliged to put aside the cup that was offered, for the first time, to her parched soul in the dreary desert of her life. She leaned her forehead against the mantel-piece, and, without trusting herself to look at Conrad, she said, in a low but steady tone, 'You must go; there is no more peace or safety for us together. So long as I did not know your secret I was guiltless. God knows, I never suspected it till this morning; we have been so calm, so happy; but that is all past now, and will never return. Do not attempt to come back again; we can never be again as we have been; it is idle to dream of it. You will find again the peace of mind you have lost. My life was dreary before you came, and when you are gone,'—her voice failed, but she recovered herself, and continued abruptly, 'It is a forbidden thing for us to be happy as we have been, and we must both pay the price of having learned what we ought never to have known. I cannot innocently see you again. I must not remain here; let me go.'

He seized one of her hands as she turned away, and flinging himself on the ground, clasped her knees: 'Alice! Alice!' cried he, wildly, 'do you know the meaning of "for ever"? God alone has the right to condemn to a "for ever". You know not what you

are saying. Tell me I am not to return for a month—for a
year—for two years,—but fix some term when I may come back
to look on you.'

'Conrad! Conrad!' cried Alice, in despair, 'do not break my
heart! It is you who should strengthen me; you must have
strength for both. Do I look as if it made me happy to send you
away for ever?—to know that we must never see each other
again? Do not lead me into wrong: let me go; I must go; I will
go.'

Disengaging her hand, and without daring to look at him she
left that room. Conrad remained in the same spot, prostrate on
the ground, unable to tear himself away from where he had last
seen her. The candle had long since burned out, and the cold
gray morning began to break the darkness. He madly kissed the
ground where she had stood, and staggered to his bed-room,
where, exhausted, he flung himself on the bed.

He had arranged to depart early, and was in hopes he should
escape without seeing Bryant; who, however, was already in the
breakfast-room, where the shutters had just been opened and a
hasty breakfast set out, when Conrad descended.

'Conrad, my boy! I did not see you last night. Alice could not
get up to see you, she is very ill. I sat up late writing letters last
night, and when I went up stairs at a little after two o'clock this
morning I found her lying on the couch in her dressing-room.
She has been having shivering-fits and fainting away the whole
night. I shall go with you to the coach, and then bring home the
doctor to see her, for I am very uneasy about her.'

Fortunately, Bryant was too much engaged to notice Conrad's
haggard and disturbed countenance, or to perceive the agitation
into which the mention of Alice threw him. Nevertheless, to
hear of her suffering was the only consolation of which he was
just then susceptible. He felt a secret joy at knowing that he did
not suffer alone.

'Now, my boy, we have not a moment to lose,' cried Bryant,
rising and swallowing his cup of tea; 'the coach starts at a quarter
to six.' Casting one look at the desolate room, Conrad followed
him.

CHAPTER XII

At first Alice felt Conrad's absence a relief,—he loved her, he had told her so, and she was satisfied. The deep thirst of her heart was appeased, she felt it was well for both he should be away. Then began the deep vacuity of absence; that weight, 'heavy as lead, and deep almost as life':* it enveloped her and her whole existence as with a cloud of thick darkness,—'darkness that might be felt'.* She shut herself up in the house—refused to see any one, refused to go out. She could not bear to look on any object associated with him. When she walked in the garden, the very trees seemed to nod their heads, and mock her dumb agony. She sat nearly always in the inner drawing-room. Sometimes she tried to continue the ottoman she had worked on when he was there, and forced herself to take a few stitches; then, flinging down the frame, as a pang of memory shot through her mind, she would fall back in a fit of vehement hysterical weeping, which increased upon her every day, till her health became seriously affected. At other times she would go to a small book-case, and taking down the Wordsworth he had given to her, sit looking at it without reading, wildly pressing her lips to a mark on one of the pages. Sometimes she would make a desperate struggle to free herself. She determined to crush this passion out of her heart; and once actually began to destroy the presents he had given her from time to time, the box of paints, a little Swiss basket, and the rest. But such a host of memories came with each—the kind words, the pleasant occasions on which they had been presented—times, before she had eaten of the tree of knowledge, when she was calm, happy, ignorant of passion—that her courage failed her. Hastily snatching the little carved basket from the flames, she took all her treasures and hid them in the secret drawer of a cabinet, in the inner drawing-room, firmly resolving that she would never visit them, or look upon them again; and that same night, after she had retired to rest, came down stairs, to be sure that no one had meddled with them! She struggled, helplessly, under a weight that seemed glued to her very soul. A sense of remorse pursued her like a fiend—every kind word uttered by her husband went to her heart—a thousand times she was on the point of telling him every thing—the pent-up agony of her soul was more than she could bear—the feeling of her duplicity was, perhaps, after all, the most intolerable of her sufferings. She longed to tell her husband, in order that, at least, she might stand true in his eyes; but then she feared to compromise Conrad; she hesitated, and, after all, it was but one emotion out of the thousand that tore her soul. Her health failed, her temper failed; it became unequal, passionate, morose. She was in misery; misery that no words could express; and, at times, she was near suicide, as the only escape from her intolerable suffering.

Bryant was, at that time, a great deal from home, or he must have suspected some cause for this extraordinary change. He saw she was dull, and out of spirits. He pressed her to invite some friend—she pettishly refused. He proposed she should go from home, with his sister, for change of scene—she sullenly refused to stir. When he spoke affectionately, she repulsed him. He could not account for the change that had come over her, and at length quietly bore it; hoping that, in time, she would recover her equanimity. She was touched by her husband's patient forbearance, and made many efforts to be more amiable towards him; but she was in misery, and when she thought that she was never to see Conrad more, she was in a frenzy of grief, that drove, for the time, all the better movements from her heart.

A strong emotion—a real feeling of any kind, is a truth; no matter whether it be compatible or not with received maxims of right and wrong.

A married woman, in love with a man not her husband, is a fact worthy of all reprobation—worthy of the anathemas which are deserved, by either men or women, who have taken on themselves engagements, and fail in the fulfilment of it. Still, when all the anathemas have been expended, the fact remains the same; she is under the dominion of a real feeling, deep as life, and overpowering as death. It is a fact, and requires to be exorcised by something as deep, strong, and vital, as itself. It will not stir for being called hard names, it does not recognise them; it stands on its own affinity with reality; otherwise, it could not hold its place against the torrent of shame, fear, remorse, and all kinds of confusion, which, like a wild deluge, sweeps over the soul it hath entered, driving before it all the rules of action, principle, and thought, by which life had previously been shaped and organised. It has taken possession in right of being stronger than any thing already there; it is proof against evil report, danger, shame, death itself, when they are denounced simply as penalties for the offence. A true woman would cheerfully risk her own salvation for the sake of him she loves. There must be an appeal to some higher motive than mere personal considerations, if a woman, once under the influence of passion, is to be brought back to a sound mind. Alice had no one to speak a word of strong counsel to her, she was left to be tossed amongst her own shifting and vacillating emotions,—to her own weak passionate heart. She had never been possessed of any real sense of the paramount reality and importance of duty. Among all the maxims she had been taught, and the vague, misty, religious doctrines she had learned, there was not one, which now, in this hour of temptation, presented itself, as appealing to the realities of things. She had a vague notion of being very bad, and very wicked, but what she was to do, or how she ought to right herself, never occurred to her. She sat down, helpless and miserable, humbled to the dust by a sense of guilt, and yet clinging to her passion for Conrad, without even an effort to conquer it. The constant aspiration of her poor, tossed, trembling heart, was, 'Oh, that I had any one to counsel me, to tell me what I ought to do.' Her instinct was to tell her husband—to take up her true position with him. This instinct she did not dare to follow; she thought it would be more *prudent* to conceal it.

Things went on in this miserable, distracted manner for nearly two months, when Bryant, who had been much worried by business, had to go from home in consequence of the failure of one of his correspondents. He never was in the habit of plaguing Alice about his business anxieties; they often rendered him silent and abstracted, but never cross or harsh. Alice had been too much absorbed in her own misery to notice the deepened shadow that had come over him. He told her at breakfast one morning that business of importance required him to leave home for some days.

'Oh, do not go; you must not go,' cried Alice, passionately.

'What is the meaning of all this?' said Bryant, in a surprised tone.

'Do not leave me alone,' said Alice, still more vehemently; 'have you not seen me ill, suffering, and you are going to leave me! You love your business more than any thing else. You care not what comes to me. You would never miss me; you would live equally contented if I were dead: you have never loved me, and now you are leaving me alone!'

'Alice, Alice,' said Bryant, sternly, 'what fantastic nonsense is this? You are worse than childish; you fancy yourself ill, and you give way to your temper, till your humour becomes absolutely insupportable. You see me worried and anxious about matters of indispensable importance, and you choose this time for reproaches,—which you know are not deserved.'

'Oh do not speak unkindly to me!' cried Alice, piteously; 'I cannot bear it; I am ill, weak, wicked, but do not leave me; or if you must go, take me with you, do not leave me by myself.'

Bryant was so accustomed of late to see Alice in violent fits of excitement, and of a most variable and uncertain humour, that he did not attach any sort of importance to this outburst of feeling. He only replied in a cold, decided tone.

'You are asking what is quite impossible. I am going on business that must be attended to, and you would be in the way. I am quite tired of these scenes, and I wish you would try to get a little more reasonable before I return.'

He left the room as he said this, without any attempt to soften its severity or to console Alice.

'I should be in the way,' sobbed she, as soon as she was alone, 'he is quite tired of these scenes—business, business, always business—I am nothing, or at best of secondary importance. Well, be it so, be it so; I need feel no more remorse; he has lost me by his own fault.'

Bryant was to go that evening. When he returned to dinner he tried to make amends for his harshness in the morning, but Alice remained sullen and indifferent. He was fully occupied about the affair that called him from home; and after a few attempts to conquer her ill humour, he left her to recover her temper (as he considered it) at her leisure. Alice saw him depart with a strange mixture of feelings. She had no definite purpose of evil in her heart; but for the first time she began to justify herself, and to reason down her remorse. She ceased to struggle with her own thoughts, and gave in headlong to the passion that was consuming her.

The devil never fails to take advantage of every evil or weak movement, and asserts himself at every 'damning opportunity'. Bryant had to see Conrad in London, and to tell him of the awkward turn affairs were taking; with trembling lips Conrad asked after Alice, and learned that she had been ill and seemed out of spirits. To Conrad this revealed much; he felt that absence had befriended him; and he resolved to present himself before her, sure that he would not be repulsed.

Bryant had been gone four days, and Alice was sitting in her accustomed place in the inner drawing-room, when she heard a ring at the bell which she well recognised. It made her heart stand still. She thought they would never open the door. She feared that through some stupidity *he* would be refused on account of 'Mr Bryant not being at home'. Steps approached, the drawing-room opened, and 'Mr Conrad Percy' was announced. He did not advance till the door was closed behind him and the servant had time to retire; then trembling, and as much agitated as Alice, he stood before her.

Alice neither spoke nor moved, but a flash of gladness like sunlight passed over her face. Neither of them spoke. A passionate, guilty joy was in their hearts; they were interpenetrated with each other's presence.

As the melting fire burneth,

honour, conscience, every barrier that was between them was destroyed; they only felt they were together; neither regret nor doubt intruded. THEY WERE TOGETHER. That was the one reality into which their whole life was absorbed.

'You love me now, Alice,' said Conrad, at last, in a low voice. Alice did not reply, but the hands he held grasped his.

'You will never send me away again.'

'Never!' said Alice.

Conrad had a perverse sense of honour. He was deterred by no scruple from gaining the affection of his friend's wife; but when assured of his triumph, he shrank from the man on whom he had inflicted such a grievous wrong: he insisted that Alice should leave her husband's roof, and fly with him that very evening. At first, Alice refused; she had confessed her passion to him, but intended to stop there. Women always intend to stand very firm, after they have given in the first step; but the 'pomp of virtue', as Mr Rowe calls it, did not come to her rescue. Conrad endeavoured to invest the step he was proposing with an air of uprightness. He knew that if he could make her believe that she had kept her faith with Bryant, in remaining faithful to him so long as she continued under his roof, and that in going away openly she was acting uprightly, he should be able to shield her from the reaction of remorse or regret. He knew her well enough, to be sure she would shrink from no blame or scandal, or loss of reputation, so long as she could to her own conscience throw the least varnish of rectitude over her crime; and, besides, he really wished to conduct matters as honourably as circumstances would allow.

Alice, who believed that, in loving him, she had already committed all the sin possible, and that no redemption for her remained, at length consented to fly with him—to leave her husband's roof within an hour! To avoid rousing the suspicions of the servants, they agreed to leave the house separately. Conrad departed to make arrangements for their flight, and was to await her at the gate in half an hour.

'Be firm, my Alice. You will not fail me; I trust my life, my honour, all my future in your hands!'

'You need not fear for me,' said Alice, with desperate calmness. 'I know that I have lost my soul for you. I know the punishment on wives who are faithless—I know there is no pardon or remission of sin for me in this world or the next. I have lost myself for you, and would do so again a thousand times, to give you but one moment's gladness. I will not fail you.'

When Conrad was gone, Alice, like one in the stupor of drunkenness or in sleep-walking, went to her dressing-room. She made no preparation for her departure, she determined to take nothing with her—she locked her drawers and her dressing-case, which contained her jewels, and made the key into a parcel addressed to Bryant. This reminded her that she ought to write to him to explain what she had done, and she sat down to her desk and began to write, in the same state of stupified excitement. It seemed to her as if she were transacting a dream.

Meanwhile, Bryant, by one of those coincidences that occur so often in real life, and which sound so unreal in books, had been able to return home earlier than he expected. He thought he would not write to tell Alice, but would give her a surprise. After Conrad had been gone about a quarter of an hour, he arrived. Surprised to find the hall door on the latch, he entered without ringing; and meeting one of the servants in the hall, he reproved his carelessness in leaving the door open. 'Is your mistress within?' continued he.

'Yes, sir; she is in the drawing-room, along with Mr Percy.'

Bryant proceeded there, but found no one. He went up stairs, fancying she might be in her own sitting-room; but when he reached the landing-place he saw, through the half-open door, Alice, in her dressing-room, seated at her desk.

CHAPTER XIII

BRYANT entered in the dusk. Alice had not heard his arrival, and did not look up from her writing.

'My own Alice,' said Bryant;—she looked up and saw her husband standing over her. She uttered a shriek of terror, and fell senseless at his feet.

'I ought to have remembered her weak, nervous state, and not have ventured to surprise her,' said he, to himself, as he tenderly lifted her on the couch and tried every means to restore her to sensibility. He succeeded, at length; but it was only to see her seized by frightful spasms, which contracted and convulsed her whole body; her cries were piercing; her delicate limbs were tossed and contorted; her head rolled violently from side to side, and no trace remained in her features of the fair and gentle Alice. In a few minutes the violence of the attack subsided, but was followed by immediate insensibility. Bryant was in despair, and terrified beyond expression at this frightful seizure. The whole household, alarmed by her cries, came rushing up stairs. He despatched three men on horseback in different directions for medical assistance, whilst her own maid and the housekeeper got her undressed and, assisted by Bryant, laid in bed, without rousing her from the death-like swoon in which she was plunged. When Bryant returned to the dressing-room for a moment, he for the first time perceived the half-finished letter over which she had been occupied when he entered. There was enough written to tell him all that had passed during his absence. Every sorrow in life seemed to be let loose against him at once. A deep flush mounted to his temples, and the veins swelled and throbbed to bursting, but no sound came from his compressed lips. He read the paper over twice; then lighting a taper on the hearth, he held the paper in the flame till every particle was destroyed; a gust of air carried the light black ashes up the chimney, and he returned to his wife's room. She had by this time recovered her senses, but seemed in violent terror, and trembled extremely. She caught a glimpse of her husband through an opening between the curtains and screamed with fear, hiding and cowering under the clothes;

the spasms returned more severely than ever; and a horrible suspicion darted into Bryant's mind that she had taken poison. In a state of mind amounting to frensy he sat beside her bed, trying to shut out from his ears the sound of her cries. At length, after an interval that seemed an eternity, two medical men arrived, one of them the physician who attended the family. Bryant, who could not bear to stand by whilst they consulted, went to the dressing-room, and hiding his face with his hands, sat in a convulsed and desperate calmness till they came to him. The old family physician, who was also a friend, at length entered.

'Well, sir?' said Bryant sternly.

The old man came up to him, and putting his hand on his shoulder, said, in a voice trembling with tears:

'You must be a man, Bryant. It may be averted even yet, but we fear the worst. That sweet creature'—and here the old man fairly burst into tears.

'Tell me what is the matter,' said Bryant, imperiously; 'I will know; I insist on having nothing kept from me. What is this sudden and frightful seizure?'

'A most severe attack of hysteria, complicated by spasms of the stomach; and, from her extreme delicacy and the great general debility under which she is labouring, we fear the worst. It is not necessarily fatal—but—but—I dare not say that we are sanguine.'

'You are telling me the truth!' said Bryant, fiercely. 'I will not be trifled with. Do you swear to me that it is natural—that she has not taken—that no one has given her—that it is not from—from—medicine'—

'No, no; my dear friend, calm yourself; it is quite natural; it is a frequent form of malady with women, not often so severe. But what do you suspect it arises from? Has she had any strong mental shock or violent emotion to bring it on?'

'Thank God!' said Bryant, fervently, and drawing a breath as of one relieved from intolerable fear. 'No, no; I know of nothing, I can account for nothing, and I will have no questions asked;—do you hear? I hate that prying into every act of the past weeks or months, and straining every insignificant point to yield a reason or a meaning. You will ask nothing, and seek to know nothing. It is enough that she is ill—dying—that you cannot restore her precious soul. Tell me, will she, do you think, be able to recognise me?—to endure to see me?—shall I hear her sweet voice again? Oh, let me but be able to speak to her once more, if it be only for one moment,—let her but be able to hear and understand one word, and I ask no more! Tell me, may I hope for this?'

'We must hope so; we must hope the best; but you will need all your firmness, so much depends on your calmness. You must not see her now; the least excitement would be fatal.'

The old doctor grasped his hand and returned to the bedside of Alice, whilst Bryant remained all that night and the next day sitting at the door of the dressing-room, listening to every sound that proceeded from his wife's room. At length, late in the afternoon, the old doctor came to him; he had been in from time to time to speak such words of comfort as he could, but to compel him to take some food to induce rest was beyond his power. Bryant sat motionless as an Indian Faqueer, rigid in sorrow. He looked up with dull eyes as the doctor appeared.

'If you wish to see her, come now; but be very calm.'

'Let every one else leave the room,' said Bryant, as he followed the doctor, and stood beside his wife. She was lying calm and sensible, but entirely exhausted; her eyes were sunk, and looked preternaturally large, surrounded with a large violet circle; she trembled when she saw Bryant, and cowered down amongst the bed clothes.

'Am I then so very hateful to you, my poor child?' said Bryant, mournfully.

She did not speak, but looked up in his face with an expression of touching, deprecating helplessness.

'Alice! Alice!' said Bryant, 'let me speak to you. I feared you should die without my being able to tell you, not of my pardon, but of my love; poor child! how much you have struggled and suffered, and I was ignorant of it! Why did you not take refuge with me? I would have sheltered you from yourself; you might have trusted me, Alice. I could have sympathised with your temptation, and you should not have been left single-handed to struggle, and to fall at last. Who could have loved you as I did, who could have pitied and sympathised as I would have done? You should not have fallen, I would have won back your heart with such love as must have won you. Oh why did you feel so little confidence in me? Why did you not lean on me in your helplessness? It was not your fault that you were tempted, and I should only have loved you more for your peril; dear child, I do not blame you now. I love you; do not look on me with dread. Think of me as one who loves you better than any earthly thing.'

Alice put out her hand to him, and he took it almost timidly.

'Bryant,' said she, in a whisper, 'one thing I want you to know: you are not dishonoured—in that one sense, at least, I have been faithful to you. Do you believe me?'

'I do,' said Bryant, earnestly.

'Would to God!' continued she, in gasps, as her weakness would permit her—'would to God I had confided all to you. I was a hundred times on the point of doing so. You could have brought back my heart to you;—but I did not know you—I did not dare to trust you. I see now all the evil I have wrought. Forgive me; you *can* forgive me, can you not?'

Bryant bent down over her. She looked timidly up to him. He lifted her up in bed, and laid her head upon his bosom, as she had been a child.

'I have no right here now,' said she.

'Ever your resting-place!' cried Bryant, fervently. 'Would I had sought more to draw you here in love and trust. It was my blame—I ought to have sought you more;—but, Alice, I love you—I have always loved you—I love you as a father, mother, husband, all that the world has of most tender and protecting. I will not fail you;—cling to me, trust to me;—I love you far more than you can love yourself.'

Alice clung to him, like a frightened child.

'Let me die here, Bryant, let me die here; I have no other wish.'

'You shall get well darling—you shall not die, now that we have just found each other again.'

'No, no, no,' said Alice, 'it is very merciful thus—it is more than I deserve—to die, and to be taken away from all the evil I have done.'

Her tears were falling fast;—at first, they came like a painless gentle rain; but they became more violent; the convulsions returned, and though not so severe as at first, she had not strength to rally; fainting followed, and at length she fell into a dead, heavy stupor, from which she never awoke. She died in the evening,—as nearly as could be ascertained, about the hour she was first seized.

The broken lily lies,
The storm is overpast.*

CHAPTER XIV

BRYANT sat in his room of business the day after Alice had expired; his head rested upon his arms; a pile of business-letters, with their seals all unbroken, lay beside him. He was plunged in a deep waking stupor of grief. He had been so overwrought with agony, that the last point of sensation had been passed. Wretches have been known to fall asleep on the rack in the interval of their tortures. A number of thoughts, all more or less irrelevant to the one great thing that possessed him, crawled forth, like rats from their hiding-place, and careered over his desolate mind, exciting no effort on his part to chase them away. From the window he could perceive a half-finished building. His dull eyes followed the men as they went up and down the ladder, carrying their hods of mortar and bricks; the round of one of the ladders broke, near the top, as the man was stepping upon it, and he and his load of bricks fell to the ground. It did not move him; he looked on, as though he were reading it in a book. His eyes caught a spot on the carpet where it was much worn, and he mechanically began to follow the lines and patches, and to count the spots which formed the pattern. The frenzy of grief had subsided, and left him in a lazy stupor of reverie.

A knock came to the door; which he heard, well enough, but did not answer. It was repeated; and the butler entered, to tell his master that he was wanted in the drawing-room. Bryant gave a dull vague stare; and, like one under mesmeric influence, rose, and followed the servant, who held open the drawing-room door and closed it after him.

Bryant advanced listlessly. Conrad stood at the window place, with his eyes fixed on the door. For an instant his features seemed galvanised by a spasm, as the man whom he had so much injured came in; but they became immediately still and rigid; all the traces of mental anguish and fiery passion seemed to have been arrested in their working, and left stamped there with the grim emphasis of death.

Bryant did not raise his eyes, nor perceive him, until he had reached the middle of the room. The men stood face to face, each bearing traces of strong agony, but utterly stilled now, and unable to manifest either life or passion.

Conrad spoke first; his voice came sharp and grating, as if it came from a piece of mechanism.

'Mr Bryant,' said he, 'I might have blown out my brains for myself, but that it had become your right to do so. I know that you must be aware of what happened in your absence, and I have no wish to elude your vengeance. Now make an end speedily. I am at your service, to meet you when you please.'

Bryant's eyes gleamed fiercely at Conrad, and he looked like a wild beast in sight of his prey.

'I have only one word to say,' continued Conrad, 'it may make you think less hardly of *her*. On me alone your curse should fall. She was pure in heart, and never guessed my passion till I revealed it. She drove me away from her, she might have escaped if I would have let her. I hunted her down, she had no chance. Ask yourself, did you protect her? When she was struggling, did you stretch out your hand to save her from the toils? She was left to her own strength. Had you taken her away when she entreated you, she had been saved; but your business, your money, your time, your cursed convenience, made you refuse her harshly,— blind fool that you were! She was struggling to be faithful to you—to save your honour, and you saw it not. She was dying with the struggle and you left her to her fate; to save a miserable "contract", you left her. You left her in my power; the blood of her soul is on your hands as well as on mine. Oh, when you refused either to remain with her, or to take her away, to whom else could she go but to me who loved her?'

His voice had gradually risen into an hysterical shrillness; the words he uttered came with pain and gashed his soul as though they had been knives. Bryant at first seemed to listen as though he heard not, but the iteration of the words, 'You left her, you left her,' seemed to rouse him to madness; he crushed his hands together till the blood started beneath the pressure of the nails, and then, as if a pent-up torrent had broken loose, bearing down all before it,

'Man, man,' he cried, in a voice hardly human in its agony, 'what gave you the right to torture me? can you say aught I have not said to myself? Do I not know that she was pure? do not I know her worth? Are you a stranger of yesterday to come and teach me her worth; do I not know all, all—what can you know? You who would have degraded her—who only knew her in her fall! Was not her whole life mine, and *you* talk of her!—you, you, you, oh God! that such a thing should be able to mention her name—*you* school me to think less hardly of her!'

After a moment's pause, he seemed to constrain himself by a violent effort, and continued in a calm, bitter tone:

'Listen to me, sir, and take this to heart all the days of your miserable life, and know what it is that you have done. She thought I did not love her, because I had no words like you. She was the very life within my heart. She was the soul of my life. By nature I was cold and proud. I could not make a demonstration of my feelings, but I loved her all the more, because it was her way to show much. You are a gentleman. You taunt me with my attention to business. When a man spends his life in doing a thing, he generally gives his attention to it. You do not know what you talk about when you reproach me with my business. I must have given my mind to it, or have been ruined, and made her a beggar. Perhaps I was too much engrossed. Such things grow on one. I knew not that she was pining for more love, more sympathy, than I had power to show. I knew it not; I guessed it not, God knows. You came, sir; you were a man of fashion, a man of gallantry, a man of intrigue. This thing you have attempted is nothing in the eyes of your own set; it would not live a week in one of your scandalous journals. The device by which you obtained a footing in the family, and blinded my eyes, will cover you with applause; it will be a jest, a good after-dinner story for a month; and this will be all the trace it leaves in your horizon—it is a very little thing, an episode of three months; and, to furnish food for your ennui, you have consumed the life and soul of a woman, on whom God had bestowed His most precious things. You have degraded a man who only sought to do you good. You have uprooted me from the face of the earth. What I shall be in another world, God alone knows; you have made me an outcast in this; and you will make a jest of it. I am become the legitimate object of a jest; I am become—what you have made me.'

Hitherto he had controlled himself, but now a multitude of thoughts were roused; an intense hatred entered into him like a demon, and he felt powerless to give it utterance.

'Killing you,' he exclaimed, 'would not slack my hatred.' But his words were lost in an inarticulate gurgling.

'God knows,' said Conrad, 'I have no wish to escape your vengeance; I came to offer you my life; it is all the atonement I can make. Your lot is enviable compared to mine; to revoke the last six months I would willingly never have lived.'

The ravages that misery had made on the young and handsome features of Conrad struck Bryant even at this desperate moment.

'I am not going to fight you,' said he, more calmly; '*her* name shall not be sullied; your death in a duel would cause inquiries, comments, in the newspapers. You must live, as I shall have to do. I believe that you are sorry, now that you have to pay the penalty of your sin; but go, or the devil within me will be roused again—I should kill you where you stand. Let me see you no longer—go.'

'Are you a coward, then, that you refuse to fight me? What more can I do?'

'Go—let me never see you more.'

'I cannot live, I will not live!' cried Conrad, passionately.

'*She* shall not be made the subject of slanderous gossip—*she* shall have peace in the grave, where you have laid her. You talk of death! What have you done to earn such a blessing?'

'Bryant, you may safely fight me. What cowardice, what folly is this—we must fight.'

'Have not I to live also?' rejoined the other, sternly. He pointed silently to the door. Conrad quailed beneath the deep, scornful misery that looked from his eyes. He felt constrained to obey; but when he reached the door he stopped, and, with a sudden impulse, turning round, he flung himself on the floor at Bryant's feet, exclaiming, in quick, broken tones—

'Be merciful, and kill me—or, if you will have me live—I will swear to do so: but as life is your sentence, for the love of Heaven be merciful—let me look on her once more. I will swear to go hence to redeem the future. I will live—live. You understand—I will be your galley slave, and live my life out to the end. But think what it is you lay on me. I have no claim to what I ask; but, as one prays to God in deepest need, I implore you to let me look on her once more. As God shall hear you—and surely you have sinned against Him—as you hope to be heard by Him, let me see her. I am kneeling to you—let me see her. As you are a man, look on my misery—let me see her, and I will swear to live.'

His agony of entreaty could not utter itself in words: but that tone of intense supplication, addressed by one human being to another, was almost fearful. In the midst of his own wrongs and hatred, Bryant could not help feeling a sort of pity at the sight of the young man's desolation. Death had taken away all littleness from his sorrow; he was moved; and, placing his hand on Conrad's shoulder, he said, in a husky voice, 'Come with me.'

They passed up the large staircase, and stood before the chamber of death. Bryant took out a key, unlocked the door, and they entered together.

There, on the bed surrounded with heavy crimson draperies, lay the white, cold form of Alice, utterly insensible to the misery of the two beings whom she had loved best in life. There was something frightful in the changeless calm of that which still bore the semblance of passionate humanity. Conrad uttered a sharp cry at the sight of her, and fell, in strong convulsions, over the footboard of the bed.

In the midst of his own sorrow, Bryant felt a flash of triumph to think that in death she was all his own; and that Conrad, the intruder, the usurper, stood there an alien, without the power to take a last look except by his permission.

It was beyond his strength to remove Conrad, but with the assistance of the butler he was taken to another chamber. He went not near him himself, but, with proud, Arab-like hospitality, ordered medical assistance and every needful attention for him, and then locked himself in the room where the dead lay. There, sitting beside the bed, one hand clasping that of Alice, he watched all night, feeling that she was all his own once more.

Men must lose some dear object by death before they can realise the invisible world: we must have a stake in it before we can believe it.

Sitting there, beside his dead wife, Bryant was admitted to the threshold of the unseen state. What now to him was the dream of life, with all its highly-coloured appearances?—hope and fear were alike dead: he sat in the presence of the Invisible, and calmness came gradually to his soul.

Alice's weakness—Conrad's treachery—his own wounded pride—all seemed now hushed to insignificance in the presence of the great, mysterious fact of Death; even his grief seemed small and idle. What was he that he should complain? The tumult and glare which had surrounded all things subsided before the cold, colourless light of death, with whom 'neither variableness nor shadow of turning' may dwell.

He left that chamber in the early dawn of the next morning with some portion of the eternal calmness on his own soul.

He did not trust himself to see Conrad, who lay in a brain fever. He ordered that he should receive all needful attention, and a regular nurse was hired for him.

Bryant left the house immediately after the funeral.

It was many days before Conrad recovered sufficiently to leave his room. He had been dealt with by a hand not of man, and when he left his sick room years seemed to have passed over his head.

He entreated the old butler to let him once more enter the room where he had seen Alice dead. The old man gave him the key, and he repaired thither alone.

The hangings of the bed and all the arrangements of the room were the same as before, but Alice had passed away—even the lifeless form that had been there was now hidden for ever from the eyes of all men.

He stooped, and reverently kissed the pillow on which he had seen her laid, and left the room without looking back.

CHAPTER XV

THE walls of the town of B——were all placarded in large letters, of every colour in the rainbow, with the 'Immense Attraction, for five Nights only, of Mademoiselle Bianca', who would make her first appearance that evening in her celebrated character of *Juliet*, in Shakespeare's play.

Bianca arrived about the middle of the day, and found herself for the first time on the scene of her early struggles; she had not visited the town since she left it in the train of Mr Simpson's equestrian troop. Had she been asked then, her position of to-day would have seemed the realisation of her most fabulous dreams; and yet now she was as little able to sit down and rest as she had been then. The stars in heaven all seem the same distance from us, all of them seem to us to be let into the smooth solid-looking vault that roofs the earth, and *we must get up there* before we can believe in the very terrestrial sort of glory it would be that we should find.

With all this, however, Bianca felt a whimsical sort of satisfaction in returning under such different auspices; she had attained an object by dint of her own resolute efforts, and there is always a complacent feeling in success of any kind. It is always more satisfactory to learn even the worthlessness of an object by success than by failure.

Bianca had to proceed at once to rehearsal, which proved a long and wearisome affair. After it was over, she proceeded on foot to find out the old lodgings where she had formerly resided. There had been so many changes in the neighbourhood, that she had some difficulty in finding her way. The old court was still standing, but most of the former inhabitants had passed away, and altogether the place was much more desolate-looking, and the people of a lower and rougher description than when she left it: to be sure, eight additional years of total abstinence from paint and whitewash had materially darkened the face of things, and accounted for the dilapidated, demoralised look of the place; it had become, as the policeman told her, 'a very low neighbourhood'.

She addressed a disorderly, good-natured woman, who was standing at an open door, surrounded by several other women, who were gazing at her in great curiosity, and inquired where Mrs Mullins lived.

For some time nobody could tell any thing about Mrs Mullins, and the whole court was gathered together to hear what was wanted. At last a heavy black-looking man, who was leaning lazily against a door-post with a pipe in his mouth, announced that 'if it were the woman whose husband used to be the ostler at the "Black Swan", she was gone to the House, for her master had got a kick from a vicious horse, which had lamed him entirely, and when they could carry on no longer they had to go to the House.'

'What house? Where?' asked Bianca, bewildered.

'Why the Union,* to be sure,' answered the man; 'I reckon it is only poor folks who knows where it is.'

'Aye, aye, poor folk must be thankful for any thing,' said one of the women in a scolding tone; 'they have pig-sties like these to live in whilst they can work hard, and the House to prison them when they are wore out.'

Bianca turned away, glad to escape. As she went, she gave a trifle to a child, whom she saw assisting an aged woman, probably its grandmother, to crawl up and down the flags in the sunshine, that came slanting over the roofs.

'I have to be thankful for much that I was nearly forgetting,' thought she, as she emerged into the main street.

Her next visit was to find the old priest, who had been her friend. She soon reached the dark low house attached to the little chapel; it was situated in a very poor and densely populated neighbourhood. She was shown into his little parlour by the housekeeper, not the one Bianca remembered. The priest looked up from his writing as she entered.

'You have forgotten me, father,' said Bianca; as the priest seemed searching his memory.

'Do you remember a young girl in the circus here some years ago?'

'Ah!' said the old man, with an indescribable reserve.

'I am she. You have not forgotten how kind you were to me and to my mother; and here is the little book you gave me with your own name in it, and you told me to be always a good girl; this is the first time I have been in the town since.'

'Ah, indeed, yes,' said the old man, putting off his spectacles; 'I remember you now, but I should not have known you. And how is the good lady, your mother?'

'It has pleased God to take her away from me,' replied Bianca.

The priest's face assumed a look of gravity, as if it were the habitual expression on the receipt of such intelligence. 'I will say a prayer for her to-night.'

'Thank you, father.'

'Well,' rejoined the old man, 'and what have you been doing all these years? It was a bad way of life you were in, I trust you have quitted it.'

'I have left the circus,' said Bianca, smiling; 'but I fear I am still in a way you will not approve of—I belong to the theatre still.'

'Well, well, many of your class when they become weary of the world to which they have dedicated their best days, have grace given them to renounce it, and to hide themselves in a cloister; and many I could name have become shining examples of piety; we must despair of no one; even Mary Magdalene, you know, was honoured to become a saint, though no one could have led a worse life.—Grace may find you anywhere.'

Bianca felt inexpressibly chilled and disappointed by the old man's tone; she had come to seek him with her heart overflowing with the recollection of his kindness, and rejoiced like a child at the thought of seeing him once more. The utter absence of every thing like human nature in his manner,—the frigid professional tone of his exhortation,—threw all that back upon her heart. He had become a PRIEST, and nothing more; and she knew no spell by which she could penetrate through the dry filigree work with which his heart was incrusted. It was another phase of her past life blotted out of the golden book of recollection: she had attempted to bring it back into the present, and the whole vanished like the figures in a magic mirror, on the attempt of the beholder to approach and grasp them. The old priest—the fatherly friend, whose image she had so gratefully cherished—was gone: a dry, bigotted old man, who had lost all interest in her, remained in his place. And yet it was only the natural indifference of old age, aided by the total absence of all human affections (for the old man had no relatives), which had wrought this change; he now did his duty with a single eye to his own salvation, and considered that the less mortal feeling mingled with it the better. Every thing that centres in *self*, even if it be the saving of our own soul, makes a very barren and uninteresting result.

'I have prospered in the world since you saw me, father, and I have brought you a small offering. I cannot go amongst the poor myself, and I prefer its passing through your hands; if amongst your poor there is any one situated as I was, let her have a double portion. If there be any good work in which you are interested, I shall rejoice to aid to the extent of my ability.'

'Ah!' said the priest, brightening up at the sight of the handsome sum Bianca had placed in his hand,—'this will be a great help to the Sisters of Mercy,—they are very poor.'

'Have you established a House, then?' asked Bianca.

This was touching the right chord; and with more cordiality than he had yet shown, the old man asked her if she would like to visit it. Bianca eagerly assented. She had never seen a convent, but often when weighed down with sorrow, or wearied with labour, she had indulged in vague thoughts of ending her days in one; especially since her disappointment in Conrad, the idea of a convent had hovered before her like a haven of repose after she should have finished her labours.

He took her to a small house adjoining the chapel, where the sisterhood were located, until such time as a suitable dwelling should be erected to receive them.

The lady superior, a severe, majestic-looking woman, received them with much civility, but from behind an indescribable wall of reserve, that separated her as completely from those she addressed, as if she had been an inhabitant of another world made visible.

At Bianca's request they were conducted over the house. It was 'the hour of recreation', and the sisters were seated at a long table, some of them writing, some reading, but most of them engaged in needle-work. They all looked very picturesque, for the Catholic understands costume; but there was a stony sweetness of expression on their faces, as if all spontaneity of thought and will had been petrified into a placid negation. Bianca experienced a sense of something almost like fear, at the aspect of so much humanity quelled down and buried beneath a concrete of inflexible obedience to an artificial authority, through which no blade of genuine spontaneity could spring. All aspirations of devotion, even the very works of mercy to which they had dedicated themselves, seemed to have been drilled to rules, till they weighed down on the soul like a nightmare. Bianca felt stifled in that low, close house, tenanted by these bodies destitute of a will! She placed an offering in the poor's box, and hastened to quit the place.

'Farewell, daughter,' said the old man; 'and, remember, when you are weary of the service of the world, Holy Church will open her arms to receive you to a quiet resting-place.'

Bianca drew a deep breath, when she was fairly in the street. 'Any thing but that, any thing but that,' said she, to herself; 'no amount of weariness or suffering shall induce me to commit moral suicide,—I am free, at least, to lead my own life, and suffer my own sufferings! I will never dream of a cowardly escape again!'

When she reached her hotel it was late; and she had barely time to dine, and repose for half an hour, before it was time to proceed to the theatre.

Whilst she was dressing, her maid told her that a respectable looking young woman had been inquiring for her, and seemed so much disappointed that she could not see her, that the maid had desired her to call the next morning, at nine o'clock. Bianca listened to all this with great indifference, and as at that moment she was called, she did not make any inquiries—indeed, had quite forgotten the whole matter, when the next morning, as she was sitting at breakfast, the door of her sitting-room was thrown open, and the waiter announced, 'A young woman to speak to you, ma'am.' Bianca looked up, and recognised Simmonds, Alice's maid, who had been very kind to her when she was Alice's *protégée*.

'Why, Simmonds! is that you? I am very glad to see you—come and sit down, and have some breakfast, and tell me how you left your mistress—is she here? have you brought me any message from her?'

'Oh! Miss Bianca, my poor missis, my poor missis!' exclaimed Simmonds, passionately.

'What of her? tell me quick,' cried Bianca, remarking, for the first time, the deep mourning of the woman's dress, 'has she lost her husband? is Mr Bryant dead?'

Simmonds sobbed more violently, and did not reply; at length she said, 'No, no, he has lost missis, and if ever there was an angel in the world she was it.'

'Alice dead!' said Bianca, stupified.

'Ah! indeed, yes, ma'am, I knew you had a respect for her, and that made me come and tell you; I thought, may be, you had not heard. I saw your name on the walls, and I felt sure it must be you.'

Bianca poured out a cup of coffee, and handed it to Simmonds, who, like all women of her class, now that the violence of her emotion had subsided, began to feel the consolation of talk.

'Ah! Miss Bianca, missis was very fond of you, and often used to speak of you to me; she would have shown more to you, only master said you were an actress, and he did not like his wife to know you. Ah! in my opinion, this would never have happened if you had been there.'

Bianca, still stunned with the intelligence she had just heard, sat dimly conscious that Simmonds was speaking. At length, putting her hand to her head, she said, like one speaking out of a dream:

'Did you say just now that Alice was dead?'

'Indeed I did, ma'am, it is only too true; but oh, Miss Bianca, don't look in that way, it hurts me to see you, indeed it does.'

'Tell me, when did she die?' said Bianca.

'A month ago last Wednesday,' replied the woman. 'Master is just heart-broke now it is too late. He left the house after the funeral; but Mr Conrad is still there, and quite out of his senses.'

'Mr Conrad Percy!' said Bianca, quite bewildered, 'what has he to do with the matter?'

'Well, Miss Bianca,' said Simmonds, mysteriously, 'I don't mind speaking to you, for I know it will go no further; but there is not another mortal person to whom I would say what I am going to tell you. I think it is nowise honourable for a servant to go and spread reports about the family; a confidential servant, too, as I may say, for the missis told me any thing—nothing passed in the house without my knowing, and I have my own thoughts about things. Well, then, ma'am, if I must say it,' continued she, lowering her voice, and looking round mysteriously, 'Mr Conrad and missis were great companions;—master was always busy with his own affairs, and did not know how to manage her; he would leave her alone for days together, and perhaps hardly speak to her sometimes for a week. I have seen missis often and often come up into her own room and cry about it, though she never said a word to me; but she could not help my seeing; and Mr Conrad was very fond of her, he worshipped the ground she trod upon; my opinion is, that he went into partnership with master, only to have an excuse to come to the house—though, of course, I would not say so to any body in the world but you. As to missis, she was as innocent as a lamb; but it killed her—I know it was that and nothing else. She never had those dreadful spasms before; and if master would only have opened his eyes and taken a little notice, she might have been alive now. With my own ears I heard her ask him to take her away with him, when he went to Paris, and he refused, because he was going on business. "His business" came before every thing, and missis was hurt at always coming second to a parcel of rubbishing iron. He is sorry enough now, poor man!'

'Well,' said Bianca, more and more bewildered—

'Well, ma'am, it is not a thing one ought to say lightly, but my mind misgives me that missis was going away with Mr Conrad. He came again after master went to France. I met him in the hall just as he was going out; he looked quite strange and bewildered; he took me for Mrs Lauriston (master's sister), and said something that Mrs Bryant was ill, and could not see me. I went straight to the parlour, and saw missis, who was going up-stairs. I shall never forget her face whilst I live, so stony and desperate looking. Ah! poor thing, she never came down those stairs again, till she was carried in her coffin!'

Simmonds burst into fresh tears at the end of her recital. Bianca sat without speaking, utterly stupified by what she heard. Simmonds continued—

'Whilst missis lay dying, Mr Conrad roamed like a spirit round the house; he never darkened a door, but wandered up and down the park like a man beside himself. He climbed up to the window of her room once; I saw him, and went down to speak to him. It would have made a stone pitiful to see him, with his hair all matted on his forehead, his eyes like glass, and his face quite dreadful to look at—twenty years seemed to have passed over his head. Master took on dreadful, too; but it was his own fault, in one way,—if he had only shown more what he had felt, none of this would have happened. Missis was like a child, and a kind word was more to her than a fine present. She and master were quite reconciled at the last, and she died quite composed; but she suffered dreadful tortures. I am sure my heart is almost broke to think of all the misery there was. Master let Mr Conrad see her after all was over, and it nearly killed him. Master behaved very handsome, and said every thing was to be done for him; but the poor young man is not long for this world, I am thinking. I don't know who is most to be pitied. Master looked dreadfully ill when he went away; they say he is gone abroad. All the servants had their wages paid them, and a quarter over, and the house is to be shut up; only Mr Thompson, the butler, is left in charge of it. Every thing looks so strange and desolate, even in this short time, that you would hardly know the place, Miss Bianca.'

Bianca had concealed her face in her hands, and remained silently leaning her head on the arm of the sofa. Wounds, hardly closed in her own soul, were opened afresh; and she staggered under a bewildering sense of misery which seemed to encompass her about on all sides. She could not weep: her whole being was parched with torture, every thing was blotted out in the world; it seemed to her that she alone remained a living thing in it, and that her whole vitality had diminished down to a single point— the consciousness of pain.

'Dear, dear Miss Bianca! do not you take on so,' said the sympathising Simmonds, fancying that Bianca was weeping, the only manifestation of sorrow women like her can understand.

The waiter entered with letters, and said that a person was waiting to see Bianca on business.

'Show the person in,' said Bianca. She had no more time for the indulgence of emotion, her sorrow had to be imprisoned in her heart, till she was at liberty to return to it. The business of life is imperative, and will not stop till we are consoled; it rolls along day by day, like a great Juggernaut, indifferent whether we are carried in its train or crushed beneath its track.

'Well, Simmonds,' said she, when the waiter departed, 'if you have not suited yourself with a better situation, will you like to remain with me? My present maid has more than she can do, and will be very glad of a companion. I should like to have you with me, for you were very faithful to her who is gone. Will you stay with me?'

'Indeed! indeed, Miss Bianca, I will be only too glad if you think I shall suit you, for I always liked you, and so did poor missis.'

'Then it is agreed,' said Bianca, 'that you come to me on the same terms. You may go now. Can you be ready to come to-night, or will to-morrow suit you better.'

'Just when you please, Miss Bianca; I think to-night, if it is all the same to you, for I feel quite low-spirited by myself; and now I will wish you good morning.'

Simmonds curtseyed herself out of the room, with a flutter of satisfaction, for which she reproached herself as hard-hearted: but the truth was, that Simmonds had always cherished a secret wish to see something of the world; and now, to be engaged as own maid to a great actress, and to have the prospect of seeing a play whenever she pleased, was an immense satisfaction, that insinuated itself into her heart, whether she consented to its admission or not.

CHAPTER XVI

CONRAD left that room, crushed under a weight of unutterable misery, sensible of nothing but the blind desire to get away from the house which had been cursed for his sake.

There was something weird-like and menacing in the desolate stillness of that deserted place. It seemed, to his morbid fancy, that he had left the living world, and passed 'into the land where all things are forgotten', and where the souls of men await in gloomy half consciousness, the judgment for 'the deeds done in the body'.

'How soon can I have a chaise to take me away from here?' asked he.

'In an hour, if you wish it, sir,' replied the old man. 'But, are you quite sure that you are well enough to travel? The last orders that master gave were, that you should not go till you were quite recovered.'

'And where is your master?' asked Conrad.

The butler shook his head, as he replied—'Master went away the day of the funeral, and we none of us know where to. I do not think, somehow, that he knew himself. All the servants were discharged, and only I and my sister, who lives at the lodge, were left in charge of the things here. I cannot say when master will come back. I have lived in this place, man and boy, nigh fifty years, and it hurts me to see things gone so desolate. He is a good man, Mr Bryant, and it is a sore heart he has taken away with him!'

Conrad groaned—it was as if a hot iron had been thrust against him.

'See that the chaise is here as soon as possible. I must go hence to-day.'

'If you are quite determined, sir, there is a letter master left with me, desiring that you might have it before you went.'

The old man left the room, and shortly returned with a sealed letter. So soon as Conrad was alone, he broke the seal and read as follows:

Conrad, do not waste your time in useless grieving. If we never meet again, I tell you now, that I forgive you. Waste no more of your life, but do somewhat that shall redeem the past. I wish you to live, and to make yourself respected. You are still young, and may hope that much time lies before you.

JOHN BRYANT.

A few words had been added just before the signature, but they had been carefully blotted out.

Conrad bowed his head upon his hands and wept bitterly.

In about half an hour the butler announced that the chaise was at the door. Conrad wrung the old man's hand, without speaking, and flung himself back in the vehicle, covering his face to avoid the last look of the home he had rendered desolate.

Conrad had formed no plan for himself; he mechanically ordered the horses' heads to be turned towards London. His lodgings were there, and so was his servant; otherwise there was no reason why he should have gone there, rather than to the other end of the world. He belonged to no one—his kindred were not nearly related to him, and he had never been on terms of intimacy with any of them. The journey passed over in one vague gloomy reverie. He was unconscious of all the incidents that occurred, although he mechanically performed his part at the different stages.

It was nearly dusk when the chaise drove up to the door of his lodgings, and his appearance caused some commotion in the house. He was evidently not expected; his servant was from home, and his landlady ushered him herself, with many apologies, into his sitting-room, which wore the half dull, half dirty look, which all lodgings in town are prone to assume. The furniture, all in its wrong place, stood stiff and uncomfortable against the walls; no fire was in the grate; the windows had not been recently cleaned, and the foggy remains of daylight dimly struggled through them. A pile of letters, visiting cards, circulars, and bills, lay on the table beside his meerschaum, and a half emptied box of cigars, whilst a faint odour of tobacco lingered on the close, cold atmosphere of the room.

Conrad was too weary and too miserable to take any special note of the discomfort, although in general he was very sensitive to such influences. He threw himself on the sofa, until such time as his servant should return.

It was now become quite dark, and the gas-lights from the streets were glaring on the walls, making both the light and the darkness look equally harsh. He knew not how long he had lain when his servant entered with the lamp. He started back at the first aspect of his master, who was so changed by his illness as to be hardly recognisable. 'Good Heaven! Mr Conrad, sir, you are come back looking like a ghost! I had grown quite unhappy about you: I did not know where you were to be found, and so could not forward your letters. I had only just gone out, and have not left the house for more than a week before.'

'How long have I been away?' asked Conrad, abruptly.

'Five weeks to-morrow, sir,' replied the man, surprised.

'I thought it had been a hundred years. What day of the week is it?'

'Thursday, sir.'

'Ah, indeed!' said Conrad, endeavouring to recollect.

Nature is a benevolent mother; our weakness is at once our limitation and our deliverance; when our sufferings become utterly unendurable, she bewilders our perception of it, and steeps our senses in forgetfulness.

Conrad was thus stupified; staggering, too, under the weakness of a recent illness, he gave in like a baffled swimmer, and ceased to struggle with the deep waters that were overwhelming him.

'I am sure, sir, you are very ill,' said the man, compassionately; 'you will be better in bed.'

'No, no,' replied Conrad, impatiently, turning away his head and closing his eyes, 'let me alone, let me alone.'

'But, sir, you look in a high fever, and must really let yourself be led.'

Conrad made a fretful gesture, but the man persisted, and at length succeeded in getting him to his room; he was like one drunk with misery.

'Shall I leave you a light, sir?'

'No, darkness, darkness, let me be in cold and darkness for ever.'

The servant retired, but determined that if his master were not more like a reasonable being in the morning he would fetch a doctor on his own responsibility.

The next morning, when he proceeded to his room, he found Conrad in a heavy stupor, from which he could not arouse him.

The doctor arrived and declared congestion of the brain to be imminent, and proceeded at once to strong measures.

For many days after this, Conrad lay utterly unconscious of all that was going on around him; and even when out of danger he had such a tedious and precarious convalescence, owing to several severe relapses, that it was several weeks before he could leave his room. No condition in life can well be more desolate than that of a man without either mother or sisters, falling ill in lodgings. Conrad, however, was fortunate in having a servant who was much attached to him, and who tended him very carefully. He had lived with him many years, and of course knew all his affairs rather better than his master himself. He contrived, from various indications, to discover where it was that his master had been during his late absence (for Conrad had carefully avoided giving him any clue), and then he pretty well surmised all that had taken place. He had, indeed, settled in his own mind how matters would end long before either Conrad or Alice dreamed of their danger. People in his class do not understand delicate distinctions; they have a rough, coarse way of judging of things, which, however, often comes nearer to the actual truth than a more subtle philosophy would have led them.

Conrad remained plunged in an apathy from which nothing could rouse him, and the gloom thickened every day.

One morning he entered his master's room with an air of suppressed importance; a happy thought had struck him.

'Dear heart, sir,' said he, as he was dressing him, 'I wish you would see some of your old friends, many of them called whilst you were lying ill. I did not tell you yesterday (speaking of your friends reminds me of it), that whilst I was in at the confectioner's buying some grapes, Miss Bianca came in; she knew me directly, and began to speak to me quite kind and pleasant, and I made bold to tell her how ill you had been, and she seemed quite put out of the way about it.'

Conrad did not speak, but he looked as if he were listening, and Walters went on.

'Do you know, sir, I think Miss Bianca is a very kind, nice young lady, and I think it is a great pity you never see her now. It would do you good to talk to her, she seemed so sorry as never was when I told her about your illness.'

Walters said no more, but he had touched the only chord which in the present state of things could move Conrad. After Walters had left him, it seemed as if the desire to see once more Bianca began like a spark of life to assert itself. He waited until Walters next entered the room (for he had not energy to ring the bell), and then desired him to bring the cab round and prepare to drive him to Bianca's house.

Walters brought him his hat and gloves, put his cloak around him, and placed him in the cab, as if he had been a child; for at the last moment Conrad shrank back, it looked so impossible to go.

Bianca was not at home when they arrived, but Conrad was coaxed into waiting for her. The servant ushered him into a pleasant parlour, the windows of which opened to the ground and looked into a small garden tastefully though rather fantastic-ally laid out; it was Bianca's usual sitting-room. It was very simply furnished; but it had a bright home look with its fresh chintz hangings, and book-shelves all round the room, and stands of plants and vases of choice flowers. A bust in marble, beautifully executed, of her old friend, stood on a pedestal, and the pure bright sunlight streamed full upon it.

As Conrad lay on the couch before the window, he felt himself gradually penetrated with a sense of pleasure at the change from his own large, dim, heavy-looking rooms to this cheerful region.

Suddenly he heard Bianca's voice in the hall—a rush of mingled feelings made him wish that he could sink into the earth to hide from her eyes. Bianca entered in the midst of his misgivings; without speaking, she went up to him, and they grasped each other's hands in silence. Much as Bianca desired to control herself, the tears gushed from her eyes at the sight of the ravages the last few months had wrought upon Conrad. His hair had grown quite gray, his figure was bent, and almost reduced to a skeleton; his thin pale face was stamped with a look of settled pain. For some time they were both unable to speak.

'I am come back to you, Bianca,' said Conrad at length, in a voice hardly audible.

'And to whom else should you go in sorrow?' replied she, in a kind, calm voice, for she had regained the mastery over herself, and did not wish to agitate him; she sat down on the sofa beside him.

'Oh! Bianca, if I had never left you, I should not now be thus,' said Conrad.

'Hush!' said she, gently, 'let the past be past, we will not speak of it.'

'Would that it might indeed be past,' said he, gloomily,— 'but nothing can die that has once been!—Bianca,' continued he, after a pause, 'I felt that I must come to you again—do you forgive me?'

She looked at him with the tenderest pity in her large clear eyes.

'There is nothing to forgive between friends,' said she; 'you are come to seek me when you were in sorrow, what more could you do? Do not let your thoughts dwell on the past; think of me as your mother, as your sister.' She rose, and began to arrange the pillows for his head, as if he had been a sick child. 'Now, you must be very quiet; you are not strong enough to talk.'

Conrad obeyed; her manner was inexpressibly tender and maternal; he felt soothed and comforted, as Orestes might have been when he was beside Electra.* Her grief had given to her features that expression of refinement and softness which nothing but sorrow can give. She then took her netting, and seated herself on a chair beside the couch.

'Bianca! are *you* Alice?' said Conrad, suddenly,—'you had *her* face this moment.'

'No, no, dear Conrad, you are dreaming,' said she, soothingly, for she began to fear that his mind was unsettled.

'You are so strangely like her,' persisted Conrad. 'How wonderful, if her soul should have passed into you, in order to come back and comfort me!—You never used to look like her.'

'You did not perceive it, perhaps,' replied Bianca; 'if I am really like her, it is not so strange as it appears—there is a secret I never told you.'

'Is there?' said Conrad, absently, for he was still filled with the sense of awe which the resemblance inspired. Since Bianca's sorrow it had indeed become strikingly developed.

'Do not go away from me, Bianca,' said Conrad, as she rose from her chair.

'No, dear friend, I am not going to leave you, I only want to show you a picture.'

She went to her desk and took thence a small miniature.

'Have you never seen a picture like that?' said she, giving it to him.

'Alice had one in her room—a portrait of her father'—

'And that is a portrait of my father also.'

'Who and what are you then?' asked Conrad, wildly.

'Alice was my half sister, although she was ignorant of it.'

'But, Bianca, explain all this—tell me every thing; why did you keep this from me? tell me quickly, but come back and sit beside me; do not go so far off.'

She complied, and returning to her seat beside the couch, she told him the history with which the reader is already acquainted.

'Oh, Bianca,' he exclaimed, when she ceased to speak, 'how strangely all has happened! I cannot tell you the good it does me to know this; but I also have many things to tell you, and that which you must know before I can feel sure that you have forgiven me.'

'Not today, Conrad; you have been already too much agitated. Besides, I already know much of what you would tell me.'

Dinner was now brought in.

'Now, Conrad,' said Bianca, 'remember you are my patient, and I shall be a most despotic nurse; you must eat what I give you.'

'If you have poison for me I will drink it,' said Conrad.

'Well, that is quite right, only just now some of this fowl and a glass of Madeira will do you more good.'

After dinner Conrad fell asleep for near an hour. Bianca gazed upon him with the kind of yearning tenderness a mother might feel towards a storm-tossed, misguided son, who after many wanderings should return destitute and broken to the shadow of his home. The deep life-long affection she had cherished for him was recompensed at last, although in a different mode to what she had once expected. Still it was an inexpressible consolation to feel that it had not been wasted; he had recognized her love when he fell into sorrow, and it was beside her that he had come to find rest. It was abundant recompence and consolation for all she had suffered. Her affection for him had, it was true, changed its character. All passionate emotion had passed away; she was disenchanted of all her illusions with regard to him. He was no longer the idol before whom she worshipped, and to whom she vainly dedicated her gifts. The fiery pain in which her soul had been steeped on his account had passed away, and it was now become as if it had been written in a book concerning another person.

She felt a mournful presentiment that he was wrecked for life—that his career was finished in the midst of his days; and, with her heart purified from all personal emotion, and selfish feeling, she made a vow in her heart, to be to him henceforth— mother, sister, friend. When he awoke he seemed refreshed—the look of deep pain was lightened.

The day was beginning to decline, and Walters appeared with the cab, to take his master home before the evening set in.

'I am sure you must be an angel from heaven, Miss Bianca,' said the man, in a low voice; 'Master looks better already. May I bring him again tomorrow?'

'Oh, yes,' said Bianca, with a smile, 'if he does not come of his own accord.'

Life does not end in a catastrophe like a book or a play. We may, and do feel, after some occurrence which has shaken our being to its centre, as though we had reached the end of the world, and that our next step must be out on sheer nothingness; but it is not so. Life goes on until death receives it; made up of the same stuff as heretofore, and filled up with natural occur-rences. The day after that one, which once seemed to us as though it must be the end of our being, comes as fresh, and unscarred, as the first that dawned on Eden.

Both Bianca and Conrad had each touched a point in their experience beyond which it seemed impossible for life to pro-ceed. But neither their sorrow, nor their passionate despair, had been realities. The darkness which hung over them had dis-persed; and Life still stretched before them with a Future hung in the distance, and shrouding the end as of old.

CHAPTER XVII

WHILST these things were going on in England, Lord Melton, utterly unconscious of them, was wandering hither and thither with great perseverance. He had been to Egypt, seen Ali Pacha, inspected the Pyramids, and all the wonderful remains of tombs and temples and statues. The Egyptians, who deified LIFE—that one notion of religion running through all their forms of worship—were the people who erected the most gorgeous dwelling-places to DEATH, its twin mystery. He also made excursions into the Desert; took sundry family dinners with Bedouin Arabs, whose encampment he fell in with; made a collection of shawls and pipes, and any curiosities he fancied Bianca would like, or that would amuse her. He had constantly written long letters to her, and to his sister, detailing his adventures; but as curious readers have had all manner of the very best Oriental details in 'Eöthen, and Warburton* they can the better afford to go without them now; at least it satisfies our conscience for not purposing to give them any; we really cannot go so far out of our way. We only wish to find Lord Melton, who, after ten months' wanderings, arrived in Athens. He had quite made up his mind that letters would be awaiting him from his sister and from Bianca: but whether his directions had not been sufficiently precise, or whether his various correspondents had nothing to say which they considered worth foreign postage, or whether their precious letters had gone to enrich the treasury of the moon (the paradise of lost things), it is impossible to say; all we know is, that not a single letter or newspaper had arrived for Lord Melton, and that his lordship was, as his valet expressed it, 'very much put out of the way' in consequence. People must be in a foreign land, and counting the days until they reach the place where their letters ought to be, before they can know the dead, sickening blank, of hearing that there are none. An incredulous disappointment, and a disposition to storm the post-office, or to bribe the clerks to any amount to unsay their intelligence and find a letter, seems a feasible miracle. If people only knew the amount of suffering entailed by negligence, they would not allow a small amount of hindrance to prevent their letters being as certain as sunrise. Lord Melton was bitterly disappointed; and the consciousness of feeling himself a very ill-used man, with the full privilege of unlimited sulkiness, was a very poor compensation. Added to which, the heat of the weather, and the fatigues of his journey, threw him into a high fever. He had been unwell for some days, but on the night of his arrival at Athens, he became so ill that he had to send for a physician, and submit himself during many days to medical discipline. When he was again able to travel (indeed almost before it was prudent), he proceeded to Constantinople, although he heard that the plague was going about like influenza. Constantinople was the next place where he had directed his letters to be sent, and he would have gone if there had been fifty plagues instead of one.

When he reached Constantinople, he immediately despatched a messenger to the embassy for his letters and newspapers. This time he was not disappointed. He eagerly opened a closely written letter from Bianca, and read it all through; but the veins stood out on his forehead, his countenance was flushed, and his lips compressed, till all their colour was driven back. When he had finished reading it, he looked carefully to see whether under the seal, or in a postscript, there might not be some word or line he had overlooked; but he found none. Then, with a gesture of rage, he crumpled the letter in his hand, and flung it vehemently to the other end of the room.

For a few moments he seemed literally choking—he flung his arms above his head, and then walked rapidly up and down the room, as though he would, by motion, calm the rage which was convulsing him.

'What a fool I am!—what a double fool, to let myself be so played upon. That cursed Conrad! Oh, that I could kill him, stamp the life out of him! To come crawling back to her, after he had insulted her, abandoned her, because he saw another valued the prize he flung away! And Bianca!—but all women are alike; none have truth, none have sense; she knew, and had proved what he was, and now writes to me that he has come back to her, with a cursed bland complacency, as if it were the most natural thing in the world! Why did she not invite me to the wedding-breakfast at once—or to assist at the ceremony and give her away?—it needed but that to be complete! She cares for nothing but herself when it comes to the point.'

His words, which came like a torrent, broken by rocks and obstacles, instead of calming him, seemed to lash him into fresh fury. There was something fearful in the sight of one usually so self-controlled, thus moved. The whole purpose and hope of his life seemed violently thrust aside, for the idle caprice of a man, who, he knew, set no real value on the prize he was thus coldly wresting from his grasp. All the pure and constant affection he had lavished on Bianca was suddenly turned to mockery, and, even in his own eyes, made him seem a blind, weak fool. The whole world, to his distempered fancy, seemed combined to turn all that had been generous and trusting, all his best qualities, to his own discomfiture.

The whole of that night he passed in a state of bitter anguish he had never known before.

His hope of winning Bianca had grown almost to a certainty;— he had felt sure, when all obstacles were removed, that such love as his was, must, in the end, win her; and now it was violently wrenched away, and a blank despair, with which he could not struggle, invaded and took possession of his soul.

Lord Melton was not one of those who had ever played at being 'sad as night'; he had never gone through any species of mental convulsion: he was a fine, sound, healthy-toned character, with a great deal of good sense, and a singleness of mind and motive, a directness of purpose, that had kept him clear of all metaphysical perplexities; he was always intensely in earnest, which gave a child-like directness to his whole character. His passion for Bianca was part of himself—no external circumstances could touch it—so long as Bianca remained what she was, so long, hopeless or not, would his affection for her remain un-altered. The fierce passions that were now roused within him— the dark, terrible despair that filled his soul, absolutely terrified him; he was, as it were, taken prisoner by the powers of darkness, and the sense of the reality of these powers crushed and bore him down; he was overpowered, and all idea of escape or struggle seemed vain.

As the night deepened, the dark aspect of his position became more exaggerated and fantastic; visions of Conrad and Bianca, in their home, where, by some mysterious power he also was condemned to dwell, haunted him; he seemed to have caught the trick of Conrad's way of speaking, and of Bianca's mode of thought, which served to give a colouring of reality to his most bitter and fanciful imaginings; he ceased to distinguish that it was he himself who embodied these fancies, and attributed them to Conrad, to Bianca; his mind was dragged along by his imagination, as wretches of old were bound alive to the chariot of their victors, and dragged along the ground. After a while all his perceptions became confused; he no longer discerned the objects around him. His valet found him delirious in the morning; his fever had returned with ten-fold violence, and it was many days before he recognised those around him. Having a fever and being delirious are easy and compendious phrases for those in health to use, and to them it conveys an idea of illness, perhaps of danger; but the fearful suffering from the visitation of those inhabitants of the realm of madness,—the intense reality of those delirious wanderings are never recognised.

> Deeds to be hid, which were not hid,
> And all confused, I did not know,
> Whether I suffered, or I did,
> But all was guilt, and fear, and woe.

At length Lord Melton was convalescent—his misery had become less dark—it was a suffering that had to be borne, and he recognised it as such.

Never, for an instant, did a doubt of how it would all end intrude upon him. It must be remembered, that he was entirely ignorant of the sad and fatal drama which had occurred during his absence, and which separated Conrad and Bianca, as by a gulf of fire, from all possible return to their old relations.

Still further was he from surmising the deep radical dissimilarity and discrepancy of character which every day developed between Bianca and Conrad. He did not know that Bianca, set free from her first engagement, and become accustomed to his refinement, and clear, keen judgment, had involuntarily erected himself into the standard by which she judged and measured all others. Bianca was not aware of it herself. Lord Melton did not know, either, that Conrad, broken and weary, had gone to

Bianca, as the only living being who would endure the weight of his desolation, without any trace of his old passion, but with an immense and intuitive reliance on her indestructible affection, which no absence or ill treatment could efface. He did not know that it was an unconscious tribute to the worth and reality of her character:—and, above all, he was ignorant of that well-spring of tenderness and devotion, which, in a woman who has truly loved, survives all the more earthly and selfish emotions of passion. The living principle of love remains, when all passion is dead; and then it takes that deepest and broadest form of manifestation, which has its foundation woven into the very fibres of a woman's nature—the sentiment of maternity.

The sentiment of motherhood is latent in all women, and is a far stronger instinct than any passion for a lover. Let a man they care for ever so little come before them ill and suffering, and this instinct is instantly aroused—they are capable of any exertion or any sacrifice in his behalf: it signifies no sort of passion, and is compatible with utter personal indifference. When the need of sacrifice and exertion is gone by, the mere collapse from a state of occupation may set a woman thinking and dreaming, and the transition to sentimentality is very short and easy; but then it must be a new untried affection, and not, as in Bianca's case, a sentiment on each side thoroughly worn out. It was the sincerest tribute Conrad could pay to the intrinsic worth and nobleness of Bianca, to come to her with an unerring instinct that she would receive him; and that no thought of her own dignity, or her own position, no self-love, or vanity of any kind, would hinder her.

But Lord Melton knew nothing of metaphysics, and still less of psychology; neither, as we have seen, did he know any thing of the facts of the present case; so, naturally enough, all the reason and judgment he endeavoured to bring to bear on the matter, only made the conclusion he arrived at more elaborately wrong.

If we would only condescend, when we are dealing with reasonably conscientious people, to believe what they tell us, we should generally arrive nearer the truth than by asserting our claim to shrewdness and cleverness by drawing our own inferences.

Lord Melton had hitherto implicitly believed Bianca in all she said. In this instance she had told him the exact truth about her own sentiments for Conrad. She could not in a letter venture on details, and Lord Melton fell bankrupt in faith, or, perhaps, we should say, there was a strong run on his jealousy, which did not allow his faith fair play, and he got into a most complicated state of misery accordingly.

The old theologians were quite right in making faith the primeval virtue of religion—the granite rock of its foundation; it is a divine inspiration of heart, a clear insight into things, to which neither knowledge nor reason can reach; 'it is high, they cannot attain unto it.'

In Lord Melton's case faith was just the only virtue which could bring its own reward with it. There were many excuses for him, still excuses cannot redeem any one from the consequences of his own act, so Lord Melton was miserable all the same. When he was well enough to travel, he ordered his departure, but previously he wrote to Bianca, what he considered a highly proper and dignified letter. In it he remarked, somewhat sarcastically, on 'her forgiving spirit', and said that women were fond of forgiving, and that 'unless a man behaved like a scoundrel to them, he had no chance of rousing either their heroism or their generosity'. He concluded rather grimly, with his best wishes for her happiness, 'wherever and with whomsoever she might fix her choice'! He casually mentioned that he should travel for some time further, and omitted to furnish her with his address; a piece of dignity which at the time rather soothed him, though like all other dignity, it weighed heavily on him afterwards.

The next day he departed for Trieste, intending to make up his mind to his further destination when he arrived there.

Thus had a source of distrust and change crept into an attachment which he believed could never either die or fade until he himself should die. Between these two beings formed for each other, deeply and purely attached! For Bianca loved him, although her love was yet like the young corn, hardly showing its gentle green above the ground, and she did not recognise it till it had struck its roots in her heart. The devil, who is the father and furtherer of all evil, the hater of unity, and the promoter of division, had succeeded in inserting a wedge of dissatisfaction and distrust between Lord Melton and Bianca!

CHAPTER XVIII

ALL this while, Conrad continued to come frequently to Bianca; her calm, clear spirit soothed and sustained his weak and shattered soul; he fell into the habit of her society, whilst he continued to go to her house without giving a thought to the various rumours and interpretations that would be likely to arise from it. In effect a great deal of gossip was the result. Reports of all kinds were afloat, from the sedate paragraph in the daily papers, containing an official announcement of the 'Hymeneal altar',★ down to passages in scandalous prints, of a far more questionable tendency: jokes, innuendoes, and circumstantial reports, containing every quality in the world except truth, were rife concerning her. Bianca could not be unaware of all this, neither was she so hero-ically superior to humanity as to be indifferent to what was said of her. No woman can be indifferent to evil reports of her good fame: but whilst Bianca's proud heart was blistered by find-ing that her name was running the gauntlet of all the infamous things that papers dependent on high-seasoned scandal choose to invent, still she did not feel at liberty to draw back; she felt that without her, Conrad's life or reason would have failed, and she did not dare to let a thought of herself stand in the way. 'I will live all that down hereafter,' she said to herself, and in the meanwhile, neither by look nor sign, did she show to Conrad that she had the least cognisance of all the reports that had been raised. Conrad was too absorbed in his own feelings and his own sorrows, to think of any thing of the sort; if he had been aware of it, he had too much gentlemanly feeling, and too much real regard for Bianca, to have subjected her to it for any selfish consideration of himself.

Gradually, however, he came to her less frequently, and a change, the nature of which she could hardly have defined, came over him: at first she thought it was out of consideration to her; that he had become aware of the painful reports, and was endeav-ouring silently to extinguish them, and she felt pleased and grateful for his delicacy: but it was not long before she perceived that some other and far deeper feeling was at work within him, but as he shrank from all conversation that seemed to question him on that point, she was obliged to leave him to time.

One evening she was driving to a large dinner-party that had been made expressly for her. Many of her leading acquaintance—indeed, nearly all of them—had magnanimously countenanced her during the storm that had arisen, for which they one and all took great credit to themselves; never failing, however, when they mentioned the fact, to go over a tolerably long list of highly unexceptionable people who kept them in countenance. Bianca, in this, was very fortunate, for if only one had given way, it is a chance but that the whole circle would have gone, like a row of children's soldiers, of which, if you touch but one, they all fall in succession. Bianca continued to be invited to the most unexceptionable dinings and tea-drinkings. She would much rather have stayed away from most of them; but in this world it is one of the social rewards, and criterions of 'perfect respectability', to receive admissions to the heaviest and solemnest reunions that can be drawn together; whilst exclusion from them, is 'to lie under the ban of the empire'. As an estimable old lady once said to us, in the depth of a dreary party, 'there would cease to be any reward for virtue, if we admitted both the good and the bad indiscriminately to our social intercourse'.

But all this is an immense digression. Bianca was going, on the evening in question, to a most unexceptionable dinner party. There was a momentary stoppage in the street, as they were passing the doors of a dissenting chapel;* it was evidently some special occasion, for large bills were posted on the wall, and the name of some noted preacher was underlined. Bianca half smiled to see how extremes met, and that she and the preacher who would, no doubt, have considered her in a high state of reprobation, were both pressed on the public by the same mode. A crowd of people were pouring in, and a long string of sober-looking carriages blocked up the way. Bianca looked out with some curiosity, and her eyes caught Conrad's, as he was turning to enter in. He seemed slightly annoyed at being recognised, but he immediately came to the carriage-window to speak to her.

'Where have you been all the week? and what is there here to-night to make such a concourse?'

'Are you then coming?' asked Conrad, with surprise.

'I? No; I want to know what it is at all.'

'A very noted and eloquent preacher, and a very holy man,' replied Conrad, gravely. 'He is a new friend of mine.'

'Well,' replied Bianca, smiling, 'do not let him make you forget your old ones.'

The obstruction had now ceased, and the coachman drove on. Bianca thought with some surprise on the utter change that must have passed over Conrad to induce him to enter a dissenting meeting; he had never been at all addicted to going to church under any circumstances, and she had heard him express the most unmitigated contempt for all kinds of Methodists and Dissenters; but she had reached her destination, and had no further convenience for speculation. The evening passed over in stately decorum; but she learned casually that Lord Melton was in Vienna, and talked of making an excursion into the heart of Bohemia; that he had been in Vienna some weeks, and was going about a great deal into the very gayest society.

'How very strange that he has never written,' thought Bianca, and a vague discomfort of heart seized on her.

It seemed as if all her intelligence of Lord Melton's movements had been frozen up, and were suddenly set free like the words heard by Pantagruel and his companions;* for the next day, a lady whom she had not seen before that season, called upon her. After some ordinary talk, the lady suddenly said, 'By the way, I am not to forget to tell you, that my brother returned last week from Vienna, where he left your old friend, Lord Melton, who is become the gayest of the gay. Frank says that he goes into an immense deal of society, "*la crême de la crême*", as Mrs Trollope would say.* He was said to be madly in love with the prima donna who is making such a sensation there, La Fornasari; who, by the way, Frank declares to be wonderfully like you; perhaps that may be the reason why Lord Melton has fallen in love with her. Frank can talk of nothing else but her beauty, and her wit, and her eccentricities; he says she does every day, the maddest things possible. I hope she will come here, I do so like people out of the common way.'

'That depends on circumstances,' said Bianca, laughing: 'I know nothing so disagreeable as people who set up to be out of the common way; they are so prosaically fantastic, and as stupid as a labyrinth of which one knows every turn.'

'Oh, but I assure you that La Fornasari is not one of that sort; she is as full of caprices as Undine before she got her soul,★ and has turned the heads of all the young men in Vienna: she has ruined I do not know how many, and one young Polish noble-man has committed suicide on her account; he and his most intimate friend were both in love with her, and they came to a quarrel in consequence; there was to have been a duel (Frank was asked to be one of the seconds), but the night previous to the meeting, this poor young man shot himself, because he would not fight his friend. He left a most beautiful letter, Frank says, and a farewell waltz, which he dedicated to the Fornasari. His friend was so affected that he renounced her, and left the city the next day. It made a great sensation, and even the Fornasari was touched. She wrote some words to his air, and sang them herself; and made a vow, for his sake, to treat the very next lover who presented himself with great consideration. Lord Melton, seem-ingly, has been that one, for he came on with her directly afterwards. Frank brought me a copy of the air and the song. I will send them to you. Is it not a romantic history?'

'Highly so, indeed,' replied Bianca, absently.

'The Fornasari will never keep Lord Melton long,' said Con-rad, who was present, 'nor any one else, except those who follow her for the fashion. She has no more heart than a wicked fairy. If she came to England she would not succeed. I should be sorry to see one so utterly shameless even in the theatre. She is not fit to be spoken of.'

Both Bianca and the lady looked surprised at this burst of energy. The lady, however, very shortly after rose to take her leave.

After she had departed, Bianca sat silently, making up a bou-quet, which she was to wear in one of her scenes that evening. Conrad, who was sitting opposite to her, in a large chair, was struck with the peculiar expression of her countenance.

'I do not believe one word of all that chattering woman has said!' said he, suddenly. 'Melton is not the one to get entangled with a bad meretricious woman; if your friend, who was speaking of her so lightly just now, had only known one half of what I do, she would be struck dumb with shame for her own levity.'

'When did you know her?' asked Bianca.

'Some years ago, in Italy. She had then just made her *début*. I saw her the first night of her appearance; she certainly is as much like you in person, as she is different from you in mind.'

'How was it you never mentioned her to me?'

'Bianca, if you only knew how loathsome those years of vanity and folly look to me now, you would not wonder that I shrink from recalling them; and yet, perhaps, the lengths and depths of sinfulness to which I have been permitted to go, were necessary to my complete humiliation, so that I might walk in penitence and self-abhorrence all my life, and, being made to see my own weakness, never trust in my own heart more.'

'What a singular mode you have taken up of expressing yourself lately,' said Bianca; 'you seem to have quite a new way of thinking on all subjects.'

'Not a new way, dear Bianca; I have only found, I trust, the old way—the way that alone can conduct us to rest and peace.'

Bianca looked puzzled—but she had become accustomed to hear him speak mysteriously, and attached no particular importance to it: to-night, however, he seemed singularly grave and sad.

'You are not well, to-night, Conrad; you are not yet strong enough to venture into these crowded places at night. If you must go to church, go in the day time. By the way, you have not told me any thing of what you heard last night. Preachers have such power when they are eloquent. The pulpit, next to the press, is the most powerful instrument for influencing the minds of men, and in these days it has quite lost its power. Men have not now their hearts stirred within them from the pulpit, for they know beforehand all that the preacher is allowed to tell them.'

'I wish you would not speak in that way, Bianca, you do not know how it jars upon me. I consider that the man who is called to the ministry is called to a perilous honour, which places him higher than the angels—inasmuch as they only contemplate from afar the mystery of which he is a partaker.'

'You are growing quite a mystic!' said Bianca, winding a silver wire round her flowers: 'look, are not they lovely?'

'To come from the fresh dew and the sunlight, where they were placed, to wither in the glare and heat of the theatre!' said he, looking mournfully at them and at her.

'And why not in the theatre as well as in a ball-room?' said Bianca, impatiently.

'Just as well and just as ill,' said Conrad, gently; 'both (to say the least of them), are equally vain and weary modes of existence for an immortal soul, which may be called at any moment to give in its account of "the deeds done in the body". If I felt regret that those fair perishing flowers should exhale their beauty and their perfume on such service, how much more great and terrible must seem to me the waste of you, with all your gifts of genius (given for far higher purposes), your noble faculties, and fine qualities, sacrificing night after night at the shrine of that world which rewards its votaries with bitterness and self-contempt, which lures them on, to leave them desolate and deceived at last! Believe me, dear Bianca, no worldly success, no earthly glitter, will ever satisfy a human heart—they all "leave an aching void the world can never fill".'*

'Conrad, you are not well,' said Bianca, kindly: 'I am not going to argue with you, because what you say is quite true, only you seem to have taken it up in a strange perverted way; all you say about sacrificing to the world is very true, but it does not touch me: if one has work to do one must do it; no one worth the name of a rational being ever dreamed of living for the sake of amusing himself. If you tried my life for a month, you would find it real hard work, and no amusement at all.'

'We do not understand each other, Bianca,' replied Conrad; 'some day it will perhaps be given you to know what I mean.'

'Meanwhile, I must go to the theatre; my time is up. When shall I see you again?'

'Will you let me find you alone at eleven o'clock to-morrow, if I come?' asked Conrad.

'Make it ten o'clock, and then you will be sure to find me disengaged,' said Bianca; 'but if you are going home, shall I set you down?'

'No. I will be here at ten o'clock to-morrow.'

Bianca was tying her bonnet, and did not remark the peculiar manner in which Conrad spoke; she nodded her head to him as she left the room, and desiring the coachman to drive very fast, as they were late, she sprang into the carriage.

Conrad remained where she had left him, apparently in bitter reflection. After awhile he started up like one stung with pain,

and began to pace up and down the room. He stopped opposite
the window which opened into the garden. It was a rich June
evening; it was beginning to get dusk; a clear air tint that seemed
like light from neither sun nor moon, but rather a transparent
darkness, was spread over all. An expression of intense pain
knitted his forehead.

'Thirty years old to-day!' exclaimed he, bitterly; 'and this is all
the good that my life has done me! utterly wrecked, utterly
bankrupt! Sorrow I have brought on all who have known me,
bitter, never-ceasing remorse on myself! these are the goodly
fruits of all the labours I have done under the sun!'

'Oh!' groaned he, as in utter anguish of spirit,—'A lost life,—a
lost life,—a lost life! to what purpose has been all this waste?
Would to God that I had never been born!'

He clasped his hands above his head with a gesture of despair,
and flung himself on the couch, which shook under his convulsive sobbings. After a while they ceased, and he lay calmed and
stunned; but then again, as impelled by some fury, he sprang from
the couch, and began again to walk, with writhing steps, up and
down the room.

'She has rest in the grave where I have laid her—where I have
laid her. Yes, yes,—"Woe to thee that spoilest, and thou wast not
spoiled—and dealest treacherously and they dealt not treacherously to thee;—when thou shalt cease to spoil, thou shalt be
spoiled—and when thou shalt make an end to deal treacherously,
they shall deal treacherously with thee." '

He uttered these words in a dull, absent tone, like one speaking
in a trance, or as if he had used a voice that was not his own.

'Aye,' continued he, in a sharp, quick tone, 'that is my doom;
those are the words written against me, and none can take them
away. None can take them away.'

One of the servants entered hastily with a light; he had heard a
sound of talking, and knowing that his mistress was not at home
he was alarmed. The sudden flashing of the lamp dazzled the eyes
of Conrad, but he instantly recovered his self-possession, and
coldly bidding, the man bring his hat, he left the house.

CHAPTER XIX

THE next morning, when Bianca descended to breakfast, she found Conrad already arrived; but she started back at his strange aspect. He seemed utterly transformed, and for a second she hardly recognised him. He was dressed in a coarse iron-gray coat, made something like a Quaker's; his linen, about which he had always been singularly fastidious, was of the very coarsest description, though perfectly white and clean. The whole of his dress, which was of the same iron-gray colour, seemed to have been made by a tailor who worked for artizans, so rudely and clumsily was it fashioned; his shoes were thick, with nails in the soles, and coarse gray woollen stockings were seen above them.

'What on earth is all this about, Conrad? What are you going to do with yourself at all in this guise?'

'I have many things to say to you, Bianca, and we have no time to lose in idle surprise.'

'Well, sit down and have some breakfast, and tell me what it is that has come upon you.'

'A change of heart which will lead to a changed life, I would fain hope,' replied he, gravely.

'You are speaking parables this morning,' said she, trying to speak cheerfully, although a vague fear that his mind was getting unhinged oppressed her. 'What shall I give you? I can recommend this chocolate; I had a quantity given me the other day. It is real Spanish.'

'Thank you, no, I have already eaten; delicate food no more shall pass my lips.'

Bianca, more and more surprised, began to sip her chocolate in uneasy silence, waiting for what he should next say. He did not speak, however, until she seemed to have finished her breakfast; he appeared to be considering in what manner he might best unfold his errand. At length he spoke, in a slow, grave voice.

'I am come to say farewell. I have not told you of my plans before, because I feared you would oppose me and harass me, by painful entreaties. You know all the folly of my past life—you know all the sin of it—you know the deep sin of all that lies on my soul. You have been very good to me; if you had not stood beside me in the beginning, I must have lost my reason, which has been spared me to work out my repentance. When that was done, your work ceased. You wished to have restored me to peace and comfort, but that was not for me. What have I done that I should ever know peace again? How could I live at peace, when she is in the grave, where I have laid her? But, Bianca, when I was helplessly crying "What must I do to find peace?" I strayed by chance, not knowing whither I went (you see I was guided there by a power not my own), into that chapel where you saw me entering the other night, and there I heard the message intended for me. I was told there that I had lived in self—that I had been dead in pleasure, dead in sin, and that there was a woe against all those who lived at ease, forgetting God—forgetting their brethren, the poor of this world. I knew I had done all this—I knew that I had bestowed on the needy none of the good things which I had thought mine, but of which I now heard I was only steward. I had kept all for myself, and my soul was weighed down with a curse. Oh, Bianca! you know not what it is to open your eyes suddenly, and see yourself utterly steeped and polluted with sin; to be obliged to abhor yourself more than the most loathsome thing you ever gazed on before;—but you must know what you are—it is the first step out of the abyss. I went to this chapel often; I heard what my soul thirsted to hear. You could not speak those words to me,—good, and kind, and devoted, you were still blind yourself. At length I spoke to the minister from whose lips I had first heard what I was. He showed me what I must do. The time past of my life shall suffice to have wrought folly—henceforth, I give myself to try to do good, as I have before done evil. Of myself, I can do no good thing; but help will be given me. I have sold all I possessed. Henceforth, I will wear no elegant clothes, I will eat no delicate food. I am the steward of my fortune—the possessors of it are all those who are in hunger, and want, and wretchedness. I go to live amongst them, to minister unto them.'

'But, Conrad, that is pure fanaticism, and nothing else. With your education, and your talents, to go to live entirely with rude, miserable wretches, is throwing yourself away; it is not using your gifts to advantage.'

'Do not talk to me, Bianca, you know not what you say. I came to speak to you for the last time, therefore do not distract me from what I have to say. I would fain exhort you to quit your mode of life, for one better befitting an immortal creature; but I am not worthy to exhort you, you are far higher and better than I am; you will have another teacher sent to you. I have better wishes for you than you have for yourself; something tells me you will be led into the right way before you die. Now, Bianca, farewell,—God bless and reward you for all you have been to me.'

His words choked him, and the tears streamed from his eyes, as he rose and took her hand.

'You have been a dear and precious friend to me,' said he, in a voice broken with emotion; 'forgive me all the sorrow I once brought on you.'

'Surely you are not leaving me in this way, Conrad!' cried Bianca, fearfully,—'where are you going?—why are you going?—it must be some dream,' said she, with a bewildered look.

'It is no dream, Bianca,—the Conrad you knew is dead.—The last day of my old life closed yesterday—to-day my new life has arisen.'

Bianca put her hands to her head; he took one of them, and said, gently, 'All this tumult and confusion will pass away. You should rejoice that I have found the true and the right way, and not sorrow that I have left my old life behind.'

'But you will let me hear of you—you will come and see me, sometimes, at least?'

Conrad shook his head.

'If ever you should be in want or sorrow, and should need me, then I would come:—a note to the minister of that chapel would always find me. Bianca, Bianca!' continued he, whilst his whole frame shook with the emotion he endeavoured to suppress, 'do not weep thus,—it breaks my heart to see you, for I cannot help you. You are good and kind, and would do all things for me; but you cannot help me; you cannot heal my wounded soul. I *must* go—"there is a task laid on me which I must fulfil." '

He grasped both her hands in his, and with lips cold as death he pressed one long kiss upon her forehead.

'I have left you, Bianca, some books and things that you will keep for my sake; and this I have brought you, too; you may keep it innocently: and now, farewell.'

He laid a small morocco miniature case upon the table, and without again venturing to look at it, he left the room.

CHAPTER XX

LORD MELTON, in the course of his wanderings, found himself
at Trieste. He was undetermined as to his course; he could not
resolve to return to England, and he had put off making up his
mind until he should reach Trieste. It was a relief to him, that,
until he arrived there, he need decide on nothing; he flung
himself into the chapter of accidents, like one trying a '*sortes*'* for
something to determine his steps.

When he had settled himself at the hotel, he strolled towards
the sea. He sat down, at length, listlessly enough, to survey the
busy and vivid scene before him.

Suddenly a loud scream arose, from a group of children who
were at play in a boat, which was secured to the shore by a cable
twisted several times round a stone pillar. The boat had been
swayed to and fro by the ripple of the waves, and their movements in their game, in a way that rendered it difficult for them
to keep their balance. A dispute arose, and the biggest of the
children seized another angrily; in the struggle, both fell over
into the water, between the boat and the shore. Both disappeared, and were drawn by the waves under the boat. Before,
however, Lord Melton could reach the spot, a young sailor who
was lounging near, had dived like a water-dog after them, and in
a few moments re-appeared with one of the children hanging,
drenched and lifeless, across his arm. Lord Melton promptly
relieved him from his burden, and he again disappeared beneath
the surface to search for the other. This time he was less successful, and had to come up to take breath more than once. At length
he appeared with the other; it had got entangled in a heap of
sea-weed under the boat, and life was quite extinct. Lord Melton
had carried his burden into a cabaret which stood near the quay,
and was anxiously watching, beside the bed, the application of all
the usual remedies, when the second victim of the casualty was
brought and laid down beside the other, who was now beginning
to show some symptoms of restored animation. All the bystanders
assisted, and seemed instinctively to turn their eyes to Lord
Melton for directions. He had with difficulty succeeded in calming

the tumult and bustle of many advisers, and introduced orderliness into their proceedings.

'I fear,' said he, putting his hand on the child's heart, 'that this poor little thing is past our care; we can but try. Is that water still warm?'

An answer being returned in the affirmative, he directed one of the bystanders to place him in it, and then turned to continue his cares to the one under his hands. On lifting the left arm to rub it more conveniently, he observed the mark of a small cross pricked on the inner side in blue ink, whilst several initials were printed in different colours at each of the angles. He had no leisure to bestow much attention upon this, as his ears were at that instant assailed by loud lamentations, mingled with the shrill clamour of many female voices, speaking at once in varied tones of deprecation and sympathy. The door of the apartment burst open, and a tall masculine looking woman, in the dress of a Hungarian peasant, violently disengaged herself from the grasp of her companions, who strove to soothe her, and rushed to the body of the dead child, which had been removed from the bath, and strained it frantically to her bosom.

'It is the mother—the mother of them both,' said some one in the group, in an almost unintelligible *patois*.

'Tell her,' said Lord Melton, 'that she is losing the only chance of recovering her child. She must be quiet.'

A dozen voices were raised at once; the woman seemed not to heed, but sat with a stony gaze, rigidly clasping the form of her child.

Lord Melton, much affected, endeavoured gently to remove her, and to draw her attention to the one he had succeeded in restoring, but she pushed him angrily aside, and regarded the now calmly breathing form of the rescued one with a shudder of despair and affright, whilst she fiercely resisted his attempt to disengage the child she still convulsively clutched.

'They were both your children,' said Lord Melton, 'and you must be thankful for the one preserved to you.'

She stared at him wildly, without understanding a word he said.

The voices of several women were again raised to enforce his words.

'It is false, it is false,' said she, wildly: 'this one is my son; what is the other to me? I have lost my soul for it, and now it has cost me my son.'

'She is mad, the poor Monica!' said a woman, compassionately; 'the one that lies dead was her favourite; she never favoured the other, she would not have cared had the other been the victim.'

'I am not mad, I tell ye,' cried the mother, fiercely: 'this one is my child—my precious son; the other—how should I know who owns it—it has brought evil on me from the beginning:' and muttering still wilder words, she went off in a violent hysterical seizure, and had to be removed to a distant room.

Lord Melton's patience was at last rewarded by seeing his little patient fall into a peaceful slumber. With some difficulty he continued to clear the room, and remained still watching beside the bed. He might have sat there about half an hour, when a servant returned, saying that the woman, the mother of the children, earnestly desired to see him.

'Is she better?' asked Lord Melton—'this little fellow is doing well.'

'His mother rambles and talks wildly—it seems to be little she cares for this one; she calls the other her child: but she asks to see you, and will not rest until your lordship is good enough to humour her.'

'By all means I will go; and you will see that the doctor and the landlord understand that I am responsible for all expenses, and so forth. The sailor who jumped into the water after him, should have something; but that I will see to myself. Remain here beside the child until I return.'

Lord Melton was shown into a miserable garret in the auberge, and on a low pallet the wretched woman lay. A priest was beside her, and several women were standing round the bed, which was covered with marks of blood: in her paroxysm of grief she had broken a blood-vessel, and she seemed on the point of death.

'Here is the good English prince who has saved your child,' said one of the women.

'Let him come close, that he may hear me,' said she, in a whisper.

'Your son is alive, and out of all danger, and will be at play again before evening,' said Lord Melton, cheerfully.

'I am dying,' said the woman, 'with a deadly sin on me,—will you help me to lighten the curse?'

'I will do every thing possible,' replied he, kindly; 'but you are not in a state to talk.'

'Yes, I am; every body stay to hear what I say:—that child is not mine—I was persuaded to keep him—the priest will tell you all how it was. You are rich; you can go where you will; you can find its mother, and deliver me from her curse.'

The woman spoke in gasps, and in a patois hardly intelligible; but her eye was fixed upon him in an agony of entreaty, anxiety, and terror, that was terrible to endure.

'My good woman, what can I do? You are deceived in my power to help you.'

The woman groaned, and with a look of despair to the priest, she said, 'Father, tell me how to make restitution—do not let me die under its mother's curse.'

The priest said a few words which he intended to be consoling, but they had no effect: the poor creature sprang up in bed, and seizing Lord Melton's arm, said, with a shriek that vibrated through the whole house, 'Promise, promise;' a violent fit of coughing drowned her voice, and a dark stream of blood gushed from her lips; her head fell back—all attempts to restore her were in vain: after a few moments' struggle all was over, and she lay dead before them.

Lord Melton had never seen any one before at the moment of death, and the horrors of the deathbed he had just witnessed were an appalling addition to the thrilling mystery which invests the event, even when the transit is most peaceful. He felt as if under the influence of a terrific dream, from which he could not deliver himself.

'You are unequal to this sight, my lord,' said the priest, compassionately, 'you had better retire, whilst we perform the last offices:—at another time I will explain the miserable woman's words.'

He gently led him outside the door, and guided him down the rickety stairs to the open air, which somewhat relieved the deathly faintness that oppressed him.

'I must go now, my lord, but I will see you this evening, if you will allow me.'

'You will find me at the Golden Lion,' replied Lord Melton, giving him his card—'and will you see that the rescued child wants for nothing,' added he, placing a sum of money in the old man's hand.

'Be quite sure that every thing needful shall be done;—can I see you at five o'clock if I call?'

'At any hour that will suit your other engagements.'

'At five, then, I will not fail to be with you,' replied the priest, courteously, as he turned to enter the auberge.

Lord Melton walked back to his hotel, shocked and stupified by the events of the morning.

As he entered, a travelling carriage drove up, and a gentleman in deep mourning, evidently an Englishman, alighted.

Pre-occupied as he was, Lord Melton could not avoid remarking the look of deep settled grief which rested on his countenance.

'Do you happen to know who that gentleman is that arrived just now,' asked he of his valet.

'His name is Bryant, my lord.'

CHAPTER XXI

LORD MELTON was sitting at the open window of his apartment in the hotel, which commanded a view of the sea. He was smoking with great diligence. Of all human inventions smoking is the greatest resource for any sort of perplexity; Sancho Panza's benediction on him who invented sleep,* may be reiterated with emphasis on the man who invented smoking—it calms his irritation, it soothes his sorrow, it unravels his perplexities, it inspires his genius; and difficulties which seemed impossible at the beginning of a cigar, grow to look quite tame and manageable at the end of it. Lord Melton had met with an incident that might either lie dormant for ever, or like the grain found in the sarcophagi of mummies, be destined after years of darkness and oblivion, to germinate a preternaturally abundant harvest of adventures. He was interrupted by the old priest, who came punctually to his appointed time. In his hand he led the child, which had now quite recovered from its accident, but was crying bitterly after its mother and little brother.

Lord Melton received the old man very cordially, and comforted the child with some sweetmeats.

'What is to be done with him?' said he. 'Having saved his life I feel bound to do something towards making it worth his living.'

'I have been myself thinking of the same thing,' replied the old man; 'poor little fellow, he has already had many vicissitudes. I have written down the confession of her who died this morning, along with the dates, which may be useful. So many extraordinary coincidences occur in life, and we are so often brought in contact with people strangely connected with events, from which they seemed for ever divided by accidents of distance, time, and country, that there is no saying what influence you may exercise over that young creature's destiny. I do not believe that we any of us stand alone in the world; we are all more or less connected with each other, and whoever we have once known, never passes away from us entirely; incidents are continually occurring to bring them again across our path.'

'I have often thought so,' replied Lord Melton; 'but it seemed too vague a fancy to make a maxim about, or to petrify into a fact.'

'Yes,' said the priest, 'it requires some courage to stake an action on the faith of that which is not seen. We call the whole human family our "brothers" as a *façon de parler,*★ but most of us only believe in the connexion we may chance to make with those who cross our path; we cannot risk an action on the faith of that bond of unity, which lies underneath all apparent diversities of interests, nations, and races. A practical faith in the Providence which gathers together in one all the families of the earth, seems to you enthusiasm or perhaps insanity.'

'Well,' said Lord Melton, good-humouredly, 'whether I accept your theory or not, at least I am not going to abandon this little one so strangely thrown in my way,—and to come back to the first question, what had better be done with him?'

'The superior of the monastery of St Lazarus would receive and educate him; but I am too poor to pay the fee.'

'That is very easily settled,' said Lord Melton, greatly relieved by this simple solution of the question.

'Now you see how we are all fitly joined together,' said the old man, smiling; 'what to you seems so easy, to me was an insuperable obstacle. Men would fail in nothing, if they would only work together.'

Lord Melton did not know what to make of the priest and his childish belief in his own theories. He inquired where this monastery of St Lazarus was; and hearing that it lay near, he proposed to walk thither at once, and arrange the business; to which the old man assented, and they accordingly set off.

'I am only remaining in this place until to-morrow,' said Lord Melton, as they went along; 'and according to your theory, I have been brought here for this purpose.'

'Who knows,' replied the priest, 'why you have been brought? It is not in man that walketh, to direct his steps. We never know what we do at the time when we are doing it: we seem to be following our own business or our own pleasures—and when the event is completed those are proved to have been but mere tools.'

By this time they had reached the monastery. The business that brought them was soon despatched. Lord Melton paid a sum that would maintain the child until he was old enough to be put to a trade, and the old priest promised to take him the next morning.

The next morning also saw Lord Melton start for Vienna.

He had many friends in Vienna, most of them in distinguished positions in society, so that on his arrival, he was welcomed into all the fashion and gaiety going about at that season.

After his desultory, wandering, and yet lonely life for so many months, he was surprised to find how extremely pleasant all the dissipation proved in which he found himself thus suddenly involved.

In fact, he had had quite enough of his own company; and sociability is a much deeper feeling in human nature, than any sort of misanthropy, sulkiness, or exclusiveness in which even an Englishman may please to rejoice. For a season one may wish to escape the sight and sound of our species, but after a while one is always very glad to go back to them.

Two nights after his arrival, one of his acquaintance burst into his room to carry him off to the opera. It was the first night of the Fornasari's appearance in 'Semiramide',* and tickets were worth more than their weight in gold.

Lord Melton was startled at the name; it was precisely the one that figured in the narrative the old priest had given him.

Of course he offered no objection, and they went accordingly. The house was filled to the ceiling with an enthusiastic audience, but Lord Melton did not go with the multitude. He saw in the Fornasari a beautiful woman, who at first sight startled him by her resemblance to Bianca; but it produced a singularly unpleasant effect upon him; her bold, insolent, defiant look, for an instant almost shook his faith in Bianca. It did not seem possible for them to be so much alike and yet different. Even her singing and acting disgusted him. She had a magnificent voice, and showed flashes of genius in her personation of the character, but all was marred by the constant intrusion of herself. Music, singing, acting, all seemed nothing but so many vehicles for the glorification of *herself*. It was no realisation of Semiramis, the demi-god, the wondrous, half-fabulous Queen of Babylon; but an intrusive manifestation of an unmentionable woman. At least so Lord Melton thought, until the scene with Arsace, after she discovers that he is her son; and then there was a touch of deep feeling and reality, which contrasted strangely with the meretricious character of the former portion of her performance.

'How do you like her?—what do you think of her? does she not realise your idea of a syren?' were questions that burst like a waterfall over the ears of Lord Melton as soon as the curtain fell.

'To me she seems perfectly hateful,' said he; 'and I could not have conceived it possible that any one so beautiful, so gifted, and with a voice I never heard approached (much less equalled), could produce such an utterly disagreeable impression. She did not suggest the idea of a syren to me in the least, but something far less classical; all the time she was singing with that fierce, cruel, insolent, and yet enticing look, I could think of nothing but Delilah beguiling Samson to betray him to the Philistines.'

'It is her receiving night, and I was about to ask you to go there with me to supper, but with those sinister notions you will hardly like to venture,' said his friend.

'Do you mean to say that you could present me?' asked Lord Melton.

'Decidedly, if you like to come.'

'Well, then, she certainly is a phenomenon I should like to view more nearly; so if you think I shall be received, I should be very glad to go.'

'You are an Englishman, and will be received quite well, there is no fear. She has a great desire to sing in London, and so is very civil to all the Englishmen who come in her way, as a matter of speculation; but come along, for we shall be late.'

As they went along Lord Melton said,

'I should think that woman must have a history—where does she come from?—who is she?'

'Oh,' replied the other, 'those sort of women have seldom any antecedents worth knowing.—They drudge till they come into notice, and then one is too much taken up with the present to go back to the past. I can tell you nothing about her, except that she has turned the heads of the whole city, and that men ruin themselves, make fools of themselves, and now and then shoot themselves, to her great glorification, for she does not in the least distress herself about those accidents: and yet, now and then she shows a gleam of feeling that astonishes one, and makes one wonder whether she is the frivolous, heartless, creature she seems; in fact, she is an enigma beyond my power to solve, and that, I suppose, keeps up the enthusiasm about her: but here we are arrived—now for your reception!'

They were admitted without delay, and were conducted by a servant in gorgeous livery up a handsome, well-lighted staircase, to an anti-room, filled with all sorts of curiosities, bijouterie, pictures, statues, bronzes, porcelain, &c., &c.; they had no time to stay to examine them, as they were immediately ushered into a smaller room adjoining, where about a dozen men of different ages were assembled.

The room was hung in panels of rose-coloured silk, with a wreath of gold flowers in the centre of each:—no expense or luxury had been spared, and yet the result was rather whimsical than tasteful, and Lord Melton fancied it bore the impress of the character of its possessor. The room was neither Gothic, nor Grecian, nor Chinese, nor Medieval, nor of the Renaissance; and yet it was a mixture of them all, and every style had sent some object to represent it. One or two immense mirrors were let into the wall, so that in the daytime those presenting themselves for admission could be perceived and recognised.

The room was lighted with a profusion of wax lights, but shaded into a pleasant silvery radiance; the atmosphere was heavy with perfume that arose from a stand of flowers, which in that room seemed not without a certain meretricious look, as if they had become demoralised from their associations; in fact, they had composed the innumerable wreaths and bouquets which had been flung to her on the stage the previous evening. Card-tables were laid out in different parts of the room, for the Fornasari was said to be addicted to high play, amongst her other virtues.

Lord Melton was presented by his companion to the guests already assembled, who were mostly men of some consideration.

'I ought to have told you that there is always play after supper, but you need not join unless you like.'

The Fornasari just then entered, and prevented the need of a reply: she was plainly and quietly dressed, and was accompanied by her sister, a pretty enough insignificant young woman, who was her *dame de compagnie*.* She seemed tired and out of spirits, and made a much better impression on Lord Melton than he would have believed possible five minutes previously. She received him with something almost like kindness, and placed him beside her at supper, which was announced almost immediately in an adjoining apartment.

Every thing was served in excellent style, and the conversation was loud and lively; but the Fornasari sat very absent and silent, joining only by fits and starts in what was said.

'This is one of your days for being in low spirits, madame; one of the eclipses with which you shroud your brightness in pity to your worshippers,' said one of the guests, a fat middle-aged man, with an air of faded gallantry.

She did not take the trouble to reply; but her sister, with a half officious, half pert air, said,

'Ah, yes, that makes you value us more when we shine; it is only politic to be invisible sometimes.'

'If we have finished supper, let us go back to the other room,' said the Fornasari, abruptly. 'Do you play?' asked she, turning to Lord Melton.

'Not unless I am wanted to make up a game.'

'Ah, that is right; then you will sit and talk to me. I shall not play, either.—Count de Rossi, you must have your revenge another night.'

The company dispersed themselves about the room, and made up their parties to the different tables. The Fornasari seated herself on an ottoman, and signed to Lord Melton to sit beside her.

She began to converse with him about his travels, and showed a degree of shrewdness and good sense in her observations that surprised him. Afterwards she asked him many questions about England, about the theatre, and about the estimation in which performers were held.

'But I suppose,' said she, bitterly, 'that there, as elsewhere, people think it due to themselves to *exploiter* all the beauty, genius, or powers of pleasing, possessed by those whom evil stars have doomed to live by them, and afterwards to despise those who have amused them, with all the majesty of stupidity. Do you know, I have often envied the power exercised by stupidity; it has a weight far beyond that of genius. Genius may break its heart in the endeavour to infuse a spark of sensibility or sympathy with its efforts; and stupidity can stand unmoved, unruffled, utterly invulnerable, and coming off decidedly the best in the encounter.

"Against stupidity the gods themselves fight in vain";* and, as for me, who am a mere mortal, I am absolutely frightened at its leaden superiority to all my genius,—such a strange mystery attaches to silence and stupidity!'

Lord Melton laughed. 'Is that intended as a tribute to my English impassivity?' said he.

'No; it is a tribute to truth, for once.'

'Your perception of the dignity of stupidity, in your dazzling position,' replied he, 'looks somewhat like the taste of a monarch for black bread and a peasant's hovel. You would both be satisfied with a short life. Those once accustomed to a brilliant position can never desire another, except as a carnival disguise.'

'Yes,' said the Fornasari, with something like bitterness, 'my life is like the last scene of a pantomine, or a display of fireworks; there is a very flat and smouldering result—but the audience will have dispersed before then.'

'This is the anniversary of a great sorrow,' continued she, after a pause; 'several years have passed since it befel me; but, at these times, all this glare and noise is very sickening. You have a kind face, and it is a comfort to me to see you here to-night.'

Lord Melton said something about his good fortune in having been presented to her, and turned the conversation on her performance of the 'Semiramide'. 'I was startled,' said he, 'in that scene with your son. You invested it with a feeling I could not explain. What was your idea in it, if I may ask?'

'ENVY,' replied the Fornasari, abruptly. She rose as she spoke, as though to break off the conversation; and, approaching one of the tables where two of her guests were playing *écarté*, she staked a heavy wager on the one who was losing. It was getting late, and Lord Melton rose to leave, feeling much more in charity with his hostess than he would have believed possible two hours previously. 'Ah! you are going,' said she, turning her head towards him. 'Well, I hope you will come again.'

Lord Melton bowed; and then he added, involuntarily, 'Will you give me a private audience to-morrow if I come?'

'I will,' replied she. 'Be here to-morrow at eleven o'clock, and I will see you.'

Several things had struck Lord Melton as coinciding with the facts mentioned in the priest's note; and, at least, it was worth while to try whether the Signora Fornasari in his note, was the same person as La Fornasari of the evening before. Punctually, at the appointed time, he presented himself at the gate, and was admitted by the *concierge* without hesitation. He was shown into the room he had before seen: the daylight came softened down to a *tendre jour*,★ through blinds of rose-coloured crape. The Fornasari herself, in a most becoming morning-dress, was trying over an air in a new opera, which was shortly to appear. She ceased at his entrance.

'All you Englishmen are punctual,' cried she, gaily. She seemed quite to have lost the depression of the evening before, and Lord Melton began to feel a return of the disgust with which she had at first inspired him. He even thought that his poor little half-drowned *protégé* would be better without a mother to the end of his life, than to be restored to the arms of such a questionable parent. She saw that she failed in producing an effect; that the good feeling with which he regarded her the evening before had passed away; and like a woman accustomed to success, she determined not to let him depart until she had recovered her ground. She was one of those women cursed with gifts which result in the ruin of themselves, and the misery of those who come under their spell. She had a passion for subjugating all who came within her reach, for the gratification of her own vanity; and for this miserable result she displayed powers almost miraculous. She seemed to know every turning and fold of the human heart; to carry in her own nature the key of every different character. She could turn and govern men at will. Had she been a noble woman, she might have made them into heroes; as it was, she was contented with making them fools, for her sake. She was so largely endowed and organised, that in herself she seemed the epitome of the whole sex; but all her gifts were limited and vulgarised by being centred in herself, and by the total absence of all elevation of thought or feeling. She had tasted the intoxication of the subtle sovereignty which women like her can exercise, and to hold her empire to the latest moment was her only aim. She saw Lord Melton did not admire her levity of tone, and fell gently back into the half-confidential melancholy of the evening before; which, after all, had for once been a genuine expression of the feeling of the moment: but mobile as she was, the same mood never lasted an hour.

'It is the misfortune of women like me,' said she, in reply to some slight compliment from him, 'that those who come near us never seem to see any thing worth respecting; and that makes one feel towards them as if they were natural enemies, and show them no mercy. Why should one trust them, or treat them well?—they would only make one suffer for it. You have some feeling, some humanity in you; but it makes me mad with contempt and hatred to see the crowd of those who come round me, for the gratification of their own egoism and vanity. They get what they can from me; and if my beauty were to fade, or my voice to fail, they would allow me to sink down to straw and a hospital without remonstrance or regret, if they only found another who could fill my place. Do you think that I am blinded by all this luxury and adulation that surrounds me? Do you think I do not know that they are all fairy gifts, which when breathed on (as they will one day be) by age or sickness, will vanish, and I shall find myself like an awakened dreamer, in rags and starvation in a garret. It is written on every panel in the walls—there is not a day in which it does not cross my fancy;—the thought is like a familiar spirit always within call. It will be my fate. I am not a coward to fear it, but it gives a zest to the present moment and keeps enjoyment from palling. What should men like you know of the fierce intoxication contained in the exhortation of "Let us eat and drink for to-morrow we die." '

'The fate you sketch,' replied Lord Melton, 'seems to me much less fearful than the state of mind you describe. Power is power, and may be turned to one purpose as well as another. If you were to use the influence you sway to a better purpose, the consequences would not be so bitterly reckless as you represent them. On your own showing, what you call "your fate" is of your own working.'

'Oh, I know I am a gilded Ishmaelite,' said she, laughing; 'but I will not fall, until I become old and ugly, and have lost my energy, and then it will not much signify what befalls me. We all change so much that what seems very terrible at one time, is quite supportable at another; there is always room to walk upright under troubles that at first seemed as if they must crush us to death. Besides,' added she, speaking in a tone of natural feeling, 'one sometimes has had a great sorrow, after which we feel quite sure nothing again can ever give us any pain; we have endured the worst and live. But I can keep you no longer now, for I am wanted at the opera.'

'I have already intruded too long,' said Lord Melton; 'but it struck me that you might be the person referred to in this memorial; if so, you will find information that highly concerns you; if not, pardon my officiousness.'

He placed the paper on the table and departed. The Fornasari sat for a moment after he left the room like one buried in painful thought; then negligently taking up the paper, she began to read; but her negligence was soon changed into the most vehement agitation. An expression of fear and hope was in her face, her lips were apart and colourless, her eyes dilated, and a nervous spasm shook her frame. Her sister came running in alarm, having heard her sobs of hysterical weeping in the next room.

'You will never be able to sing if you sob in this manner, Julietta,' said her sister; 'what has come to you?'

'Read, read,' cried the Fornasari.

That same night there was a terrible *émeute** at the opera. The Fornasari had departed, and no one could tell whither.

CHAPTER XXII

SUCH was the substance, from which the reports that reached Bianca, of Lord Melton's intimacy with the singer, had their origin. It would have annoyed him excessively to have known that his name was mixed up with a style of woman he detested so thoroughly. He felt very sorry for the Fornasari—sorry to see so many good gifts laid waste—but he was too much of an Englishman in all his notions to entertain any philosophical charity for her, and he did not feel called upon to exert himself to rouse the small leaven of good which even he thought he discerned, amid all her sins, against the laws of good morals and good taste. Indeed, the judgment human beings pass on each other, has often more to do with the outrage offered to the idiosyncracies of personal taste and feeling, than to their dereliction from abstract principles of morality.

When people commit sins with which we individually have no sympathy, and which press inconveniently upon us, we are apt to give them over to absolute reprobation; they are utterances of humanity we do not comprehend. But if it were possible that any one man should arise, who could thoroughly know all that was in man, we should be struck dumb with the immense tolerance, sympathy, power of reconciliation, and of guiding to good, which he would manifest for all orders and degrees of men— from the Pharisee, with his broad phalactery of respectability, down to the most hardened outcast of Norfolk Island,* who has sinned himself down to the level, and almost to the likeness, of a brute. Meanwhile, it is a great comfort to believe that there exists a higher judgment, which will revise the rash and compendious mode by which so many are given calmly over to reprobation by their fellows. This, however, is a digression.

Lord Melton continued in Vienna, going, as has been represented, a great deal into society. He gradually grew into a more healthy frame of mind—he was carried out of himself and his own sensations. He began to feel that he had no right to allow even the overthrow of his dearest hopes to engross his thoughts. He had preached this doctrine to his conscience often enough, but now he began to feel and believe in it, and to make a strong determination to act upon it. He was one of those deep, constant, Othello-like natures, which form but few attachments, and those few are so interwoven with the very stuff out of which their life is formed, that when one of them is violently broken, their whole nature receives a shock, from which it slowly and with difficulty (if ever) recovers. It is almost impossible for them to replace an old affection with a fresh one. To many it may seem a very small thing which had befallen Lord Melton, and it may seem foolish and weak that it should have so completely prostrated him; but that which is only a scratch to one man, proves a mortal wound to another. After the first natural pang of wounded self-love had passed away, his affection for Bianca re-asserted itself in its full force. He did not judge her conduct, he did not even blame her; he recognised, in her indestructible affection for Conrad, a nature like his own. He only felt a sorrowful satisfaction (which no one can call selfish) in the conviction that she would now need more than ever the brotherly, disinterested affection he had vowed her—for no amount of faith, hope, or charity, could enable him to believe that Conrad was either worthy of her, or sensible of her worth. He vividly foresaw the bitter disappointment in store for her, when she should discover the cold limitations of his nature, which she had mistaken and revered as proofs of his power to guide her.

It was an immense relief to him when the sentiment of his own self-love was silenced, and he had given up all thought of his own dignity. A great part of his suffering had arisen from the struggle between his pride and his affection, the intense yearning to forgive Bianca the slight she had offered him, and to care for her as of old, with the harassing sense of his own discomfiture, which seemed to prescribe a dignified estrangement from her for the future, as his only possible course. But now that he had succeeded in imposing silence on his wounded *amour propre*, and was restored to unity within himself, he felt almost happy again, and able to bear his disappointment like a man. He determined to return to England very shortly. He was first to make an excursion into Bohemia. He had heard some curious details of a singular race of people inhabiting a wild and almost unknown district; about whose roads, and inns, and things to be seen, no guide-book had as yet been written. He felt a strong desire to explore them, and being so far on his way, it seemed too fair an opportunity to be lost, after which he felt fully determined to return home and do his duty as an English nobleman and landholder, and no longer discharge them through his steward.

All this time the *habitués* of the opera were in despair, at the prolonged and unexplained absence of the Fornasari. The whole public came to a sense of its insulted majesty—'by disappointment every day beguiled'; and it magnanimously determined to crush her under the weight of its just displeasure, in case she should now be even ready to return. Apparently she knew her own power better than the public did; for one night she suddenly re-appeared more resplendent than ever, singing and acting as she had never done in her life before. Till she came back to them, the audience had hardly realised the loss they had sustained; the sense of their dignity was not proof against the sense of their own amusement; they allowed her to proceed, and at the close of the opera sealed her pardon by calling her before the curtain, when their gracious forgiveness was turned into enthusiasm by the graceful air with which she seemed to thank them at once for their applause and their forbearance.

That same day, Lord Melton received two notes, one from the old priest at Trieste, informing him that the child, whose life he had saved, had been given up to a lady who had claimed him, having given reasonable proofs of being his mother, and appealing to Lord Melton whether that did not convince him of the truth of his doctrine, that we were all one family on the earth. The other note was from the Fornasari herself, overflowing with gratitude to him for his humanity to her child, and requesting him to come and see her very soon.

Lord Melton was on the point of entering the carriage to leave Vienna, and he did not feel tempted to delay his departure, to pay a visit to receive thanks; he therefore wrote a polite and stately note, excusing himself from obeying her commands. He had an indescribable sort of spite against this woman, for reminding him so disagreeably of Bianca; she seemed an odious libel upon her, both in her life and profession.

But the chapter of accidents and adventures having once opened on Lord Melton, did not seem destined to close very soon.

At the close of the first day's journey, the road, which led through a wild and thinly-peopled district, turned off through a dark wood, principally of pine trees; large masses of rock, covered with long moss, lay scattered about on each side of it, and piled up in all directions, bearing witness to some long past convulsion of nature. The fading daylight with difficulty pierced the close shade of the trees. Lord Melton desired the postillions to hasten their pace, which they actually did, and in consequence came up with a smart shock against some dark object which was lying across the road, and which proved to be a travelling-carriage that had been overturned. A German postillion, whose natural amount of stupidity had been increased and perfected by the black beer he had obtained that day, was helplessly trying to disengage the passenger within the vehicle, and whose groans proved him to be suffering severely. A couple of horses, with their broken traces still hanging to them, were lazily picking what fodder they could find on the road side.

Lord Melton succeeded in calming the torrent of objurgation which arose from his own postillion, at this untoward event, for the postillion of the other carriage was too much stupified to reply. He then got out of his own vehicle to offer his assistance.

Pushing aside the drunken man, he addressed the person whom he presumed to be inside, in French, which was replied to, but with a decidedly English accent.

'I think we are countrymen,' said Lord Melton; 'I rejoice to have come up at such a conjuncture. How can I next assist you?'

'By getting me out of this place if you can,' replied the other. 'I am much bruised, and my arm is caught on the other side. Have you any people with you to help?'

The Englishman spoke in evident pain, though there was a singular composure in his manner. Lord Melton was shocked to find that his arm, which had been placed out of the window of the carriage, in the attempt to open the door at the moment it overturned, had been caught beneath it, and though fortunately a small piece of rock had left a space between the side of the carriage and the ground, still there was reason to fear the limb would be severely crushed.

With the assistance of his own postillions, Lord Melton succeeded in liberating him from his painful position. On emerging from the depths of the carriage he recognised the Englishman whom he had seen at the door of the hotel at Trieste, who was really no other than Bryant. He was in a state of extreme suffering; his left arm was broken, and he was, besides, so much bruised as to be hardly able to stand.

'You had better proceed at once with me, Mr Bryant, without waiting for the assistance your messengers will bring; they will contrive to get the carriage along, somehow, and you ought not to lose any time in getting your bruises looked to.'

Bryant started at hearing himself addressed by his own name, in the middle of that wild, desolate place, and nearly in the dark besides.

'You have proved yourself a friend in need,' said he: 'I did not expect you were an acquaintance, also. If I could take out my writing-case, I should be inclined to follow your advice, but it contains papers I dare not leave out of my sight.'

'We will get out the case if you will trust us,—but—'

Bryant, who had supported himself with difficulty, tottered a few steps, and would have fallen, had not one of the postillions caught him in his sturdy arms.

'Carry him, and place him carefully into the other carriage,' said Lord Melton, 'whilst I look for the writing-case.'

As they had not been able to lift the carriage, the search was neither easy nor successful; he looked everywhere, but the case was not to be found, and fearful of keeping the injured man longer without medical assistance, Lord Melton was obliged to order the carriage to proceed; he left his own servant with strict injunctions not to permit any thing to be touched or removed, and to bring the broken vehicle along as soon as possible.

The pain of removal had roused Bryant from his insensibility, but he still seemed unconscious of every thing but his own suffering. It was not until he had been laid in bed at the small miserable inn, and his arm set, that he asked after his writing-case, and manifested the warmest anxiety when he found it had not been brought. It was almost necessary to keep him in bed by force.

'I will go back, and superintend the removal of the case from the chaise, if you will only tell me whereabouts you placed it.'

'In the back of the carriage—it is a small panel that opens with a spring; if you will add this to the other favours you have already conferred, it would be a great comfort to me to know you were on the spot, and that no one had access to the inside but yourself.'

To calm his anxiety, Lord Melton good-naturedly complied, and turned out in search of the carriage, which he found in the same place, the assistance having not arrived.

This time he was more successful, and securing the case, and some books that were also with it, he began to retrace his steps a second time;—the distance was not more than a league. On arriving, he found Bryant in a high fever, and quite delirious. He addressed Lord Melton as 'Conrad', and ordered him to leave the room. He raved a great deal about 'Alice'. That which no power on earth would have induced him to mention to his dearest friend, he, in the defenceless state of delirium, talked about incessantly. Lord Melton watched beside his bed all night, and in those unconnected wanderings he found the solution of all that had been tormenting and perplexing himself.

CHAPTER XXIII

IN the meanwhile Bianca was fulfilling her vocation, but not at
all with satisfaction to herself. She was still engrossed with her art.
But other feelings had taken possession of her, and prevented its
being the only object of her life. The old actor was quite right in
saying, that 'when women got hold of a love affair they made that
their business, and let every thing else go to the devil.' It is a sad
truth, not at all creditable to the sagacity of the female mind; but,
alas, so it is; and Bianca, with all her strength, was only a partial
exception to the general rule. Lord Melton's continued silence
perplexed her. She had a profound consciousness that she had not
behaved too well to him, and she began to feel terribly afraid he
had succeeded in regaining his liberty, at the very moment when
she was better disposed to him than she had ever been before.
Such is the perversity of human affairs. The kindness, and tenderness, and more than a mother's thoughtfulness, which he had
always shown her, and which she had at the time considered
matters of course, became now to be looked back upon as things
vainly and mournfully precious; which she had allowed to pass
away from her, unconscious of their value, and with a stupid
indifference.

She had been much worn by her attachment to Conrad. She
had been obliged to supply affection both for him and herself
also. There had been nothing reciprocal in it; or, at least, she had
given so much more than she had received, that a weariness of
soul remained, which made her shrink from all violent or strong
emotion. She fancied that she had become indifferent for ever;
when, in fact, she was only gathering strength, breaking up the
ground for a calmer and more lasting attachment, that should
embrace the whole life; in the existence, and under the broad
shadow of which she might dwell at rest and peace; in which she
might put her whole trust, without needing to feel anxiety as to
the meaning of each word and look, clinging with painful tenacity lest she should be thrown off, to fall, she knew not whither.
She needed to dwell under the influence of a large, calm, loving
nature, which should, as it were, sheathe her more vehement and

impetuous spirit. She now awoke to the consciousness of all that Lord Melton would have been to her. But he had come before her when she had no strength to accept the love he offered—like water found too late, by wretches perishing in the desert of thirst. Now, when she would have stretched out her hand to the blessing, it appeared to have passed, and she was smitten with 'that curse of life—too late'.

Every day now increased her intense desire to regain the friend she had allowed to depart. She reproached herself for her former coldness and indifference, as if, at the time, she could have been other than she had been. Every day the recollection of the time when he had been her friend, came to her, as dreams of a golden time, which had passed away because she did not know its worth.

She endeavoured to give her whole soul more and more to her art; tried to make herself believe, that to live a calm, self-sustained existence, dedicated like that of a priestess, cold, strong, and pure, to the utterance of the oracle confided to her, was indeed the noblest and highest vocation she could embrace. But it would not do, she needed some more human motive to sustain her. She could have felt capable of everything, if Lord Melton had been there to approve of it, and sympathise with her actions. But standing alone, with only an abstract motive in life, all was cold, hollow, and dead. She was alone in the world, and all the ties she had endeavoured to weave for herself, had been broken in sunder. Often when she went into private society, and sat in the midst of family groups, saw them bound together by ties of kindred, and of natural affection, and felt herself like Ruth standing 'amid the alien corn',* a stranger received amongst them from courtesy, from kindness it might be, but having no part nor lot amongst them, no right to take a share in their joys and sorrows, living, like a mendicant, on voluntary affection, without a claim on the love of any one,—the yearning thirst for natural affection, for some one to belong to, became so intense, that, after an evening spent 'in a friendly way', as the phrase is, she would go home and weep bitterly, from the mere sense of isolation. Her position was as brilliant as ever; her reputation, if possible, stood higher. She had acquired a fortune amply suffi-cient for all her wants; but her whole being was drooping in the glare of her success; her heart was aching with desire for that common blessing, which yet is more precious than life—the natural affection of friends and kinsfolks; which comes from God, and is given when men enter on this weary life, to be a rest and refreshing for them, and that they should not walk through the desert alone.

Bianca did not, however, fold her hands in indolent low spirits; she tried hard to drown the voice of sadness which rose up in her heart with the hum of work: and that sadness was good for her too, for it kept down all thoughts of glorification and self-complacency; the voice of praise could not beguile a soul that was listening for words of affection. She who looked with a species of envy on those women who were occupied with the common duties of home, was not likely to have her heart hardened by a success that set her only further from their daily sympathies.

One day she received a letter from Lady Vernon, who was the nearest approach to what she fancied a relation must be; the letter was as follows, we give it entire:

'My dear Bianca,—Why on earth do you not write to me a little oftener than you do? but there seems to be a natural perverseness in human nature, which induces even the best people to stand still, the moment you tell them earnestly you wish them to go on. I believe if I had never told you that I delighted in your letters, and desired to have as many as ever you could write, that I should have been better off—you would not have put me off with such a short allowance; decidedly the broad basis of humanity,—bah! I was going to make you a treatise on metaphysics instead of telling you of my worries as a friend ought to do. I am in a very bad temper, as you will have discovered ere you have read thus far. When I am very cross I always fancy it a symptom of not being well, and dutifully confess it to my medical man along with my other items. My dear! either every thing in this world is very precious indeed (even the things we have despised) or else nothing is of any importance at all, not even those things we have considered the most important; only figure to yourself that at my time of life I have to begin to revise all the ideas that have carried me thus far on my journey! It is as bad as having to suspect my old butler of making away with the plate, or being obliged to turn away my woman who has lived with me for twenty years, at a moment's warning. The same question applies to both distresses—where am I to look for fresh ones? You see one's own convenience is the primeval granite foundation of our nature after all! Well, I am coming to the subject of my letter with the most graceful minuet step I can master, for to walk straight up to the fact of owning myself in the wrong is beyond my virtue. Do you remember that girl who you said sang so well on that evening, when you went with me to my school?—and have you forgotten how you preached to me that she was a genius, and ought to have her musical talent cultivated? I dare say, also, that you remember how I declared that I would have no singing women in my school? and how I said many more very sensible things? Well, my dear, I am obliged to confess that I was quite mistaken, and to come round to the opinion you then expressed. Ignominious, is it not, to turn all my old ideas about the fitness of things out of doors? However, I cannot help thinking women are happier and better when they are the centre of a home, and can live there contented amongst their duties, leaving the world outside for men to dig and delve, and make a garden of Eden of it, if they can. Still, if God is pleased to give a woman faculties, I suppose she must cultivate them. There will be no successful going against nature, until the Millennium, "when the lion will eat straw like an ox"—though I do not think he will much relish it, even then; and the diet evidently would not suit him in the present state of things. I have been attempting to make my lion and my lambs lie down together, and the experiment has failed. You foretold it. I think you offered, in case that girl's musical faculty grew too strong for me, that you would get her admitted into the Academy—and I would be really glad to claim your promise now. That girl will do no good if she is thwarted any longer. I have kept her down—put her to severe studies—cultivated her in history and geography, all to no purpose. She is a dunce at all but music; and for the credit of my management, I blush and grieve to say that she made an attempt to run away! Fortunately, she was discovered, as she was scaling the garden wall, and brought back. When questioned as to what she intended to do, she said, "Sing in the streets, to earn money to go to Italy!"—a precious prospect, after all our teaching and instruction in the cardinal virtues! It is a clear case, that there is no good to be got by going contrary to such decided tendencies; we must make the best of them, and train them as well as we can. She has always been a good girl in all that does not concern the singing; but she has grown wilful and sulky, and eccentric, of late, so the sooner we put her in the way of following her humour honestly the better. Will you take steps to make all the needful inquiries and arrangements, and write to me, as to what you think will be the best way of placing her. Can you not come down to me for a week? I want to see you very much; and I have been so worried with the affair of this girl, that I really need something pleasant to take the taste of it out of my life. So, finally, in the hope of being helped out of my troubles by you,

　　　　I am, my dear Bianca, ever your friend,

　　　　　　　　　　MARGARET VERNON.

Bianca laughed heartily over her old friend's whimsical distress, at finding a musical genius developed on her hands; but she was very well pleased at such a good opportunity of putting some theories of her own in practice, about the training of women for a profession. She answered the letter immediately, offering to take the girl altogether off her hands, promising to put her in the way of making herself independent, and to take charge of her in the meantime.

'I have,' said she, in conclusion,

'your own wholesome mistrust of all patrons and *protégés*. Those who are very helpless are generally incapable of being helped, they will not walk, but require to be carried—a mode of proceeding very unadvisable. All one can do is to set people in the right way, if they cannot hit upon it for themselves, and then they must use their own faculties for getting along. Still this is a legitimate opportunity for being useful, which I shall rejoice to embrace. I have been very successful in my own career; I have so much for which I have reason to be very thankful, that I feel a need to bestow on some one else the blessings I have received myself. You have heard me speak of my old friend the actor, who was almost like a father to me in my early life. I could never make any return to him for all his goodness. I must repay my obligation by befriending some one who needs help now as much as I did then. I undertake this for his sake, and if he were alive now he would understand and accept my work. You have no weariness or caprice to fear from me. I am discharging a sacred obligation, and if my efforts in this girl's behalf bear good fruit, she in her turn will find some one to whom she may repay the benefits she will have received from me. To be able at the same time to relieve you from an embarrassing charge is a great additional pleasure. I am not going to give her a royal road to success; she must give golden work if she wishes to attain it; but she shall have a good starting point, so that she may be free to apply all her powers to the prosecution of her art, and not have to spend her strength in fighting with sordid difficulties, which wear the life and soul out of one to no profit. She will *begin* at a point which I had to attain wearily, working in the dark upwards out of deep mire. She shall begin in the daylight, I am resolved. Let her come to me at once, I wish to study her powers and her character a little before I take any decisive steps about her. To you I will be always ready to render a strict account of your delegated responsibility. My engagement will terminate in three weeks, and then if you will invite me to Willersdale Park for a holiday, no child would be more delighted to come. I desire to see you once more quite as earnestly as you can wish to see me. I shall look out for this young lady in four days at the furthest. You know my impatience when I once take an idea into my head until I can get it realised, so show some sympathy with my natural impetuosity!

Ever your affectionate

BIANCA.

P.S. What *is* become of your brother? I have received no letter from him for a very long time, and I fear—

The words '*I fear*' were blotted out, for Bianca could not frame the sentence.

At the end of a week from the day she wrote the letter to Lady Vernon, that excellent lady's butler arrived at Bianca's house in attendance on a young girl of about sixteen.

They were ushered into Bianca's morning-room, where she was writing.

'Ah! Mathews, is that you?' said she, looking up and smiling on him, 'I am very glad to see you; how did you leave Lady Vernon?'

'Her ladyship is quite well, thank you, Miss Bianca, and I hope you are the same. She sent this letter and this young lady under my charge, and ordered me to deliver both without fail into your own hands.'

'And how are you, my child?' said Bianca, kissing the young girl, who stood nearly fainting with timidity. 'I am very glad to see you—you have not forgotten me, have you?'

'Oh, no, and never shall!' was the reply that came, scarcely audible, through the blushes that burned her cheeks.

'Well, Mathews, you are a capital knight, and have done your errand well. How long can you remain here?'

'Why, ma'am, her ladyship said I was to return directly; but, that if you asked me very much, I might remain over to-morrow.'

'Then you are to consider yourself asked quite enough to keep you here. You must make yourself at home—and I think you will find an old acquaintance down stairs.'

Bianca rang the bell, and her own maid came—the one who had lived with her before the advent of Simmonds.

'Here is a visitor, Agnes, you must take him down stairs and introduce him.'

Mr Mathews and Agnes smiled on each other, in the best pleased manner possible, and left the room together. Bianca then turned to the young girl, who sat on the sofa, gazing timidly around the room.

'Now, are you tired with your journey? Will you lie down a little before dinner? If you will, come with me, I will show you your room. Do you think you will be rested enough to go to the Opera to-night?'

'The Opera! oh!' ejaculated the young creature, as if a glimpse of Heaven were suddenly disclosed to her eyes.

'You have never seen one?' asked Bianca, smiling at her childlike gladness.

'No, never; and it seems too good a thing to happen to me. I have learnt airs out of "Norma" and "Medea",* and they have been so beautiful, that I thought to see a whole opera, and hear it all well sung, would be the very grandest thing in the world. I used to think about it at night, after I was in bed, and wonder how it would be. I used to be glad when bed-time came, that I might be able to build castles about the Opera.'

'Well, you shall go to-night. This is your room. You have been taught, by Lady Vernon to be very orderly, and I am glad of it, for I do not like having any but very orderly people about me. I shall come in every morning to see that you do not keep your things in a litter.'

'Such a beautiful room! How good you are to me. I will do any thing you bid me,' replied the girl, delightedly. The room was, indeed, very pretty, and Bianca had taken some trouble in preparing it for her *protégée*. The walls were hung with a neat fresh paper; the furniture was painted green, and the curtains were of snowy whiteness. The window looked into the garden, and a splendid American creeper grew almost into the room. There was a dressing-room beyond, which had been fitted up for a chamber of study; it contained a small book-case and a neat cottage piano. The paper and furniture corresponded with those in the bed-room. A neat, plain writing-desk stood on a small table in the centre. The window opened into the garden, like the other. 'These rooms are entirely your own; you can come here to sit whenever you are disposed, and you will practise here.'

'Oh, I shall be so happy!' cried the girl; 'it will be like living in a fairy tale!'

'But your fairy must be hard work, my child; you are not coming here to play. However, just now rest yourself; Simmonds shall come and help you to unpack your things, and put them into the wardrobe. Whatever you want, apply to her for, if I am not at home. They shall come and tell you when dinner is ready.'

Bianca kindly and considerately left the girl to calm herself at leisure, and to get a little accustomed to her new environments before she attempted any conversation. On going to her own room, she found Simmonds at work, and commended the young damsel to her special care.

The opera that night was 'Don Giovanni'. Donzelli was in London,* and singing that season. The house was full, and very brilliant—nothing could be imagined more dazzling than the spectacle—and yet that light and radiance seemed only the appearance produced by some glorious reality beyond. It requires a person to be drilled into life, and to know thoroughly all the pitiful details which go to make up both the decorations and the spectators, before he can lose the idea that they are the utterance and manifestation of some more exceeding excellence; the enchantment is over, when he feels convinced that all the preparation has been to produce an appearance only. To this young girl, however (whose name we may as well say was Clara Broughton), every person in the house, down to the very box-openers, seemed gilded with glorious mystery. They had a box on the first tier, close to the stage. Clara timidly touched the satin curtains, and then touched herself, repeating, softly: 'I am here at this minute!'—as if she expected to be spirited away—and she was willing to give some pledge to her memory, that she might be sure she had really enjoyed such blessedness!

At length the curtain drew up, and the opera began. Clara had never been inside a theatre in her life before, and was bewildered between the make-believe of the scenery, and the reality of the actors. But all outward things were speedily to be swallowed up for her, in the entrancing sounds of the music; every nerve seemed strained to the utmost tension, that it might bear the weight of rapture which increased every moment, till she felt that madness must follow the attempt to contain it all. Her senses were too small to comprehend the immense, the unutterable, delight that was placed before them. It was painful to feel that there was so much she could not grasp. At the end of the first act, Bianca was terrified at the wild wrapt expression of her face. She spoke to her, but could obtain no answer—she seemed in a trance with her eyes open.

'I wish you could manage to obtain a glass of water,' said Bianca, to the gentleman who was with them; 'we shall be having this child in a fit of apoplexy, if we do not take care. I had no idea she was so excitable.'

'With her musical temperament, it is enough to drive her mad, to come here, if she be not used to such places.'

'She only came from school in the country this morning, and I do not feel to have done at all a wise thing in bringing her; do go and get some water.'

The opera at length ended; Clara drew a long breath, and threw herself back in her chair. The glittering house, the dazzling spectacle, were now become nothing to her; she was like one who had been gazing on the entrance of Paradise, and found the vista suddenly darkened. She was miserable—as all people are, when a great enjoyment has passed suddenly away from them, broken off with no prospect of return.

When the ballet began she felt nothing but disgust.

'How can the people stay to look at this sort of thing when they have just been listening to music!' cried she.

'Would you like to go home?' asked Bianca.

'Ah, yes, and then I can think of what I have heard!'

The next day was Sunday, and Bianca took her to Warwick Street Chapel, where she attended. There the music was of a different nature, and produced even more effect than the opera. She concealed herself in the pew from all bystanders, and remained dissolved in tears, which alone had the power to give inarticulate utterance to all the emotion that was stirred in her soul. Bianca recollected her own sensations at the first glimpse of the manifestation of her own art.

Bianca determined that her *protégée* should see every thing that was most remarkable, for as she said to Lady Vernon, 'If girls who have been allowed to grow up without unhealthy stimulants can be taken, when their faculties begin to ripen, to see the best performances on the stage, and to hear the best music, it gives an impulse to their intellect, and a development to their ideas that makes both their existence and their character stronger and more complete.'

On this theory Clara was taken several times to the theatres. She saw Bianca act, and once or twice accompanied her into society. At the end of a month she had received a mass of sensations and ideas which it would need many years of life to elaborate and unravel.

One day Bianca went to her room when she was practising. 'Oh,' cried she, 'this is an air I have been trying the whole of the day, and I cannot sing it as I wish, will you listen to it?'

'Willingly,' said Bianca.

The girl sang it with an intense feeling and expression, though her voice and intonation were very unfinished.

'Well, there is a quality in that singing I like very much,' said Bianca; 'but you need a great deal of study yet, and now I want to talk to you a little. Tomorrow you are to begin your studies regularly. You will not go out so much as you have hitherto done; you must earn your right to go into society by your own endeavours. You have a career before you. You have been shown what excellence in the arts is, and you see how much you have to do before you can be worthy to be a companion of eminent artists. Measure yourself always with the highest, and never do less than your best. That has been the only rule I have known through life. Another thing, my dear child, remember, that strong and sterling qualities of character are needed to make the brightest genius of any more worth than the gold and purple clouds of evening, which turn to leaden coloured mists. People are sometimes apt to think that genius is like the kingdom of Heaven, which, if you have, all other things will follow of course. But, my dear girl, unless you cultivate an iron resolution to follow a purpose once conceived steadily out to the end, an industry and perseverance, which are proof against all self-indulgence, a spirit of loving-kindness and single-mindedness, you will find your genius of little worth, except to lead you into splendid mistakes. You must strive to be a complete and well-balanced character, if your genius is to do its perfect work and to attain its full growth. You have a rich and fertile nature—you have genius for music; therefore, watch over it as a precious responsibility committed to your charge, and know that every time it is desecrated to your own personal glorification its force and quality are deteriorated. You must be faithful to your charge if you would have your genius reach the fulness of its strength. I have given you a long lecture, but recollect it is my own life that I am giving you to profit by. Now let us come down to dinner, and then to-morrow I will give you the plan according to which I should like you to apportion your time, that you may make the most of it.'

Bianca was rather stern at times, she felt so earnestly when she had any instruction to give; but no one could be more gentle and affectionate, when there were no principles to be insisted upon.

Clara Broughton had a fine rich nature; the seeds of good principles and good habits had been already inculcated in her, and with Bianca her intellect was daily developed, and her good habits strengthened. To Bianca it was an intense pleasure thus to watch over and form the mind of this young girl, and to train her for her career in life; it took her thoughts out of herself, and was a wholesome occupation, by which her own being was strengthened and calmed.

Instead of going down to Willersdale Park for her holiday, Lady Vernon came to her, as she did not wish to break up Clara's regular mode of life so soon; but it was settled that they should both spend the Christmas holidays there. When Bianca had got the better of her restlessness, and was throwing all her energy into her actual life, and as little as possible allowing herself to

> Sit at Fancy's door,
> Calling shapes and shadows to her,

then, as always happens in life, when one is resigned to going *without* some dearly desired object—it always comes to us.

One fine morning the postman brought Bianca the letter from Lord Melton, she had so long and so vainly looked for! The contents were every thing her heart could desire, and she felt more contentedly happy than she had ever been before.

When people make a great fuss about 'happiness our being's end and aim',* it is a very vulgar affair, and rather impertinent to the toiling, busy world, which has plenty of its own complicated affairs to mind. Still, when any one has worked and endured so long and constantly as Bianca, people are apt to feel rather glad when she obtains a little spell of happiness—she has earned it.

CHAPTER XXIV

FOR two days Lord Melton remained watching beside Bryant, who lay sometimes in a state of stupor, and at others in delirium. He talked of past scenes, and mingled names and circumstances, some of which, like a touch on a secret spring, revealed to Lord Melton the explanation of Bianca's conduct, which he had so long wearied himself to find.

During the second night, whilst Bryant slept, he again referred to the last letter he had received from her, and which, although crushed and torn in his first jealous fury, he still kept and cherished with a perverse tenacity. He now read it again, and as it seemed with enlightened eyes; for he now discerned all that seemed before so dark in her allusions, and which he had fancied was only her manner of breaking the weight of his annoyance at her intelligence. Now that he saw what she really had meant, he was astonished at his own stupidity and want of faith. But no martyr ever gave himself to the flames with the cheerfulness with which he endured the reproaches of his own conscience; he rejoiced in every fresh light he was able to throw on his own harshness and false judgment; he was so thankful to find himself in the wrong, that he would willingly have compounded for a great deal more remorse than fell to his share: no saint was ever so glad to be justified as he was to feel condemned. One only misgiving tormented him, and that was lest Bianca, out of patience at his neglect, should have allowed her interest in him to grow cold. Then that there might be some reaction to this flood of gladness, he began to fear lest from some transcendental idea of generosity, she might have allowed herself to be prevailed upon to join her fate to Conrad's for life, in order to save him from the passionate effects of his remorse; as he was one of those weakly impulsive characters who can neither resist a temptation, nor endure the consequences. He knew that the brightness of Bianca's life had been overcast, and he did not know whether she might not take refuge in a life of austere self-sacrifice; accepting a fate she had once passionately desired, but from which all love and hope had now departed, in the same spirit as other wounded and weary hearts had taken refuge in a cloister. The more he pondered upon this the more probability did it assume. He knew her affectionate heart, and he knew also her lonely and isolated life. He determined that the moment Bryant was sufficiently recovered that he might be left without inhumanity, he would proceed straight to England and see if a chance were still open to him.

During the second night Bryant, who had been for some hours in a peaceful sleep, awoke; he withdrew the curtain and perceived Lord Melton sitting in a large arm-chair.

'How long have I been in bed? and have you been watching beside me all this time?' asked he.

'How do you feel now? Better for your sleep? Here is the portfolio I got from the carriage, it has not been opened.'

These words seemed to cause a spasm of memory to the wounded man.

'Ah!' said he, with a slight shudder, 'you are very good to have charged yourself with it; but how fatigued you must be, will you not retire to bed?'

'Oh, I assure you, they have made me up a capital bed in the corner of the room, and I have taken all sorts of good care of myself; but the doctor desired that you might have this draught so soon as you awoke, and you were not to talk. He could not judge of the state of your hand and arm until the fever had a little abated. Are you in much pain?'

'Rather; but it is bearable now. Will you tell me one thing,' continued he, with a sort of embarrassment: 'have I rambled much?'

'You certainly have had delirium; but what then? words uttered in delirium mean nothing. One might as well catechise a dream. Do not torment yourself whilst you are so weak. Be assured you have said nothing you ought not.'

This was intended to tranquillise his mind, although it was not precisely what he would have considered the truth. He only half believed it, but it was soothing to be told so; besides, he felt a desire to sleep, and he again fell off into a quiet slumber before he had summoned the energy sufficient to ask any more questions.

The next day, when the doctor came, he pronounced the patient much better; but two of the fingers of the left hand were so much crushed as to render amputation needful.

Bryant bore the operation with great firmness. When both the doctor and Lord Melton complimented him upon it, he said, with a look of inexpressible gloom, 'It is possible, in some cases, to find even severe bodily pain a relief from worse suffering in the mind.'

He was again removed to bed, and ordered to be kept very quiet, as his system had not recovered from the shock it had received. Lord Melton continued with him, although it required some self-denial to spend long silent days beside the couch of a stranger, when he desired so ardently and impatiently to commence his journey to England. About three nights after the operation had been performed, Lord Melton was on the point of retiring to rest, when Bryant said:

'Do not leave me just yet; I have strength to ask you a question now, which I want to have answered out of the road. Will you tell me, as briefly as may be, what stuff it is that I have actually talked during these last days?'

'What you have said has been very incoherent. I can really hardly give you any account of it. You talked about some lady named Alice, and about one of your friends, whom you called Conrad, with whom you seemed to have quarrelled.'

'And could you divine on what account?' asked Bryant, eagerly.

'You are still feverish and excited,' said Lord Melton, 'you are not yet able to carry on a connected conversation. You have said nothing that can betray what you would wish to conceal. Do not ask any more questions to-night; in a day or two you will be stronger, and then we will talk as long as you please.'

Bryant, with his sensitive suspicious nature, which so seldom opened to voluntary intercourse, felt abashed by this speech, and, turning his face to the wall, uttered a half-sullen 'Good night.'

Lord Melton saw what was passing in his mind, and considered over the best, the most practicable means of setting him at ease—for, certainly, to come to the knowledge of a man's secrets through the medium of his being delirious, is something like unwittingly reading a letter left lying about.

The next morning, when he went to visit Bryant, he found him embarrassed and reserved; he still felt awkward at the species of rebuff he had encountered the evening before; but he was decidedly getting on very well, his fever was abated, and his hand was doing well. After a few common-place remarks, Lord Melton sat down beside the bed (for Bryant could not yet bear to be moved), and looking at him with his frank blue eyes, he said, after a moment's pause: 'If you are well enough, Bryant, I should like to have a little conversation with you this morning; will it tire you?'

'Not in the least, my lord, I shall be happy to listen to you,' said Bryant, somewhat stiffly.

'I have been thinking a great deal of what you said last night, and I think I had better tell you frankly how much I have learned from your delirium, and then you need feel no more annoyance about the matter; but first I shall have to trouble you with a history of some affairs of my own. I am too much of an Englishman to feel at all inclined to talk to every body about private matters;—in fact, it is bad taste, and I know you feel with me on that point; but it will explain to you how I happened to pay any sort of attention to that, which, in another state of mind, you would never have told me. The fact is, that I found myself a party concerned. You mentioned the name of a man I have long known, and your unconnected ramblings threw light on a matter which has cost me great suffering.'

Lord Melton then entered into rather a minute detail of the manner in which Conrad had crossed his path. He compelled himself to go into particulars, in order that Bryant might be relieved from the galling consciousness, that whilst his secret had been surprised, he was utterly ignorant of every particular connected with the charitable stranger, who had shown him a degree of kindness, which, under those circumstances, was rather oppressive. Lord Melton began at the beginning of his intercourse with Bianca, and her engagement to Conrad; he told him how, in a lady whom she called Mrs Bryant, and whose name was 'Alice', she had discovered her half-sister.

'Ah! that is strange,' said Bryant, 'and must be some one else—my—Alice, I mean, had no sister, she was an only child; and, now I recollect, she had a *protégée*, some young actress, whom she insisted on befriending in spite of my dislike to those sort of people; and, if she be the same party, she must have imposed upon you by a false tale. Alice would have told me if she had had any such relation.'

'Pardon me,' replied Lord Melton, 'Mrs Bryant was ignorant of the fact. Bianca, knowing your prejudice against her profession, did not wish to embarrass her sister, and therefore determined not to disclose it until she should have reached such a position as not to discredit her. Subsequently she found, that even her distinguished reputation would not secure her a cordial reception with you; and therefore, although her whole heart was yearning towards this sister, who knew her not, she had the magnanimity to conceal it. You do not know Bianca, or you would not speak of her in that tone. As to your being ignorant that Mrs Bryant had a sister, it is very possible; as, when men marry, and have legitimate families, they are generally silent about former events. Bianca's mother was an Italian lady.'

'Ah, that will explain matters,' said Bryant.

Lord Melton then went on to tell him all he had suffered, from hearing of the renewal of Conrad's intimacy with Bianca, and how the things he had vaguely uttered in delirium, had enabled him to see the meaning of all that had so painfully perplexed him.

'When you know the weight from which your words have delivered me,' concluded he, smiling, 'I can hardly think you will have the heart to regret that I was here to profit by them.'

'You are a good fellow, Lord Melton, and I respect you. Thank you for all you have done for me, and thank you for all you have just said, more than all. If it has done you good, I am very glad you have been here to hear every thing. What you say of Conrad, proves, that he is, what he has always been, a plausible, good-for-nothing fellow, thinking of no one but himself, and bringing sorrow on all who have trusted him. I never knew any good come from those fellows with such a pretence of fine feeling and refinement, yet. What they gain in smoothness they lose in honesty. I remember, years ago, when he first came to us, how he went sneaking after this girl. His father came down and put a stop to it; and, I must say, I persuaded him to get his precious son out of the country. But the girl seems to have been only too good for him.'

'Indeed you are right there,' replied Lord Melton, 'there are few men for whom she would not be too good.'

'I should like to hear something more about her if you can tell me. If she were really her sister,' but here his voice faltered, and he stopped abruptly.

Lord Melton was glad of an opportunity of speaking of Bianca; he desired to make her worth known to all the world: beside, talking of her was an indulgence he had not engaged for a long time, and he did not need to be asked twice before he began a most elaborate and detailed biography, lengthened with his own comments. Bryant was a very patient listener; to be sure he did not hear above one-half of what was said, but he did not interrupt the narration, and that was the grand point. He heard enough, however, to feel an interest in her: opposite as were their modes of life, there was that in the heart of Bryant which recognised her worth, and responded to her energetic perseverance and strength of purpose.

'Ah!' said he, when Lord Melton at last ceased, 'she must be a very remarkable young woman, quite superior to her station. I had no ill-will against her, I wished to do right, and an actress did not seem to me a desirable companion for—but no matter, I see now how mistaken I have been in many things which I thought proper and prudent. If I had known what she was, it might have been the means of avoiding a great deal of misery, but I did for the best; I thought how strange it would seem to let an actress into the family. Nobody else knew any thing of her. I could never endure to have observations made on my actions. She seems to have been a very well-conducted young woman indeed.'

The surgeon now came in, and Lord Melton left the room.

'You must not allow your patient to talk much,' said he, to Lord Melton, when he departed; 'the system is very much excited, and he must be kept very quiet.'

Lord Melton did not attempt any more conversation during the day, and indeed Bryant did not seem disposed for any. He appeared to sleep a great deal, but he only took that method to disembarrass himself from all looks or inquiries. For more than forty years he had been a taciturn, reserved man. Within the last few days all his habits and ideas had been violated, and notwithstanding all his friendly feeling for Lord Melton, he suffered under the painful impression which made itself felt through all the real sorrow that was on his heart, of having lowered himself, of having done foolishly. People of his character are morbidly sensitive of ridicule, the fear and dread of which pursues them to their remotest thoughts, and cramps all spontaneity of action. They are utterly unable to understand impulsiveness of utterance. To make themselves remarkable is their supreme dread; good, true, upright, excellent, as men of this sort are, they are prone to be suspicious, and to take a disgust at the least action that does not appear in the measured formal guise to which they are accustomed.

Bryant, notwithstanding his burst of good-will to Lord Melton, suffered from the reaction of his shy, reserved nature; but the ice was fairly broken, his sorrow had borne down all the petty ideas that once held him in bonds, the desire for human sympathy,—that deep primeval sentiment of humanity, asserted itself; he was away from England, and all that had been the world to him. The re-action of his old nature subsided.

Lord Melton did not go into his room until the next morning; he sat down and began to converse about indifferent things: particularly he began to make inquiries of Bryant about this district in Bohemia which he had been about to explore,* and spoke of continuing his journey in a few days.

'It is very dull for you staying here,' said Bryant, 'and you have been very good already, but can you not stay, as you are here, until I am able to move, and then we can travel together. I was on my way to our iron mines, which are further in the country. I know the district you mean well, and if I were with you I could show you the country better than you would be able to see it for yourself.'

'Why for the matter of that,' said Lord Melton, 'I do not now think of going at all, for I feel anxious to get back to England.'

'Ah! you have something to go back for!' said Bryant, mournfully. 'I shall never endure to live in England again.'

'I know you have had a great sorrow,' replied Lord Melton. 'I saw you at Trieste, and felt drawn to you there—although I was far from suspecting we should so soon be thrown together.'

'And you have heard what I never thought would be uttered by me to mortal man. My lord, you are a man of honour, and I will not insult you by the request to keep secret all you know. You have told me a great deal about yourself, and I thank you for your confidence. I feel a comfort in talking to you, I have never known in talking before; and we are mixed up together in a very singular way. I have been thinking a great deal of what you said of Bianca. I am very sorry I never judged of her for myself; but I thought she was artful and scheming, and I took part with old Mr Percy against her and against his son: but it has come home to me. I did it for the best, as I said before. It would be a great comfort to me to see her now; what is she like?—is she handsome?'

'Extremely handsome,' said Lord Melton, 'with black hair, and dark gray eyes.'

'*Her* hair was nearly black too.—Well, my lord, if you marry her be kind to her, and do not let any worldly matter come before her in your mind; women feel such things—they are very tender-hearted, and have nothing to occupy them as we have; and do not hide your feelings from her, do not be ashamed of showing how much you love her. You deserve to be happy; but break off her acquaintance with Conrad, it will do her no good.'

Lord Melton listened in silence, and in some surprise to these expressions: he did not know that, trite and common-place as they seemed to him, they were utterances taught by the sufferings of a life laid waste; that they had been burnt into his soul by an experience the most terrible. Had he known all, he would no longer have wondered at the oracular earnestness with which they were delivered.

'You said, I think, that she had no relations,' continued Bryant, after a pause, 'that she had been left all her life to struggle by herself?'

'Just so,' replied Lord Melton.

'Well, that is a pity. Poor thing, she must have had a hard time of it! Will you let me see her when you are married?—and,' continued he, speaking with an effort, 'will you tell her that her sister's husband earnestly desires her to consider him as a brother? If she had only left a dog behind, I should have cherished it—much more her own sister,' added he, as if to herself.

'You little know the blessing you are sending,' said Lord Melton. 'I, who know the yearning affection with which Bianca regarded her sister, the desire she had to be known to her, and the generous forbearance which induced her to keep silence, can answer for the satisfaction your kind message will bring to her. You will, you must, return to England, and let her know you, and love you herself.'

Bryant shook his head, mournfully.

'My dear lord, I am not a young man, and I have no more strength to hope. My life is broken up. I do not complain,—one must endure whatever is sent to us. Sometime, perhaps, I shall return to England, if I live, and then it will be a comfort to see *her* sister. There are some events that leave one like a mountain shivered to the base; it may look, outwardly, a very narrow crevice, but it goes all the way to the foundation, and nothing can unite it. I am on my way to our iron mines. I shall stay there to superintend them. In that distant place I shall see nothing to remind me of the past. As long as I live, I must be doing something. I do not care for making money now, it is the work I care for. I shall live in the mountains among the miners. Since I have been in sorrow I have thought of many things that never struck me before, especially since I have been lying here. We have many hundred workmen in our employ—we paid them their wages—they did our work—the rest was their concern. I think we should have considered something more than making our money out of them. They are a sad wild set. I have not much faith in benevolent schemes, but I shall see what can be done about them. I can do things for any one but myself just now. I have no plan, but I shall look into their condition a little. When I have the heart to go back to England I shall see what is to be done there. I must live out my days, Lord Melton; and I shall be, I hope, submissive to my Maker; but I do not feel as if any thing could make me either glad or sorry again.'

'You shame me, Mr Bryant,' said Lord Melton. 'My conscience reproaches me for all the little use I have made of my position and influence. I shall often think of you, and try to follow the example you set me.'

'With a happier heart, I trust,' said Bryant, smiling mournfully.

In a few hours afterwards he again addressed Lord Melton, who had been writing letters at a little table in another part of the room.

'I have been considering,' said he, 'that I was very ill advised, and very selfish, to ask you to delay longer. You ought not to write to England, you ought to return thither: now that all your doubts are cleared up, and a faithful heart is awaiting you, do not allow a light thing to keep you from going to claim it. Perhaps, too, she is suffering from your absence. Oh, when there are so many uncertainties in life, do not kill an opportunity of easing the heart of one who is suffering; it may pass away and leave you a remorse.'

Lord Melton looked up. 'I believe you are in the right,' said he, quickly; 'you have spoken the word, and I will act upon it. I dare hardly hope in the bright picture you draw, but any way I will go home. I have behaved unkindly; and as you say she may be suffering; I am brute enough to hope that it is so.'

'And when will you depart?' said Bryant, not without a pang at finding his words so promptly acted upon.

'Oh, I shall not go until you are all right again. I am not going to leave you in this hole, not half recovered yet. I shall not stir a step until you are able to travel; and then, the day you can proceed towards your mines, I shall set off towards England, as fast as the horses will take me. I have been away, and kept a sulky silence so long, that a week of absence, more or less, will not be felt. I have written a letter, which I hope will get me forgiven. Even now, I fear more than I hope.'

Bryant was not disinterested enough to combat this resolution. Lord Melton continued a fortnight longer; at the end of which time Bryant was well enough to travel. During that period, a warm esteem, and sincere friendship, had arisen up between these two men, so strangely thrown together.

Bryant's whole life had been too rudely shattered to allow of any thing like a feeling of happiness springing up in it—but it seemed less arid and desolate—a friend had been sent to him in a world where he thought himself alone. He felt stronger, and better able to endure his lot.

Lord Melton departed with a heart full of hope, in spite of all he said and thought to the contrary.

'Farewell,' said he, as he wrung Bryant's uninjured hand, 'and remember that you belong to us when you return to England.'

'I do—I will. God bless you for all the comfort you have been to me,' replied Bryant.

In a few moments they were both on their several routes.

CHAPTER XXV

IT was now near Christmas, and, in a few days Bianca was to go down to Willersdale Park. Her heart whispered to her, that she would there see again the one being who had for a long time past entirely filled her thought, either as a latent unacknowledged influence, or in the more decided guise of regretful reveries. Even since the receipt of his last letter, she had felt all her doubts set at rest; she knew that he would return the same as he had departed. But after the first gush of joy, she had become restless and impatient. She began to fear that some accident would intervene, to dash down her cup of happiness, now that it was nearly within her grasp. In her hours of sorrow she had often wished that she might lie down and die; and, on the occasion of an epidemic, which carried off a great number of persons, she had looked with a species of envy on the funerals constantly passing the streets. 'Amongst so many, why am not I included?' was her regretful aspiration. But now, she was seized with a strange horror, lest her unhallowed prayer of those 'days of darkness' should be heard and answered. She, who had been so brave and patient in times of sorrow, had become a coward during the season of suspense and expectation, which preceded the dawning of her day of hope. Hopes are only inverted fears; but it requires more strength of faith and resignation to the decree of a higher will, to wait calmly the solution of a theory of bright hopes, than to stand firm and resolved under the shadow of threatening ill.

Bianca was not one, however, to allow herself to be lightly carried away by every gust of feeling, and she struggled hard to regain the mastery over her mind, but with very moderate success.

A few days before the one fixed for her departure, the music-master whom she had engaged for Clara requested an interview. Bianca, who fancied that it only had reference to some arrangement about her employment during the vacation, was puzzled to understand the embarrassed tenacity with which he continued in the room after all business had been settled and dismissed. She was impatient for his departure, and not at all disposed to find agreeable conversation to prolong his visit. She relapsed into silence; during which she continued to pack her dressing-case, the occupation she had interrupted on his entrance.

At length the poor man, grown desperate, said, with the perspiration standing on his forehead, 'When did you say I might have the pleasure of renewing my lessons to my very talented pupil?'

'We shall be absent a month, and I will write to you on our return.'

This was definite enough, but it seemed to convey no intelligence.

'There certainly is one thing I have neglected to inform you of, madam, and that is, my own intention to proceed to Italy early next season. I think, if Miss Clara were to study in Italy, it would be of the greatest advantage to her—indeed it is necessary. She has great talent and genius; I would almost say——'

'I intend her to have every advantage, and I am sorry she is likely to lose the advantage of your instructions.'

'I was going to ask, madam, with all deference to your superior judgment, whether you think an attractive young woman ought to appear in public without the sanction and protection of a husband?'

Bianca looked up,—a gleam of the worthy man's meaning (for worthy he was) began to dawn upon her, but she was not going to help him in its development; so she replied, 'Well?'

It is astonishing sometimes how little serves for an answer; it is like parrying a thrust in fencing, the least touch diverts the course of a weapon. Bianca's 'Well?' served the purpose of bringing a very general proposition into a definite form, though still painfully expressed, as if he were badly off for a language. It was to the effect that he being fully impressed with a sense of Miss Clara Broughton's charms, genius, and virtue, wished to become, in his own proper person, the 'husband who was to give the sanction and protection' required for her appearance on the stage, and that he was most anxious to obtain Bianca's support and influence with Lady Vernon.

'You are aware that Miss Broughton has relations; I can say nothing in this matter, except that I will mention your proposals to Lady Vernon, and speak favourably of you as far as I know.

You are older a great deal than Miss Broughton. Have you spoken to her?'

'No—a thousand times no!—for whom do you take me, madam? You are the first to whom I have opened my lips. I can offer the young lady a good position; she might fall into the hands of those who would marry her on speculation for her talents, as heiresses are married for their money. I can offer her a home, and whether her future keeps the promise of the present or not, it will make no difference in my feelings towards her.'

'Well, I can give you no answer, except as I said before, to lay what you say before Lady Vernon, to whom I think you had better write yourself.'

The good man retired with all the gratitude that such good hopes were likely to excite.

'So, Clara's romance of life seems likely to be soon and safely decided,' said she to herself, when left alone; 'certainly a worthy, honest, sensible man for a protector will be a great advantage, and smooth many difficulties in her course; but I prefer my own struggles to all the patent safety that could have been secured to me. I wonder what Clara's instinct will be about the matter!' She, however, resolved to say nothing until she had seen Lady Vernon, and talked over the matter with her.

Lady Vernon was standing in the hall waiting for them, when they arrived.

'My dear child, how glad I am to see you again! both Christmas and the New Year will realise their ordinary "compliments of the season", now that you are really come back to me—and is that Clara? Why, mercy on me, how you are grown and improved! you are looking quite womanly. I suppose you have been thriving upon having gained your own way; but, come along, for dinner has been waiting I do not know how long. I have had your own old rooms prepared for you,' said she to Bianca, as she led them along the gallery, 'do not stay to make any toilet, for we have to keep Christmas alone. I have invited no one. I thought a little real quiet would be a blessing to you.'

Bianca, who had been hoping and expecting she hardly knew what, felt a strange chill of heart at these words; all the delight of Willersdale Park had vanished; for a moment she felt as if she had been entrapped into a prison, from which she longed restlessly to escape. Lady Vernon went chattering on in the extremest spirits; either Bianca kept her countenance with wonderful success, or else her ladyship's penetration was not on the alert.

They descended to dinner. The old-fashioned dining-room, ornamented with evergreens, with its oak panels, and rich crimson draperies—the sideboard, loaded with massive plate, all lighted up with a dazzling fire, and a profusion of lights,—looked like a scene of old English Christmas time; but Bianca, who had been unaccountably hoping she knew not what, felt a chill disconsolateness at finding that Lady Vernon had spoken the literal truth, and that there was actually no one besides themselves.

'I have not done you the honour of having a fire lighted in the drawing-room for you,' said Lady Vernon. 'I thought, in this bitterly cold weather, we should be more comfortable in my sitting-room, and there I have ordered coffee; but I believe it would have broken the heart of Mathews if we had not dined in state. You completely turned his head that time he stayed with you in London. He speaks of it as of the "three glorious days" of his life. After awhile, I must hear Clara sing.'

'She has been a very good girl, and made great progress,' said Bianca. 'I am very well satisfied with her.'

Bianca was listening for the name of Lord Melton, to whom his sister had, as yet, made no allusion; but she continued talking on, about every thing else in the world except the one thing Bianca was sickening to hear. When they reached the sitting-room, Lady Vernon wheeled round the sofa to the fire.

'There now, Bianca, do you take your own old place, and I will sit here, in Melton's chair. Poor fellow! I wonder when he will come back to occupy it again! I had half a hope that he would take us by surprise, and be here for Christmas; but he has neither come nor written. He is making an unaccountably long tour. I do not think that men with large estates like his ought to be so long absent.'

'Then you do not know when he will come back?' said Bianca.

'Not the least in the world, my dear, any more than yourself.'

There was a pause, during which they drank their coffee; then Lady Vernon, turning to Clara, asked her if she could sing so soon after dinner. Clara went at once to the instrument, and for nearly an hour sang in her fresh rich voice, all the pieces she fancied she sang the best.

'Upon my word she has not lost her time,' said Lady Vernon; 'I can hardly believe that she is the same Clara I sent to you, half in disgrace, six months ago. You see you were right, my dear, and I was wrong.'

The hall-bell at this moment was rung, though Clara's singing had prevented them hearing the sound of wheels along the avenue.

'What can that be?' said Lady Vernon, 'at this time of night?—surely no accident at the school-house.'

Bianca's heart beat violently—she could utter no suggestion.

'This way, my lord—the ladies are here,' said the old butler, flinging open the door.

The next moment Lord Melton, wrapped in furs to the chin, stood amongst them!

CHAPTER XXVI

'WHAT a perverse fellow you are, Maurice,' cried Lady Vernon, when the first greetings were over, and Lord Melton had quietly subsided into his accustomed chair, 'you are like all other very good people, who reject the recognised "arts of tormenting", but who still contrive to smuggle their desire to be disagreeable into circulation! Here I have been abusing you to Bianca, and saying the wisest things about your long silence, and still longer absence, and you come back to contradict them at the eleventh hour, and force me to feel so glad to see you, that I have not the heart to persist in them; but you have behaved very shamefully all the same!'

'When criminals are condemned to death, the judge always reads them a homily; but when they can prove their innocence they only receive congratulations. You are speaking a speech not set down for you, my lady—I appeal to Bianca whether I deserve scolding?'

The blood rushed to Bianca's face, and her voice would not for a moment obey her, but she replied at length,

'Your friends must all be delighted at your return, though they might still have rejoiced had you come earlier.'

Lord Melton did not answer, he began to disturb the slumbers of his sister's Persian cat, which was stretched luxuriously before the fire.

The conversation became general, he had much to tell, and he seemed in high spirits. Bianca was struck with the change that had come over him: he looked much older than when she last saw him, and his ideas were more firmly knit and developed; he did not seem less good and kind than of old, but a latent sternness and determination was perceived through all his sweetness of temper and gentleness of manner. This was precisely the one charm he had always needed to gain influence over Bianca's fancy. She had felt too completely her power over him, now it seemed his turn to assert his ascendency over her.

Whilst he told them his adventures with a brilliancy and *abandon* she had never seen in him before, or asked his sister a multiplicity of questions on all that had happened during his absence (declaring that he had seen no newspapers for the last six months, except some files of the *New Zealand Herald*), Bianca sat silently listening, intensely happy to be once more in his presence, but still with a vague fear lurking in her mind lest all this disengaged easy talk should portend that he had recovered his freedom. Lord Melton, on his side, made no attempt to draw her into conversation, or to attract her attention; and although his sister had vacated her place on the sofa beside Bianca, he did not take possession of it.

'People never meet exactly as they parted,' said Bianca to herself, as she retired to rest.

She apparently was destined to prove the full truth of her aphorism, for though she could find no positive fault with Lord Melton's manners, still there was an indescribable something about them that did not satisfy her; in fact, in comparing them with what they had formerly been, she fancied he had become more distant and formal than she had ever known him.

The fact might be, that they had fallen out of their old habit of brotherly intercourse, such as it existed at the time of Bianca's long visit to Willersdale Park; but more especially it arose from Lord Melton being fully possessed with the idea that he had Bianca entirely to win, and he was so much afraid of spoiling his cause by being too precipitate in the renewal of his proposals, and, by asking too much and too soon, throw himself further back than ever, that he perhaps fell into the contrary extreme. Besides, he was very well content with the actual posture of affairs, for he had Bianca all to himself, and there was no one to interfere with him, or to excite his jealousy: so they read, and rode, and walked, and talked together as of old, but they were seldom alone, for either Lady Vernon or Clara were generally of the party.

Bianca's heart smote her, when one morning, about a week after her arrival, she found a letter on her breakfast plate, from Clara's music-master and admirer, desiring, in the most pathetic terms, to know his fate, and entreating her to use her influence with Lady Vernon, to incline the heart of the young lady towards his suit.

Bianca had not exactly forgotten her promise, but she had put off speaking to Lady Vernon, thinking that the man would write himself; and now it seemed that he had, with desperate patience, been awaiting the result of her mediation.

She was aroused by hearing Lady Vernon saying, in her clear, quick tones,

'My dear Bianca, what does all this mean? What is it at all that you ought to have told me, but which you have not told me? I cannot find my way through the mystery of this letter; just look at it, and see if you know who has written it.'

Lady Vernon gave her the letter in question, which was from the unhappy music-master, full of expressions of 'respect', 'anxiety', and 'honourable intentions', and begging her favourable decision on the proposals he had the honour of submitting to the Signora Bianca the day before her departure from town, and which she had kindly promised to lay before her ladyship.

'Well, are you as much in the dark as myself?'

'Alas! no,' replied Bianca. 'I see my own omissions with distressing clearness. If you will come into my room after breakfast, I will explain all I ought to have told you as soon as I arrived.'

'Is it a lover of your own who is praying for my good offices?'

Lord Melton looked up quickly from his newspaper.

'No, no,' said Bianca, blushing.

'Well, I am all impatience to hear,' said the good lady, who, with all her virtues, was the least in the world of a gossip. 'So now, Maurice, you must amuse yourself this morning; we are about to hold a cabinet council in our own regions, and shall be invisible till luncheon.'

'It is not for me to make any objection,' said Lord Melton, rather stiffly, for he felt unreasonably annoyed at not being taken into their confidence. He held open the door for them to pass, and then returned to his newspaper, which he threw aside at the end of ten minutes. He stood over the fire, looked out of the window, and had all the air of a man who does not know what to do with himself;—at length, catching the tones of Clara's piano, he took himself to the music-room.

'Well, now, Bianca, let me hear the history of the mystery,' said Lady Vernon, seating herself in a comfortable bergère on one side of the fire-place, having first arranged a small table for herself, to hold her many coloured wools. Bianca took possession of the couch opposite; but she did not employ herself to any purpose, she only pulled a piece of packthread into every species of entanglement.

'Our correspondent is the music-master I engaged for Clara; he professes to be attached to her, and to wish to marry her. I promised to lay the case before you, and to say all the good in my power of him. You see it is as prosaic a piece of business as possible. I thought that I had better speak to you before I disturbed the child's young head with the affair. She suspects no more than your worsted work.'

'Well, but, my dear, let me have full particulars. To have that girl well married, would be an infinite relief to my mind, for ever since there has been a chance of her singing in public, I have felt responsible for all that may befall her; and to know her in the hands of a good, sensible man, who will take care of her, would take away half the objection. To me, there seems something revolting in an unmarried girl singing in public. I mean nothing disrespectful to you, my dear—you are an exception to all rules to the contrary.'

Bianca then went into a more detailed account of the affair.

'How old is he, and what sort of a looking young man is he?'

'He is about thirty, and what most people would call rather handsome. A light German looking young man, with a very kind, amiable face.'

'So far, so good; if she can fancy him I think it is quite as good a match as she can reasonably look for. So, finally, I think we should tell the child and hear how she stands affected; and although she has no parents, she has relations, who ought to be consulted.'

'I have some letters to write,' said Bianca, 'so I will leave you here, and send Clara to you. Poor child, she seems very young to have her destiny sealed for life!'

'My dear Bianca, do not be romantic! if she dislikes him she shall refuse him, but for the rest she may be very thankful to marry a steady, sensible young man who can take care of her. I have seen a great many love matches in my time, and they have none of them turned out so well as to make me anxious to see a young woman in whom I take interest, marry headlong for love. Girls at her age can get up a fancy for any one.'

Bianca went to the library to write her letters; on the way she met Clara, and sent her to Lady Vernon, glad to get the responsibility removed from herself.

Whilst she was writing Lord Melton entered: she did not perceive him, and he flung himself without speaking on one of the couches where he could watch her movements in a large mirror.

She wrote letter after letter; Lord Melton lost all patience, he thought she would never stop; the scratching of her pen on the paper irritated his nerves until he could bear it no longer. He exclaimed pettishly,

'Who on earth are you writing so many letters to, Bianca?'

She turned round in surprise at the sound of his voice, she could not see him as he was hidden by the back of the sofa. He arose as he spoke.

'Ah!' said she, 'is that you? I did not hear you come in; how long have you been here?'

'For a long time. I intended to wait patiently until you had finished, but it seemed as if you were about to write on to all eternity, and I was listening for every stroke to be the last. Who can you have to write so many letters to?'

'Most of them are on business,' said Bianca, 'I have neglected every thing since I came here. My holiday will be over soon, and I must think about work.'

'So you wish to get away?' said Lord Melton, bitterly. 'Do you know, Bianca, it is a very great failing of yours, that of never being easy unless you are moving about.'

'I assure you I never felt so little inclined "to move about", as you call it, in my life.'

Lord Melton's heart beat violently; he did not speak, but began to walk up and down the room;—at length he came and sat down at a little distance from her.

'Bianca!' said he, in an unsteady voice, 'a long time ago you said you loved me as a sister; that will not content me; tell me, are you still the same?—can you give me nothing more? I cannot go on in this way. I cannot live as we have lived together, since I came home. If you cannot give me any hope, tell me so, and I will trouble you no more.'

He did not dare to look at Bianca, who trembled too violently to speak.

'Answer me, Bianca. I will not be importunate; I know you will mean what you say; but give me one word.'

Still Bianca did not say that word. She could not utter a sound, although her lips trembled.

'Bianca!' cried Lord Melton, in a tone of passionate entreaty, 'I do not ask you to speak—only give me your hand, as a sign that I may hope.'

Bianca placed her hand tremblingly into Lord Melton's. 'I will be any thing you wish,' she said, 'only do not leave me again.'

Lord Melton could hardly believe the evidence of his senses—he was giddy with joy.

'But, Bianca, do you love me?—or is this only your generosity, that cannot bear to give me pain?'

'No, no!' said she, in a low voice, 'it is not generosity. I know now, that my whole soul is bound up in you. It would kill me to lose your love.'

'But it is not as a brother you love me?' persisted he. 'I wish there were no such relation to deceive one! Will you ever tell me that I am your brother again?'

'What would you have?' said Bianca. 'You possess my whole soul—every thought I have is yours. I cannot tell when I began to love you—it has come like daylight. When you were so long absent, and so long without writing to me, I suffered very much. I feared lest you should have wearied of me, and left me. I found, then, that you were part of my life. I have been quite unhappy enough about you to satisfy your utmost scepticism, that at last I do love you as you desire to be loved! You deserve that I should tell you all this,' said she, looking at him through the tears that were blinding her, with an expression of radiant happiness, like sunshine through a silver mist. 'I have made you suffer as well as myself; but until you were gone, I knew not how much you were to me. Do not leave me again—let me belong to you, so that nothing may ever part us more!'

Lord Melton drew her towards him, and whispered,

'That nothing may ever part us more!'

CHAPTER XXVII

LADY VERNON went to the library to take Bianca's opinion of the letter she had written to Mr Meyer (which, by the way, was the name of Clara's adorer), and also of the communication she had made to Clara's uncle, but she found the room vacant; she then went to find her in her own sitting-room, but with equally little success. The bell rang for luncheon, but neither Lord Melton nor Bianca made their appearance. Clara, too, had vanished—to dream over the new prospects the morning had disclosed to her, and to find out whether she really could be in love with Mr Meyer. She fancied she should greatly prefer Lord Melton; and wondered whether he 'meant any thing', by coming into the music-room, and listening to her whilst she practised that morning; and thought how very handsome and fascinating he was, so superior to every one she had ever seen before in her life.

Accordingly, Lady Vernon found herself left completely alone, which rather annoyed her, as, at that moment, she felt herself much in need of that woman's true consolation—a long confidential gossip about the events of the morning.

The first dinner bell rang, and yet no one appeared; but, whilst she was dressing, a tap was heard at the door; it was Lord Melton's servant, who came from him, to request that her ladyship would allow him to come to her dressing-room for a few moments' conversation before she went down to dinner.

'Certainly,' cried Lady Vernon, who overheard the message; 'say that I shall be disengaged in five minutes.'

Her 'five minutes' were of reasonably conscientious length for a woman finishing her toilet—that is to say, not more than ten elapsed before she entered her dressing-room, where she found her brother, who declared he had been waiting there more than half an hour.

'My dear Maurice, where have you hidden yourself all the morning? and do you chance to know what has become of Bianca; but,' cried she, looking at him with surprise, 'what good news have you heard that makes you so radiant?'

'Something that I hope you will consider as "good news", too, Margaret—Bianca has consented to become my wife; and all that is needed to my perfect happiness is, that you should feel as happy as I do.'

Lady Vernon could not reply for an instant, then she said:

'You know how anxious I have always felt for your marriage, but I always doubted whether you would find a woman to deserve you. Bianca is a noble creature; and though I do not like actresses, and I wish she had been any thing else in the world, still you may feel very proud to have won her. I love her as if she were my own daughter; and you, both of you, have my best blessing!'

The old lady then fairly burst into tears; as, somehow, people are always prone to do, when they hear that a dearly loved relative is about to marry: but she soon dried her eyes, embraced her brother, and went off to Bianca's room. She found Bianca, who had not begun to dress, sitting before the fire, rather anxious as to the first effect of Lord Melton's communication; she knew the good lady's family pride, and she had a vague fear that the almost overpowering happiness of the morning must be shaded by some mortal mixture of disappointment, but all shadows vanished before the maternal kindness with which Lady Vernon pressed her to her heart. For a minute both were too much overpowered to speak.

'God bless you, my dear child,' said she, at length, 'I am glad to have you for a sister, though I shall always feel more as if you were my daughter; Melton has told me every thing; he deserves that you should make him happy.'

'I who have been alone all my life, am finding all my kinsfolk in one day,' said Bianca, leaning her head on the old lady's shoulder. 'I will be your sister or daughter, or any thing you will. I cannot love you more than I do. You have been all goodness to me, and now you are still adding to it;—tell me again, will you have me for your sister?'

'Indeed, yes, my darling,' said Lady Vernon, taking Bianca's face between her hands and kissing her forehead. 'Maurice may be thankful to gain you for a wife, and I am glad to receive you into our family,' concluded she with affectionate dignity.

'Now, my dear, you must come to dinner, it has been waiting at least two hours, never mind dressing.'

'I will not be a second,' said Bianca. 'I shall be dressed by the time the bell has been rung.'

'Well then, I will leave you, to see what has become of that child Clara.'

The dinner was at last actually on the table. Mathews, the old butler, and one of Bianca's most devoted admireres, had somehow penetrated into the secret; he considered that he belonged to the family, and had a right to take interest in all that concerned it, and there was something almost paternal in the attentions he bestowed on Bianca that day. Nobody talked much, but it seemed as though they spoke to each other without words, for no one felt silent. Poor Clara soon found all her vague fancies about Lord Melton scattered like mist; and she, with that spider-like instinct which is very strong in mankind, especially in the young, began to weave reveries almost as bright of which the attainable Mr Meyer was the centre.

It had been arranged by Lady Vernon that Clara should go to spend a few weeks with her uncle and aunt, and there Mr Meyer was to come and make his suit in person, for as the old lady sagaciously said, she would be much more likely to view him dispassionately when seen from her own level than when she was liable to be dazzled by the accidental position in which she found herself at Willersdale Park. In the course of a few days a most satisfactory letter came from her uncle, who was a veterinary surgeon in a market town in Essex; and under the escort of Mathews, Clara once more took a journey. She was to spend the remainder of the holidays with her uncle, and then go up to town to Bianca. Clara's affairs once off her hands, for the present at least, Lady Vernon became very anxious that her brother's marriage with Bianca should take place without delay, in which idea Lord Melton quite coincided. Bianca pleaded for time to acquit herself of her professional engagements. The point of time was stoutly contended, but in the end Bianca found herself obliged to yield, especially when Lady Vernon said,

'My dear Bianca will not, I am sure, refuse the first request made by her sister; which is, that she will not again appear on the stage, now that she belongs to us.'

'So be it, then,' said Bianca, gracefully; 'arrange all as you wish it to be, and I will be conformable.'

'That is being a good child!' said Lady Vernon; whilst Lord Melton, as in duty bound, expressed all the gratitude it was possible for man to feel.

Three weeks afterwards, all the newspapers contained announcements of the marriage of 'Viscount Melton, of Melton Hall, in Staffordshire, and of Fort Vernon, in Scotland, with the celebrated actress Bianca'. As Parliament was not sitting, and there were no very exciting public events going on, the public were not deprived of any particulars, from the bride's veil of Honiton lace, down to all sorts of anecdotes and incidents of her professional career, as many biographical sketches as could be collected, criticisms on the different characters in which she had appeared, estimates of her genius, tributes in prose and verse to her virtues and accomplishments, with bitter lamentations for the irreparable loss the stage had sustained from the abdication of its high-priestess,—all which was the only drawback to Lady Vernon's complete and entire contentment at the event, which was celebrated at Willersdale Park.

As her own marriage so much sooner than she had anticipated, put it out of Bianca's power again to take charge of Clara, Lady Vernon obviated the difficulty by promising to receive her until some other arrangement could be made. Clara soon spared every one any further anxiety about her by an ecstatic letter to Lady Vernon, in which she declared her profound affection for Mr Meyer, and stated, that with the approbation of her friends, she had accepted him, and that they were to go to Italy immediately. Clara's cup of happiness seemed brim full. Bianca felt half afraid that the journey to Italy had some share in her enthusiasm for Mr Meyer; but Lady Vernon declared that it was a very promising looking affair, and a letter coming also from her uncle, in which he expressed his perfect approbation of the match, and a great deal of gratitude to Lady Vernon for all her kindness, Bianca resigned herself to letting matters take their course. She made Clara a present of all the furniture of her house in Brompton, and sent her a splendid wedding-dress beside. Lady Vernon, also, gave her a handsome present; and Clara was married, and departed with her husband for Italy with as bright prospects as any young woman could desire.

Bianca and her husband proceeded to Fort Vernon, intending
to reside for some months there.

It is a great mistake to suppose that genius is shown in one
special mode of manifestation alone;—it inspires its possessor,
and enables him to feel equal to all situations.

Bianca might have been born to her new position, so easily she
sustained her dignities, and so well ordered and appointed was
her household.

One evening, about six months after their marriage, Bianca and
Lord Melton were in the library at Fort Vernon. It was a splendid
room; the ceiling was panelled with emblazoned escutcheons and
armorial bearings, the walls and book-cases covered with black
oak carvings.

> Full of fancies, strange and sweet,
> All made out of the carver's brain.

Lord Melton had been reading aloud, whilst Bianca was working a cushion in crochet for Lady Vernon. The fading light,
which was rendered still more dim by coming through the
panes of curiously stained glass, prevented him continuing his
employment. He ceased to read, and silently watched Bianca, as
she strove to finish the row she had begun, in spite of the
increasing gloom. He stirred the fire, and the flashing light
danced on the gorgeous ceiling, and the quaint dark mouldings
round the room.

'Bianca,' said her husband, as if he were asking the most
ordinary question in the world, 'in how many former states did
you live, before you came into this world? I have never mentioned it to you, but I have been wonder-struck at the prudence
and dexterity with which you have adapted yourself to what must
be such a new order of things—the orderliness, the—what shall I
say?—house-keeping qualities, which have developed in you are
so marvellous, as to make you seem what the Scotch folks would
call "not canny".'

'Why, you Turk, you heathen, you unbelieving Jew!' cried
Bianca, flinging down her work—'is this positively the first time
you have discovered that I am a clever woman? You are like all
the rest of men, and have no faith in a woman's genius, until it is
shown in the practical manifestation of arranging your breakfasts,

dinners, and servants. There is no wonder in the matter; the simple secret of filling any position, great or small, consists in just giving your mind to see and understand what are the peculiar requirements of it, and in doing them heartily. But with all that,' continued she, looking at him affectionately, 'you cannot think how it pleases me to hear you say that I manage my house well, and that you like what I do.'

'Bianca! will you tell me one thing?' said he, after a pause. 'I may be "a curious impertinent", for asking; I ought, perhaps, to remain content with my present blessedness, without seeking further; but still, will you tell me, did you love Conrad as much as you love me?'

'No,' replied Bianca, firmly. 'He would not have permitted me to love him as I love you; he would always have been putting himself between us. I should have always been struggling to follow my own nature—to be, in short, what I am now—and he would have been tired to death, and I should have worn myself out in the attempt to make his affection what I desired to find it—to make it what alone would have satisfied me. I should not have discovered until it was too late, that it was not in his nature to be what I desired; not until I had broken myself against the irremediable incompatibility of our characters; in the end, I should have been forced to recognise that I possessed a larger and more devoted nature than his own, which would have been an entirely fatal thing to me, for a woman can only love when she fancies that on the whole the object is endowed with a greater and nobler character than her own. It may be that she possesses individually more beauty, more genius, more brilliancy, than the man she chooses; but there must be a preponderating character in him. She must find in him something that supports her best and noblest impulses, and which strengthens her weakness. I should not have found this with Conrad. I have had opportunities of studying his character well since the days when I loved him; he had sympathy with nothing but his own arbitrary notions. Instead of being able to live easily and freely beside him, all my strength would have gone in efforts to avoid collision, and to obtain marks of affection; till, wearied and worn out, I should have ended by making him as wretched as myself. I can see now how well it is for us that we are not allowed to choose our own lot in life. I tremble when I think of all my own headstrong wilfulness. We are none of us, or to speak more modestly, *I* am not, wise enough to be trusted with my own wishes.'

'Then you are happy with me, Bianca?' said her husband.

'Upon my honour I am too contented to know whether I am happy or not. I have never thought about it. I only know that I would endure again all that horrible uprooting of my life, which at the time seemed as if it must tear the very soul out of me, and endure as much more added to that as nature might support without loosing her hold on life, if in the end I might be as I am now, to know you as I do, and to possess the priceless treasure of your love. It was good for me, necessary for me, that I should suffer all that horrible anguish. My love for you grew out of that chaos, from the wreck of all on which I had built myself up. Oh, if we could only have faith enough, at the time we are suffering, to resign ourselves to the will of Him who orders all things, to take His will for the best and wisest; and "though he slay us to trust in Him", it would be the true, the only wisdom. I am humbled to the dust when I think how little I have deserved all the happiness that has come upon me. I would not now for all the world have been without that great sorrow, although at the time it well-nigh overwhelmed me. Sorrow is our matriculation in humanity, and no one who has received its mysterious baptism would ever wish to have been spared what has been laid upon him. My love for Conrad was true and devoted; my whole life was bound up in him at the time, and it kept me from much evil: but I could not give up my idol; and when it was taken away I had no faith to trust a Higher Will, and that made my suffering.'

'But,' said Lord Melton, 'if you had ceased to love Conrad, how could you show such devoted kindness to him in his sorrow? You must have had some love for him remaining, or I should not have had the instinct to feel so jealous.'

'It was a different sort of thing altogether,' said Bianca; 'the feeling had completely changed its nature, and there was nothing of which you need have been jealous.'

'That I believe, now; but how could I feel sure at the time? We are all wise enough after the fact. Do you know where he is now?'

'I do not. He completely broke all connexion with the world, and I suppose he is still working out his idea of expiation, and of wearing away the remorse that consumed him.'

It might be about a fortnight after this conversation that Bianca said one morning at breakfast:

'In spite of all the fine things I said the other evening about the vanity of wishing, I have fallen a victim to it myself.'

'Well, tell me what it is about, and then we shall see if it be possible to compass it?'

'I want to go to Italy. It is my own country, and I should so much like to see it again. Will you take me there?'

'We will see what can be done towards winter; at present, I must live at home a little.'

'Ah, yes!' said Bianca, remorsefully; 'and when I think that it was I who banished you for so long, I feel glad to suffer a little of the penalty; but you will take me some time? I feel a yearning to go there I cannot express.'

It was not likely that Lord Melton should thwart such a very moderate desire of his wife's. They went to Willersdale Park in the autumn, to pay a long-promised visit to Lady Vernon; after which they were to proceed to Italy.

On their journey from Scotland to Willersdale Park they remained all night at Newcastle. When Lord Melton entered to breakfast in the morning, he found Bianca sitting so absorbed in a play-bill that she did not perceive his entrance.

'What have you found to interest you so much?' said he, looking over her shoulder.

'How strangely things come about in this world!' said she. 'Mr Simpson and his company are performing here in all their glory; this is a bill of their performance for to-night. This is the very town where my mother fell ill. Conrad and Mr Simpson extricated me from my distress. It was the first time I ever saw Conrad, and he spoke Italian to me, and seemed like an angel from heaven. I have lived out that romance, I am going back to Italy which I had then just left, and here comes Mr Simpson to witness my exit in the same way as he presided over my entrance on life in England. All rounded in ten years! it seems like a dream!'

'It is a singular coincidence,' said Lord Melton. 'What is this Mr Simpson like? I should rather like to see him.'

'And so should I, very much,' said Bianca; 'he really was a very good man in his way, and very kind to me; he might have been my father, only he paid me so ill; and he had so much real feeling and zeal for his calling. I would go and see him, only—'

'Only what?'

'Only, that I know him to be quite capable of exhibiting me in a grand transparency, and getting up a drama on my romance of real life! No, I know him too well to venture to glorify him in any such manner; but, if you will come out with me, after breakfast, we will buy the most sumptuous breastpin to be found, at any jeweller's in the town—I know his taste—and I will send it as an anonymous tribute to his genius. Now, I am quite sure you must have finished your breakfast, so come along.'

As they were proceeding up one of the principal streets in the town, they encountered a grand equestrian procession, the rear of which was brought up by Mr Simpson himself; not on a lofty phaeton, as of old, but in a magnificent private carriage, almost worthy of a lord mayor, and drawn by eight beautiful horses.

'Look! look!' cried Bianca, 'that is Mr Simpson; he is a little older than he used to be, but he is very little changed. I dare say he has set up the carriage because he considers that it looks more patriarchal than his former resplendant phaeton. I wonder whether his wife be living still—I would send her something too. Is not our identity a strange thing?'

They had now reached a jeweller's shop, and Bianca chose the most radiant brooch she could find, as a present to Mrs Simpson, and a very handsome gold snuff-box for the hero himself. She desired that they might be sent forthwith to Mr Simpson's lodgings. She wrote, herself, on the envelope, that they were the gift of one who had sincere respect for his character, and admiration of his genius.

'I wish I could be by, to see his astonishment,' said she, laughing, when they got out of the shop. 'I can just fancy him; and then how happily and complacently he will settle down in the conviction, that the dawn of his fame has arisen!'

'Well, my angel, but we shall be late; the carriage will have been waiting an hour.'

After remaining a short time with Lady Vernon they went to Italy, to her birth-place, but Bianca found no one living there who remembered her. At Milan they saw Clara and her husband—both supremely happy. Clara's voice kept its promise; and, with the instruction she was receiving, there was every reason to expect that she would take the lead amongst English singers on her return, and raise the credit of the English school.

Bryant came to England, and paid Lord Melton and Bianca a visit. He never rallied from the deep depression of spirits which Alice's death had left: he continued to superintend his vast mining concerns, but it was for the sake of ameliorating the condition of the workmen, which seemed the only object in which he felt any interest. His clear sagacity and businesslike habits enabled him to be very useful to Lord Melton, in his plans for the improvement of the peasantry on his Scotch and Irish estates. At first, Bianca seemed to awaken many painful recollections, and he avoided her; but afterwards he grew very much attached to her.

Conrad never re-appeared in the world. Some years after her marriage, Bianca received a letter in an unknown hand, informing her of his death. It was from one of his own sect, who had been desired by him to communicate the fact to her. He had fallen a victim to typhus fever, which was ravaging the courts and alleys amongst which he was constantly pursuing his mission.

Lady Vernon lived to a good old age, and her school flourished to the last. After her death Bianca continued it, and set up others on its model.

Lady Vernon left all her fortune, with the exception of some legacies and annuities, to her brother, with directions that it was to descend to his younger children. Bianca and Lord Melton lived long and happily together; every year seemed to increase the perfect union between them. They had several children, who inherited the sound character of their parents.

If the reader insists on a moral being tacked to the end of a story, to save him the trouble of extracting it himself, we can find nothing better than those words of Shelley.

Gentleness, Virtue, Wisdom, and Endurance,
These are the seals of that most firm assurance,
  Which bars the pit over Destruction's strength;
And if, with infirm hand, Eternity,
Mother of many acts and hours, should free
  The serpent that would clasp her with his length,
These are the spells by which to re-assume
An empire o'er the disentangled doom.★

THE END

EXPLANATORY NOTES

Dedication: despite her friendship with Geraldine Jewsbury, Jane Carlyle was initially uneasy about having the novel dedicated to her, apparently because it seemed to her, and particularly to her husband, as redolent of 'George Sandism' (see Introduction; also *Letters and Memorials of Jane Welsh Carlyle*, ii. 30–1, and Norma Clarke, *Ambitious Heights*, 186–8). Elizabeth Newton Paulet was another of Jewsbury's long-standing friends, and had collaborated with her in the early stages of the writing of *Zoe*.

5   *if you have any friends*: in the nineteenth century, 'friends' often implied relatives as well.

6   *assize time*: the time when judges of the superior courts held one of their periodical sessions, trying civil and criminal cases.

7   *a true Englishman's silence*: a foreshadowing of one of the novel's recurrent themes—the English character, and how it contrasts with the Italian.

10   *I will give her ten shillings a-week*: not a very generous salary—albeit it seems to have become twelve shillings by Chapter VII. Performers could have high outlays on temporary lodgings, meals, and fares. On the other hand, Simpson's offer to pay for Bianca's stage clothes is generous, since these normally had to be provided by performers themselves. (See Tracy C. Davis, *Actresses as Working Women*, 24–35.) Simpson is portrayed throughout the novel as a kind of lovable skinflint.

   how are you called?: the un-English turn of phrase is perhaps meant to remind us that Conrad is speaking Italian. The Italian for 'what is your name?'—*come ci chi ama?*—translates literally as 'how are you called?'

13   *An engraving of the Princess Charlotte, and another of her husband*: Princess Charlotte (b. 1796) was the only child of George, Prince of Wales (later George IV) and Caroline of Brunswick; she married Prince Leopold of Saxe-Coburg in 1816. But she died on 5 November 1817 after giving birth to a stillborn boy, and was much mourned by the British public.

15   *I paid eightpence for a letter for you this morning*: until the introduction of the penny post in 1840, letters were paid for by the recipients, and charged for by weight.

16   *his father would not hear of a Papist for a daughter-in-law*: British Protestants in the nineteenth century were often prejudiced against Catholics, and 'Papist' was a derogatory term for them, reflecting Catholics' allegiance to the Pope (rather than the British monarch).

18   *a word of abomination as great as that of Socialist*: the word 'Socialist' only came into use in English in the 1830s; it derived from the French *socialiste*, and was associated with the ideas of the Comte de Saint-Simon (1760–1825). Charles Lambert, the man to whom Geraldine Jewsbury proposed in 1847, was a leading French follower of St Simon, while the following year she visited Paris where a revolution partly inspired by Socialist ideas had broken out.

20   *objects of vertu*: objects of worth, value.

24   *exigeante*: exacting.

36   *tracasseries*: fusses, irritations.

39   *the oxy-hydrogen microscope*: a microscope where the object was illuminated by a bright light caused by hydrogen burning in oxygen.

40   *Sismondi's Literature du Midi*: *De la Littérature du Midi de l'Europe* (1813; published in English in 1823 as *Historical View of the Literature of the South of Europe*), by Leonard Simonde de Sismondi (1773–1842), a French historian of Italian descent and close friend of Madame de Staël. Like her fascination with paintings, particularly that of the Spanish convent (Vol. 1, Chapter VIII), Alice's interest in this book reflects her attraction both to the arts and to the world beyond the stifling middle-class life of the English Midlands.

42   *'first, last, midst, and without end'*: echoes a line from a Wordsworth poem, published in 1845, which describes the natural phenomena he experiences on descending the Alps as 'Characters of the great Apocalypse, | The types and symbols of Eternity, | Of first, and last, and midst, and without end'. The passage was later incorporated into *The Prelude* (1850)—see Book vi, 11. 625–40.

50   *family receipts*: recipes.

     Mrs Ellis's novel: Sarah Stickney Ellis (1796–1874) was a prolific writer, famous mainly for her conduct manuals for women, *The Women of England* (1838), *The Daughters of England* (1842), *The Wives of England* (1843), and *The Mothers of England* (1843). These,

like her many novels, inculcate the ideas about women's upbringing and role which Alice's story is designed to challenge; Geraldine
Jewsbury's letters contain several attacks on Mrs Ellis and her ideas.

52   *ennuyé*: bored.

53   *savans*: scholars, scientists (modern French *savants*).

54   *Some are born stupid, some achieve stupidity, and some have stupidity
     thrust upon them!*: a parody of 'Some are born great, some achieve
     greatness, and some have greatness thrust upon them'. This is not
     from Bacon, but from Shakespeare (*Twelfth Night*, II. iv). It is
     not clear whether the misattribution is Bryant's or Jewsbury's—or
     a joke based on the long-standing but discredited theory that
     Bacon really wrote Shakespeare's plays.

55   *au naturel*: unadorned, in the raw.

     *he will be held up as a heathen man, and be attacked for his insidious
     principles*: although Darwin's *The Origin of Species* was not pub-
     lished till 1859, there was already in the 1830s and 1840s con-
     troversy about the inconsistencies between the biblical version of
     history and that suggested by the geological record. The term
     'Asses' Bridge' referred originally to the first difficult proposition
     in Euclidian geometry—hence, by extension, to a well-known
     idea which a stupid person might be proud of discovering.

56   *voyage autour de la chambre*: voyage around the room.

57   *the land of Goshen*: the fertile part of Egypt where the Israelites of
     the Old Testament lived, and where they were protected from
     the plagues (see Genesis and Exodus).

58   *Amory's 'Life of John Buncle'*: *The Life and Opinions of John Buncle,
     Esq.*, by Thomas Amory (?1691–1788), published in two volumes,
     1756 and 1766. The eponymous hero travels through the moor-
     land and mountain scenery of northern England, which is de-
     scribed in much detail.

     explored . . . by turnpike commissioners, if not by railway surveyors: in
     the late eighteenth and early nineteenth centuries, many im-
     portant roads in Britain had become turnpike roads—those in
     wheeled vehicles had to go through a toll-gate, or turnpike, and
     pay a toll. But by the late 1840s revenue from these roads was
     falling with the rapid expansion of the railways, generally seen as
     an indicator of technological and economic progress.

     *'as man is no longer an individual, but a species,' as Fanny Wright tells
     us*: Fanny Wright (1795–1853) first attracted attention with her
     Views of Society and Manners in America (1821), and became famous

as a lecturer on a wide range of religious, social, political, racial, and women's issues; her tendency to question received truths no doubt appealed to Jewsbury. Central to Wright's thinking was the idea that people were weak as individuals, but strong when they co-operated with each other to improve society.

59 *personalities*: used in the unusual and now-obselete sense of personal qualities or characteristics.

60 *table d'hôte*: here, a buffet supper.

Corinne: see Introduction.

65 *Dr Gregory*: Dr John Gregory (1724–73), author of *A Father's Legacy to His Daughters* (1774). Written originally to guide Gregory's already-motherless daughters after his own death, this book was still popular enough in the nineteenth century to be familiar to someone as little given to reading as Mrs Helmsby. A strange mixture of the high-minded and the calculating, its advice, if expressed less crudely than hers, is sometimes along the same lines. Here she is recalling Gregory's comment in his chapter on 'Friendship, Love, Marriage':

> If you love [a suitor], let me advise you never to discover to him the full extent of your love; no, not although you marry him: that sufficiently shows your preference, which is all he is entitled to know. If he has delicacy, he will ask for no stronger proof of your affection.

Gregory goes on to say that, even after marriage, 'that reserve and delicacy which always left the lover something further to wish, and often made him doubtful of your sensibility or attachment, may, and ought ever to remain' (1822 edition, John Sharpe: London, pp. 71–2, 99).

68 *listened with Desdemona-like avidity*: in Shakespeare's *Othello*, Desdemona falls in love with Othello as a result of listening to him recount his travels and exploits as a warrior. See Act I, scene iii, especially ll. 128–70.

69 *all the heroes of the 'Niebelungen Lied'*: this thirteenth-century German poem dealing with figures of Norse legend contains several heroes, including Siegfried, Gunther, Etzel, and Hildebrand, not to mention the warrior-maiden Brünnhilde. To Mrs Helmsby, Alice's marriage is the big 'heroic' adventure of her daughter's life.

Harriet Byron, who married Sir Charles Grandison: *The History of Sir Charles Grandison* (1753–4) is one of the novels of Samuel

Richardson, best-known today for *Clarissa*. Still much read in the
nineteenth century, *Sir Charles Grandison* was none the less far
longer than even the standard three-volume novel of the time:
when the hero Sir Charles eventually marries his beloved Harriet
in book VI, the wedding is described in copious detail, including
the bride's wedding clothes.

70   *embonpoint*: stoutness, fullness.

71   *My dear John*: an inconsistency on Jewsbury's part—Bryant was
     initially introduced as William.

     chefs-d'œuvre: masterpieces.

74   *empressement*: eagerness, enthusiasm.

77   *accès*: attack, fit.

     épanchement du cœur: outpouring from the heart.

78   *Mais allons*: But let's go.

81   *An ampler ether, a diviner air*: from Wordsworth's 'Laodamia'
     (1815), l. 105. Wordsworth was Poet Laureate at the time of
     writing. A jocular reference, but Conrad's familiarity with Words-
     worth will become significant later in the novel.

82   *Magnus Apollo*: Great Apollo—Apollo was the Greek god of the
     sun, thought to make it rise and set by driving his chariot across
     the sky.

83   *rencontre*: encounter.

89   *He was a bright particular star*: an allusion to the soliloquy by Helena
     in Shakespeare's *All's Well That Ends Well*, I. i. 91–117, which
     Bianca, significantly, finds the only Shakespeare passage she can
     think of when auditioned by Montague St Leger later in this
     chapter. Helena expresses her love for Bertram, Count of Rousil-
     lon, whom (at this point) she considers beyond her reach as a
     husband, largely because of the social distance between them. The
     most relevant lines are:

                    my imagination
     Carries no favour in't but Bertram's.
     I am undone: there is no living, none,
     If Bertram be away. It were all one
     That I should love a bright particular star
     And think to wed it, he is so above me:
     In his bright radiance and collateral light
     Must I be comforted, not in his sphere.
     The ambition in my love thus plagues itself:

> The hind that would be mated by the lion
> Must die for love. . . . (ll. 94–104)

Although the plot of the novel by no means follows that of the play, Bertram's contemptuous attitude to Helena when she is given the opportunity to marry him does foreshadow Conrad's later behaviour to Bianca.

90   *recherche*: stylish elegance.

93   *one of Calista's speeches*: Calista is the heroine of *The Fair Penitent*, a tragedy by Nicholas Rowe (1674–1718), first produced in 1703 and still popular on the early Victorian stage. In love with Lothario, Calista is obliged by her father to marry Altamont, but her affair with Lothario is exposed, Altamont kills him, and she eventually dies. Her speeches run the gamut from rancour to remorse, from passion to despair, and thus provide an actress with great scope to display her talents—but, in view of his later intentions towards Bianca, St Leger may be thinking more of how easily Calista was seduced.

96   *pour se fair valoir*: so as to make the most of himself.

116   *retenue*: modesty.

   a *'Roman Triumph'*: in ancient Rome, a solemn and elaborate procession celebrating the victory of a successful general.

117   a *bonne fortune*: a bit of good luck.

118   *King Ahasuerus-like designs*: the connotations are of lechery and a desire to exert power over women, both applicable to St Leger. King Ahasuerus of Persia in the biblical book of Esther repudiated his queen, Vashti, for refusing to appear before him when summoned. He then had many beautiful virgins brought into his harem, finally choosing as the new queen the Jewess Esther. Bianca suffers a similar fate to Vashti, but does get her revenge.

124   *whose speech betrayed him a Quaker*: that is, his use of 'thee' rather than 'you'. The Quakers (more correctly, the Religious Society of Friends) were a religious group established in the mid-seventeenth century, when English usage still distinguished between a familiar form (thou, thee, thy) used to family, friends, and social equals and inferiors, and a polite form (you, your), used to social superiors and strangers. The Quakers had used the familiar form to everyone, in order to demonstrate their tenet that all were equal in the sight of God, and had retained this form into the nineteenth century, although it had died out in general use.

(In this instance, the chemist should have used 'thou' to be grammatically correct.)

127   *the force du sang*: the force of blood.

128   *c'était faire au même temps le bien publique et privé*: it was doing good publicly and privately at the same time.

129   *froissé*: hurt, bruised.

132   *gêne*: embarrassment.

133   *the bearers of a bar-sinister*: the illegitimate. In coats of arms, a diagonal bar going from right to left (/), rather than the other way round, was thought, not always rightly, to signify illegitimacy.

     the part of Mrs Haller: a standard role for nineteenth-century actresses. Like that of Calista, it bears witness to audiences' fascination with seeing represented on stage the kind of woman likely to be repudiated in real life. Mrs Haller is the leading female character in *The Stranger*, a play adapted by playwright R. B. Sheridan in 1798 from *Menschenhass und Reue*, by the German dramatist Kotzebue. An adulterous wife abandoned by her lover and overcome with remorse, she gains her husband's forgiveness before her death.

134   *flétrie*: stained, blighted.

147   *thrice is he armed, who hath his quarrel just*: Shakespeare, *Henry VI, Pt. 2*, iii. ii. 233.

     icicle of Dian's temple: a garbling of a passage in Shakespeare's *Coriolanus*, where the eponymous hero (with none of St Leger's contemptuous tone) describes his wife's friend Valeria as 'chaste as the icicle | That's curdied by the frost from purest snow | And hangs on Dian's temple' (v. iii. 65–7). 'Dian' is Diana, the Roman goddess of chastity.

     It soothes the awkward squad of the rejected | To find how very badly she's selected: from Byron's satirical poem *Don Juan* (1819–24), Canto XII, stanza 287—describing the rationalizations of the many unsuccessful suitors in English fashionable life when an heiress finally chooses a husband.

159   *Hazlitt's Essays; Schlegel's Lectures . . . those German translations from Schiller and Goethe*: all indications of Conrad's and Bianca's excellent, indeed advanced, literary taste. William Hazlitt (1778–1830) was among the best literary critics of the nineteenth century, whose works include *Characters of Shakespeare's Plays* (1817) and *A View of the English Stage* (1818). August Wilhelm Schlegel

(1767–1845) produced a distinguished German translation of Shake-speare's plays, as well as a collection of lectures, *Über dramatische Kunst und Literatur* (1809–11, translated in 1815 as *Lectures on Dramatic Art and Literature*). The multifarious achievements of J. C. F. von Schiller (1759–1805) and J. W. von Goethe (1749–1832) are too many to do justice to here, but both were dramatists, while the diffusion of knowledge about both in England was much attributable to Jewsbury's friend Thomas Carlyle.

166   *Abelard and Eloïse*: the famous lovers Peter Abelard (a notable twelfth-century French theologian), and his pupil Héloïse. Separated after the exposure of their affair, both took to the monastic life, but exchanged letters which became celebrated and were often published in conjunction with Alexander Pope's poem of 1717, 'Eloisa to Abelard'. It is actually Héloïse's letters which are the passionate ones.

168   *coulisses*: wings, backstage.

169   *Covent Garden*: Covent Garden and Drury Lane were the most prestigious theatres, and, till 1843, the only ones in London allowed to perform 'serious' drama such as Shakespeare's plays.

178   *déjeuners*: lunches.

185   *bijouterie*: jewellery.

186   *Ernest Maltravers*: a novel of 1837 by E. L. Bulwer Lytton, one of the most prolific, popular, and respected novelists of the mid-nineteenth century. Valerie de St Ventadour is briefly the object of Maltravers's love: she is like Alice Bryant in being unhappily married, but M. de St Ventadour is a complete fool, and Valerie a worldly and fashionable beauty.

189   *prononcé*: pronounced, obvious.

194   *minauderies*: simperings.

195   *amende*: apology.

207   *portière*: door-curtain.

208   *écarté*: a card game fashionable in the nineteenth century.

       par hasard?: by any chance?

       Van Amburgh's half-tamed tigress: Isaac Van Amburgh was an American famous for his lion-taming and his menagerie. He had a season of 115 nights at Drury Lane in 1838–9, and in 1847, when Jewsbury was writing *The Half Sisters*, a painting of him by Edwin Landseer was exhibited at the Royal Academy.

tant soi peu: ever so little.

209   *Pour moi*: as for me.

211   *fade 'into the light of common day'*: Wordsworth, 'Ode: Intimations of Immortality from Recollections of Early Childhood' (1807), l. 77, describing the adult's loss of the child's vision of Nature.

    he could have waited seven years, like Jacob, and found them as seven days: in order to win Rachel as his wife, Jacob served her father Laban for seven years, but they seemed to him only a few days (see Genesis 29).

212   *Dulcinea*: in Miguel de Cervantes' novel *Don Quixote de la Mancha* (1605, 1615), Dulcinea is the village girl whom the elderly knight of the title adopts as his ideal love.

213   *a passion . . . 'ne renaît jamais dans la même place ni pour la même personne'*: a passion . . . 'is never reborn in the same place nor for the same person'.

214   *mais cela suffit*: but that's all.

215   *Don Giovannis*: Don Giovanni, the protagonist of Mozart's 1787 opera of the same name, is an insatiable womanizer with hundreds of conquests. (Bianca and her protégée Clara Broughton go to see the opera in Chapter XXIII.)

217   *Lord Byron's 'Curse of Darkness'*: a remarkable poem of 1816, called simply 'Darkness', and showing darkness descending on the world as humanity destroys itself.

222   *Acteon-like*: in classical myth, the huntsman Actaeon was punished for seeing the goddess Diana bathing by being turned into a stag and torn to pieces by his own hounds.

224   *Queen Katherine in 'Henry the Eighth'*: the part of Katharine of Aragon, the first wife of Henry VIII, was considered one of the great female Shakespearian roles in the nineteenth century—albeit some of the play, including much of Katharine's role, is now thought to have been written by John Fletcher. Katharine generates pathos through her dignified response to Henry's divorce proceedings against her.

235   *Sir Symond d'Ewes*: a seventeenth-century antiquary (1602–50) who transcribed numerous monastic registers and early wills, records, and cartularies, plus journals of Parliaments under Elizabeth I.

246   *Une mère en permettrait la lecture à sa fille*: a mother would allow her daughter to read it.

251   *chiffonnage*: rubbish.

258   *non ragionam di lor*: let us not speak of them, from Dante's *Divine Comedy* (early fourteenth century), *Inferno*, iii. 51.

266   *Whose dwelling is the light of setting suns*: Wordsworth, 'Lines Composed a Few Miles Above Tintern Abbey' (1798), l. 97. The reference is to 'something far more deeply interfused', which the speaker of the poem sees as pervading both natural phenomena and 'the mind of man'—just as Alice feels united in spirit with the clouds at sunset.

272   *eat the bread of carefulness*: Psalm 127—the gist of this being that labour and effort are futile unless under God's guidance.

274   *Naiad*: water-nymph (in classical mythology).

281   *heavy as lead, and deep almost as life*: again from Wordsworth's 'Ode: Intimations of Immortality', l. 129, slightly misquoted (the original reads, 'heavy as frost'). The line refers to the way 'custom' gradually damages the child's powers of perception.

       darkness that might be felt: slight misquotation of Exodus 10: 21, 'darkness that may be felt'—referring to one of the plagues of Egypt.

292   *The broken lily lies, | The storm is overpast*: from Shelley's 'Adonais' (1821), an elegy on Keats's premature death (at 25). Jewsbury here divides one line (54) into two.

300   *the Union*: under nineteenth-century Poor Laws, a group of parishes would make up a 'union' administered by a Board of Guardians, and would contain a workhouse for the destitute. Being sent to the workhouse usually meant living in harsh conditions and separated from one's family, so it was a fate much dreaded by the poor.

313   *as Orestes might have been when he was beside Electra*: the significance is that Orestes and Electra were brother and sister. According to Greek legend, when their mother Clytemnestra stabbed to death their father Agamemnon, Electra prevented Clytemnestra from killing Orestes as well.

316   *the very best Oriental details in 'Eöthen' and Warburton*: Eöthen: or Traces of Travel Brought Home from the East (1844) was by Alexander William Kinglake (1809–91), and dealt with his experiences in what is now called the Middle East. Kinglake's friend Eliot Warburton also enjoyed great success in 1845 with *The Crescent and the Cross: or Romance and Realities of Eastern Travel*.

322   *Hymeneal altar*: marriage (Hymen being the Greek god of marriage).

323   *a dissenting chapel*: the name of 'Dissenters' was formerly given to members of Protestant denominations outside the Church of England, which was the official or Established Church. These denominations (such as Congregationalists, Baptists, Presbyterians, Quakers, and Methodists) generally considered the Church of England too worldly, and both Conrad's viewpoint here and his tone are characteristic of Victorian Dissenters, albeit inflected with the extremism of the recent convert. Dissenters also worshipped at 'chapel' rather than 'church'.

324   *frozen up, and . . . set free like the words heard by Pantagruel and his companions*: in chapters 55 and 56 of *The Fourth Book of the Heroic Deeds and Sayings of the Good Pantagruel* (1552) by François Rabelais, the giant Pantagruel and his companions encounter frozen words: when they melt they become clarion notes, horses neighing, and sounds of battle, while some sting and draw blood.

    'la crême de la crême', as Mrs Trollope would say: Frances Trollope (1780–1863) achieved notoriety with her *Domestic Manners of the Americans* (1832), partly because it presented all but the highest reaches of American society as lacking good manners, culture, and civilized values. Although a prolific and successful writer in her day, Mrs Trollope's fame has since been outstripped by that of her son Anthony.

325   *Undine before she got her soul*: referring to the well-known romance *Undine* (1811) by Friedrich, Baron de la Motte Fouqué. Undine is a water nymph who can only gain a human soul by marrying a mortal; she does so, but is snatched back into the water when he proves faithless.

327   *leave an aching void the world can never fill*: from William Cowper's well-known hymn, 'Oh for a closer Walk with God' (1772). The speaker regrets his severance from God and His Word, and recalls:

> What peacefull Hours I then enjoy'd,
> How sweet their Mem'ry still!
> But they have left an Aching Void
> The World can never fill.

333   *sortes*: drawings of lots (Latin).

338   *Sancho Panza's benediction on him who invented sleep*: in *Don Quixote de la Mancha*, pt. 2, ch. 68; Sancho Panza is Don Quixote's very down-to-earth squire.

339   *façon de parler*: manner of speaking.

340   *Semiramide*: an opera by Giocchino Rossini, first produced in Venice in 1823.

342   *dame de compagnie*: lady companion

344   *Against stupidity the gods themselves fight in vain*: a translation of 'Mit der Dummheit kämpfen Götter selbst vergebens', from Schiller's play *The Maid of Orleans* (1801), III. vi.

345   *tendre jour*: subdued light.

347   *émeute*: riot, disturbance.

348   *the most hardened outcast of Norfolk Island*: the late eighteenth and early nineteenth centuries saw the transportation of thousands of convicts to Australia; those whose behaviour was considered still unregenerate after arrival were confined to Norfolk Island, off the Australian coast.

355   *felt herself like Ruth standing 'amid the alien corn'*: in the Book of Ruth, the widowed Ruth leaves her own country to follow her mother-in-law Naomi to Beth-lehem-judah, and works in the corn-fields of Naomi's kinsman Boaz. (That she later marries Boaz foreshadows Bianca's fate.) But the phrase 'amid the alien corn' comes not from the Bible but from Keats's evocation of Ruth in 'Ode to a Nightingale' (1820), l. 67.

360   *airs out of 'Norma' and 'Medea'*: two popular nineteenth-century operas: 'Norma' (1832) by Vincenzo Bellini and 'Medea' (1843) by Giovanni Pacini.

361   *Donzelli was in London*: the tenor Domenico Donzelli, presumably singing Don Ottavio, as Don Giovanni is a baritone role. Donzelli sang in London in 1829, 1832, and 1833. This doesn't square with Clara's reference to the 1843 opera 'Medea' two pages earlier, but dating events in the novel as a whole is difficult.

365   *happiness our being's end and aim*: Alexander Pope, *An Essay on Man* (1732–4), Epistle iv, l. 1.

372   *this district in Bohemia which he had been about to explore*: given Bryant's rather contemptuous attitude to the world of the arts earlier in the novel, 'Bohemia' may here stand as much for this world as for the region of central Europe.

397   *Gentleness, Virtue, Wisdom, and Endurance . . . An empire o'er the disentangled doom*: ll. 562–9 of the last Act of Shelley's verse drama *Prometheus Unbound* (1820).

TROLLOPE IN OXFORD WORLD'S CLASSICS

ANTHONY TROLLOPE

An Autobiography
Ayala's Angel
Barchester Towers
The Belton Estate
The Bertrams
Can You Forgive Her?
The Claverings
Cousin Henry
Doctor Thorne
Doctor Wortle's School
The Duke's Children
Early Short Stories
The Eustace Diamonds
An Eye for an Eye
Framley Parsonage
He Knew He Was Right
Lady Anna
The Last Chronicle of Barset
Later Short Stories
Miss Mackenzie
Mr Scarborough's Family
Orley Farm
Phineas Finn
Phineas Redux
The Prime Minister
Rachel Ray
The Small House at Allington
La Vendée
The Warden
The Way We Live Now

HANS CHRISTIAN ANDERSEN	**Fairy Tales**
J. M. BARRIE	**Peter Pan in Kensington Gardens** and **Peter and Wendy**
L. FRANK BAUM	**The Wonderful Wizard of Oz**
FRANCES HODGSON BURNETT	**The Secret Garden**
LEWIS CARROLL	**Alice's Adventures in Wonderland** and **Through the Looking-Glass**
CARLO COLLODI	**The Adventures of Pinocchio**
KENNETH GRAHAME	**The Wind in the Willows**
THOMAS HUGHES	**Tom Brown's Schooldays**
CHARLES KINGSLEY	**The Water-Babies**
GEORGE MACDONALD	**The Princess and the Goblin** and **The Princess and Curdie**
EDITH NESBIT	**Five Children and It** **The Railway Children**
ANNA SEWELL	**Black Beauty**
JOHANN DAVID WYSS	**The Swiss Family Robinson**

The Oxford World's Classics Website

www.worldsclassics.co.uk

- Information about new titles
- Explore the full range of Oxford World's Classics
- Links to other literary sites and the main OUP webpage
- Imaginative competitions, with bookish prizes
- Peruse *Compass*, the Oxford World's Classics magazine
- Articles by editors
- Extracts from Introductions
- A forum for discussion and feedback on the series
- Special information for teachers and lecturers

www.worldsclassics.co.uk

American Literature

British and Irish Literature

Children's Literature

Classics and Ancient Literature

Colonial Literature

Eastern Literature

European Literature

History

Medieval Literature

Oxford English Drama

Poetry

Philosophy

Politics

Religion

The Oxford Shakespeare